Charles Janeway Stillé

Major-General Anthony Wayne

and the Pennsylvania line in the Continental Army - Vol. 1

Charles Janeway Stillé

Major-General Anthony Wayne
and the Pennsylvania line in the Continental Army - Vol. 1

ISBN/EAN: 9783337409722

Printed in Europe, USA, Canada, Australia, Japan

Cover: Foto ©Andreas Hilbeck / pixelio.de

More available books at **www.hansebooks.com**

MAJOR-GENERAL

ANTHONY WAYNE

AND

THE PENNSYLVANIA LINE

IN THE

CONTINENTAL ARMY.

BY

CHARLES J. STILLÉ,

PRESIDENT OF THE HISTORICAL SOCIETY OF PENNSYLVANIA.

PHILADELPHIA:

J. B. LIPPINCOTT COMPANY.

1893.

PREFACE.

It has often been remarked by students of American history (in this part of the country at least) that in both popular and standard works on the Revolutionary and pre-Revolutionary eras there is a singular failure to give any adequate account of the part taken by Pennsylvania in the struggles of those days, or of the influence of her statesmen and soldiers in moulding the national policy.

Impressed with a belief that such opinions are not without foundation, and with the hope of calling the attention of students to what I venture to term certain "lost" chapters of our American history, I prepared some time ago a biography of that illustrious Pennsylvania statesman JOHN DICKINSON,—a man who for various reasons is little known to this generation, but who, in the formative period of our history, so guided the policy of the country that his controlling influence is readily recognized as shaping that policy from the date of the Stamp Act to that of the Declaration of Independence.

With the same object in view I now present another chapter of that neglected history, that which relates to the achievements of a most distinguished soldier of Pennsylvania,—GENERAL ANTHONY WAYNE.

The materials for a memoir of General Wayne,

which are exceedingly abundant and valuable, have been preserved with great care by his family, and are now deposited with the collections of the Historical Society of Pennsylvania. A study of these papers has enabled me to give to the public a full and, I hope, a trustworthy account of the career of General Wayne. These papers embrace copies of the letters written by him during his campaigns, or rather the rough draughts of those letters, letters received by him from the most eminent personages of the Revolution, and many other documents illustrating his life. My object has been to allow these letters to tell their own story, connecting them only by such an account of the events of the time as may seem necessary to explain the true value and character of General Wayne's achievements and those of the men he commanded,—for the most part officers and soldiers of the Pennsylvania line.

On the death of General Wayne in 1796 his papers passed into the possession of his son, Colonel Isaac Wayne. Colonel Wayne was a man deeply imbued with filial reverence for the memory of his father, and with a very high conception of the glory which he had achieved by his military exploits. In 1829 he printed in a magazine called "The Casket" a brief memoir of his father, illustrated by numerous letters of the general, then, for the first time, made public, which were at once recognized as extremely valuable and interesting contributions to our Revolutionary history. Not satisfied with this, however, he asked at different times two of his friends, the HON. CHARLES MINER and the HON. JOSEPH J. LEWIS, of West Chester, to complete the work which he had begun. Neither of these gentlemen seems to have been able to comply fully with his request, although it appears that each of them wrote portions of a memoir of General Wayne. The "Supplementary Chapter" in this book was prepared by MR. LEWIS, and I think no one who reads it can help feeling regret that he did not write "The Life of General Wayne" with the same spirit which inspired this chapter of it.

The only printed account of any of General Wayne's achievements which is fully illustrated by his own letters is the story of the capture of Stony Point in 1779 by the late MR. HENRY B. DAWSON. This work is in the shape of a paper read before the Historical Society of New York in 1863. It was privately printed,—only two hundred and fifty copies having been struck off. It seems to me one of the fullest and most satisfactory narratives of a great historical event with which I am acquainted.

The gentlemen above named have left their work unfinished. They have given us but a glimpse or an outline of the character and career of our illustrious soldier. With the material at my disposal I have felt it a duty which I owed not only to the memory of General Wayne, but also to the reputation of the State whose son he was, to make an effort to complete the work which others have begun, and to portray the general as he appeared to our fathers,—a typical hero.

It is much to be regretted that the material for illustrating the career of many of the brave men he commanded has not, after diligent search, proved as abundant as that which has been preserved for bringing before us the life of their chief.

I must express my great obligations to the librarian of the Historical Society, Mr. F. D. Stone, for his careful supervision of the text of my book, as well as to those kind friends of the Society who have aided me in completing the work while suffering from an attack of illness.

March, 1893.

CONTENTS.

SUPPLEMENTARY CHAPTER.—(*Pages* 349–373.)

APPENDICES.

MAJOR-GENERAL WAYNE.

CHAPTER I.

EARLY TRAINING AND DISCIPLINE.

THE renewed interest which has of late been awa-
kened in the study of American history, and especially
in the history of the Revolution, has drawn attention
to the wonderful career of General Wayne.   By many
his memory is cherished as that of a popular idol ; still,
not much seems to be known of his character and
achievements even in his native State, where his fame
should have been preserved as a precious heritage.
Some, it is true, recall the strange *sobriquet* of " Mad
Anthony" by which he was known in his lifetime, and
are curious to know how it happened that a man who
accomplished such great deeds should have been called
a madman.   Others have not forgotten that he was the
most brilliant and picturesque figure in the Revolutionary army, with the possible exception of the young
Marquis de La Fayette.   Those also who have read
in the history of the Revolution of the most striking
and wonderful exploit of the war, the midnight assault
of Stony Point under Wayne's leadership, or of the
manner in which he restored the fortunes of the day at
Monmouth, or of the extraordinary ability with which,
supported by an insignificant force, he contrived to
rescue the State of Georgia from the British and their

Indian allies in one campaign of three months' duration, naturally seek to know something of the character of a man whose life was rendered illustrious by these and similar exploits.   Here is a man whose career extends from fighting with well-trained British soldiers in Canada to the successful blockade of the English garrison at Savannah, from the desperate conflict at Monmouth to the final conquest and subjugation of the Indians of the Northwest ; who, beginning as a surveyor and a simple farmer of Chester County, raised one of the first regiments in Pennsylvania for the Continental army, and closed his career twenty years later as the General Commanding-in-Chief of the Armies of the United States, appointed to that high office by Washington himself; yet, according to the editor of the most voluminous and accurate history of the country which has been published, "his life is yet to be written."   It seems that the time has come when an effort should be made to portray him as he really was, and not as he appears in the popular legend, which in many respects is misleading, and to give some account of his career, gathered chiefly from his correspondence, which presents his career not merely as a soldier, but as a patriot, in the most striking and attractive light.

    To get a true view of Wayne's life, however, we must at the outset divest our minds of certain prepossessions concerning his career which usually make up the whole of the picture presented to us, but which form in reality only the background of that of which Wayne is the central figure.   There is a general impression, for instance, that he was simply a *beau sabreur*,—a sort of reckless dare-devil, who could be relied upon, and was at all times called upon, to lead with unshrinking courage the most desperately dangerous operations. People forget that he many times proved to the satisfaction of his great chief not merely that he was impetuous in action, but that while he was quick in conception and prompt in execution he was most cautious and careful in preparation and unfailing in resources. If we are to judge Wayne simply as an intrepid leader for whom personal danger had a certain positive charm, and not as a great soldier possessing that rare combination of qualities which go to make up the illustrious general, we shall fall into great error. We might as well regard Sheridan, for instance, as he restored the fortunes of the day and rallied his army in the valley of the Shenandoah, as having thereby established his fame as a great general, or judge Grant as a general by the brilliant operations which led to the surrender of Donelson.

The very brilliancy of Wayne's reputation as a fighting general has somewhat blinded the eyes of his countrymen to those military qualities which he possessed in common with all great soldiers. For the moment it is only necessary to say that no important strategetical movement was undertaken by Washington while Wayne was under his command without consulting him. His illustrious chief knew that he could trust him thoroughly for the execution of his part in any plan assigned to him, for his heart was in his work; every faculty of his mind was bent to its accomplishment, and he never disappointed those who trusted him.

The career of General Wayne has for us in this State a special interest. Not only is his fame part of the heritage of glory in achieving our national independence of which we, as Pennsylvanians, may justly claim our share, but we can never forget that his great deeds were achieved by the aid of the men of Pennsylvania, whom he had trained as soldiers, and who, under his command, throughout the Revolution formed a *corps d'élite* in the American army called "the Pennsylvania line." The services of these men, rendered with a courage which never failed amidst all the dangers and trials of the Revolutionary campaigns, have been in a great measure unchronicled, or the story is told in documents and correspondence which have never been printed. It seems that the present is a fit time, when, as we have said, a new interest appears to have been aroused in our Revolutionary history, that an effort should be made to do away with that self-reproach which always oppresses us as we stand over the graves of our forgotten heroes and strive to bring before our minds a true picture of the deeds of those who suffered and died that we might live. Surely State pride, if not reverence for their memory, founded upon gratitude for their services, should teach us to honor these men by recounting their achievements as well as those of their intrepid leader.

The family of Wayne was originally of English stock, and at the time of the outbreak of the Revolution it had been seated for three generations in Chester County. The grandfather of the general during the reign of Charles II. had removed his family from Yorkshire and had taken possession of an estate in the County Wicklow in Ireland. He was a Protestant, and joined the forces of William of Orange in his

contest with King James II. He commanded a troop
of dragoons in the service of King William at the
battle of the Boyne, and he greatly distinguished himself by his gallantry in that decisive battle. It is said
that the ancestor of General William Irvine, Wayne's
distinguished Lieutenant, had been an officer in the
same battle. Wayne was not of the race called, in
our classification of the population of Pennsylvania, the
Scotch-Irish, as were so many of his friends and neighbors in Chester County, Wicklow being a part of Ireland into which the translated Scotch never penetrated.
For some reason which it is now impossible to explain,
his grandfather gave up his estate in Ireland and came
to Pennsylvania in 1722, one of the years in which a
great tide of Scotch-Irish emigration flowed in upon us
from the northern part of that kingdom. The elder
Wayne brought with him four sons, who are said to
have been carefully educated at home, and with them, it
would appear, a considerable worldly substance. In the
year 1724 he purchased an estate in Chester County
of nearly sixteen hundred acres on the border of that
most beautiful of valleys, the great valley of that county,
which he called Waynesborough. Upon his death this
estate was divided among his sons; his youngest, Isaac,
the father of the future general, receiving as his share
about five hundred acres, which, by a strange coincidence, lay near by the spot known in after-years as the
scene of the Paoli massacre. Isaac Wayne is described
as having been a man of strong mind and of great industry and enterprise. He frequently represented the
county of Chester in the Provincial Assembly, and as a
commissioned officer distinguished himself in expedi-

tions against the Indians.[1]   After a long life of usefulness to his country, to his family, and to his friends, he
died in 1774, leaving one son and two daughters.[2]   His
only son, Anthony, was born at Waynesborough, in the
township of Easttown, in Chester County, on the 1st
of January, 1745.

Of Anthony Wayne it may be said, if it can be truly
said of any one, that he was born with the instinct of
a soldier.   He had all his mother's force of character
and his father's love for military adventure and enterprise.   He seems from the first to have been a manly
and self-reliant boy, although hardly taking kindly to
the course of instruction designed for him by his father.
His uncle Gilbert, whose pupil he was, found that he
had little taste for the study of the ancient languages,
then, as it is now, the basis of all truly liberal education, but that he made great progress in the elementary
mathematics.   As a boy his ambition seems to have
been to lead the life and do the work of a soldier.   His
uncle writes to his father, "What he may be best qualified for I know not.   He may perhaps make a soldier.
He has already distracted the brains of two-thirds of the
boys under my charge by rehearsals of battles, sieges,
etc.   During noon, in place of the usual games and
amusements, he has the boys employed in throwing up

[1] Captain Isaac Wayne was a captain in the Provincial service,
commissioned by Governor Morris, and was stationed during the
winter of 1756 first at Nazareth and afterwards at Fort Allen.   He
married Elizabeth, daughter of Richard Iddings, of Chester County,
who is spoken of as a woman of remarkable force and earnestness of
character.

[2] Moore's Life of Wayne, p. 8.

redoubts, skirmishing, etc." Thus early did the hero of Stony Point show the unmistakable bent of his genius. We may remember that many generals in embryo, Napoleon foremost of them all, have been distinguished in their boyhood by just such decided tastes ; moreover, that the preference of such boys has generally been for mathematical rather than for classical studies.

Wayne's wise father, while probably recognizing the very strong bent of his son's mind for a military life, was perfectly aware that no such career was open in the British army for a provincial without a home influence such as he could not command. He therefore made up his mind to try once more to train him in classical studies. He was accordingly sent, when sixteen years old, to the Academy in Philadelphia, no doubt with the expectation that a change of school studies would bring about a change of tastes. Apparently the hoped-for result was not attained.[1] His fondness for an out-of-door life and for mathematical studies was at this time his strong characteristic, and led him at last, as his hopes of becoming a soldier vanished, to adopt the profession of a surveyor. In those days this occupation resembled in this country more nearly that of a soldier than any other, and the adventurous life which the surveyor was forced to lead in the wilderness in the practice of his profession, the discipline in which he was trained by the dangers, hardships, and constant vigilance which made up part of his daily occupation, formed an excellent preparation for his future work as

[1] His name is not found among those of the matriculates of the Academy.

a soldier. Such was the school in which Washington was trained, and in it Wayne acquired the qualities of a true soldier. In those days the country in which the surveyor was called upon to do his work of tracing courses and distances and settling boundaries was for the most part a dense and untrodden forest, often occupied by hostile Indians. While thus in the performance of his duty he led a life of constant exposure and hardship, his body became hardened and disciplined, and his mind ready and resourceful in times of difficulty.

Young Wayne seems to have gained reputation as a surveyor rapidly. We find that before he was twenty-one years old he was employed to survey and settle—that is, to colonize—two vast tracts of wild lands which had been purchased by Dr. Franklin and his associates, capitalists in Philadelphia, in Nova Scotia. No better proof could be given of the character which he had already established than that he, a mere boy in years, should have been employed upon such an errand of colonization by a man as sagacious as Dr. Franklin. These lands had been purchased in 1765 under the impression that the peace of 1763 opened a large and profitable field of English enterprise in that quarter.[1]

Wayne was sent to Nova Scotia by these gentlemen not merely to survey their lands and to fix their bound-

[1] It appears from the records of the Crown Land Office at Halifax that on the 31st of October, 1765, a grant passed under the seal of the Province for one hundred thousand acres on the St. John's River to Alexander McNutt, Matthew Clarkson, Edward Duffield, Gerardus Clarkson, John Nagle, Benjamin Franklin, Anthony Wayne, and various others, and on the same day a grant was made to the same parties of one hundred thousand acres on the Piticoodzack River.

aries, but also to establish upon them a colony of settlers who would cultivate them,—a most remarkable
proof, as we have said, of the confidence which Wayne
as a young man was able to inspire.   Of course
Nova Scotia at that time was an untracked and unknown wilderness, and it speaks well for Wayne's
courage and adventurous spirit that he was willing
to embark on so formidable an undertaking.   We are
unfortunately without the means of knowing the course
he pursued in overcoming the obstacles which were
interposed in the way of performing the duties assigned
to him, but it is very clear that he could only have
maintained himself at all in his position by the exercise
of great force of character.   As the agent of the company he seems to have justified the confidence reposed
in him.   The following are the points recommended to
this boy to be observed, by the principal agent of the
associates, Mr. John Hughes, a great favorite of Dr.
Franklin's, who had been appointed through the Doctor's influence distributor of stamps for this district.
He was told to ascertain whether "the land proposed to
be bought and settled upon was, 1. Good & supplied
with navigable waters.   2. To observe where were the
heads of navigation in Rivers, that is, the tide.   3. Convenient places for ferries.   4. Passes through the mountains.   5. Iron ore & cole mines.   6. Mill Seats &
other waterworks.   7. Places where the roads meet.
8. Beaches or islands with black sand washed up.   9.
Mast lands or pure swamps.   10. Lime stone or other
stones.   11. Meadow lands and marsh.   12. Large
Springs or any mineral Springs."   A pretty extensive
catalogue of subjects to be investigated and reported

upon by a boy, even if he was as promising as young Wayne.

In the course of a year he had not only made a first survey of the lands, but had led into the wilderness and settled in their new home a colony abundantly provided with implements of husbandry and provisions. He continued in charge of this settlement until 1767, when the company, finding, it is said, its operations menaced by the controversy which had arisen between the mother-country and the Colonies, abandoned its scheme of colonization. It is worth while to recall this period of Wayne's early life, for what he went through during the two years he was engaged in this work proved invaluable in the military career he was destined to follow.

Having given up his position as superintendent of the Nova Scotia lands and returned home, he was married in May, 1766, to the daughter of Mr. Bartholomew Penrose, a prominent merchant of Philadelphia. From that time until the outbreak of the Revolution he cultivated his farm at Waynesborough, and established, besides, an extensive tannery upon it. He was regarded by his neighbors, young as he was, owing to his extensive experience, as an expert surveyor, whose professional opinion upon the various perplexing questions which arise in a newly-settled country in regard to boundaries was received as of final authority. During these years he grew in the affections and confidence of his neighbors, and was recognized as a leader among a population of unusual intelligence and public spirit. He was chosen to fill several unimportant county offices, and when the first murmur of resistance to the minis-

terial measures was heard in 1774, his counsel was regarded as that of a recognized interpreter of public
opinion in Chester County.   His father died during
this year, and he is spoken of in the address of con-
dolence sent by the officers of the regiment which the
son was then organizing, as a "man conspicuously
friendly to the great cause now depending between
Great Britain and her Colonies."   From this address,
and from other circumstances, we may infer that the
father was a shining example of that patriotic devotion
with which the son's whole career was inspired.   The
death of his father, of course, brought new duties and
responsibilities to the future general.   His inheritance
increased his stake in the country's destiny, but neither
the responsibilities which he incurred by the course of
action which he pursued, nor the dangers which menaced his private interests, cooled for a moment the enthusiasm with which he resisted the claims of ministerial
oppression.

The immediate cause of the outbreak of the Revolution was, it will be remembered, the retaliatory measures taken by the British Ministry to punish the town
of Boston for the destruction of the tea sent thither
in December, 1773, and the refusal of its people to
make any compensation to the East India Company
for the loss thereby incurred.   The method taken by
the Bostonians of protesting against sending taxable
tea to that place, by permitting a mob to throw it into
the harbor, and afterwards refusing to compensate the
owners of the tea for its loss, was not generally approved by the malcontents outside of New England,
or, indeed, even outside of Boston itself.   The country

had been practically unanimous in its opposition to the
measures which had led the Ministry to permit the ex-
portation of the tea to this country, and in all the Colonies on the sea-coast arrangements had been made to
prevent an attempt to land it and to enforce its with-
drawal. The object of the patriots at this time was to
keep strictly within the limits of law and order, hoping
thereby that their petitions for a redress of grievances
would be more readily listened to. The riotous conduct
of the mob in Boston disappointed these hopes, and the
destruction of the tea and the refusal of compensation
were regarded as "untoward events" by meetings held
throughout Pennsylvania, as well as by the Assembly of
that Province. The steadiness of the people here in
their opposition to the measures of the Ministry was
not affected by these proceedings. Still less was there
any disposition manifested to follow the example of
Boston. We had in Philadelphia prevented the landing
of the tea sent to this port in a different way.

It is most important, in order to understand the course
of the events in the early history of the Revolution, to
remember that different sections of the country were
led into the revolt by different motives, and that they had
different objects which they hoped to accomplish by it.
Thus, the destruction of the tea was not regarded here,
as we are told it was in Boston, by the latest New England writer of American history,[1] as a "colossal event"
and as "the most magnificent movement of all," but
rather, so far as the influence of such acts upon the
most important of all questions of that time was con-

---

[1] See Fiske's American Revolution, vol. i. p. 85.

cerned, the union of the Colonies in opposition to the Ministry, as constituting a stupendous blunder. We had no intention here, at least, to vindicate what is called "the supreme assertion of the most fundamental principle of political freedom" in this way.

Still, here, as in all parts of the country, there was deep sympathy for the distress into which Boston had been plunged by the riotous conduct of some of her people. She was punished, as is well known, by every means which the ingenuity of the Ministry could devise "to chastise her insolence," as it was called. She suffered all the evils incidental to a modern state of siege, which, to a commercial town like Boston, meant ruin. It was felt that she was indeed suffering in the common cause, and people here, without stopping to inquire how much of all this was due to her own act, felt that the best method of relieving her was to send her provisions in her distress and to urge the repeal of the Acts of Parliament which had made such a state of things possible.

In Philadelphia in the June of that year (1774) a town meeting was held in which such was the line of opposition to the ministerial measures marked out. Committees of Correspondence and of Safety were named, and vigorous efforts were made to organize the popular sentiment of the Province in a constitutional opposition to the acts of the Ministry. The attempt was successful. The Assembly in September, 1774, although many Quakers were members of it, with surprising unanimity adopted the Whig policy of asking for a redress of grievances, and the first Continental Congress in its proceedings pursued the same policy, although it was induced by a false rumor of the bombardment of Boston by General Gage to promise to support her cause by force.

The policy adopted during the summer of 1774 in Philadelphia was quickly responded to from all parts of the Province. Nowhere was the counsel which the leaders in that city had given more quickly followed than in Chester County, and in no man in that county was the determination to resist the action of the Ministry with arms in his hands, if necessary, more completely embodied than in Anthony Wayne. He was emphatically the leader of the opponents to the ministerial acts. He was chairman of the County Committee which proposed the resolutions condemning the course of the Ministry adopted by the freemen of that county on the 13th of July, 1774. He was also chairman of the committee appointed to carry out the recommendations of the Assembly in reference to a military organization and non-importation agreement; he was a member of the Provincial Convention which met in January, 1775, to encourage domestic manufactures in anticipation of the effect of the non-importation of English goods; he was the author of the proposition in May, 1775, that the freemen of the county should be organized for military purposes. In June he became one of the members of the Provincial Committee of Safety, in July a member of the Provincial Convention, and in October a member of the Committee of Correspondence. He was put forward in December by his friends as a proper person to represent his county in the Assembly for the next year. During the whole of this busy year, and while engaged in these methods of organizing the opposition, he was occupied also in recruiting a regiment in Chester for the Continental service, in pursuance of the Act of Congress calling upon Pennsylvania for her quota of troops. By the close of the year the ranks of this regiment (Fourth Battalion) were filled, and on the recommendation of the Committee of Safety he was, on the 3d of January, 1776, appointed its colonel, and Francis Johnston its lieutenant-colonel.

Wayne at this period must have been a singularly attractive person, very unlike the commonplace people who at that time made up an average farming community. Everything about him seemed calculated to draw public attention to him and to render him popular, as it is called, in the community in which he lived. He was just thirty years of age, a handsome, manly figure, and free and bold in the outspoken declaration of his opinions. He was a man of better education and of a wider knowledge of the world than most of his neighbors, and this superiority was recognized by them. He inspired confidence and gained adherents whenever he expressed his political opinions. He was known by all (a great point then, as it is now) to be absolutely disinterested. We can recall but two of the higher officers of the army who served throughout the war, General Washington and the Marquis de La Fayette, who left larger private fortunes to risk all in the public cause than General Wayne.[1] Removed in this way

---

[1] The following memorandum was found on one of General Wayne's ledgers, dated March, 1784: "Mr. Shannon has sunk for me since the beginning of January 1776, upwards of £2400 in stock, exclusive of the interest for near eight years. Had he managed my

from any temptation to seek public office from sordid motives, he was trusted throughout the war by all whom he led,—his neighbors and townsmen as well as his soldiers. Certainly in the military family of no other general of the army was there to be seen such an affectionate intercourse as existed between Wayne and his subordinates.

He had, of course, his failings and his weaknesses, conspicuous even in his early manhood. He seems to have been constitutionally a vain man, and to have expressed himself from the beginning too often in an over-confident and boastful style, which was not always in good taste. Vanity is usually combined with offensive pretension, but Wayne all through his life was the type of truth, honor, and frankness; and it may be remembered, too, that a good deal of his manner was due to a certain impetuous eagerness and impatience of nature which did not allow him always to measure his words. Of his perfect sincerity when he assumed this tone (which he did only when he proposed daring and hazardous deeds) there could be no doubt. His peculiarity was so well known in the army that he was never thought of merely as boastful when he adopted it, but simply it was looked upon as his method of urging desperate plans which seemed perfectly feasible to his ardent and impetuous temper. People may have laughed at his manner, but no one ever thought that he was less terribly in earnest in any scheme which he proposed because he used the language of hyperbole.

stock in trade to the advantage which others have done in the course of the late war, I ought to have had at a moderate computation seven thousand pounds in stock in place of nothing.   A. W."

The record of the life of a man during the year of the outbreak of hostilities who afterwards occupied so prominent a position in the public service as did Wayne is indeed a most interesting and instructive one. It not only proves the depth and earnestness of his political convictions and the energy with which he maintained them, but also exhibits the methods by which the armed opposition to the home government in this Province was organized under Wayne's direction. It will be observed that at the beginning of the year 1776 there were soldiers of two distinct kinds raised in Pennsylvania. The one was composed of battalions of "Associators," so called, in the Provincial service, the organization of which resembled that of the militia of the other Colonies, except that the men composing the battalions were all volunteers. Of these battalions, fifty-three had been raised by this time in Pennsylvania, of which five came from Chester County. There were, besides, regiments enlisted here for the Continental service, and they differed from the Provincial battalions chiefly in this, that the men were to serve for a longer term, that the discipline was stricter and more regular, and that they were directly under the authority of Congress. In Chester County such was the patriotic ardor of the people that during the year 1775 the ranks of both the Provincial and the Continental battalions were rapidly filled. Of the five battalions of Associators raised there, commanded by Colonels Moore, Hockley, Lloyd, Montgomery, and Thomas, three were present at the battle of Long Island. They were stationed in the advance on both flanks of the army, with the Pennsylvania regiments of Atlee and Miles, and although they were nearly

3

cut to pieces and many of the survivors were captured, they displayed a steadiness and courage in maintaining their position against overwhelming numbers which excited the admiration of the army. Caleb Parry, a Chester County man, and lieutenant-colonel in Atlee's regiment, who was killed in this battle, is said to have been the protomartyr of the Revolution among the Pennsylvania officers.

As Wayne was recognized as a leader by the patriotic men of his county, he was chosen by the Committee of Safety, without hesitation, colonel of the regiment which he had done so much to raise. He was known to all as a man of high character and of considerable substance, who at a great sacrifice had proved his patriotic zeal by outspoken acts of resistance to the Ministry, and whose loyal and persistent devotion to the cause through good report and evil report might be confidently expected. He and the officers of his regiment seem to have been animated by the same spirit during the war. Many of his subordinates became famous for their gallantry during the Revolutionary campaigns as officers in the Pennsylvania line. Johnston, Wood, Robinson, Frazer, Moore, North, Church, Lacey, and Vernon are familiar as the names of those who acquired by their deeds fame for themselves and credit for the State which had sent them to the field during the war, and they all began their military career as officers of Wayne's regiment.

Different portions of the country were, as we have said, differently affected by the conduct of the Ministry previous to the Revolution. Although all agreed that their measures should be resisted, the methods and

time and extent of that resistance were subjects concerning which, up to the date of the Declaration of
Independence, scarcely any of the widely-separated
sections of the country could agree.

It is worth considering for a moment how and why
the revolutionary excitement had so deeply affected a
population like that of the farmers of Chester County,
who had suffered no practical grievance, and who, there
is no reason to doubt, were at that time (as they say in
their resolutions in July, 1774) thoroughly loyal to the
British crown, as to lead them to take up arms to maintain their opinions.   Wayne's action at this time is
typical not only of his own opinions but of those of his
neighbors and fellow-farmers, and indeed of the rural
population throughout the Province, and some account
of their political ideas affords the best explanation of
what may seem inconsistent in their conduct.

No portion of the population in Pennsylvania was
more completely law-abiding than that of Chester
County.   It was largely made up of Quakers, the descendants of the most prosperous of Penn's followers,
many of them men of Welsh blood, with a sprinkling
of Irish Protestants.   From the reverence of these
people for law, nothing seemed to them more illegal,
and therefore wrong, than the enactment by Parliament
since 1763 of no fewer than eleven statutes the main
object of which was to give the English Ministry
absolute control over the Colonies.   This was their
grievance, and to redress it, with no ulterior view whatever, they thought, as their English ancestors had done,
that the best plan was to negotiate with arms in their
hands.   Neither Wayne nor any of his neighbors were

in any sense revolutionists or adventurers, nor, in the new-fangled phrase of the day, " Sons of Liberty." Wayne was their natural leader, but all his surroundings made him a conservative. He was a young man who had just come into a handsome landed estate, who had been recently married, and who, if he had any political ambition, no doubt looked forward to maintaining that position in life which the influence of his wealth and education would command among his neighbors. Certainly he could never have dreamed of military distinction for himself as the possible outcome of the quarrel of which he had become a champion. His surroundings spoke of peace as the necessary condition of maintaining the material prosperity which was everywhere apparent. Even now, as one looks upon the fair prospect which opens before him in " the Great Valley" and its surrounding region, of cultivated farm, of comfortable homestead and picturesque woodland, stretching in the far distance towards the Schuylkill, everything around him suggesting thrift and a well-ordered community, he feels that there must have happened something like a moral earthquake to rouse such a people to embark in the vicissitudes and calamities of war. And when he reflects that this valley was occupied at an early date by men of Anglo-Saxon blood and traditions, he finds an explanation of the two apparently contradictory expressions of their opinions at the outbreak of the Revolution, the one adopted July 13, 1774, the other in September, 1775.

The first asserted the absolute right of every English subject to the enjoyment and disposal of his property, and that no power on earth could legally divest him of

it; and again, that the attempted invasion of that right
was a grievance which should be redressed by constitutional means. What was meant by constitutional
means is shown by the resolution adopted by the
Committee in September, as follows:

> "In Committee.
>
> "Chester Co., Sep. 25, 1775.
>
> "Whereas, some persons evidently inimical to the liberty of
> America have industriously propagated a report that the military
> associators of this County in conjunction with the military associa-
> tors in general, intend to overturn the Constitution by declaring an
> independency in the execution of which they are aided by this
> Committee and the Board of Commissioners and Assessors with the
> arms now making for this County, and as such report could not
> originate but among the worst of men for the worst of purposes,
> This Committee have thought proper to declare, and they do hereby
> declare their abhorrence even of an idea so pernicious in its nature,
> as they ardently wish for nothing more than a happy and speedy
> reconciliation on constitutional principles with that State from
> whom they derive their origin.
>
> "By order.
>
> "Anthony Wayne,
>
> "*Chairman.*"

These resolutions, while they express the opinions of
a man who from the beginning to the end of the war
never sheathed his sword, also show how much more
slowly the people of Chester County, and of Pennsylvania generally, arrived at the *ultima ratio* than those
of New England, and by what different routes. And no
wonder. Here, with all earthly blessings around them,
they had thus far suffered nothing from actual wrong
committed, but they were roused by the violation of
a constitutional principle, which begot a fear lest evil

might happen to them in the future should the claims
of the Ministry pass unchallenged.   Their commerce
had not been destroyed, the capital of their Province
was not, like Boston, in a state of siege, no attempt had
been made so to change their charter as to place them
more fully under the control of the Ministry, their town
meetings had not been forbidden, their system of selecting juries had not been interfered with, nor was the
choice of officers once made by the people transferred
to the appointment of the Ministry.   Still, they took
up arms, and protested, as Wayne's grandfather might
have done when he joined King William's forces at the
battle of the Boyne, "that levying money for or to the
use of the Crown by pretence of prerogative without
due authority was illegal."   And on this opposition to
arbitrary methods they staked the issue, and sympa-
thized with Boston as suffering in the common cause.
Wayne, with a deep and abiding conviction that the
only way to secure redress was to extort it, was a true
conservative from the beginning to the end of the war.
His letters, which are filled with expressions of undying love for his country and of evidences of a self-
sacrificing devotion, will be searched in vain for a single
revolutionary sentiment.   At all times we shall see that
this "Mad Anthony" was the slave of law.   Nor must
it be forgotten that neither Wayne nor his companions
fought any the less earnestly or less successfully in the
contest because such was their political creed.

During the winter of 1776 Wayne was engaged at
Chester in preparing his men for active service, and
in bringing them under proper discipline.   He began
by punishing desertion severely.   Before his regiment

left Pennsylvania no less than six of its members were punished, some with fifteen and others with thirty-nine lashes, for this offence. All through his career Wayne was known for the strictness with which he enforced discipline, and to this practice was doubtless due in a great measure the efficiency of his men. Like many other officers in the army of the Revolution, Wayne appears to have studied, before he held command, the principles of strategy as laid down in such books as " Marshal Saxe's Campaigns" and " The Commentaries of Cæsar on the Gallic War," and in his letters are frequent allusions to the opinions of these masters of the art. There was a painful consciousness of ignorance on the part of many of the officers of the highest rank in the service on this subject, which sometimes led them to an indecision which was fatal, or, to what was almost as disastrous, a confidence in the opinions of Generals Gates and Charles Lee, who passed in the army of the Revolution as officers educated in a scientific knowledge of the art of war as practised in Europe. But a large fund of common sense, experience, and perfect coolness in emergencies, rather than books on the art of war, tempered the zeal of Wayne, so that towards the close of his career, and especially during the campaign in Georgia, he was justly regarded as an accomplished strategist.

There was one little piece of pardonable vanity with which he was charged in the beginning of his career, the details of which seem amusing enough when we recall the rough, hard work which his regiment had to do, and that was his apparent anxiety for the military appearance of the men of his regiment. In a letter to

Washington he says, "I have an insuperable bias in favor of an elegant uniform and soldierly appearance, so much so that I would rather risk my life and reputation at the head of the same men in an attack, clothed and appointed as I could wish, merely with bayonets and a single charge of ammunition, than to take them as they appear in common with sixty rounds of cartridges. It may be a false idea, but I cannot help cherishing it." The disastrous campaign in Canada did not change his opinion of the necessity of keeping up appearances. In his orders of July 9, 1776, he tells his regiment that "a barber for each company shall be nominated for the purpose of shaving the soldiers and dressing their hair," and that "the colonel is determined to punish every man who comes on parade with a long beard, slovenly dressed, or dirty;" and again, "he hopes the officers will think it their duty to see that their men always appear washed, shaved, their hair plaited and powdered, and their arms in good order." It is characteristic of the care of Wayne for the appearance of his men that at the time this order was issued his regiment had just gone through a campaign in Canada (as will soon appear), where they had suffered from the roughest and hardest usage, and where they had lost almost everything belonging to them save their hair and their beards.

THE WAYNE HOMESTEAD.

CHAPTER II.

THE expedition to Canada in the spring and summer of 1776 was the first campaign in which the regiment of Colonel Wayne was engaged. It formed part of a brigade of Pennsylvanians commanded by General William Thompson, composed of the Second Battalion, under Colonel St. Clair, the Sixth, under Colonel William Irvine, and the Fourth, under Colonel Wayne. It was sent by order of Congress to reinforce the army under Generals Montgomery and Arnold, which had been repulsed at Quebec.

It is not easy fully to understand why such prodigious efforts were made in the beginning of the Revolution to induce the Canadians to join us in the revolt against the English government. There is no doubt that it was hoped not merely by the majority of the members of Congress, but also by men of the sagacity of Dr. Franklin and the calm judgment of Washington, that some signal advantage would be gained to the American cause by the expeditions under the command of Montgomery and Arnold and the capture of Quebec. Faith in the result must have been very strong when the best troops under the bravest officers were sent on this far-distant and dangerous expedition, when the issue of the siege of Boston was as yet uncertain, when New York was threatened by the enemy, and when the ardor and zeal of the new levies before Boston had grown so cool that many of them were disgusted with the service and were ready to leave the army on the very day on which the short term of their engagement ended. It is true that Canada was poorly defended at the time, and had there been any prospect of our maintaining possession of the country there might have been some excuse for sending so many troops, commanded by our most gallant officers, to conquer it. But in our eagerness we forgot that it was easy, whenever the St. Lawrence was navigable, to send by that river an overwhelming force brought from England against us. The impression seemed to be that once within the walls of Quebec, Canada was ours. Besides these miscalculations, we fell into two capital errors in planning such an expedition. One was that the Canadians were to the last degree discontented . with the English government, owing to the provisions of the Quebec Act of 1774, and, secondly, that as good Catholics and Frenchmen they were thoroughly dissatisfied with remaining under the control of a foreign and Protestant government.

The Quebec Act, by which the Province was governed, provided, with what has since proved singular wisdom, that as the body of the population was French it should be governed in the French and not in the English way. There was no representative assembly ; the people were ruled directly by the king through a governor appointed by him ; the old French law was recognized, especially in its regulation of land-tenures ; posts of honor were conferred upon the French Catholic nobles, and, more than all, for the first time since the Reformation the large Catholic Church estates, the continued possession of which had been guaranteed by the treaty of 1763, were confirmed by the Act to the clergy. There was, it is true, much discontent on the part of both the French and the English inhabitants, the latter of whom were few in numbers compared with the former. The French, of course, disliked a foreign and alien rule, and the English felt that the great guarantees of liberty had been sacrificed in order to keep the Province tranquil. Congress, with the inborn instinct of English freemen, supposed that because the Quebec Act was distasteful to the thirteen Colonies it must necessarily be so to the people of Canada. Under this delusion the invasion of the Province was undertaken, the expectation being that the invaders would be greatly aided by the discontented inhabitants. This hope was in a great measure disappointed, and the result was that our troops were repulsed from the walls of Quebec, leaving no trace of their work there save the undying remembrance of their heroic valor. Congress was a good deal puzzled to account for the want of support given to the invasion, especially by the Catholic clergy, whose influence was all-powerful with the French population. They sent a commission to Canada to clear up the mystery, composed of Dr. Franklin, Mr. Carroll (afterwards Catholic archbishop of Baltimore), and Judge Chase. These gentlemen soon discovered that the clergy declined to interfere, thinking that the exercise of their religion, and especially the possession of the Church estates, would be safer under the guarantee of the treaty of 1763 than under the promises of religious toleration made by the American

Congress. No doubt these priests in so acting were wise in their generation.

Such was the condition of affairs in Canada when the second expedition was undertaken. Its principal object was to reinforce the troops already in that Province; but where they would be found, or in what condition, no one could tell. A portion of Wayne's regiment was hurried forward by companies, but in such an unprepared condition that it was not until the first week in May, upon reaching Albany, that they were provided with arms. Five companies of the regiment, under Lieutenant-Colonel Johnston, were detained on Long Island as late as May 15 without arms, and without any prospect of receiving any other weapons than "d——d tomahawks," to use the energetic language of their commander. On the 5th of June they reached the fort at the mouth of the Sorel in Canada, about half-way between Montreal and Quebec, and there they found the remnant of General Montgomery's army, which had retreated from Quebec, and the Pennsylvania Brigade, under General Thompson, which had preceded them in the retreat, the whole under the command of General Sullivan. The British force, under General Burgoyne, was at Three Rivers, some distance down the St. Lawrence. The army having been collected at the Sorel, Sullivan ordered General Thompson with the Pennsylvania Brigade to attack the British at Three Rivers. As this was the first battle of the Revolution in which Pennsylvania troops fought almost alone (Maxwell's small New Jersey battalion being brigaded with it), and as it was Wayne's maiden battle, we annex his own account of it.

Colonel Wayne to Dr. Franklin and others.

CAMP AT SOREL 13th June 1776

DEAR SIR,—After a long march by land & water varied with De-lightful as well as Gloomy prospects we arrived here the night of the 5th Instant and on the 7th it was agreed in a council of war to attack the enemy at Three Rivers about 47 miles lower down, whose strength was estimated at 3 or 4 Hundred. Gen'l Thompson was appointed for this Command, the Disposition was as follows 4 attacks to be made at the same time viz Col Maxwell to conduct the first, myself the second, Col St Clair the third, & Col Irvine the 4th Lie't Col Hartley the Reserves.

On the same evening we Embarked and arrived at Col St Clairs Encampment about midnight—it was intended that the Attack shou'd be made at the dawn of day—this we found to be Impracticable, therefor we Remained where we were until the 9th when we to the number of 1450 Men all Penns'lvanians except Maxwells Battalion took boats

About 2 in the morning we landed nine Miles above the town, and after an Hour's march day began to appear. Our Guides had mistook the road, the Enemy Discovered and Cannonaded us from their ships, a Surprise was out of the Question—we therefore put our best face on it and Continued our line of march thro' a thick deep swamp three miles wide, and after four Hours Arrived at a more open piece of Ground—amidst the thickest firing of the shipping when all of a sudden a large Body of Regulars marched down in good Order Immediately in front of me to prevent our forming—in Consequence of which I Ordered my Light Infantry together with Capt Hay's Company of Riflemen to advance and amuse them whilst I was forming; they began and Continued the attack with great spirit until I advanced to support them when I ordered them to wheel to the Right & left and flank the Enemy at the same time we poured in a well Aimed and heavy fire in front as this—

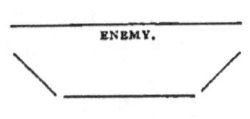

they attempted to Retreat in good Order at first but in a few minutes broke and ran in the utmost Confusion. About this time the Other Divisions began to Emerge from the swamp except Maxwell who with his was advanced in a thicket a Considerable Distance to the left—our

Rear now becoming our front &c At this Instant we Rec'd a heavy fire in flank from musketry, field pieces, Howitzers &c &c which threw us into some confusion, but was Instantly Remedied— We Advanced in Column up to their breast work's which till then we had not Discovered—at this time Gen'l Thompson with Cols St Clair, Irvine & Hartly were marching in full view to our support. Col Maxwell now began to Engage on the left of me, the fire was so hot he could not mantain his post—the other troops had also filed off to the left—my small Battalion composed of my own & two Companies of Jersey men under Major Ray amounting in the whole to about 200 were left exposed to the whole fire of the shipping in flank and full three thousand men in front with all their Artillery under the command of Gen'l Burgoyne— Our people taking example by others gave way— Indeed it was Imposible for them to stand it longer— Whilst Col Allen and myself were Employed in Rallying the troops Let. Col. Hartly had advanced with the Reserves and bravely Attacked the Enemy from a thicket in a swamp to the left, this hardiness of his was of the Utmost Consequence to us—we having rallied about 800 men from the Different Regiments —we now sent to find the Gen'l and Other field Officers—at the same time the Rifle men of mine & Irvine's kept up a galling fire on the Enemy—the Swamp was so deep and thick with timber and underwood that a man 10 yards in front or Rear wou'd not see the men Drawn up—this was the Cause of the Gen'l, Col St Clair, Maxwell & Irvine missing us—or perhaps they had taken for Granted that we were all cut off—Col Hartly who lay near by retreated without a Discovery on either side, until he Crossed our line near the left, which caused our people to follow him—Allen and myself were now left on the field with only twenty men & five Officers, the Enemy still Continuing their whole fire from Great and small guns upon us—but afraid to venture from their lines, we thought it prudent to keep them in play by keeping up a small fire in Order to gain time for our people to make good their Retreat in Consequence of which we Continued about an Hour longer in the field, and then Retreated back into the woods which brought us to a Road on the far side of the Swamp. We followed this Road about two miles when we cut loose from our small party & reached the Place where our people had enter'd the swamp by which means we soon Collected

6 or 700 men with whom we Retreated in good Order but without
nourishment of any kind. The Enemy who were Strong in number
had Detached in two or three bodies about 1500 men to cut off our
Retreat. They way laid & Engaged us again about 9 miles from the
field of Battle, they did us little damage. We Continued our march,
and the third day almost worn out with fatigue, Hunger, & Difi-
culties, scarcely to be paralleld we arrived here with 1100 men, but
Gen'l Thompson Col Irvine Doc'r McCalla and several Officers are
prisoners at Three Rivers— Col St Clair Arrived alone last night
Their Separation from the Army (which appeared Indeed to be lost)
was the cause of their misfortunes—I believe it will be Universally
allowed that Col Allen & myself have saved the Army in Canada.
Capt Robinson has proved himself the Soldier and the Gen'tm. his
Conduct has outgone the most Sanguine hopes of his friends, out of
150 of my own I have lost more than the One Quarter part—together with Slight touch in my Right leg—which is partly well
already, we shall have more business soon, our People are in high
spirits and long for the Other bought as well as your H'l S't—

ANT'Y WAYNE.

So much for the battle of the Three Rivers. We
now come to the retreat of the beaten army, and the
prompt and skilful efforts made by Colonel Wayne to
cover with it the escape of Arnold from Montreal, to
which place the British army, successful at the Three
Rivers, pushed forward at once. Arnold, on learning
the approach of the enemy, had retreated from Montreal, and sent his aide-de-camp, Wilkinson, to Sullivan
to ask that some of his men should be detached to
aid him. In his search for Sullivan on the line of
the retreat Wilkinson found the men whose aid he was
sent to implore in a pitiable condition. We cannot do
better than borrow his graphic account of what followed
(Memoirs, vol. i. p. 51 *et seq.*): "I found every house
and hut on my route crowded with straggling men

without officers, and officers without men. The first
officer of my acquaintance whom I met was Lieutenant-
Colonel William Allen,[1] of the Second Pennsylvania. I
informed him of my orders for a detachment. He replied, 'Wilkinson, this army is conquered by its fears,
and I doubt whether you can draw any assistance from
it; but Colonel Wayne is in the rear, and if any one
can do it he is the man.' On which I quickened my
pace, and half an hour after I met that gallant soldier as
much at his ease as if he was marching to a parade of
exercise. He halted at the bridge and posted a guard,
with orders to stop every man, without regard to corps,
who appeared to be active, alert, and equipped. In a
short time a detachment was completely formed and in
motion for Longueil (on the route to Montreal). The
very men who only the day before were retreating in
confusion before a division of the enemy now marched
with alacrity against his main body." Shortly afterwards it was discovered that Arnold had escaped without the aid of Wayne's troops, and they were pushed
on to join Sullivan. "Then," says Wilkinson, "our
detachment was discovered advancing on the bank of
the Sorel two miles below the fort. We were taken
(by Sullivan) for the enemy, and great alarm and confusion ensued, the drums beat to arms, and General
Sullivan and his officers were observed making great
exertions to prepare for battle. Colonel Wayne halted
his column, pulled out his glass, and seemed to enjoy

---

[1] Colonel Allen, who behaved so gallantly at the battle of the
Three Rivers, was one of the four sons of Chief Justice Allen, of
Pennsylvania. After the Declaration of Independence was adopted
he resigned his commission and entered the British service.

the panic his appearance produced," etc. These operations, disastrous in their results in many ways, seemed
to show that there was at least one man in that army
with the stuff of a true general in him. The coolness
and readiness of resource which he exhibited, and the
courage with which he was able in a short hour to recall
a fleeing and panic-stricken rabble to the duty and discipline of soldiers, find scarcely a parallel in the history
of our Revolutionary campaigns. To understand fully
Wayne's position, it must not be forgotten that in this
battle and retreat Wayne commanded for the first time
men who were brought also for the first time under
the fire of the enemy. General Thompson and Colonel
Irvine having been taken prisoners at the Three Rivers,
and Colonel St. Clair having been wounded, the command of the Pennsylvania troops during the difficult
retreat from the Sorel to Ticonderoga devolved upon
Colonel Wayne, himself, as we have seen, slightly
wounded. They were closely pursued from St. John's
to Lake Champlain by a British division under Burgoyne, and it required all the activity and vigilance of
the commander to enable his men to reach in safety
first the Isle aux Noix, and afterwards Crown Point
and Ticonderoga, where they determined to make a
stand. The enemy, however, after destroying Arnold's
fleet on the lake, and threatening Ticonderoga, de-
ferred further operations until the next season.

These operations in Canada had established the reputation of Colonel Wayne as an energetic officer, and
no doubt led to his appointment on the 18th of November, by General Schuyler, to the command of the fort
at Ticonderoga with its dependencies, the second most

important military post, as Wayne regarded it, in the country. The garrison consisted of about two thousand five hundred men, who were under his command during the winter. His labors, trials, and anxieties while stationed at this post are most graphically described in his letters. They were written to private friends, who were naturally very anxious to know how he and his two thousand Pennsylvanians were faring while guarding this distant frontier. The style of these letters is very free and unconventional, but they are interesting as presenting a very striking picture of garrison life and its surroundings. The ever-confident and even at times boastful spirit so characteristic of Wayne is very conspicuous in these letters, but it does not overshadow the real earnestness and enthusiasm of the patriot and the soldier. They embrace a great variety of subjects, including the position of the garrison at Ticonderoga, the condition of the Pennsylvania regiments there, the unhealthiness of the post, the difficulties arising from short enlistments, observations on the anarchical condition of things then prevailing in Pennsylvania, and so forth. It is not possible to arrange them in a strictly chronological order, so as to make the story they tell clearer, but it seems to us that a selection from them will prove, in their unadorned simplicity, full of interest to those who desire to know how people felt and acted in the army and in Congress in the dark days of the Revolution. We copy those sent to his wife and to his brother-in-law, Colonel Penrose. The details he gives of his garrison life are interesting. The others addressed to Dr. Franklin and other friends on the military and political situation are given because they are

highly characteristic of the man, and show what work
the Pennsylvania troops were doing on the Canada
frontier.

Colonel Wayne to Mrs. Mary Wayne.

TICONDEROGA 12th Aug't 1776

DEAR POLLY,—I wrote to you by the —— and sent a small present—he will be able to give you a particular acc't of this place
and Army—but he will paint matters worse than they realy are—
within these two days we have been Re-enforc'd by three Thousand
new England militia; fresh provision is become more plenty than
salt; & our people have Recovered health and spirits—I have now
the finest and best Regiment in the Continental Service—we are
viewed with admiration and pleasure by all the Officers in the Army,
and we have render'd our camp almost Impregnable—

Fortune has heretofore been a fickle Goddess to us—and like
some other females changed for the first new face she saw— We shall
once more court her in the face of all the British thunder, and take
her *Vi et armis* from her present possessors— A Major Bigelow—who
was sent with a flag to Canada—Returned just now from the Enemy's
advanced post who treated him with a Cold distant Civility—he
has brought with him the Orders of the day Issued by General
Carleton—they are Bombastical, Insolent, & empty—you'll shortly
see them published by Congress— . . . The fall may turn up something,—we are prepared for the event, and Death or Glory will attend
us— I wou'd write to several of my old friends & neighbours but
for want of time;—you'l let them know they live in my grateful
memory, and I shall always esteem myself happy in Rendering them
every service in my Power.

I hope yet to pass many an Agreeable hour in your and their
Society—but if the fate of war shou'd Order it otherwise—they will
Remember I fell in the support of their Rights—and the Rights of
Mankind

Adieu my Dear Girl

ANT'Y WAYNE.

Colonel Wayne to Mrs. Mary Wayne.

TICONDEROGA 3d Jan'y 1777

DEAR POLLY,—I don't know where this will meet you. The Rapid
progress of the Enemy through Jersey only reach'd us last evening—

perhaps they may now be in Phil'a and Ravaging the Country for many miles Round

The Anxiety we are under on acc't of our families and friends is much better felt than expressed— Should you be necessitated to leave Easttown—I doubt not but you'l meet with Hospitality in the Back parts of the provinces— The *British Rebels* may be successful for a time ; they may take and Destroy our Towns near the Water and Distress us much But they never can—they never will subjugate the free born sons of America. Our Growing Country can meet with Considerable Losses and survive them : but one Defeat to our more than Savage Enemy Ruins them for ever :

A number of unhappy Circumstances have Contributed to their success thus far, but let not that in the least Dispirit you. We shall soon learn to face them in the field and the day is not far off when we shall produce a Conviction to the World that we Deserve to be free—

I expect every hour to be Relieved with Orders to march to the Assistance of Gen'l Washington : I have 1500 Hardy Veterans left who will push hard for Victory and Revenge—they are second to none in Courage (I have seen them tried) and I know they Equal any Regulars in point of Discipline—I hope soon to meet their Sanguine Wish—that is to lead them on to Death or Glory

Kiss my little boy and Girl for me— Give my kindest Compliments to all friends and believe me ever yours

A. WAYNE.

[MRS. M. WAYNE.]

Colonel Wayne to Colonel Penrose.

TICONDEROGA 23rd Aug. 1776

We Remain in the same state as when I wrote you last, with only this Difference—I begin to get me in flesh ; wine, punch, porter, Venson Mutton Beef Potatoes Peas beans Butter & Cheese begin to make their appearance in Camp ; of these good Creatures I the more freely partake—as man can not live by bread alone ; *there are but few who live in this way* tho' all wou'd wish it, provided they cou'd obtain it without much expense—but that is Impossible here for it appears to be the last part of the world that God made & I have some ground to believe it was finished in the dark—that it was never Intended that man shou'd live in it is clear—for the people who attempted to make any stay—have for the most part perished by pestilence or the sword.

I believe it to be the Ancient *Golgotha* or place of Skulls—they are so plenty here that our people for want of Other Vessels drink out of them whilst the soldiers make tent pins of the shin and thigh bones of Abercrumbies men—

[COL. PENROSE.]

Colonel Wayne to Dr. Franklin.

TICONDEROGA 29th July 1776

DEAR SIR,—We are so far Removed from the seat of Govern't of the *free* and *Independent* states of America—and such an Insurmountable Barrier, Albany, between us that not one letter, or the least Intelligence of any thing that's doing with you can reach us. Through the medium of my Chaplain (the Rev Mr Jones), I hope this will reach you as he has promised to blow out any man's brains who will attempt to take it from him

Naturally, I must own I have some Apprehensions for the Brave and Generous sons of America who will be obliged to bear the brunt of the day.—A raw Undisciplined Militia crowding in upon them will in a few Weeks become Impatient of Command & Subject to many Disorders fatal to an army—an artful enemy will wait the favourable moment to make approach—Howe is not unacquainted with the wretched Condition our people were in at Cambridge— he lost the Opportunity—he'l not be guilty of the like soon again—

Burgoyne will attempt a Junction. He'l not effect it without the loss of much blood—Col St Clair, Dehaes, & myself are in possession of Montcalms lines. We shall render them more formidable than they ever were in a few days. We are to be joined by Col Hartley. The whole of the Pennsylvanians in this Country will amount to 1600 men fit for duty Officers Included— Our lines are extensive—but Rest assured, If Burgoyne makes an attack upon us —the British arms will meet a worse fate than when under Abercrombie— They'l find an enemy fertile in expedients, and brave by nature, who will push them hard for Victory, & Revenge for the unfortunate affair at the Three Rivers—I am almost tempted to say with MacDuff, Gracious heaven ! cut short all Intervention and front to front set those sons of War and ourselves—if they then escape may heaven forgive them too—

The Eastern troops are stationed on the East and Opposite side of the lake—on a peninsula Inaccessible except at one spot—which they are beginning to fortify— These are composed of three Brigades, we of one under Col St Clair, who with myself are Engineers in chief. We amend, form, and Alter such part, and parts of the French lines as we think proper, a plan of which is here Inclosed—

I believe the whole amount of our Army fit for duty may amount to about 3500 men—we expect a Reinforcement from Connecticut shortly of 1500, and we are Indefatigable in preparing to meet the Enemy by water—the superiority in a naval force on this Lake is an Object of the first moment— It has been we think shamefully neglected—but now we have Information of 100 Carpenters from the Eastward and 50 from Philadelphia, being at Skene'sboro', and all at work in building Gondolas— At present we have three little schoners, and one sloop well Rigged—and man'd with people drafted from the Respective Regiments, they carry from 8 to 16 Guns each. These with four Gondolas already built will be a formidable fleet in *this sea*—on which I think we may ride Triumphant if we please. The Enemy on the Other hand are Industriously Employ'd in building vessels, Batteaus &c &c so that in a few days we shall put the matter to the test. We have Rec'd two days fresh Provisions and have a prospect of being better supplied—our people begin to recruit in health and spirits—but are still Destitute of almost every necessary fit for a soldier, shoes, stockings shirts and coats are articles not easily done without—yet they cannot be Obtained—

I am sorry to have Occasion to write in this manner but when Objects of Distress hourly strike the eye—Objects that look up to me for Relief, I can't but feel for their situation although unable to help them— Can't some means be fallen upon to send a speedy supply of these articles—

The *State* of Mass'ts Bay has Established a post to this place & all letters carried free to the Army—as you'l see by the Inclosed note. Can't you procure a similar one to pass in our *State*—or are we less worthy than the Gentlemen from the Eastward—be that as it may—an Inquiry into the cause of this shameful Conduct in some of the

Different posts or Offices is a matter not to be neglected, as it may in the end be attended with bad and fatal Consequences.

Dr. Rush to Colonel Wayne.

PHILAD'A Septemb'r 24th 1776

My dear Sir,—I have not been unmindful of you since we parted. No man rejoiced more than I did in hearing of your gallant behavior at the Three Rivers, and General Sullivan can witness for me that when He repeated any anecdote that related to our Army in Canada in which your name was mentioned with respect, I felt, and showed the same satisfaction that I should have done had he been lavishing encomiums upon a brother.—You will hear before this reaches you that the command of General Sinclair's regiment was given to Col: Wood. I lament with you Col: Allen's resignation, and loss to our Army, but I believe you have been misinformed as to his motives in that transaction— His family suffered no indignities in this State but such as they in some degree merited by their opposition to the institution of a new government, and the declaration of Independence—I have constantly made great allowances for gentlemen of moderate sentiments, and still class several of them among the worthiest of my friends, but I think it no breach of charity to suppose that a family so much affected in power, and property as the one above mentioned were actuated only by low, and interested motives.—

My seat in Congress has subjected me to many cares to which I was a stranger when my whole business consisted in reading—writing—& feeling pulses.—I am obliged daily to hear the most melancholy accounts of the distresses of our troops from wants of every kind—I have felt a large share of the pain & shame brought upon our arms by the desertion of Long Island, and evacuation of New York. The military spirit of our country men seems to have subsided in that part of the continent, and a torpor seems likewise to have seized upon the citizens of America in general. I apprehend we have overrated the public Virtue of our country. If this is the case, let us not repine at misfortunes— They are necessary to the growth & existence of patriotism. History shows us that States like individuals have arisen to importance only when their foundations were laid in difficulties & adversity. We received so many pledges during the last Campaign of the favor and protection of Heaven that it would seem a species of infidelity to doubt our success in the issue of the present controversy.

A convention has at last formed a government for our State. Herewith I send you a copy of it [Constitution of 1776]. It is tho't by many people to be rather too much upon the democratical order, for liberty is as apt to degenerate into luxuriousness, as power is to become arbitrary. Restraints therefore are as necessary in the former as in the latter case. Had the Governor and Council in the new constitution of Pennsylvania possessed a negative upon the proceedings of the assembly, the government would have derived safety—wisdom & dignity from it. But we hope the Council of Censors will remedy this defect at the expiration of seven years.

My present situation requires that I shou'd possess a thorough knowledge of the state of the armies of the Continent. Let me beg of you therefore to furnish me every week (if possible) with the history of every material occurrence in the Northern department. Tell me all your wants whether they relate to provisions, clothing, tents—ammunition or medicines— I could wish you would go further, & inform [me] what officers, and what brigades, or regiments stand highest with you for courage—conduct, and military discipline. Duty & inclination will prompt me to do every thing in my power to remedy abuses—correct delays—and reward merit of every kind in the Army.

My Comp'ts await Gen'l Gates, and Gen'l St. Clair. Tell the latter that I have done nothing since I took my seat in Congress with greater pleasure than giving my Vote for making him a Brigadier and I wish for nothing more than to do the same justice to the merit of my friend Col: Wayne. *Inter nos*—an attention in you to Gen'l Gates may facilitate this matter if it should soon come before Congress.

Adieu, my dear Anthony, God bless you! & bring you back in safety to our native province in which I hope to spend many days with you in the enjoyment of that freedom for which we are both making sacrifices in the cabinet & field.

Yours sincerely
B. Rush.

Colonel Wayne to Dr. Franklin and Mr. Morton.

TICONDEROGA 2nd Oct. 1776.

DEAR SIR,—I have the same plea for not answering yours of the 16th of Aug—as you had when you wrote—i.e want of time— I observe we have an extraordinary House or Convention and as an extraordinary Bench of the peace—but the old Adage holds—that a Desperate Disorder—requires a Desperate cure— Our Constitution was Convulsed—these may be the most proper state Physicians to restore it to its native vigor—I hope they will effect it— I am totally unacquainted with your Politicks I shall therefore waive the subject—and like uncle Toby ride my own hobby— We are not a little surprised at the evacuation of Long Island—the surrender of that was the opening the Door to the Island of New York—our people can't possibly hold that place when the North & East Rivers are free for the enemy's fleet. They will even have it in their power to land troops on the Back of our ports—an Event which I fear they have not properly Guarded against. If so the sacrifice of 4-5 or even 10,000 men in my humble Opinion ought to be made rather than to have given up ground for a small Misfortune—that will not only supply the Enemy with Every necessary and afford them Winter Quarters—but reduce us to the hard necessity of making a Winter Campaign in the open field to watch their motions—

As to us—unless the Enemy can prevail over our fleet—which I think will be no easy matter, we having greatly the advantage in point of time and materials for this purpose, which Advantage we have Industriously Improved—& on the land side our lines are strengthen'd with Redoubts—they can not Carry by Storm—and the Season is too farre Advanced for a Regular Seige add to this our people are in high spirits—tho' poorly and thinly clad—yet they will sell their Lives & Liberty dear—the fatigue they have undergone in this place is Inexpressible, yet they go thro' all without a murmor—

*   *   *   *   *   *   *   *   *

ANTH'Y WAYNE.

Colonel Wayne to Dr. Rush.

TICONDEROGA 18th Oct'r 1776

MY DEAR SIR,—I shall not attempt to give my Opinion of what Regiments or Officers stand highest in Esteem for military Discipline or Conduct—until the fortune of War Determines whether

Americans or Britains are to remain masters of this Ground—an event which in all probability will be known before this Reaches you perhaps in a few hours—they have prevail'd over our Fleet,—and are within fifteen miles of this place—the first fair wind brings them up—when I am Apprehensive they will Oblige us to meet them on Open Ground—our rear being in a great measure neglected—for we always depended on our Fleet—as the Rear Guard—that Depend-ence is now at an end—and if they Attack us in that Quarter we shall have warm work—it will not be cool to them as they will be exposed to the fire of two Batteries—upon the whole I am Rather Inclined to think they will strive to make the Assault on the Penns'a lines as it is the Ground which Commands all the Other works—if they shou'd be so hardy—I am almost Confident of success—

Our Army don't Amount to more than 6000 Effective men—of which something less than One half i e about 2600 will bear the brunt of the day—the Remainder being on Mount Independance on the Opposite Side of the lake—I can't in Justice Omit mentioning one hundred Pennsylvanians who arrived here last Evening from lake George—where they were lately sent for the Recovery of their health to the Gen'l Hospital—on hearing of the defeat of our Fleet they Immediately returned to this place Determined to Conquer or die, with their Country men—these poor Emaciated worthy fellows are Entitled to more merit than I have time or Ability to Describe.

I could write you a long letter Cont'g a list of Grieveances, & such Intelligence as you Require but the Enemy will not permit me —and I am Call'd to Arms by an Alarm this moment Given—

Adieu my Dear friend & believe me yours &c

ANT'Y WAYNE.

Adjutant Harper to Colonel Wayne.

ALBANY Janu'y 31 1777

DEAR COLONEL,—Your Regiment march'd from this Place yester-day morning—but the Soldiers were so dispersed through the Town that It was with the Greatest Dificulty that wee got them together— The place was so full of Recruiting Parties Endeavouring to enlist them that two thirds of them were drunk— The Recruiting Officers here Rather than miss a Pennsylvanian would sit and drink with him all night—they Even have Gone into the Hospitals and enlisted Our

Sick, some of whom were Re-enlisted before Viz Short of Capt. Poth Company and Jones a Silver Smith of Capt. Morris, they tried two Days ago and are to be punished—

*   *   *   *   *   *   *   *   *

Colonel Johnston to Richard Peters, Secretary of Board of War.

Oct 20, '76.

If you shou'd think proper, you may publish the following Paragraph, in regard to our Penn'a soldiers—" It appears to me that the Pennsylvanians were originally designed for Soldiers, their Vigilance, assiduity & resignation to bad Usage, fatigue & ye strictest Discipline convinces me—their bravery too & enthusiasm in the Service are equally remarkable—

"'There is an Anecdote respecting them, which I cannot omit mentioning—as soon as the News of the Defeat of our Fleet reach'd Fort George, the Pennsylvanians who had been laid up in the Hospitals emaciated with Disease & Sickness of the most malignant kind, even some of them with Discharges in their Pockets, without Orders or the least compulsion, fix'd on their Military Accoutraments & crossed the Lake to our Assistance, swearing by every thing sacred they wou'd have ample revenge—

" As two Privates of the first Bat'n Commanded by Col. De Haas pass'd thro' our Encampment on their return, they were asked if no more of the Penn'as were coming to w'h they answ'd with Indignation 'Yes, blast your Eyes, every sick man amongst us that cou'd possibly crawl, but we lead the Van from our Rank'—this they Did while other pusilanimous wretches had their whole thoughts entirely bent upon Home—"

I can add no more, as the Divine says, so present my Love to Mr & Mrs Delany & God bless you both—

I am sincerely Yours &c

F: Johnston.

Colonel Johnston to Colonel Wayne.

Albany 17th Nov'r, 1776—

Dear Col'l,—I rec'd your agreeable Letter of the 12th inst't from the Hand of Col: Lewis   Its Contents serve as a farther Proof of the friendship you bear me—

I shall ever embrace the opportunities put in my way, of acknowledging the several kindnesses you confer on me—& use my utmost diligence to repay them—

I find you have engaged the Interests of Gen'l Gates St Clair & Col: De Haas in my favor I shall never forget this signal piece of service— I have been assiduous in my Endeavours to enlist, but all such as are fit for the service are already engaged, the Others are only *Food for Worms*—miserable sharp looking Caitiffs, hungry lean fac'd Villains &c &c.

Your Letter, joined to the services w'h I apprehend I can perform in Penn'a, have determin'd me to proceed— Let me add to this Poor Tom [Robinson] is so weak yet, that I must not part with him— On my Arrival, I propose to open my Quarters near Chester & send out trusty Serjeants for the purpose of recruiting our Regiment; As Wallace & Funk cannot join us again with propriety, I suppose I may Venture to promise a worthy fellow an Ensignsy, & Dispatch him thro' the Country in search of Recruits—

I find myself greatly recovered but still continue weak—riding on Horse back will fully effect my Cure— I shou'd most assuredly have visited *Tye* this week, but your Letter induces me (as I before observ'd) to go on— I cannot part with you thus— The news of this place I must transmit you—

It is said here that Howe's Army have cross'd over to the Jersey side, & that our Army means to accompany them wherever they go— It is likewise reported, that a Strong Detachment of the Enemy are in the rear of Fort Montgomery, w'h you know is totally undefended— It is very observable, that all the American Fortifications are defenceless in the rear & ever left unguarded— Oh the *miserable* State of this Country ! As we are obliged to place our Dependance on such *miserable* Engineers—

Whether this be Albany News w'h I have just related, or real fact I know not, but certain it is ; Orders have been issued that all the Batteaus, Boats &c &c shall immediately be sent down the North River to transport our Army— Indeed I have heard that the Batteaus in & about Lake George must be carried in Waggons to Fort Edw'd & from thence forwarded here—if this be true, then the Army at *Tye* will naturally retreat for want of Provisions—

I could here criticize & animadvert largely on the Conduct of great men in the service of the States, on *their Counsels*, their *Mili-*

tary knowledge &c but this is unnecessary, as you are fully capable of comparing things with each other & drawing just Inferences— My friend Sec'y Peters informs me of Col: Shee's Resignation which has completely ruin'd him— He urges me strenuously by no means to follow his Example, I trust in Heaven, I never shall, tho', I must confess it chagrin'd me to see a Dutch Tavern keeper & a fat son of Epicurus promoted over my Head— Men with calmer Passions & possess'd of more Stoicism than I, would shew their Resentment on the like Occasion— Mr. Peters further adds—"things are in great Confusion in our State, the *Conventie* tho *Damnatie Conventie* have produced a sickly Constitution, not worth defending"—however I shall not have Paper suff't to make the necessary Quotations I therefore refer you to his Letter w'h I have inclosed—

My dear Sir, I must bid you adieu—
from yours sincerely
F. JOHNSTON—

P.S. Capt'n Robinson sends a deal of respects Compl't &c to you & desires you not to neglect to mention his name in your Letters, as you may th [torn out] he merits— The ½ y'rs you sent Home p [torn out] for £5: 4—get more if you can F. J.

Colonel Wayne to Sharp Delany.

TICONDEROGA 15th Dec'r 1776

MY DEAR DELANY,—Last night has frozen Lake Champlain to the Centre—it is all one solid mass of Ice—our poor fellows severely felt the Effect of it—for my own part I was so Congeal'd that after turning before the fire for three hours by *Shrewsbury Clock*—I was not half thawed until I put one Bottle of wine under my Sword Belt at Dinner— I have been toasting you all but can't *toast myself*—for by the time that one side is warm the other is froze ; however I'll still keep to the Internal Application—here's God bless you all and now let me ask you a few Questions. Who of our friends were killed or taken at Fort Washington?—was it Carried—by Surprise or Storm?— Is Gen'l Washington still Retreating—has he lost all his heavy Cannon?—dare the Enemy venture into the Country in pursuit of him— Are our people so used to *stand behind works* that they dare not face the foe in the field— That—that is the Rock we have split on. Our time has been Intirely taken up in making lines

&c and no attention paid to Manœuvring—our Defenses by some fatality have been all so planed that when ever the Enemy could get in our Rear—   *   *   *   *   *   *

In regard to discipline we understood by this only to put a necessary Constraint on the principle of freedom to prevent it growing into licentiousness which it unavoidably would if not Curbed in an army—here I must once more call in the aid of Marshal Saxe—he says—*and he says well*—"that it is a false notion, that subordination, and a passive Obedience to Superiors, is any Debasement of a mans Courage—*so far from it*, that it is a General remark—that those Armies that have been subject to the severest Discipline *have always* performed the Greatest things"—

I could say much on this subject— I shall for my own part Endeavor to put it into practice as far as in my power as I am well Convinced that we shall never Establish our Liberties until we learn to beat the *English Rebels* in the field—I hope the day is not far off.

An other Campaign or two if our people are well Appointed, Clothed and Victualed may Effect it—present my best Compliments to Mrs. Delany and all friends and believe me D'r Sir

Yours most Sincerely

ANT'Y WAYNE.

P.S. Col Johnston & Doct'r Kennedy will give you an Acc't of our Situation— Tell Mr Sect'y of War, he shall never have my benediction unless he sends troops to relieve us soon—

Colonel Wayne to Richard Peters, Secretary of War.

TICONDEROGA 1st December 1776

DEAR SIR,—An express just arrived brings advice of Fort Washington being in the Hands of the Enemy and the whole Garrison Consisting of 2000 men being killed or Prisoners, and that our people are on the Jersey side Retreating from post to post. Is the Genius of America fled our Arms?—is she ashamed to associate with her Degenerate sons; or does She Esteem them as Aliens, unworthy her protection. Are not the Enemy as Vulnerable as us;—cuts not our Swords as keen;—pierce not our Balls as deep as theirs?—*they do*—why then this terror—why shrink as from a Gorgon's head whenever they appear. Oh! my dear Sir, I but too well know the Occasion. If you have any Regard for the Liberty

of your Country;—or the Honour of America, Embody the Southern Troops by themselves; give more Attention to Manœuvering—
and less to working and rest Assured of Success—

I thank my God we are left partly alone—I have yet 1500 hardy
Veterans from Penn'a, would to Heaven I could for a day lead them
to the Assistance of poor Washington;—I would Risque my soul,
that they would sell their lives, or Liberties at too dear a Rate for
Britons to make many purchases— I wrote to Doct'r Rush a few
days since and forgot to Enclose him the State of this Garrison—
you will please to show it him—and please to let me know which of
our friends are lost at Fort Wash'g'n— Some Catiff or Envious
Dev-l prevents any Intelligence Reaching here unless it Militates
against us— I have just now Rec'd a letter from Delany Dated
17th Sep'r—make my excuse to him for not sending an answering
it at this time. give my love to my Daughter and believe me yours
Most

Sincerely
A. WAYNE.

Colonel Wayne to General Schuyler.

TICONDEROGA 2nd Jan'y 1777

DEAR GENERAL,—I herewith send you a Return of this Garrison
as also of the Soldiers re-engaged to serve during the War—which are
but few— "Liberty to come down for one month when Relieved"
carries with it an Idea of being Immediately sent back again to a
place which they Imagine to be very unhealthy;—they say; march
us off this Ground and then we will Cheerfully Re-engage ; add to
this their anxiety about their friends in the Jerseys and Penns'a
makes them Impatient to be led to the assistance of their Distressed
Country

They likewise see the Eastern people Running away in the Clouds
of the Night—(some before and all soon as their times expires).
Col Whitcombs Regiment—all the Sailors & Mariners—the whole of
the Artificers and all the Corps of Artillery except Capt. Roman's
Company (which consists but of 12 men Officers Included) are gone
off the Ground

Notwithstanding so bad an example—and the distress of their
native *State*—the Pennsylvanians, will not leave me until fresh
troops arrive to Relieve them

Your own feelings Sir on the Alarming Situation of Affairs in Penns'a and Jersey; will best Inform you of *that of* every Other Officer and Soldier (from those States) on the Present Occasion: which causes us most Ardently to wish for an Opportunity of meeting those Sons of War and Rapine—face to face; and man to man.

These worthy fellows are Second to none in Courage (*I have seen them proved*)—and I know that they are not far behind any Regulars in Point of Discipline— Such troops, actuated by Principle, and fired with just Resentment must be an Acceptable, and *perhaps seasonable* Re-inforcement to Gen'l Washington at this Critical Juncture—

If you shou'd be of the same Opinion and cause us to be Immediately relieved—with Orders to march with all Dispatch to join the main Army—I believe we shou'd be able to Re-enlist the Chief part of our people on the way: however this may be I wou'd answer for it that they will not turn aside from Danger (altho their terms shou'd be expired) when the safety and Honor of their Country Require them to face it—

I must Once more earnestly Request you to Order up shoes and soap—we are much Distressed for want of these Necessary Articles—

Doct'r M'Crea arrived last night with some Medicine—but Hospital Stores, roots and Vegitables we are totally Destitute of

I am Dear General

Your Most Ob't

Hum'l Ser't

ANT'Y WAYNE.

[GEN'L SCHUYLER.]

Colonel Wayne to General Schuyler.

TICONDEROGA 22d Jany. 1777

DEAR GEN'L,—Col Simons Reg't Col Robinsons Reg't Consisting of about 700 men Officers Included are now Arrived together with 24 men of Col Warner's Regiment—

In Consequence I have Ordered One Reg't of the Penns'a to march tomorrow. The Others will follow as soon as Possible with Orders to Proceed in Good Order to Phil'a— I have Lately Rec'd letters from Gen'l St. Clair and other Gent'm in Gen'l Washington's Camp which made me think it Advisable to keep these Regt's Embodied until they are Dismissed by the Board of War:—their time

. expired the 5th of this Instant : they are to be settled with in Phil'a *agreeable to Promise*, when I have Reason to expect the greatest part will Reengage—

I want much to go also—it would be in my Power to do more with them in case of necessity than perhaps any other Officer : I know these worthy fellows well and they know me— I am Confident they would not Desert me in a time of Danger— If you think it would be for the benefit of the Service—I shou'd be glad to be Immediately Relieved in Command with Orders to march with the last of the Southern troops.

For the present I am using every Effort to Render this place strong. I shall soon Complete the *Abattis* Round the Old fort, and Octagons on Mt. Independence, and two New Blockhouses ; so that in a few days we hope to Render this post tenable and leave it in a much securer and better state than we found it—the manner in which I have kept our Guards and Sentries and the Constant Succession of Scouts which I have out—if followed by my successor—will Effectually prevent a surprise ; you will please to Order the Other troops Destin'd for this Garrison to be forward'd with all Possible Dispatch—

Interim I am D'r Sir

Yours Most Sincerely

ANT'Y WAYNE.

[GENL SCHUYLER.]

Colonel Wayne to Sharp Delany—Extract.

20 Feb. 77

*   *   *   *   *   *   *   *

I must now in Confidence tell you that this post has been most shamefully neglected—all the old and good Troops are gone—none here but a few wretched militia—badly armed and worse Disciplined—

This Garrison at this time Ought to Consist of at least 5000 Effective men—with a well trained Corps of Artillery—perhaps Congress thinks it does. I have not One fifth part of that number on the Ground—and I would much Rather Risque my life, Reputation, and the fate of America on 400 Good Troops, than the Whole of the present Garrison.

5

This is the Situation of the Second post in the United States—the Neighboring Governments are now roused—and I expect in a few days to be strongly Re-enforced— A body of the Enemy were Discovered a few days since marching this way by two Canadians—who are gone to Albany—this has awaked Gen'l Schuyler and Others (whose business it was to send Troops) from their Lethargy—

We may probably have some Diversion in a few Hours—I have yet some good men on whom I can Depend—and I will be answerable for the maintainance of this post until succour can Arrive. Adieu my Dear Delany, and believe me still your Friend

And most Ob't

Hum Ser't

ANT'Y WAYNE.

[S. DELANY, ESQR.]

Colonel Wayne was appointed brigadier-general in February, 1777. It was hoped by his friends that he would return home for a short season and help to bring order out of the confusion into which public affairs then had been thrown in Pennsylvania.

Sharp Delany to Colonel Wayne.

PHILAD'A 28th March 1777

MY DEAR GENERAL,—To wish my Friend Joy or congratulate him on his advancement to the Rank of B: General, would seem as if I did not thoroughly know him—but to me your merits are sufficiently known   I am firmly persuaded that office could not be better or more properly given—& *ought long ere now*— Your last gave me true friendly pain—since Sept'r & not a line from Family or Friends when to my knowledge you ought to have rec'd many— Yesterday I came from East-town & left all very well tho strong in expectation of your long wished arrival— Tho' I share in every one of your honours—yet believe me I could wish you had not left us—more may be done by you in the distracted state of our Government—than perhaps would balance the many gallant & beneficial actions you have done for your Country in Canada.   To point them out in a letter would be impossible which is the reason I have but slightly touched on them in former letters.   When I have the great pleasure to see you here—I shall give you a long talk, showing the weakness, folly, Ambition of politicians. Before matters are brought right you may be Witness, you must be witness to all of them.

I never yet flattered myself you could have been spared on Acct of the Importance of the Post you command—till properly relieved, —tho all other of your friends were sure of your coming— Gen'l Greene a few days since informed me a G'l Patterson was to take charge of Ticond'a chiefly for your coming home which only gives me the hope of seeing you—busy scenes may perhaps induce you to give your Services to your Country without any intermission—but let me my Friend, advise & beg of you, to come first home, & gratify your Friends & put new life in your Family & Mother who really pine for the beloved Husband, Father & Son. You are the only military man I know who has been so long on Duty—nor is it to be expected or thought the whole man should or could be absorbed by one line of Duty—come then once more let me ask it, & speedily to your desiring Friends, & in a time we will again restore you to the Continent. I have need of you myself for many accounts— I have been in the field, if to be as I was may be called so—would to God our militia were better regulated— I was honoured by the Assembly with the Post of Lieu't of the City with Rank of Col'l Command't so that you see I may have been at head of the militia of our State but declined it—for reasons I know will be pleasing to you, when I can see and converse with you. Mr. Johnston having but a few minutes to wait, will excuse the form & manner of this letter as I was all the week with my Family at Hunters near you—but away with excuses—as my Friend I know believes I could not neglect him—he will receive all from me as coming from a friendly Heart, which I assure will ever be so while it is the property of

SHARP DELANY.

P.S. Had I expected this opportunity, would have bro't a letter from Mrs Wayne & Mother.

The condition of the military hospitals within the territory occupied by Colonel Wayne was, it seems,

such as required immediate attention. He writes thus
to George Clymer, member of Congress:

TICONDEROGA 15th Dec'r 1776

DEAR SIR,—Before this reaches you—you will almost forget that
there are some people yet Remaining at Ticonderoga who realy
Esteem your friendship—but how long that will be the case I cannot
say;—as Death that *Grisly Horrid Monster*—that Caitiff who Distinguishes neither the Gentleman, nor the Soldier, age, Sex or *State*
is daily making dreadful Havock amongst us the Pennsylvanians:
I have buried out of my own Regiment since you left this Ground
upwards of fifty men   I believe I have once already told you that
in my Opinion it was the last part of God's work, the ancient *Golgotha*—Certain it is that the Supreme Being never Intended mankind to live in it—as few, *very few* who have Attempted to make a
Lodgment, or *any stay* survived the Sword—the pestilence or famine.

We are at present threatened by all three—notwithstanding we
shall have the hardiness to brave them out until properly Relieved ;
—for my own part if I am doomed to fall by either—I wou'd chuse
the first as being the most Honorable (altho not the most likely to
take place at the present)

This you may Depend on as fact that out of the three Pennsylvania Regiments, which I have with me, & who Marched full two
thousand Effective men into this Country, Officers Included, I shall
not bring home more than Nine Hundred ; and the most of those
Emaciated—worn out and unfit for further duty—

Perhaps keeping us here so long was not bad policy in one sense ;
as it has prevented the people at large from knowing the hardships
and Miseries these poor fellows have endured (on this Infectious
Spot) the bare Recital of which wou'd shock Humanity.   The
Regulars[1] thought Crown Point vastly preferable to this in point of
health and *Strength*—they found it Absolutely Necessary to Relieve
the Garrison once a fortnight from Crown Point—and they expended
a Million Sterling in fortifying that place—the work we have done
here would have Render'd that stronger than ever—and unless we
foreclose the *English Rebels* by taking post there next Spring, they

[1] The English army.

will give us more trouble than many Gentlemen are aware of and profit by our Mistake.

I must Request you to use your Utmost Endeavors in getting us Relieved as soon as Possible—as the time for which our people are Engaged expires in three weeks—the New England troops go home in fifteen days—the General wou'd not keep them one moment longer than the first of Jan'y. I hope to prevail on our troops to stay with me until Others come to Relieve them—but no time is to be lost, you'l not neglect to Inform Congress that we are Enlisted but till the 5th of Jan'y.

> Interim I am D'r Sir
> Your Most Ob't
> Hum'l Serv't
> ANT'Y WAYNE.

Colonel Wayne had previously written (December 4) on the same subject to the Council of Safety: "The wretched condition the battalions are now in for want of every necessary except flour and bad beef is shocking to humanity and beggars all description— We have neither beds nor bedding for our sick to lay on or under, other than their own clothing; no medicine or regimen suitable for them; the dead and the dying lying mingled together in our hospital or rather house of carnage is no uncommon sight." And again to General Gates: "We can't send them to Fort George as usual—the Hospital Being Removed from thence to Albany—and the Weather so Intensely cold, that before they would reach there they would perish—it lays much in your Power by a proper Representation to Congress to have these defects Supplied—and many other Abuses Redressed, that tend to Render the Service almost Intolerable to men and Officers, but as you are a much better Judge of those Matters than I, I shall say no more on the Subject."

Colonel Wayne to Colonel Johnston concerning his Regiment.

TICONDEROGA 12th Jany. 1777

DEAR COL.,—I snatch my pen to give you a *flemish* Acct. of your Regiment— The Commander of all Armies has taken to himself on this Ground from first to last 200—he has marked 13 more for his service which I expect he will Draft in a few days— I have sent you 87 Invalids least he should take a fancy to them and I have a few more hid Ready to send by the next opportunity— I hope to follow in a week or two with about 300, being the Remainder and as brave fellows as ever faced an Enemy: of these there are about 150 Re-Engaged during the war, and we probably may Inlist 150 more by the time we arrive in Phil'a which I believe will not be before the first of March—

We hear your city has become a Deserted Village—and that the British Rebels and their Savage Auxiliaries on their march through the Jerseys Committed the most Horrid Devastation—and were guilty of Crimes shocking to Humanity, and which modesty forbids to mention—

I expect to march at the Head of about 1200 Pennsylvanians and Jerseymen well Appointed, Disciplined and Determined who all call loudly on me to them to take a just Revenge or to meet a Glorious Death—

I am D'r Sir ever yours most
Sincerely,
ANT'Y WAYNE.

P.S. My best Compliments to Delany and all friends— Tell them it is my honest wish to meet an Equal Number of the Enemy on my March—when they may Rest Assured I shall either soon make them pay dear for their past Conduct or stand in no need of any Protection for my Conduct—

[COL. JOHNSTON.]

The following letter gives some idea of the embarrassment due to short enlistments in the Army of the Revolution, and the difficulty of enforcing discipline:

Colonel Wayne to General Schuyler.

TICONDEROGA 12th Feb'y 1777

DEAR GENERAL,—I was favoured with yours of the 7th Ultimo Yesterday—and shall, agreeable to your Desire, keep a pair of fleet Horses at a place called the Red House—about five Miles North of Crown Point, where a small advanced Post is absolutely necessary— for which purpose I shall Detatch a trusty Officer and fifteen or Twenty men—still Continuing the scouting parties as usual—

Our Garrison is now very weak. If you have any good troops— *be they ever so few*—pray send them on with all possible Despatch.

After the Jersey Troops are gone, I must in *Confidence* assure you —that I would much Rather risk my life and reputation, and the fate of America on two Hundred Good Soldiers,—than on all those now on the Ground who will be left behind them—many of whom are Children, twelve or fifteen years of age— In time they'l make good men—as yet they are too young—add to this that they have but about one month to stay—and are badly armed and the Officers Enemies to Discipline.

I am in the next place to Acquaint you that Yesterday morning at Gun fire I was Informed that Capt. Nelsons Rifle Company—who used to do duty in my Regiment—were under arms with their Packs slung ready to March and Determined to force their way through all Opposition. On my Arrival at their Encampment—I found them drawn up in Order, and beginning their March. On asking the cause of such Conduct, they began in a tumultuous manner to Inform me that their time of Enlistment was expired last month, and that they looked upon themselves as at Liberty to go home— I Ordered them to Halt—that I could not Answer them all at once— I directed their leader to step out and speak for them: A Serg't Advanced—I presented a Pistol to his Breast—he fell on his knees to beg his life—I then ordered the Whole to ground their Arms— which was immediately complied with:—I then Addressed them when they with one voice agreed to Remain until the 20th Instant and Return to their duty.

This was scarce over when a Certain Jonah Holida of Capt. Coe's Company in Col Robinsons Regiment—Endeavored to excite them to Mutiny again—as you will see by the within Deposition— Interrogating him on the Occasion he Justified his Conduct— I thought proper to Chastise him for his Insolence on the spot before the men—and then sent him to answer for his Crime to the main Guard.

The Colonel waited on me and very Innocently Informed me that he had a Complaint lodged with him against me that he was Sorry for it—but was obliged to take notice of it, and then Delivered the within paper—

On Inquiring I found it was wrote by Capt. Coe— I had him brought before me— He Acknowledged the writing—and also that he knew the cause for which his Soldier was Struck and Confined—but was of Opinion that every Soldier had a Right to Deliver his Sentiments on every Occasion without being punished upon which I Ordered him in Arrest as an Abettor of the Mutiny— I wait for your Orders to send them down to Albany—where you will take such further Measures as you may deem necessary— To try them here by their Own people would answer no good purpose—perhaps the Reverse— You'l be kind enough to excuse this long Narrative and believe me Dear Sir

Your most Ob't Hum'l
Ser't,
ANT'Y WAYNE.

N.B. I believe I shall be able to prevail on Dayton's Reg't to Remain until the first of March unless these people stir them to Mutiny—which I have some Reason to apprehend—lest they themselves should be asked to stay after the expiration of their time; for which I hope there will be no Occation.

It is curious to observe while looking over these letters, most of which were written shortly after the Declaration of Independence, that that instrument is seldom referred to in them, and that very little importance is attached to it as giving a new significance to the war. Unfortunately for Pennsylvania, the date of the Declaration coincided very nearly with that of the attempt to introduce a new government into that State unacceptable to a very large and intelligent portion of the population, by methods which were regarded by many as a simple usurpation of power. The patriots who then bore sway in Pennsylvania were identified, in the minds of many who wished well to the cause, with the party who, after a most violent and bitter struggle, had destroyed the old charter of the Province, and with it the power of those who had formed the governing class in it, and had substituted for it a new Constitution, which did not appear to any one, even those most opposed to the old system, to work satisfactorily. There were, for instance, loud complaints all through the war that Pennsylvania did not supply her troops in the field regularly with clothing and provisions, and that she neglected to pay them often for months after their pay became due, and that when she did pay them it was often in base money that had little purchasing power. Her persistent neglect in these matters, as is well known, was the cause of a serious mutiny among the troops of the Pennsylvania line in the beginning of 1781, and of constant embarrassment during the war. Of course the blame for this neglect or maladministration was thrown by their opponents upon those who then wielded the power of the State. It should never be forgotten that during the Revolutionary War the struggle was not merely between the rulers of Pennsylvania and the open enemy, the British army, but also between them and the fierce opposition of a powerful party in their own State. While their opponents denounced the ruling powers as usurpers, they retorted by confiscation and test laws, a course which rendered the war highly unpopular to many. It was the intention and result of these laws to disfranchise nearly one-half

of the population in number, and more than one-half if
reckoned by their wealth and intelligence. In short,
Pennsylvania fought in the Revolution like a man with
one arm tied behind his back, and what strength was
left her was too often employed in struggles between
contending parties in their own State rather than
against the common enemy. The Declaration of Independence was, unhappily, looked upon by many at the
time as a party triumph, and it was followed up here as
nowhere else by measures that drove from the public
service many men of the highest character who had up
to that time been regarded as the foremost patriots of
the State. It is hard to estimate how far it paralyzed
her efforts during the war.

A good deal of the clamor of those days which has
survived in history, therefore, is due to this bitter party
spirit which had been aroused between those who
favored and those who opposed the Constitution of
1776. The opponents of the government organized
by it were fewer in number than those who warmly
supported it. They belonged to various classes of the
population,—to the Conservative Whigs, to the Loyalists and Tories, to the Quakers, and even to many of
the original advocates of a revision of the charter, who
were not satisfied with the Constitution which had been
adopted. Many of those who openly expressed their
dislike of the new form of government for the State
were men of high social position who had belonged to
the governing class under the old *régime*, and they did
not hesitate to sneer at the work of the radical mob, as
they called them, and to magnify their errors and their
maladministration. The truth is that, as society here

was constituted at the beginning of the Revolution, it was hardly to be expected that the men who had always been leaders in the political affairs of the Province would give up their control without a fierce struggle. Pennsylvania was, therefore, greatly weakened in the Revolution by these internal dissensions. The correspondence of Wayne is very instructive in showing how, very early in the war, this evil spirit became a conspicuous element in the progress of the Revolution. The letters just given are remarkable, because they show that civilians like Dr. Rush and Mr. Peters, and military officers of high rank like St. Clair, Thompson, Wayne, Johnston, and Hartley, were out of sympathy in many respects with the men who formed the government they served. It is prudent, therefore, in reading of the destitution of the Pennsylvania line during the war, to remember these things.

CHAPTER III.

WHILE Wayne was in command of the garrison at Ticonderoga he was appointed, as has been stated, on the 21st of February, 1777, a brigadier-general in the army. He had evidently become tired of the life of comparative inaction which he led at that post, and was very desirous of being employed in active service and under the immediate command of Washington. On the 12th of April, 1777, he was directed by the general-in-chief to join him at Morristown, and he was at once placed in command of a brigade of troops stationed there, known as the "Pennsylvania line." In order to gain a correct notion of the character of the officers and men thus placed in his charge, many of whom followed his fortunes during the remainder of the war, a few words of explanation may be necessary concerning the organization of the Pennsylvania troops in the Army of the Revolution.

The fifty-three battalions of Associators or militia organized at the outbreak of the war had by this time been disbanded, their term of service having expired. Their whole number was four thousand three hundred, and they filled the first quota of troops called for by Congress from Pennsylvania. These were replaced by six Pennsylvania State battalions, a rifle regiment, and a musketry battalion, whose term of service expired

60

in January, 1777, they having been enlisted for one year.

A reorganization of the troops was then made. Thirteen regiments of infantry, besides some small bodies of cavalry and artillery, were enlisted in Pennsylvania directly for the Continental service, many of the men, both officers and soldiers, having been members of the old State battalions and re-enlisting in the new for "three years or the war." They were all at this time in General Washington's army, forming the Pennsylvania line. These regiments should have formed a division and been commanded by a major-general. There were then but two officers of that rank appointed from Pennsylvania,—Generals Mifflin and St. Clair,— and neither of them seems to have been considered eligible to the command, St. Clair having succeeded Wayne in the command of Ticonderoga and Mifflin being quartermaster-general at the time. Wayne was a brigadier-general when he joined Washington's army, and so he remained, it may be said, during the whole war. During all this time, from the beginning to the end, he had always an independent command, burdened with all the labors, anxieties, and responsibilities of the position, without the rank, consideration, or pay, of a major-general. Nothing seems to illustrate more fully his true magnanimity and his untiring and patriotic devotion than the cheerfulness with which he performed the duties without holding the rank of a major-general. Surrounded at all times by subordinates who were adding to his troubles by constant complaints that by the "arrangement" of the civil authorities their due rank and promotion had been withheld from them, there was not a murmur heard from Wayne on this score during the war, although he doubtless felt that he had been more deeply aggrieved in the matter of rank than any of his complaining officers. I can find no allusion to this matter in the way of complaint in any of his letters, except an indignant refusal of a request made by one of his friends, early in his career, that he should ask General Gates to recommend him to Congress as a suitable person to fill the post of brigadier-general.

The command to which General Wayne was assigned in the spring of 1777 was, as has been said, composed of eight regiments, forming a division of two brigades. The First Brigade consisted of the First Regiment, Colonel Chambers ; the Second, Colonel Walter Stewart ; the Seventh, Lieutenant-Colonel Connor; and the Tenth, Lieutenant-Colonel Hubley. The Second Brigade was composed of the Fourth Regiment, Lieutenant-Colonel William Butler ; the Fifth, Lieutenant-Colonel Johnston ; the Eighth, Colonel Broadhead; and the Eleventh, Colonel Humpton. There were about seventeen hundred men in the division when General Wayne assumed the command. The other division of the Pennsylvania line in Washington's army, under Lord Stirling's command, was made up of Conway's— formerly Mifflin's—brigade of four regiments, and of Colonel Hausegger's German regiment.

At the time that General Wayne joined the army Washington had under his command forty-three regiments, all from the States south of the Hudson. They were organized in five divisions of two brigades each, and numbered about seven thousand three hundred men. They were nearly all fresh recruits. The army was then passing through one of those dangerous crises which threatened its existence at the close of each year of the war, arising from its complete renewal by recruits who were to take the place of those whose term of service had then expired. As the soldiers of the army in most of the States had been enlisted for a single year only, there was at the end of that year substantially a new army and a new organization, or, as it was called, a new "arrangement." During the period of the incubation of this new army it was necessarily weak, and, as it was naturally to be presumed that the enemy must understand its condition, Washington was kept in a state of perpetual alarm lest an attack should be made upon him by the long-trained and well-disciplined troops of the enemy, whose numbers exceeded his own threefold. He now reaped the full advantage of the masterly stroke by which he had broken the enemy's army at Trenton and Princeton and forced it to retreat. This particular result was perhaps the least of all the advantages he gained by his strategy. Having occupied the high ground in the neighborhood of Morristown, he had there an excellent defensive position, which he strengthened by intrenchments. He was thus on the right flank of the enemy's position, and until he was dislodged no movement of Sir William Howe's army could be made towards Philadelphia without great danger of being cut off from its communications and supplies. Washington therefore thought (wisely, as it turned out) that the Fabian policy was the true one under the circumstances. Thus, while refusing to meet the enemy in the open field he safely intrenched himself on the heights at Middlebrook, and manœuvred his troops so as to threaten the flanks and rear of Sir William Howe's army should he move towards Philadelphia, or should he take the opposite direction and endeavor to form a junction with Burgoyne in the hill-country of the Hudson River. To carry out this policy successfully so as to cover the country between West Point and the Delaware a general of extraordinary activity and intelligence was needed, in command of troops of such spirit and discipline as to be able to move at a moment's warning. This general was found in Wayne, and the troops chosen for the advanced guard on this special service were the Pennsylvania line under his command. The British army was moved forward to Brunswick, and took up its quarters between that place and Somerset Court-House. Their object was to cut off Sullivan, who was stationed at Princeton, but his retreat baffled them. General Washington immediately embraced the opportunity of attacking this detachment of the enemy's forces. On the 2d of May an assault was made upon them at Brunswick. They hurriedly left their intrenchments there and retreated to Amboy. What part General Wayne and his troops had in hastening "the order of their going" is told in the following letter.

General Wayne to the Board of War.

CAMP AT MOUNT PROSPECT 3 June 1777

GENTLEMEN,—In Consequence of the Orders of His Excellency Gen'l Washington I now send Major Miller for Arms & Clothing for the first Penn'a Regiment Commanded by Col. Chambers—they never Rec'd any Uniform except hunting Shirts which are worn out —and Altho a body of fine men—yet from being in Rags and badly armed—they are viewed with Contempt by the Other Troops, and begin to Despise themselves—

Discontent ever produces Desertion, to prevent which I must in the most pressing manner Request you to Assist him and the Other Gentlemen who go on the same Errand in procuring Clothes and Arms.

The Conduct of the Pennsylvanians the Other day in forceing Gen'l Grant to Retire with Circumstances of Shame and Disgrace into the very lines of the Enemy has gained them the Esteem and Confidence of His Excellency—who wishes to have Our Rifles exchanged for good Muskets & Bayonets—experience has taught us that they are not fit for the field—a few only will be Retained in each Regiment and those placed in the hands of Real Marksmen.— I have taken this Liberty as I am Confident that you have the Honor of your State at Heart—and that you will use every means in your Power to expedite the Arming & Clothing of our People as Soldiers in Order to support it—

> I am Gentlemen with the Greatest Respect
> Your Most Ob't and very
> Humb'l Ser't
> ANT'Y WAYNE.

General Wayne to Sharp Delany.

CAMP AT MOUNT PROSPECT 7th June 1777

MY DEAR DELANY,—I have just time to Inform you that I am well—I intended to say a great deal—but His Excellency has this Moment sent for me—he has posted me in Front & honored me with the Charge of the most material pass leading to the Camp.

The Enemy are all at work in fortifying their Camp—we have fairly turned the tables on them—for whilst we are Usefully Employed in Manœuvring—they are at hard Labor— Our people are daily gaining Health Spirits and Discipline—the spade & pick axe throw'd aside—for the British Rebels to take up—they notwithstanding affect to hold us cheap and threaten to beat up our Quarters—*if we don't* beat up theirs first which is in Contemplation, but *this in time.*

I am again sent for, farewell and believe me yours

> Most Sincerely
> ANT'Y WAYNE.

6

Graydon in his Memoirs says that he received substantially the same impression after a visit to General Wayne's head-quarters at this time:

"The Commander-in-Chief and all about him were in excellent spirits, and as to General Wayne, whom I waited upon at his quarters, he entertained a most sovereign contempt for the enemy. In his confident way he affirmed that the two armies had interchanged their original modes of warfare; that for our parts we had thrown away the shovel, and the British had taken it up, as they dared not face us without the cover of an entrenchment. I made some allowance for the fervid manner of the general, who is unquestionably as brave a man as any in the army, but is somewhat addicted to the vaunting style of Marshal Villars, a man who like himself could fight as well as brag."

"General Wayne's quondam uniform as colonel of the Fourth Battalion was, I think, blue and white, in which he had been accustomed to appear in exemplary neatness; whereas he was now dressed in character for Mr. Heath or Captain Gibbet, in a dingy red coat, a black rusty cravat, and tarnished laced hat."—*Graydon's Memoirs*, p. 277.

The same day Wayne writes thus to his wife, in a more serious tone:

General Wayne to Mrs. Mary Wayne.

CAMP AT MOUNT PROSPECT 7th June 1777

MY DEAR POLLY,—I this moment Rec'd yours of the 31st May—and am extremely sorry to hear of your bad state of health—you must Endeavor to keep up your Spirits as well as possible—the times Require great Sacrifices to be made—the Blessings of Liberty cannot be purchased at too high a price—the Blood and treasure of the

Choicest and best Spirits of this Land is but a trifling Consideration for the Rich Inheritance— Whether any of the present leaders will live to see it Established in this Once happy Soil Depends on Heaven;—but it must, it will at one day rise in America, & shine forth in its pristine Lustre. I would advise you to use every possible Endeavour to get in your Harvest yourself and not put it Out on Shares on no Acc't as grain and Hay will be at a Prodigious price next winter. Have we no kind Neighbours to lend a helping hand?—I am sure the Bartholomews & Davis's families will have goodness Enough to give you their Assistance and Advice,—present my best Respects to them and all our friends & tell them they live in my grateful Memory—and that I hope at one day to Enjoy *peace,* Established on the firm Basis of *Liberty* in their Social Company

The Education of my Little Children is a matter that gives me much Concern—and which I [hope] you will not neglect—I have already hinted [that] I expect my little son will not turn aside from virtue, though the path should be marked with his father's Blood—

Farewell, God Bless you,

Yours Most Sincerely

Ant'y Wayne.

I can't be spared from Camp. I have the Confidence of the General, and the Hearts of the Soldiers who will Support me in the Day of Action.

While General Wayne was cheered by the success of Washington's tactics in baffling the plans of Sir William Howe, and grew every day more hopeful as the proofs of the discipline of the army multiplied, he received letters from his two friends Dr. Rush and Mr. Peters, which, if his temperament had not been of the most buoyant kind and his faith in the triumph of the cause had not been absolute, would doubtless have utterly crushed his spirit. Nothing could well be more depressing than the account they both gave of the political condition of Pennsylvania, then suffering from evils which, in their opinion, seemed almost remediless. The letters are given a place here for this among other reasons, that we may be reminded how many causes of deep anxiety tortured the minds of the best men during the Revolution, of which we hear but little in history as it is commonly written, and how the privations and dangers of the field were not the only trials which were borne in giving birth to the government whose protection we now enjoy. We must draw special attention to the manner in which General Wayne received these gloomy accounts of the condition of his native State and the sad forebodings of his correspondents about its future. Nothing is finer or more characteristic of him as a man of true courage and a devoted patriot than the way in which he urges his correspondents to give up for the moment their domestic quarrels and combine all the forces of the State against the common enemy.

Dr. Rush to General Wayne.

MY DEAR GENERAL,—General Sinclair who will deliver you this letter will inform you of the sickly State of the politicks of Pennsylvania. Cannon—Matlack—and Dr Young still hold back the Strength of the State by urging the execution of their rascally Government in preference to supporting measures for repelling the common enemy. A majority of the Presbyterians are in favor of the constitution, and in no part of the State do they discover more Zeal for it than in Chester County. Gen'l Sinclair—& Gen'l Thompson ha[ve given p]ublic testimony against it, I [wish you] to add your Weight to the Scale of opposition, especially in your native County. The most respectable Whig characters in the State are with us. I need not point out to *you* the danger and folly of the Constitution. It has substituted a Mob Government for one of the happiest governments in the world. Nothing more was necessary to have made us a free & happy people than to abolish the royal & proprietary power of the

State. A *single legislature* is big with tyranny. I had rather live under the government of one man than of 72. They will soon become like the 30 [tyrants of] Athens. Absolute authority should belong only to God. It requires infinite Wisdom and goodness to direct it.

Come, my dear Sir and let us weep together over the dear nurse of our childhood,—the protectress of our youth, and the generous rewarder of our riper years. "De re publicâ nunquam Desperandum." Let us unite our efforts once more and perhaps we may recover Pennsylvania from her delirium— At present, she has lifted a knife to her own throat. Your timely prescriptions may yet save her life.

Adieu—my dear friend

yours

sincerely

B. RUSH.

PHILAD'A May 19th 1777.

Dr. Rush to General Wayne.

PHILAD. June 5th 1777

MY DEAR GENERAL,—I formerly thought as you do upon the subject of our government, but I have seen so many men sacrifice their prejudices against it to an honourable or lucrative office, that I am sure nothing but the determined opposition of the old Whigs to the government prevented its execution. They now begin to *feel* as well as see its weakness, and nothing but obstinacy in a few men keeps its power from falling to pieces. Had it been Once established I am sure nothing but a civil war would have overthrown it. So strong are its ties upon the passions and interests of a part of the State that innocence and justice must have sighed & submitted— Alas! that our minds should be turned from opposing a foreign to opposing a domestic tyranny— But all will end well, and I trust you will find both fruit & shade beneath the vine and the fig tree of your farm when you return to rest your limbs after the toils of the war are over.—

The public have done you justice for your gallant behaviour in checking the prowess of Mr. Grant. When shall we have the pleasure of seeing you? Suppose you write to some of your Old friends in Chester County to concur with us in Altering the Constitution.

Nothing but a new convention will restore Union to us, and draw forth the Whig strength of the State to oppose the common enemy.

I expect to spend part of this summer with you at Camp. Is your habit of body such as it used to be? If it is I think a wound can prove mortal to you in very few places— At any rate you shall have a chance for your life if I am near you, and am allowed to combat death with my old weapons of lancet—scalpel—glysterpipe &c—

God keep you from falling into my hands in that way! and grant you many laurels and long life—

    Comp'ts to Col. Johnston

Yours

B. RUSH.

Mr. R. Peters to General Wayne.

PHILAD'A May 27th 1777

MY DEAR SIR,—I am extremely sorry that from Col Trumbul's short stay among us I have not had it in my Power to Shew him the Civilities which I would wish any Gentleman of your recommendation to experience from me. Your Situation is indeed cruel; but you will bear it with that Fortitude which you have often been obliged to exercise— I hope however some of our General Officers will relieve you & then I shall have the Happiness of taking you by the Hand— Your Family Affairs want you, our *fallen* Pennsylvania wants you too— But you are no Doubt prepared to see her in quite a different Aspect from that in which you left her. I expect however better Days which God send not only for my own, but the Sake of our Country. Some Change must be made, or the Power of this important State will never be exerted, for the Salvation of American Liberty— Sally joins me in very affectionate Regards & believe me to be

Most sincerely Yours,

R. PETERS.

General Wayne to Dr. Rush.

CAMP AT MOUNT PROSPECT 2 [torn out]

MY DEAR RUSH,—I would long since have acknowledged the Rec't of yours of the   April had I not the most flattering hope of doing it *Viva Voce*— Gen'l St Clair Delivered me that dated the 19th Ultimo [May] in which you give me a Melancholy and I fear too just a picture of the Distraction of our State, and the folly Obstinacy & Incapacity of those who Influence her Councils— Gen'l St. Clair & many Other Gentlemen of the Army can witness for me that at the first view of your Sickly Constitution—I pronounced it not worth Defending—nor do I think it would have an existence at this date were it not for the early Opposition given it— in my Opinion the Only way to open the eyes of the people would have been to try to put it in execution—the Defects would not only be seen but felt which have produced a stronger Conviction than all the Reasoning or Logick that has been used on the Occation

I must for the present Request you and every friend to his Country to exert yourselves in Calling forth the Strength of Penns'a and Completing our Battalions, which are yet very weak—let us once be in a Condition to Vanquish these British Rebels and I answer for it that then your present Rulers will give way for better men which will produce better Measures.

In my next I hope to give you some pleasing Intelligence—we shan't remain many days in this Inactive state—the Enemy don't seem fond of meeting Disciplined Troops— We Offered Gen'l Grant Battle six times the Other day he as often formed but always on our Approach his people broke and Ran after firing a few Volleys which we never Returned, being Determined to let them feel the force of our fire and to give them the Bayonet under Cover of the Smoke— This Howe who was to March through America at the head of 5000 men had his Coat much Dirtied, his Horses head taken off, and himself badly Bruis'd for having the presumption at the head of 700 British Troops to face 500 Penns'as

Present my Compliments to our friends and believe me

Yours Most Sincerely

ANT'Y WAYNE.

During the month of June Washington's army was encamped at Middlebrook, near the Raritan, strongly intrenched. Various devices were resorted to by Sir William Howe to induce the Americans to evacuate their strong position and to meet him on the plains. Washington knew too well the great advantage he held to be tempted into making any such false step. Not only was he safe in his intrenchments, but he could move with equal facility to prevent Howe's advance towards Philadelphia or any movement of his intended to form a junction with Burgoyne on the Hudson, as occasion might require. Various skirmishes took place between the advanced posts of the army, in one of which General Wayne tells us he commanded, without any serious result. At length Sir William Howe, despairing of forcing Washington to meet him in a pitched battle, decided to approach Philadelphia by sea, and for that purpose embarked his troops at Staten Island immediately upon the evacuation of New Jersey.

There was still great uncertainty in the American camp in regard to the route, or even the destination, of Howe's army. Whether it was proposed to reach Burgoyne's forces by sea, or whether, leaving him to take care of himself, Howe would undertake alone the capture of Philadelphia, could not be ascertained.

While the American army was thus without positive intelligence of Howe's movements after the evacuation of New Jersey, it was astounded to learn that Ticonderoga had been evacuated by St. Clair on the 5th of July, 1777. "An event so mysterious as to baffle conjecture," is the language of Washington. In all his arrangements Washington had supposed that fortress defensible, or at least capable of standing a long siege, and its abandonment therefore without any siege whatever deranged all his plans. It is true that General Wayne and Colonel Trumbull had called attention some months before to what seemed to them a weak spot in the defences, owing to the possibility of mounting cannon on a commanding height from which it could be reached; but no heed seems to have been given to their warning, and this height was left to be occupied by the enemy. A battery having been established on Mount Defiance, the Americans at once acted the part of those who think discretion the better part of valor, and abandoned the fort. If those who knew little of the preparations which had been made there to receive the enemy were surprised at the result, what must Wayne and his companions, who had during the past winter expended so much time, labor, and even many human lives in rendering Ticonderoga, as they thought when they left it, impregnable, have felt when they heard of its abandonment? But these are matters which concern the character of that most unfortunate of generals, St. Clair, with whose vindication it is not our business to meddle here.

It was at first thought, when the news of giving up the gates of the country from the Canada side reached the army, that an effort would be at once made to form a junction of the forces of Howe and Burgoyne on the banks of the Hudson ; but it was decided by the enemy that Howe should push on to Philadelphia, and that Burgoyne should be left to his own resources and to his fate.

The British fleet with Howe's army on board went out of Sandy Hook on the 25th of July, and at once Washington issued the following order to General Wayne :

"The fleet having gone out of the Hook, and as Delaware appears to be its most probable destination, I desire that you will leave your brigade under the next in command, and proceed to Chester County, in Pennsylvania, where your presence will be necessary to arrange the militia who are to rendezvous there."

Wayne proceeded at once to perform that duty, and, having organized the Pennsylvania militia and placed it under the command of General John Armstrong (an old man, but had in honor as "the Hero of Kittanning" in the Indian wars), he rejoined his division, which by that time had reached Germantown. The army marched through Philadelphia on the 23d of August and took post near Wilmington, it having at last been fully ascertained that, as the British fleet was over two hundred miles within the capes of Chesapeake Bay, Sir William Howe intended to approach Philadelphia by that route. On the 26th of August he wrote the annexed letter to his wife while the army was in motion. It seems to me that there is a subdued tone of sadness about this letter which would indicate a feeling that the interview he asked for might be the last which the fortunes of war would permit him to enjoy.

General Wayne to Mrs. Wayne.

BLUE BELL, 26th Aug't 1777

MY DEAR GIRL,—I am peremptorily forbid by His Excellency to leave the Army—my case is hard— I am Obliged to do the duty of three General Officers—but if it was not the case—as a Gen'l Officer I could not Obtain leave of Absence—

I must therefore in the most pressing Manner Request you to meet me tomorrow Evening at Naamans Creek—pray bring Mr. Robinson with my Little Son & Daughter along—

It may probably happen that we may stay in that Neighbourhood for a day or two—my best love and Compliments to all friends

I am, Dear Polly,

Yours

ANTH'Y WAYNE.

[MRS. MARY WAYNE, Chester County.]

While the army was encamped near Wilmington a very thorough reconnoissance was made of the route by which the enemy was advancing. It was finally decided to take post on the eastern side of the Brandywine and there meet him in open battle. In the mean time, Wayne, on the 2d of September, sent a letter to General Washington in regard to a proposed expedition against the British lines which seemed to him full of promise, and of which he hoped to be the leader. The proposal does not seem to have attracted the attention of the historians of the campaign, and it certainly was not adopted by the general-in-chief, but it none the less shows the extraordinary push and energy of its author, as well as his brave and unconquerable spirit.

General Wayne to General Washington.

CAMP NEAR WILMINGTON 2nd Sept. 1777.

SIR,—I took the liberty some days since to suggest the selecting 2500 or 3000 of our best Armed and most Disciplined Troops (exclusive of the Reserves) who should hold themselves in Readiness on the Approach of the Enemy to make a Regular and Vigorous Assault on their Right or Left flank—or such part of their Army as should then be thought most expedient—and not wait the Attack from them—

This, Sir, I am well Convinced would Surprise them much—from a persuasion that you dare not leave your Works—it would totally stop the Other part from Advancing—and should the Attack be fortunate—which I have not the least doubt of—the Enemy would have no Other Alternative than to Retreat—for they dare not hazard any new manœuvre in the face of your Army which would be cool & ready to take every Advantage of either their Confusion, Disorder or Retreat—& from which the best and greatest Consequences might be Derived—

This Sir is no new Idea—it has been often practiced with success (among many Others) by *Cæsar at Amiens* when besieged by the

Gauls, who Carried part of the entrenchments and were rendering themselves Masters of the parapet—when he sallied out with his Cohorts—threw them into the utmost Consternation & Obtained an easy Victory—

He practiced the same manœuvre at *Alesia* against the same people. —Success Justified the Measure—they were struck with a terror & surprise, which Marshal Saxe *Justly Observes* "proceeds from that Consternation which is the Unavoidable effect of Sudden and unexpected Events"

This is a General rule in war; that the Irresistible Impulse of the Human Heart, which is governed by mere momentary Caprice and Opinion—Determines the fate of the day in all Actions;—& as similar Causes Generally produce Similar Effects—I could wish to see it practiced (not only on this Occasion) but to carry it still further —and make the Assault on the Enemy without Risquing too much

The Spirit and Numbers of your Regular Troops aided by the Crowds of Militia now Drawing to your Camp, Renders success probable & will at all events be sufficient to guard against any bad Consequences in case of a *Military Check* by throwing themselves into the works and Strong Ground in your Rear—

I own Sir that I dread the Re-embarquing of the Enemy much more than any Consequence attending an Attack upon them for should they take shiping again and proceed to some Other Quarter without Attempting anything this way—you will suffer more in the march after them than you would probably do in a severe Action— besides the Certain loss of the present Militia—

Should I be happy enough to meet your Excellency in Opinion— I wish to be of the number Assigned for this business. On the Contrary I know you have goodness enough to excuse a freedom—which proceeds from a Desire to render every service in the power of your Excellency's Most Ob't

and very Humb Ser't

ANT'Y WAYNE.

N.B. Upon Mature Consideration I believe it will not answer to Annex the Militia to our Brigades—I wish it may not take place—

[HIS EXCELLENCY GEN'L WASHINGTON.]

In the formation of the army at the battle of Brandywine the division of Wayne and the artillery of Procter (both composed of Pennsylvania troops), with the
Third Virginia Regiment, were posted on the left of
the American line on the east bank of the Brandywine. This creek was fordable in front of the position at a place called Chad's Ford, and at that place
Wayne's division was stationed. The details of this
battle, especially the turning of the right flank of the
Americans by the detachment under Cornwallis, are
so well known that it seems unnecessary to repeat
them here. Wayne had in front of him, separated by
a narrow creek, the forces of Knyphausen (the Hessian
general), consisting of about seven thousand men, and
during the whole day stood his ground firmly, repelling
successfully every attempt by Knyphausen to pass the
creek, and sending Maxwell with his light infantry occasionally to the other side with orders to annoy him.
Wayne remained in this position until sunset, and until
the division of Sullivan (reinforced by that of Greene),
which had not been able to withstand the attack of
Cornwallis, was forced back from Birmingham Meeting-
House. The right flank of the army being turned by
the enemy exposed Wayne's division to the danger
of being attacked by Knyphausen in his front' and by
Cornwallis in his rear. He therefore retreated, as his
supports had been driven from the field, to avoid being
surrounded. His men were in good order and discipline, and quite ready to attack the tired battalions of the
British army had they undertaken to interrupt the retreat
of the army. There can be no doubt that his division
on this retreat saved the remnant of Sullivan's force.

The conduct of Wayne at the battle of Brandywine was, in the judgment of the military critics of the time, admirable. General Henry Lee, in his " Memoirs of the Southern Campaigns," gives him and his men great credit for the manner in which they resisted the attack of Knyphausen. He says many of the corps in that battle distinguished themselves. The most conspicuous were the brigades of Wayne and Weedon, and the Third Virginia Regiment, commanded by Colonel Marshall, to whom, with the artillery directed by Colonel Procter, of Pennsylvania, much praise was given. So General Armstrong (the younger) in his account of the battle says, " The firing on the left being the signal for Knyphausen to act, that officer began his movements accordingly ; but, notwithstanding the weight and vigor of his attack and the aid it received from a covering battery, he was unable to drive Wayne from his position till near sunset." Some of the regiments of the Pennsylvania line were highly distinguished. A letter from Colonel Chambers (First Pennsylvania Regiment) to his old commander, General Hand, gives the following picturesque account of the part taken by his regiment in the battle : "The general sent orders for our artillery to retreat, and ordered me to cover it with a part of my regiment. It was done, but to my surprise the artillerymen had run and left the howitzer behind. The two pieces went up the road protected by about sixty of my men, who had very warm work, but brought them safe. I then ordered another party to fly to the howitzer and bring it off. Captain Buchanan, Lieutenant Simpson, and Lieutenant Douglass went immediately to the gun, and the men

following their example, I covered them with the few I
had remaining. But before this could be done the main
body of the foe came within thirty yards and kept up
the most terrible fire ever heard in America, though
with very little loss on our side. I brought all the brigade artillery safely off, and I hope to see them again
fired at the scoundrels. Yet we retreated to the next
height in good order in the midst of a very heavy fire
of cannon and small-arms. Not thirty yards distant
we formed to receive them, but they did not choose to
follow."[1] This gallant soldier during this brilliant action
was wounded in the side by a Hessian bullet, which he
carried to his grave. It is much to be regretted that
no full record of the services of each of the eight regiments in the Pennsylvania line has been preserved, or,
at least, is accessible. The official report of General
Wayne cannot be found. We know that the Pennsylvania regiments suffered much in this hard-fought battle.
We know that many of the field officers were wounded;
that Colonel Grier of the Seventh, Lieutenant-Colonel
Bayard of the Eighth, Major Robinson of the Fifth, and
many other officers, were wounded; that among the
prisoners taken were Lieutenant-Colonel Frazer and
Adjutant Harper of the Fifth, who were captured two
days after the battle while reconnoitring, and that Captain Thomas Butler of the Fifth, in Sullivan's division,
received the thanks of General Washington for his gallantry in rallying broken, retreating troops. This Captain Butler was one of four brothers, all officers of the

---

[1] In Sir William Howe's official despatch he refers to the capture
of these guns, but he entirely forgets to mention that they were
recaptured by Colonel Chambers's regiment.

Pennsylvania line, and all devoted friends of General Wayne,—Colonels Richard and William and Majors Thomas and Edward, a band of heroes, of whose exploits we shall learn more in the course of this history.

One of the Pennsylvania regiments, the Thirteenth, commanded by Colonel Walter Stewart, was attached to the command of General Sullivan, and not to that of General Wayne, both at Brandywine and at Germantown. The loss of this regiment in the two engagements was but sixteen; but this would seem to be no criterion of the severity of the struggle in which the regiment was engaged. "We attacked the enemy," says Lieutenant James MacMichael of that regiment at Brandywine, "at 5.30 P.M., and we were first obliged to retreat a few yards, and formed in an open field, when we fought without giving way on either side until dark. Our ammunition almost expended, firing ceased on both sides, when we received orders to proceed to Chester. This day for a severe and successive engagement exceeded all I ever saw. Our regiment fought at one stand about an hour under an incessant fire, and yet the loss was less than at Long Island, neither were we so near to each other as at Princeton, our common distance being fifty yards." [1] In the absence of duly authenticated reports of the services of the different regiments in the battle, this is all we can tell of those Pennsylvanians who found a soldier's grave on the banks of the Brandywine.

The common opinion in regard to the American

---

[1] See Diary of Lieutenant James MacMichael, Pennsylvania Magazine, vol. xvi. p. 150.

army after the battle of Brandywine is that it was totally routed and disorganized. Such could hardly have been the case, if we recall its condition during the two succeeding days. On the night of the 11th it retreated to Chester, a distance of about twelve miles, and reached a safe encampment about ten o'clock in the evening. Starting early the next morning, it marched to its old camp near the Falls of Schuylkill, a distance of at least sixteen miles, on that day. These facts in themselves would prove that the army had not lost either its organization or its vigor, even if we had not Washington's own testimony that "it was in good spirits and nowise disheartened by the recent affair, which it seemed to consider as a check rather than as a defeat." Washington, finding the army in this temper, recrossed the Schuylkill at Conshohocken, Wayne's division being in the advance, to engage once more the enemy in the hope of saving Philadelphia. The British army had moved leisurely forward towards the north and west from the battle-field, hoping to cross the Schuylkill at one of the upper fords unmolested. On the 10th Washington found the enemy near the Warren tavern, about twenty-two miles from Philadelphia, on the Lancaster Road, and made preparations to attack him. A deluge of rain separated the combatants. On the 19th the Americans, excepting Wayne's and Smallwood's divisions, crossed to the east side of the river at Parker's Ford (Lawrenceville), hoping to intercept the enemy when it should cross with the object of gaining the Philadelphia side of the river. But Sir William Howe, after having by a feint induced Washington to suppose that he would take one of the upper fords,

by a rapid countermarch during the night fell back
to Fatland Ford, just below Valley Forge, and crossed
to the eastern side of the river, whence he had an un-
opposed route to the city.

Meanwhile, Wayne's division had been ordered to
take post between the Paoli and the Warren (names of
taverns on the Lancaster Road about two miles apart),
in order to attack the rear-guard of the British, then
encamped in the Great Valley between him and the
Schuylkill, and if possible to capture the baggage-train
under its charge as soon as it moved towards the river.
It was an expedition which required the greatest secrecy, as its success depended upon taking the rear-
guard of the enemy by surprise. Wayne took every
precaution to hide his movements from the enemy, but,
unfortunately, the position of his camp was betrayed
to the English commander by Tory spies. He was encamped on the hills above the Warren tavern on the
night of the 20th of September, when he was attacked
by an overwhelming force of the rear-guard of the
enemy, which he was preparing to assail the next day,
—a force so large that two of the British regiments of
which it was composed were not engaged in the horrible work in which the rest were so conspicuous, their
services not being required. This was the affair known
in Revolutionary history as the "PAOLI *massacre*," the
tragic character of which has not been lessened by the
legend which grew out of it. Subjoined are Wayne's
official report to General Washington, and the proceedings of the court-martial which was ordered at his request to investigate the charge that he had permitted his
post to be surprised, an accusation which, with Wayne's

fine instincts of the duty of a soldier, stung him to the quick.

RED LION 21st Sept. 1777—12 oClock

DEAR GENERAL,—About 11 oClock last Evening we ware alarmed by a firing from one of our Out guards—The Division was Immediately formed which was no sooner done than a firing began on our Right Flank— I thought proper to order the Division to file off by the Left except the Infantry and two or three Regiments nearest to where the attack began in order to favour our Retreat— By this Time the Enemy and we were not more than Ten Yards Distant—a well directed fire *mutually* took Place, followed by a charge of Bayonet— numbers fell on each side— We then drew off a Little Distance and formed a Front to oppose to theirs— They did not think Prudent to push matters further. Part of the Division were a little scattered but are Collecting fast— We have saved all our Artillery, Ammunition & Stores except one or two waggons belonging to the Commissary's Department—

Gen'l Smallwood was on his march but not within supporting distance he Order'd his people to file off toward this place where his Division and my own now lay—

As soon as we have refreshed our Troops for an Hour or Two, we shall follow the Enemy who I this moment learn from Major North, are marching for Schuylkil— I cant as yet ascertain our Loss—but will make out a Return as soon as Possible, our Dead will be collected & buried this Afternoon— I must in Justice to Col's Hartley, Humpton, Broadhead, Grier, Butler, Hubley & indeed every Field & Other Officer inform your Excellency that I derived every assistance possible from those Gent'n on this Occasion— Whilst I am writing I received yours of the 20th pr. Messrs Dunlap & Leaming with the Intelligence you wished to Communicate— It will not be in our power to render you such Service, as I could wish, but all that can you may Depend on being done by Your Excellencys Most

Obed't H'bl Serv't

ANT'Y WAYNE.

N.B. The two Letters you mention I never Receiv'd— I have Reason to think they fell into the Enemy's hands Last Nights Affair fully convinces me of it

HIS EXCELL'Y GEN'L WASHINGTON.

Wayne requested that a court of inquiry should be convened to investigate his conduct at the Paoli affair, and, not being satisfied with its finding, he asked, for reasons given in the following letter, to be tried by a court-martial :

CAMP NEAR WHITE MARCH 22nd Oct. 1777

SIR,—I must Acknowledge that the Opinion of the Court of Enquiry has given me both pain and surprise—surprise to find Gent'n go on the most Erroneous grounds in two facts from which they seem to found their Opinion i.e. with Regard to the Distance, and the Carrying off of one of the Pickets—

The Distance between the nearest part of the Enemy's Camp and where I lay—was near 4 miles which was greater than from their Camp to the Fatland ford, and Richardson ford on the Schuylkill (being the very fords at which Gen'l Howe's Army passed)— Consequently had I been farther Distant it would have put it out of my power to Comply with your Excellency's Orders—i.e. to harass their Rear—but this the Court seems to have lost sight of; and may have mistaken the Distance, but with Regard to the picket I am almost tempted to believe it could not altogether be a mistake— Sir it is notorious that that picket was not Carried off at all;—between the time that Brigade Major Nichols told me that he was missing and his Return from Col Butler—a Light Horseman whom I instantly sent to the place where the picket was posted Returned and told me that he had seen him and that all was well—when Major Nichols came back with Col Butlers answer—I did tell him with some degree of anger to go to bed—for having made a mistake—

This Circumstance I literally Related to the Court— I find they gave no Credit to my Assertion—however the Officer of that picket will be able to set this Matter in a Clear point of view— That picket was not disturbed until after the Division Retreated—the Enemy having Advanced by quite a Different Route

They have also (while very minute in Other Circumstances) forgot to mention one or two Reasons for my taking and Remaining in that position i.e. Gen'l Smallwood being on his march to join me and to whom I had sent Col Chambers as a guide to Conduct him into my Rear—where he was expected to arrive every moment from two

OClock in the Afternoon until we were Attacked—and that I had Information that the Enemy would march for Schuylkill the next morning—however they perhaps did not think proper to pay any Regard to any Assertion of mine— Yet they might have given some Credit to Gen'l Smallwoods own Letter which lay before them —as well as to the Circumstance of the Enemies Actually Marching.

They affect to give me some Credit for taking off the Artillery and for *Attempting* to Rally the Troops—*after being Routed*—they don't say that the Artillery was on the Right when the Attack was actually made—and that Orders were given to the Division to Retreat at the very time the Artillery Rec'd the like Order—they don't say that I remained with the troops on the Right which were posted for the purpose of Covering the Retreat—nor do they say that I actually did Rally a Body of the troops and Remained with them on the Ground for a full hour which Effectually Covered the Retreat of the Greatest part of the Division and of all the Artillery altho one of the pieces met with misfortune near the field of Action which Impeded us a Considerable time; these Circumstances and these facts were in full proof before them—but perhaps they did not think them worth mentioning—they were not of the Criminal Kind

After this state of facts which I pledge my Honor as a Soldier and a Gentleman to give full and Ample proof of—I appeal to Your Excellencys own feelings whether I can be easy under so severe and unjust a Charge— I must therefore beg an Immediate trial by a Gen'l Court Martial Your Compliance will much Oblige your Excellencys Most Ob't and

Very Humb Ser't
ANT'Y WAYNE.

[GEN'L WASHINGTON.]

When brought before the general court-martial the following was his defence:

GENT'N,—The Charge against me is " That I had timely Notice of the Enemy's Intention to Attack the Troops under my Command on the Night of the 20th Instant—and that notwithstanding that Intelligence I neglected making a Disposition till it was too late

either to Annoy the Enemy, or to make a Retreat without the utmost
Danger and Confusion"

The first part of the Charge "that I had timely Notice of the
Enemys Intention to attack the Troops under my Command" is
very Readily Answered—

I shall briefly Relate what these gentlemen call a timely Notice—
A Mr Jones an Old Gent'n who lives near by where we were Encamped—came to my Quarters between 8 and 9 oClock at Night and
Informed me, Col's Hartley, Broadhead & Temple that a servant boy
of Mr Clayton's had been taken by the Enemy and liberated again—
who said that he had heard some of their Soldiers say—that they
Intended to Attack me that night. Altho' this could not be Deemed
a *Sufficient Notice* upon any Military principle—yet notwithstanding
I Immediately Ordered out a Number of Videttes [horse pickets]
in Addition to those already fixed with Orders to patrol all the
Roads leading to the Enemy—   I also planted two new pickets, the
One on a by path leading from the Warren to my Camp, the Other to
the Right and in the Rear—which made that Night not less than
six Different Pickets

I had Exclusive of these a horse Picket under Capt. Stoddard
well Advanced on the Swedesford Road—and on the Very Road the
Enemy Advanced—

But the first Intelligence I rec'd of their Advancing was from one
of the very Videttes which I sent out in Consequence of the Information from Mr Jones, who had only time to go out about a mile
before he met them.

Immediately upon this the troops were all Ordered under Arms—
and I myself in Person Ordered the whole to take off their Coats
and put their Cartridge Boxes under to save the Cartridges from
Damage. [by rain] this Gent'n don't look like a surprise—it Rather
proves that we were prepared to move or Act as Occasion required—
when once we were Informed which way they should approach—
As soon as it was Discovered that they were pushing for Our Right
where our Artillery was planted—I Ordered the Division to wheel
to the Right and file off by the left along a Road leading on the
Summit of the Hill towards the White Horse—it being the Very
Road upon which the Division had moved two miles the preceeding
Evening—   The Division Wheeled Accordingly—the Artillery

moved off & owing to some Neglect or Misapprehension in Col. Humpton (which is not uncommon) the Troops did not move until a second and third Order was sent altho' they were wheeled and faced for the purpose

At the very time this Order for Retreat was given I took the Light Infantry and first Reg't and formed them on the Right and Remained there with them and the Horse in Order to Cover the Retreat. If this was making no Disposition I acknowledge I know not what a Disposition is—

These troops met and Rec'd the Enemy with a Spirit becoming free Americans but were forced to give way— The neglect or misapprehension of Col Humpton had Detained the Division too long I was therefore Necessitated to form the fourth Reg't to Receive the Enemy and favour the Retreat of the Others; this Col Butler was a Witness of.

About three Hundred Yards in the Rear I again Rallied such of the Division as took the proper Route. Those who went a Contrary way and out of supporting distance of the Artillery perhaps Col Humpton can give the best Acc't of— I call upon him to know whether he once Attempted to Rally any part of the troops, and where, and why he did not Obey my Orders in Retreating when the Troops were Wheeled and faced for the purpose:

Here I have a fair field for Recrimination were I so Disposed— I shall waive the subject and beg leave to Read the Orders which I rec'd from his Excellency from time to time.

In the eyes and Judgment of Gentlemen and of Officers I trust I stand Justified for the part I took that Evening— I had the fullest and Clearest evidence that the Enemy would march that Morning at 2 OClock for the Schuylkill. I had sent Col. Chambers as a Guide to Gen'l Smallwood to Conduct him into my Rear—he was expected to Arrive every hour from two o'clock in the Afternoon until we were attacked— At which time Gen'l Smallwood was advancing and by Orders Retreated to the White Horse—

Let me put a Question—Suppose after all these Repeated Orders from His Excellency—and the Arrival of Gen'l Smallwood I had Retreated, before I knew whether the Enemy Intended to Attack me or not, and that they should have Marched for the Schuylkill that Morning [which they Actually did]—would not these very Gentle-

men have been the first to default me—would not His Excellency
with the Greatest Justice have Ordered me in Arrest for Cowardice
and Disobedience of his Repeated preemptory and pointed Orders—
would I not have stood Culpable in the eyes of the World—would I
not Justly merit either Immediate Death or Cashiering? I Certainly
would—what line could I follow but that which I did, what more
could be done on the Occation than what was done—the Artillery
Amunition &c &c were Covered and Saved by a body of Brave
troops which were Rallied and Remained on the Ground with me
for more than an hour after that Gent'n had Effected his Escape
from Danger tho' perhaps not without Confusion—I hold it needless
to say more on the Occation—I rest my Honor, Character which to
me is more Dear than life in the Hands of Gentlemen—who when
Deciding on my Honor will not forget their own—

The court-martial was unanimously of opinion that
General Wayne was "not guilty of the charge exhibited
against him, but that he, on the night of the 20th of
September last, did every duty that could be expected
from an active, brave and vigilant officer, under the
orders which he then had. The Court do acquit him
with the highest honor." The commander-in-chief approved the sentence.

The official despatch of General Wayne to the commander-in-chief dissipates, it will be perceived, some of
the misapprehensions which have been handed down
to posterity by the popular legend concerning the
" Paoli massacre." The attack was not, as clearly appears, a surprise. The special horror attending it grew
out of the common belief that all the slaughter of that
terrible night was due to a complete surprise, and that
the bayonet alone and no fire-arms were employed.
But it will be seen that General Wayne states in his
official report that on the first attack " the enemy and

we were not more than ten yards distant," and that "a well-directed fire *mutually* took place, followed by a charge of bayonet." The whole number of Wayne's detachment was about twelve hundred men ; of these sixty-one were killed. The Americans saved all their artillery, ammunition, and stores: so that it would appear that, bloody as the fight was, the term "massacre" is misapplied.

In order to ascertain the true significance of the attack at Paoli upon the fortunes of the campaign which resulted in the occupation of Philadelphia, a somewhat minute account of the movements of Washington's army in pursuit of the enemy is necessary. That army crossed the Schuylkill on the 14th of September. On the 15th it advanced along the Lancaster Road to a point about twenty miles from the city, near the White Horse tavern. The general's object, as stated in his letter of that date to the President of Congress, was to place his army between the enemy and the Schuylkill, as it was feared that the British would attempt to cross that river at Swede's Ford. On the 16th, near the White Horse tavern, the enemy advanced upon our position. Here a skirmish took place, but, a violent storm coming up, the conflict ceased for that day. Previous to this skirmish Wayne had written on the 15th to General Mifflin, foreseeing this movement of the enemy and insisting upon the importance of attacking them before they reached the fords of the river. "We intend," he says, "to push for the White Horse this evening in order to gain their left flank as soon as possible. May they not steal a march and pass the fords in the vicinity of the Falls unless we march down

at once and give them battle?" After the skirmish of
the 16th, in which, by the way, the portion of the American army engaged did not distinguish itself, the Americans took post at the Yellow Springs, about five miles
from the Paoli, and the British in the Great Valley of
Chester County near the river. On the 17th our main
army marched from the Springs northward to Warwick, a dépôt of army ordnance, about nine miles west
of the river. On the 19th Washington reported to Congress that he had reached Parker's Ford (Lawrenceville), and that it was his intention to cross the river at
that point and proceed downward on the east side to
oppose the enemy's crossing at Fatland and Swede's
Fords. This was accordingly done.

In the mean time General Washington, in order to
facilitate the execution of his plans, detached on the 17th
from his army at Yellow Springs the divisions of Wayne
and Smallwood, with instructions to take a position
secretly in the rear of the British army, so that when the
enemy began to cross the river at Swede's Ford and
Fatland (both of which positions Washington had fortified on the east side) it might be attacked in the rear
by Wayne while the main army would resist its passage
of the fords. On the 19th these orders were repeated
with increased emphasis. Wayne was directed "to move
forward on the enemy," and was promised reinforcements from the divisions of Maxwell and Porter. On
the 21st, as appears from the following letter, these
orders were revoked, and Wayne was directed instead
of moving on the enemy to join General Washington
at once. These orders were intercepted by the enemy
and never reached Wayne's hands. Had they done so

it would, of course, have been too late, the "massacre" having taken place the night before. So completely was the communication between Washington and Wayne cut off by the British that, although they were within a few miles of each other, it is evident from the following letter, written on the 23d of September and dated "four miles from Pots Grove," that Washington had not yet heard of the affair at Paoli, for on the same day Washington writes to the President of Congress (having crossed to the east side of the Schuylkill), "I am also obliged to wait for Generals Wayne and Smallwood, who were left on the other side of Schuylkill in hopes of falling upon the enemy's rear, but they have *eluded them* as well as us;" that is, they had crossed the fords and were on their march to Philadelphia.

General Washington to General Wayne.

Four miles from POTS GROVE 23d Sept. 1777

D'R SIR,—I received your favor of yesterday morning and am apprehensive as you have not acknowledged the receipt of a Letter, I wrote you the night before [21st], that it has fallen into the Enemy's hands. By that I directed Gen'l Smallwood & yourself to march immediately with your Respective Corps by the way of Potts-Grove to join me. You will both pursue the Line thereby marked out, & which I have mentioned above. *For it is my wish that we should draw our whole force together, as soon as possible, and that I should be immediately joined by your Corps.* Should we continue detached & in a divided state I fear we shall neither be able to attack, or defend ourselves with a good prospect of success—

I am D'r Sir

Y'r Most Obed Serv't,

G'E WASHINGTON.

Ser't Bingham & Hambright Crossed at the Middle ferry in One of the ferry Boats, being two there—but no Bridge. Mr. Galloway

has the Inspection of all Market people, or Others—and grants
passes—was very Inquisitive about our Camp
The Soldiers were very free in expressing their sentiments
G. WASHINGTON.

To

    BRIGAD'R GEN'L WAYNE.

The English soldiers do not seem to have proved
themselves such savages elsewhere as they are represented to have been at Paoli. Here is an account of
their doings on the same night at Waynesborough, the
residence of the general, about two miles from the
battle-field :

EAST TOWN Sep'r 22nd 1777

    DEAR ANTHONY,—I am very glad to see a few lines from you as
we have had disagreeable Acc'ts of the [Torn] terrible Night scare.
Some said you were killed, & others, that you were a prisoner, I was
still in hopes of better intelligence ; the Night before last a number
of the British troops surrounded your House in search of you, but
being disappointed in not finding you, they took poor Robert &
James, but behaved with the utmost politeness to the Women, and
said they only wanted the General. They did not disturb the least
Article. There has been several Cannon shot heard today in this
Neighbourhood. I am very uneasy to hear the issue— God Bless
& preserve you is the sincere prayer of your

Brother &c
AB'M ROBINSON.

Sally joins in love—
To
    GENERAL WAYNE
        at
           Red Lion.

Sir William Howe's army having reached Germantown, and Washington's army being encamped in the
Whitemarsh Valley, it was determined to attack the

British as soon as practicable. Washington had learned that a considerable portion of the enemy's force had been detached to capture the works on the Delaware at Billingsport, Mud Island, and Red Bank, which, with the obstructions in the river, guarded the approach to Philadelphia by water. For obvious reasons, it was essential that this approach should be made sure and safe for the British fleet. Howe had despatched a considerable body of men to reduce the works, and Washington asked the opinion of his general officers on the 28th of September whether, while the enemy was thus weakened in Germantown, opportunity should not be taken to attack them. Generals Smallwood, Scott, Wayne, and Porter were in favor of an immediate attack, while the other ten general officers thought that it should be delayed until they had received the reinforcements which had been sent for from the Northern army. As to Wayne's opinion, if we are to judge from the annexed letter to his wife, hopeful as he was at all times, he was never more hopeful than at this crisis, which to many seemed so alarming. The letter is interesting, too, as showing his opinion of the condition of the army, which, after all the reverses it had undergone, is represented as full of health and spirits.

TRAPPE 30th Sept 1777

DEAR POLLY,—I thought that you had a mind far above being Depressed at a little unfavourable Circumstance—the Enemy's being in Possession of Phila is of no more Consequence than their being in possession of the City of New York or Boston—they may hold it for a time—but must leave it with Circumstances of shame and Disgrace before the Close of the Winter—

Our Army is now in full health and spirits, and far stronger than it was at the Battle of the Brandywine— We are daily Receiving Reinforcements, and are now drawing near the Enemy—who will shortly pay dear for the little Advantages they have lately gained— Our Army to the northward under Gen'l Gates is Victorious—matters looked much more Gloomy in that Quarter four weeks ago— than they do at this time here—it is our turn next—and altho' appearances are a little Gloomy at present—yet they will be soon Dissipated and a more pleasing prospect take place— Give my kindest love and wishes to both Our Mothers and Sisters—tell them my sword will shortly point out the way to Victory peace and Happiness—kiss our little people for me— Remove my books and Valuable Writings some Distance from my own House—if not already done—this is but an Act of prudence—and not to be Considered as proceeding from any Other Motive

Adieu my Dear Girl and

believe me Yours

Most Sincerely

ANT'Y WAYNE.

Washington on this occasion decided to take the advice of the minority of his generals, and on the 3d of October he moved his army, consisting of about eleven thousand men, from his camp between the Perkiomen and Skippack Creeks towards the enemy's lines at Germantown. According to Washington's plan, Sullivan was to command the right wing, composed of his own division and that of General Wayne. They were to march down the main road from Chestnut Hill to Germantown, sometimes called the Skippack Road. They were nominally supported on the right by the Pennsylvania militia under General Armstrong, who took no part in the action, and on the left by General Greene. The objective point was the market-house in Germantown, near which, extending along School-House Lane on the right of the Americans, and on the left on Church Lane or near by, the main body of the British army was posted. It is not necessary for our purpose to discuss the many questions which have been debated concerning the behavior of certain corps or of certain generals in this battle. It ought, however, to be understood that the left wing under General Greene, owing to the distance it had to march and the nature of the ground, was not able to engage in time the English regiments. The result was that Sullivan and Wayne were exposed to its attack besides that of the enemy's force immediately in their own front. We need only recount the part taken by General Wayne and his division in the battle, and that is one of the few points connected with it about which there never has been any difference of opinion. The best account of that portion of the engagement in which he and his division were the principal actors is given in his letter to his wife, and in the relation of an officer of the Fifty-Second English Regiment, both of which are subjoined.

General Wayne to Mrs. Wayne.

CAMP NEAR PAWLING MILL
6th Oct 1777

DEAR POLLY,—On the 4th Instant at the dawn of day we attacked General Howe's Army at the upper end of Germantown— The Action soon became General—when we advanced on the Enemy with Charged Bayonets—they broke at first without waiting to Receive us —but soon formed again—when a heavy and well directed fire took place on each side— The Enemy again gave way—but being sup-ported by the Grenadiers Returned to the Charge— Gen'l Sullivans Division & Conways Brigade were at this time Engaged to the Right or west of Germantown—whilst my Division had the Whole Right wing of the Enemy's Army to Encounter on the left or east of the Town—two thirds of our army being then too far to the east to afford

us any Assistance. However the Unparalelled bravery of the troops
surmounted every Difficulty, and the enemy retreated in the utmost
Confusion— Our people Remembering the Action of the Night of
the 20th of Sep'r near the Warren—pushed on with their Bayonets—
and took Ample Vengeance for that Nights Work— Our Officers
Exerted themselves to save many of the poor wretches who were
Crying for Mercy—but to little purpose ; the Rage and fury of the
Soldiers were not to be Restrained for some time—at least not
until great numbers of the Enemy fell by our Bayonets—the fog
together with the smoke Occasioned by our Cannon, and Musketry
—made it almost as dark as night—our people mistaking one
Another for the Enemy frequently Exchanged several shots before
they discovered their Error—we had now pushed the Enemy near
three miles and were in possession of their whole Encampment
when a large body of troops were Discovered Advancing on our
left flank—which being taken for the Enemy we retreated. After
Retreating for about two miles we found it was our own people—
who were Originally Designed to Attack the Right Wing of the
Enemy's Army—

The fog and this mistake prevented us from following a victory
that in all Human probability would have put an end to the
American War—

Gen'l Howe for a long time could not persuade himself that we
had run from Victory—but the fog clearing up he ventured to follow
us with all his Infantry, Grenadiers and Light Horse with some field
pieces—I, at this time was in the Rear and finding Mr. Howe
Determined to push us hard, drew up in Order of Battle—and
waited his Approach—

When he Advanced near we gave him a few Cannon shot with
some Musketry—which caused him to break and Run with the utmost
Confusion—this ended the Action of that day—which Continued
without Intermission from day light until near twelve O'Clock— I
had forgotten to mention that my Roan Horse was killed under me
within a few yards of the Enemy's front—and my left foot a little
bruised by one of their Cannon shot—but not so much as to prevent
me from walking—my poor horse Received one Musket Ball in the
breast—and one in the flank at the same Instant that I had a slight
touch on my left hand—which is scarcely worth mentioning—upon

the Whole it was a Glorious day— Our men are in the highest Spirits—and I am Confident we shall give them a total Defeat the next Action ; which is at no great Distance

My best love and wishes to all friends

Adieu my Dear Girl

Ant'y Wayne.

N.B. I have heard that you Intend to send *Rachel* to market— I would not have it done for One thousand Guineas—

From "History of the Fifty-Second British Regiment," by General Hunter.

"The first that General Howe knew of Washington's marching against us was by his attacking us at daybreak. General Wayne commanded the advance and fully expected to be avenged for the surprise we had given him. When the first shots were fired at our pickets, so much had we all Wayne's affair in remembrance that the battalion were out under arms in a minute. At this time the day had just broke, but it was a very foggy morning, and so dark that we could not see a hundred yards before us. Just as the battalion formed, the pickets came in and said the enemy were advancing in force. They had barely joined the battalion when we heard a loud cry, 'Have at the bloodhounds, revenge Wayne's affair !' and they immediately fired a volley. We gave them one in return, cheered and charged. As it was near the end of the campaign, our battalion was very weak ; it did not consist of more than 300 men, and we had no support nearer than Germantown a mile in our rear. On our charging they gave way on all sides, but again and again renewed the attack with fresh troops and a greater force. We charged them twice till the battalion was so reduced by killed and wounded that the bugle was sounded to retreat ; indeed, had we not retreated at the time we did we should all have been taken or killed, as two columns of the enemy had nearly got round our flank. But this was the first time we had ever retreated from the Americans, and it was with great difficulty we could get the men to obey our orders.

"The enemy were kept so long in check that the two Brigades had advanced to the entrance of Beggarstown, when they met our battalion retreating. By this time General Howe had come up, and seeing the battalion retreating, all broken, he got into a passion,

8

and exclaimed, 'For shame, Light Infantry, I never saw you retreat before, form! form! it is only a scouting party.' However he was quickly convinced that it was more than a scouting party as the heads of the enemy's columns soon appeared. One coming through Beggarstown with three pieces of cannon in their front immediately fired with grape at the crowd that was standing with General Howe under a large chestnut tree. I think I never saw people enjoy a discharge of grape before, but we really all felt pleased to see the enemy make such an appearance, and to hear the grape rattle about the Commander in-Chief's ears, after he had accused the battalion of having run away from a scouting party."

In these three engagements of Brandywine, Paoli, and Germantown, in which Wayne's division was so conspicuous, that division was composed entirely of Pennsylvania troops. They were engaged for the first time in any serious conflict in these three battles on their native soil, striving to rescue the chief city of their Province from the grasp of the enemy. General Wayne's force at no time during the campaign exceeded fifteen hundred men, rank and file, present for duty. It seems that we ought to dwell upon the military behavior of these men during the campaign, while recounting the achievements of their leader with a little more fulness than is usual. Unfortunately, our records tell us chiefly of the conduct of the field officers of the regiments, although nothing can be clearer than that many an unnamed hero fell in the performance of his duty, whose memory we are forced to leave "unwept, unhonored, and unsung." Wayne's division was made up, as we have said, of two brigades, both composed of four infantry regiments. They were commanded during the Revolution, and especially in the campaign which ended with the battle of Germantown, by men who in that day were noted in the army for their devotion, capacity, and courage. The possession of these qualities is attested by the manner in which they bore the trials, fatigues, and dangers of the campaign, and by the number of the officers who were killed and wounded during its duration of about twenty days. When we recall the steadiness with which this division held its post at Chad's Ford until the right wing of the army had been broken up and was retreating, and its brilliant charge which pursued the enemy's force for nearly three miles through the street at Germantown, and which needed only the support that it had a right to count upon, but which it did not receive, to make that battle, in the language of its intrepid commander, "a victory that in all human probability would have put an end to the American war," we may well be proud of the deeds of the Pennsylvania line in the Army of the Revolution. The hardships of the campaign in which these men were engaged is shown by this, that at its close scarcely more than half the men with which it was begun remained in the ranks.

Most of the officers who led the regiments had been fellow-soldiers of Wayne from the beginning, and experience had inspired them with confidence in the capacity of their leader. Colonel Chambers of the First Regiment, of whose exploits in recovering the guns at Brandywine we have spoken, was a veteran at that time in the Army of the Revolution. He had stood by Arnold's side when he was wounded at the battle of Bemis Heights, and had gained great credit for his gallantry in the fierce assault made on the German troops of Burgoyne's army; he had also led the regiment in

its charge upon the troops occupying the town of New
Brunswick, and had driven them out of their intrenchments. In the most hazardous service at Brandywine
he was, as we have said, wounded, and notwithstanding
he and a considerable number of his officers and men
were disabled by the fire of the enemy, they retained
steadily their position, and with the rest of the division
retreated in good order.

The Second Regiment was commanded at the battle of Germantown by Major Williams until he fell,
wounded, and was taken prisoner. Captain Howell
then assumed the command. The regiment seems to
have lost heavily both at Brandywine and at Germantown, six lieutenants besides its commander having in
these two battles been either killed or wounded.

The Third, Colonel Craig, the Sixth, Colonel Bicker,
the Ninth, Colonel Nagel, and the Twelfth, Colonel
Cook, were not under Wayne's command, but formed
Conway's brigade of Lord Stirling's division at Brandywine and Germantown. Of this brigade La Fayette
speaks in his Memoirs. He tells of the brilliant manner
in which "General Conway (the Gallicized Hibernian),
Chevalier of St. Louis, acquitted himself at the head of
his brigade of eight hundred men in the encounter
with the troops of Cornwallis near Birmingham Meet-
ing-House."

The Fourth lost half of its effective force in this
short campaign, its major, Lamar, having been killed
and six of his lieutenants wounded at Paoli. The last
words of Major Lamar on receiving his death-wound
were, "Halt, boys. Give these assassins one fire."

Of the Fifth at Brandywine, Colonel Francis Johnston

was taken prisoner, and its lieutenant-colonel, Frazer, and the adjutant, Harper, were captured the next day. One captain was made prisoner at Germantown, and the major and two lieutenants were wounded. In the Seventh, commanded by Lieutenant-Colonel Grier, he and two of his captains and four lieutenants were wounded at Paoli, and sixty-one of the rank and file of the regiment were killed, besides a large number wounded or taken prisoners. Part of the Eighth Regiment had been detached, and was acting as a rifle corps in the place of Morgan's, which had been sent to the northward. Its lieutenant-colonel, Stephen Bayard, did gallant service, and was wounded. Doubtless much the same report might be made of the other regiments of the Pennsylvania line which we have not named, but either the record of their services has not been preserved or it is too imperfect to permit us to speak of them with certainty. What Wayne said of his own officers in the official account which we have given of the affair at Paoli, of Hartley, of Humpton, of Brodhead, of Grier, of William Butler, and of Hubley, might doubtless have been said with equal truth of all his officers and their subordinates who served during the campaign, of the living as of the dead, of the prisoner as well as of the freeman. None the less the organization was much broken up by the hardships the men had undergone, and a new "arrangement," as it was called, was made at the close of the year. The appointment of the following officers to vacancies may indicate Wayne's estimate of their conduct during the campaign : *Colonels:* Nagel to the Tenth ; Bicker to the Second ; R. Butler to the Ninth ; Thomas Craig to the

Third. *Lieutenant-Colonels :* Smith to the Ninth ; Miller to the Second ; Harmar to the Sixth ; Thomas Robinson to the Seventh ; Bruner to the Third ; S. Bayard to the Eighth ; Caleb North to the Eleventh. *Majors :* Nichol to the Ninth ; Church to the Fourth ; Hulings to the Third ; James Moore to the Seventh ; Vernon to the Eighth ; Taylor to the Fifth ; Tolbert to the Sixth ; Ryan to the Tenth.

After the battle of Germantown the first subject which claimed the attention of the commander-in-chief was the strengthening of the posts at Billingsport on the Jersey side of the Delaware, and of Forts Mifflin and Red Bank on opposite shores of the river just above. The fortifications at these places, with the *chevaux-de-frise* stretched across the river which they protected, closed, as we have said, the access of the English fleet to the city. With the army at Philadelphia and the fleet below constantly striving to furnish supplies by the only route by which they could reach it in sufficient quantities, it will be at once seen that it was of the utmost importance that the Americans should maintain these obstacles to a communication between the fleet and the army. Washington at that time did not consider his force sufficiently strong to detach any portion of it to relieve the garrisons at these posts, or to draw off the attention of the enemy by a counter-movement. Left to themselves, therefore, the garrisons, with the assistance of Commodore Hazlewood of the Pennsylvania Navy, defended these posts during more than six weeks with a bravery as heroic as that displayed at any time during the war. Billingsport, the lowest post, was abandoned in order to concentrate the whole disposable force at Red Bank (Fort Mercer) and at Mud Island (Fort Mifflin). Colonel Greene was in command of the garrison of the former, composed at this time of about four hundred troops. On the 22d of October a force of Hessians twelve hundred strong was sent against it, under the command of Count Donop. Their attack, which was very energetic, was repulsed with a loss of about four hundred men, and Count Donop was mortally wounded. At the same time an effort was made to attack Fort Mifflin, on the opposite shore, by ships of war, but two of the vessels, the Augusta and the Merlin, ran aground and were burned by the Americans. This success revived greatly the hopes of the Americans of preventing the fleet from reaching the city, and strengthened their determination to maintain the possession of these forts. Howe was engaged in constructing redoubts and batteries on Province Island, on the west side of the Delaware, separated from Fort Mifflin by a strait about five hundred yards wide, to enable him to get possession of these forts. To relieve Fort Mifflin it was necessary to capture these batteries on Province Island. To effect this object would have required, in the opinion of Washington and many of his generals, a greater force than he had at his disposal, and the hope was that the fort would hold out until the expected reinforcements from the northward should arrive. Such was the condition of things when General Wayne proposed to the commander-in-chief that he should lead an expedition to capture the batteries on Province Island by a *coup-de-main*. General Washington declined to approve the plan, and on the 10th of November a combined attack by the English naval forces and the land batteries on Province Island was made on the fort, so terrible in its character, and made with so overwhelming a force, that the garrison, which had fought with heroic bravery, was obliged to evacuate the ruins. That General Wayne urged an expedition for the relief of the fort, which he was to lead, is not generally known, and, as far as I am aware, no statement of his plans has ever been made in print. General Washington's letter to the President of Congress, in which he explains why the attempt was not made, is better known. This letter, and that of General Wayne to Mr. Peters concerning his projected share in the expedition, are given here in order that the reader may compare them. It is not easy to reconcile their statements.

General Washington to the President of Congress, 17th November, 1777.

SIR,—I am sorry to inform you that Fort Mifflin was evacuated the night before last after a defence which does credit to the American army and will ever reflect the highest honor upon the officers and men of the garrison.

*   *   *   *   *   *   *   *

The only remaining and practicable mode of giving relief to the Fort was by dislodging the enemy from Province Island, from whence they kept up an incessant fire. But this from the situation of the ground was not to be attempted with any degree of safety to the attacking party unless the whole, or a considerable part of the army should be removed to the west side of the Schuylkill to support and cover it.

After explaining that a force marching down the road from the Blue Bell at Darby to Province Island would have been in imminent danger of being cut off by the enemy's force crossing the Schuylkill at Market Street ferry and attacking the rear of the American detachment, he adds,—

It was therefore determined a few days ago to wait the arrival of the reinforcements from the Northward before any alteration could safely be made in the disposition of the Army ; and I was not without hopes that the fort would have held out till that time.

General Wayne to Mr. Peters, Secretary of War.

CAMP WHITE MARSH 18th Nov. 1777

DEAR SIR,—Before this reaches you the loss of Fort Mifflin has been Announced—that Garrison has done its duty—would to God that it had been equally done in an Other Quarter !

Six weeks Investiture and no Attempt to raise the siege of that fort—will scarcely be Credited at an Other day—you'l ask what was the cause of this Supineness—an over stretched caution, which is oftentimes attended with as fatal Consequences, as too much rashness, the *present*, as well as some *past* events, fully evinces the truth of this position.

Whenever that Subject was mentioned, new Difficulties were always raised sufficient to prevent any measures being taken for that purpose—until His Excellency, seeing the Absolute necessity of making every possible effort to effect so Desirable an Object, Ordered some Gent'n in whom he could Confide to Reconnoitre the Ground in the Vicinity of Province Island, the position of the Enemies works and the Avenues leading to them—on their Return a Council was held—the practicability as well as the Immediate Necessity of raising the Siege was urged in the most clear and pointed terms—the measure was again over ruled—but His Excellency had Determined to act the General—the Army was to have passed the Schuylkill and taken post near the middle ferry [Market Street]—whilst my Division with Morgan's Corps, were to proceed to Province Island, and there Storm the Enemies lines, spike their Cannon, and Ruin their works—

There was some Difficulty, as well as Danger in the Attempt—but the success depended more on the fortitude of the Troops, and the Vigor with which the Attack was made—than upon Numbers—His

Excellency had charged me with the Conduct and execution of this business—I knew my Troops & gladly Embraced the Command, but the Evacuation of that Important fortress, the Evening preceeding the day on which the Storm was to have taken place, frustrated an Expedition which Afforded the most flattering prospect of once more possessing Phil'a and Obliging the Enemy to seek for Quarters in a less Hostile place—These hopes are now Vanished— I fear I Augured but too true when I Informed you of the probable fate of our fleet and Works on the River—nothing will prevent its taking place but his Excellency sometimes act'g without *his Council.*

It was a saying of one of the first of Generals, that whenever he Intended to do [blot] he always called a Council of War—I believe it was the surest way to do nothing—yet I would not be understood to lay Councils Entirely aside—Altho' I am well Convinced that the doubts raised, and the Delays Occasion'd by these Councils, Often prevent a General from taking the Advantage of the Most favourable Circumstances, and from Striking the most Capital Strokes— There has been more than one Instance of the truth of this Observation during this Campaign.

We have yet a Capital game to play—and if we are not too fond of keeping the Cards in our hands we may make the Odd trick—but if we should still Remain Inactive—a few days will force us from the field—Our poor naked soldiers, begin to Complain of the Cold and look up to us for Relief—I never pass along the line, but Objects strike my eye, which give a painful and Melancholy Sensation, that almost Induces me to wish I was past either seeing or hearing—Indeed Sir, Nothing but the doubtful state we are in should keep me a Single Moment in the Service that has become almost Intolerable.

I herewith send you the proceedings of a Gen'l Court Martial held on me the 30th Ultimo.   I wish to Convince my friends and the publick that I have done my Duty—and that I may Quit the Service with as much Credit as I entered into it

I am Sir Your Most Ob't and very
Hum'l Ser't
ANT'Y WAYNE.

[RICH'D PETERS, ESQR.,
   Sec'y of War.]

The three subjects which engaged General Wayne's most anxious attention during the autumn of 1777 and the winter encampment of the army at Valley Forge were—1st, the expediency and necessity of carrying on an active campaign; 2d, measures for providing the men under his command with suitable clothing and food during the winter; 3d, the necessity of filling up the ranks of his regiments, depleted by sickness, desertion, and the expiration of the term of the men's enlistment.

In his efforts to bring about an active campaign, Wayne exhibited some of his most characteristic qualities. Four different times between the middle of October and the close of the year 1777, while the army lay encamped at White Marsh and Valley Forge, he urged upon the commander-in-chief the expediency of taking the field. The letters in which he outlined his plans and advocated their adoption are found among his correspondence. They prove even to those not familiar with military science and strategy how earnest was his conviction that their adoption must aid the American cause. The first of these letters, that to Mr. Secretary Peters, dated the 18th of November, has been already given, and it is rather an expression of his opinion concerning the timidity and stupidity of those of his fellow-officers who advocated a do-nothing policy, and of patriotic grief at the results which had followed the adoption of such a system, than a suggestion of new enterprises. The other three letters are addressed to the commander-in-chief. In the first, dated October 27, in answer to the general's question whether it would be prudent in our present circumstances to attempt to drive the enemy from their works (before the surrender of Forts Mifflin and Mercer), Wayne urges, as will be seen from the letter itself, the adoption of an elaborate plan of attack, by which the enemy could be dislodged, and he insists upon the absolute necessity at any rate of making the effort. In the second, dated 25th of November, likewise in reply to a letter from General Washington consulting him as to the course he should pursue, he urges most earnestly that "your Excellency should march to-morrow morning," and he fortifies his appeal as to the immediate necessity of giving battle by expressing "solemnly and clearly" his "opinion that the credit of the army, the safety of the country, the honor of the American arms, the approach of winter that must in a few days force you from the field, and, above all, the depreciation of the currency, point out the immediate necessity of giving the enemy battle." It should not be forgotten that this letter was written at the beginning of the memorable winter of 1777–78, memorable for the agony and suffering of ill-fed and almost naked soldiers subject to the hardships and exposure (easily preventable) which they were called upon to undergo during their encampment at Valley Forge. In the third, dated December 4, also addressed to General Washington, he urges—most sensibly, as it seems to us—a modified plan of a winter campaign. These letters are very characteristic. They are filled with a certain noble enthusiasm and patriotic ardor which evidently regard no interests worth pursuing save those of the writer's country, then in the supremest hour of her distress. They should be carefully read, bearing in mind that every word he uses was carefully weighed, and that he was not only willing but anxious to do his share in the hazardous operations he recommended.

General Wayne to General Washington.

Oct 27, 1777

SIR,—The first Question you offer is " Whether it will be prudent in our present circumstances & Strength to Attempt (by a General attack) to Dislodge the enemy, and if it is, and we unsuccessful, where shall we Retreat to"— I am not perfectly acquainted with our Circumstances or Strength—I have some knowledge of it as well as that of the Enemy's which nearly meets the Idea I always entertained of it—however I might have differed with Other Gentlemen on the Occasion—when I gave my Opinion for the Attack at Germantown I did not Diminish their Numbers— In point of Position they had then much the Advantage of us—the Ground they Occupied was Strong—many Roads led immediately for our flanks— In their present position—it may be said their flanks are covered—as to ours when once we move to the Attack—we shall be under no Apprehension of either being outflanked or Enclosed in the Rear— In case of a misfortune we have every Road and the Whole Country open to favor our Retreat—the shipping at the same time may move up to favour our Attack or Retreat—the Militia from the Other Side of Schuylkill with a few field pieces will not only draw the Attention of the Enemy to them but will Annoy and Enfilade them This will also facilitate the Victory or Cover the Retreat— It may be necessary to Offer some Reasons for giving this advice—they are these Viz—if the Enemy are not Immediately Dislodged—all our Defenses and Shipping on the River will Inevitably fall into their hands—they will thereby secure to themselves Comfortable Winter Quarters, the Inclemency of the Weather will soon force your Army from the field—if you should Attempt to keep it you will lose more men by sickness Desertion and other Concomitant evils Incident to a Naked Discontented Army—than you would in the Severest Action —add to this the small prospect of Recruiting or Strengthening your Force under the present Militia acts—especially as your Officers will necessarily be Engaged in the field— For my own part I am well Convinced that on the Activity and Prowess of our present

Troops much Depends—which Induces me to wish for an Immediate
Attack—that if unsuccessful we may Retire to some Other place
best Suited to Receive us and where we may Clothe and Refresh our
Troops, and Employ our Officers on the Recruiting Service—to
attempt to prevent the Enemy from Drawing Supplies when they
are once in Possession of the River will Answer no Other end than
to fatigue and Destroy our own Soldiers—

ANTHONY WAYNE.

General Wayne to General Washington.

CAMP AT WHITE MARSH 25th Nov. 1777

SIR,—After the most Dispassionate & Deliberate Consideration
of the question your Excellency was Pleased to put to the Council
of Gen'l Officers last evening—I am Solemnly and Clearly of Opinion ; that the Credit of the Army under your Command—the Safety
of the Country—the Honor of the American Arms—the Approach
of Winter that must in a few days force you from the field, and
above all the Depreciation of the Currency of these States, point out
the Immediate Necessity of giving the Enemy Battle—

Could they possibly be drawn from their lines it is a Measure
devoutly to be wished—but if that can not be Affected It is my
Opinion that your Excellency *should march tomorrow morning* and
take post with this Army at the Upper end of Germantown, and
from thence Immediately detach a Working party to throw up some
Redoubts under the Direction of your Engineers,—this Intelligence
will reach the Enemy—they will Conclude that you intend to make
good your Winter Quarters there—and however Desirous they may
be to Dislodge you—they Can't attempt it until they withdraw their
Troops from the Jerseys—this can not be done in the course of a
night—

By this manœuvre you will be within striking distance, the Enemy
will be Deceived by your Working party and lulled into Security—
your Troops will be fresh and ready to move that Night so as to
Arrive at the Enemy's lines before day light on this day morning
—agreeable to the proposed plan of Attack—the outlines of which
are good and may be Improved to Advantage ; and Crowned with
Success—

It has been Objected by some Gentlemen that the Attack is

hazardous—that if we prevail it will be Attended with great loss—
I agree with the Gentlemen in their position.

But however hazardous the Attempt and Altho' some loss is Certain
—yet it is my Opinion that you will not be in a Worse Situation—
nor your Arms in less Credit if you should meet with a Misfortune
than if you were to Remain Inactive.

The eyes of all the World are fixed on you—the Junction of the
Northern Army gives the Country and Congress some expectations
that Vigorous efforts will be made to Dislodge the Enemy—and
Oblige them to seek for Winter Quarters in a less hostile place than
Phil'a.

It's not in our power to Command Success—but it is in our power
to produce a Conviction to the World that we deserve it—

Interim I am your Excellency's most
                                        Ob't Hum'l Ser't
                                          ANT'Y WAYNE.

General Washington to General Wayne.

SIR,—I wish to recall your attention to the important matter
recommended to your Consideration some time ago—Namely the
Adviseability of a Winter Campaign, & practicability of an Attempt
upon Philad'a with the Aid of a Considerable body of Militia to be
Assembled at an appointed time & place. Particular reasons urge
me to request your Sentiments on this matter by the morning, & I
shall expect to receive them accordingly in writing by that time.

                        I am Sir
                        Your mo Obed't Servant
                                     G'E WASHINGTON.

Dec'r 3d 1777
[BRIG'R GEN'L WAYNE.
   Camp.]

General Wayne to General Washington.

                                        CAMP 4th Dec'r 1777

SIR,—I am not for a Winters Campaign in the Open field—the
Distressed and Naked Situation of your Troops will not Admit of it.

But if taking post at Wilmington & the Villages in its Vicinity—
or Hutting at the Distance of about twenty Miles West of Phil'a by

way of Quarters (which will not only support the Honor & Reputation of your Army in the eyes of the Enemy and the States of *Europe*—but will give Confidence to America—and Cover this Country against the Horrid rapine and Devastation of a Wanton Enemy,) be Deemed making a Winters Campaign—I am then for it upon every principle of Honor—policy and justice.

The probability of a Successful Attack upon Phil'a during the Winter depends so much on time, Season & a Variety of Other Circumstances—that the Calling out the Militia in General may not be Strictly Warrantable.

Notwithstanding I wish to see a proper number Always hanging on the Skirts of the Enemy, sufficient to prevent any small parties from Committing Depredations—to save the Continental Troops from that fatigue—and should the Enemy move out in force—to give timely Notice thereof and to Assist in their Repulse—

I am your Excellency's Most Ob't
and very Hum'l Ser't
ANT'Y WAYNE B.G.

[GENL. WASHINGTON.]

Wayne felt most deeply the loss of the forts on the Delaware. He writes to Gates very much in the same strain as he had done to Peters.[1] "We have lost Fort Mifflin," he says, "after an investment of six weeks without any attempt to raise the siege, the consequence of which will be the loss of all our other works and shipping on the river. . . . I have thus given you a true picture of our present situation, over which I wish to draw a veil until our arms procure one more lovely, which I don't despair of, if our worthy General will but follow his own good judgment without listening too much to some counsel."

Of the seventeen general officers of the army whom Washington was in the habit of consulting before he

---

[1] Reed's Reed, 342.

took any important step, Wayne was always one of that gallant minority whose "voice was still for war." His notion of the duty of a soldier was that while he should not be governed by a rash foolhardiness, which as often leads to disaster as to victory, he should nevertheless maintain a steady, bold self-confidence, which recognizes that there is no successful war unless prodigious risks are taken. His temperament was not one which could feel any sympathy with the doubts and misgivings of a council of war such as Washington could convene, especially as he knew that its opinion was founded upon a contempt for the military qualities of the American soldier as compared with those which were supposed to characterize his adversary. He knew that there was something of the same feeling common among certain generals that prevailed among the officers of the Royal army when they were acting with the Provincial troops before the Revolution. He knew that victory was impossible while such a feeling prevailed, and therefore by temperament, as well as a matter of calculation, he always set an example which inspired his men with self-confidence, the principal element in which he felt they were deficient. Hence he not only advocated measures which sometimes seemed to his fellow-officers desperate and rash, but he was always the leader in their execution. And it is curious to observe that from enterprises of this description, which his own brave heart told him were feasible, depending, as he said, "not on the numbers, but the vigor of the men engaged," such as the storming of Stony Point, or the change of the fortunes of the day at Monmouth (where he was obliged to withstand at the same moment the treason of Lee and the charge of the English grenadiers), or the extraordinary presence of mind and courage which he exhibited at Green Spring, although on all of these occasions those around him felt that he was fighting his last battle, he emerged, not unhurt, but triumphant. However wearied and disgusted he was with what he regarded as the timidity and incapacity of many of the generals, nothing was more striking than his unwavering loyalty to his venerated chief under all his trials. Washington's indecision, at times, Wayne ascribed wholly to his own modesty, and to his readiness to yield to inferior men who had had more military experience than himself,—notably Lee and Gates. No one was more shocked than he by the intrigues of the Conway Cabal, and no one deserved as no one gained more fully during and after the war the unlimited confidence of Washington.

The army having gone into winter quarters at Valley Forge, Wayne was soon obliged to turn his attention to a very essential part of a general's duty,—that of providing suitable clothing for his men, and recruiting their numbers diminished by sickness and desertion. His correspondence during the terrible winter of 1777–78, showing how constant were his efforts to compass these two objects, is most interesting and instructive as confirming the traditions which have been handed down to us of the suffering at Valley Forge, and showing that the inefficiency of the service was due in a great measure to a lack of administrative capacity (at least as far as the Pennsylvania troops were concerned) on the part of the State authorities. One loses patience as he reads Wayne's complaints of the neglect of the commonest wants of the soldier, and the ridiculous excuses that were made for not supplying them. It is, indeed, humiliating to read in the Wayne correspondence the story of this great neglect,—to discover, for instance, that four months after the battle of Brandywine the officers who had lost all their baggage in that engagement had not yet been supplied with new garments ; that such were the destitution and nakedness of the troops at Valley Forge that Wayne himself purchased the cloth for the articles his men most needed, hoping— as it turned out, in vain—to have the garments made up in the camp ; that the State Clothier-General refused to issue the cloth which he had in store, through some absurd rule in his opinion justifying his action. Thus, when the proper officer called for shoes repeatedly, they were not issued because no order of council had been voted which directed them to be delivered. On the 12th of March Wayne sends Colonel Bayard to Lancaster to procure arms and clothing, but the result is broken promises only. In despair he turns to the President of the Council, or Governor, and tells him of the need of supplies and of recruits for the Pennsylvania line. He is told in reply that he should send out more recruiting officers, and that as to the non-receipt of the clothing, the delay is caused by a *want of buttons*.[1]

In order that a true view of the condition of the

---

[1] It is usual to attribute the chaotic condition of the public service, so far at least as regards the supply of the needs of the Pennsylvania soldiers, to factional strife in the Assembly. It is more probable that it was due to the inexperience, the incapacity, and possibly in some cases the corruption, of the men whom the new government had brought into power.

army at Valley Forge at that time, and of the embarrassments and difficulties which surrounded General
Wayne in his efforts to procure clothing and recruits,
may be obtained, the following letters from the correspondence are given :

General Wayne to Mr. Peters, Secretary of War.

LANCASTER 26th Jan'y 1778.

DEAR SIR,—Col. Miller in Virtue of an Appointment from me
under the authority of the Board of War purchased a Quantity
of Cloth in York Town for the use of the Officers & Soldiers of
this State,—the Officers having lost their Baggage Immediately after
the Battle of Brandywine are at present Almost Destitute of Clothing,
part of the Cloth, which the Colonel has purchased was for the use
of those Officers, and yet remains in the hands of the Merchants
who do not wish to deliver it until they know where to Receive their
pay—

The Clothier General has peremptorily refused paying Col. Miller's
Orders in favour of those Merchants—so that unless the Board will
please to give Col. Miller Credit for a Sum of Money for the pur-
pose of paying for them & to be Accountable for the same to Col.
Johnston the Clothier Gen'l of this State the Officers must suffer or
Quit the Service—

I have this moment rec'd the Enclosed. A number of Officers from
the Respective Regt's of this State are now here with the Measures
to make the Officers Clothing by but the Cloth to make them is in
York under the Circumstances I have mentioned—

I must therefor Request you to lay the matter before the Board,
and fall upon some Other mode than Orders on the Clothier Gen'l
as directed by the Within Copy—for those who have ever Rec'd an
Order in that way will never be Induced to part with their goods on
the same ground in future——

I am too much Interested in the freedom and happiness of America
to withdraw from the Army at this Crisis   I believe I have a much
greater share of Care and Difficulty than Ought to come to the proportion of one Officer— Unfortunately there is no Other Gen'l in
the Penns'a line, belonging to this Army— We Derive but little

Assistance from the Civil Authority, and every let and hindrance in the power of the Clothier General seems to be thrown in the way —so that I am almost tempted to—
but I will, at all events, provide for my poor fellows before I consult my own ease & happiness

Interim I am your Most Ob't
Hum'l Ser't
Ant'y Wayne.

[Rich'd Peters Esqr.]

General Wayne to the Clothier General.

Mount Joy 6th Feb'y 1778

Dear Sir,—Col Chambers will wait on you with a Return of Clothing, for the Serjants Drums & fifes of my Division   I wish to see them make a Decent Appearance on the parade,   at present they are Almost Naked—   if you cant Conveniently have the Uniforms made up at Lancaster—will you be so kind as to Order them to be cut out and Delivered to Col Hartley—together with the Materials for making them up—which I can have done in Camp—   the Col will pass his Rect. for the Whole.

I am Sir your Most Ob't Hum'l Ser't
Ant'y Wayne.

[James Mease Esqr
Clothier General]

Commissary Lang to General Wayne.

Lancaster Feby 7th 1778

Hon'd Sir,—You can not Conceive how Uneasy I am from want of Instructions from Council concerning the Sending necessaries to Camp for the troops   You can now be furnished with 300 pair of shoes more but they (the Council) have not fixed the issueing time as yet.   Some shirts & stockings & Good Breeches are in my possession, on which account I only await your Orders & their Leave. Application has been made by the other five Reg'ts of the state who have no Shoes as yet & represent themselves in Very great Want. Possibly this may soon Lessen the number now in my hands.   Pray

send a receipt for the 301 pairs you got of Mr Henry along with
your first order & oblige Sir your

Most Obedient Ser't

Ja's Lang

[The Hon'bl Anthony Wayne, Esq'r,
Brigad'r Gen'll at Camp,
Near Valley Forge.]

General Wayne to Mr. Peters, Secretary of War.

Mount Joy 8th Feby 1778

Dear Sir,—On my Arrival in Camp I found the Division in a
much worse Condition for the Want of Clothing and every Other
matter than I expected— I am endeavouring to Remedy the Defects & hope soon to Restore Order, Introduce Discipline and Content—all which was much Wanting and desertion prevailing fast—
I flatter myself that I have so much the Esteem and Confidence of
my Troops—that Desertion will no longer take place— I am happy
to Inform you that there is not a single Instance since my Return—

I find the Enclosed Deficiency in Bayonets which I wish an Order
for from the Board of War on *Mr. William Henry* at Lancaster—
with directions to make them Eighteen Inches long in the blade
together with an Equal Number of Scabbards and belts—I would
also wish to exchange a Number of Rifles for Muskets and Bayonets—
I don't like rifles—I would almost as soon face an Enemy with a
good Musket and Bayonet without amunition—as with amunition
without a Bayonet for altho' there are not many Instances of bloody
bayonets yet I am Confident that one bayonet keeps off an Other—
and for the Want of which the Chief of the Defeats we have met
with ought in a great measure to be Attributed— the Enemy knowing the Defenseless State of our Riflemen rush on— they fly mix
with or pass thro' the Other Troops and Communicate fears that
is ever Incident to a retiring Corps— this Would not be the Case
if the Riflemen had bayonets—but it would be still better if good
muskets and bayonets were put into the hands of good Marksmen
and Rifles entirely laid aside— for my own part I never Wish to
see one—at least Without a Bayonet— I don't give this as Mere
matter of Opinion or Speculation—but as matter of fact to the truth
of Which I have more than Once been an Unhappy Witness— I

am so fully Convinced of the bad policy of such arms that no reasoning will ever Eradicate that Conviction.

I must therefore Request you to lay the Matter before your Hon'ble board and procure me the Order on Mr. Henry

Interim I am Dr Sir

Your Most Ob't Hum'l Ser't

ANTH'Y WAYNE

Mr. Peters, Secretary of War, to General Wayne.

WAR OFFICE Feby 18th 1778

D'R SIR,—I received your Letter on the Subject of exchanging the Rifles for Muskets & procuring a Number of Bayonets for your Division— I communicated the Contents of it to the Board who are well convinced of the Propriety of the Measure & of the Justice of your Observations. But as in a former Instance they have been accused of Partiality by supplying your Division with Shoes out of the Common Line, they would wish to avoid such Imputations in future— If you will procure an Order from the General or Adjutant General so as to make the thing a general & not a partial Regulation the Board will with Cheerfulness comply with your Request— A Board of Ordnance for the Regulation of the Department in the Field, consisting of the Commanding Officer of the Artillery, the Chief Engineer & eldest Colonel or Commissary of Artillery, is appointed & they will be furnished with Money to answer all immediate Exigencies in Camp & it is hoped as they are more immediately cognisant of the Wants of the Army there will be less Complaints of their being neglected because at a Distance from the Seat of public Business—

I am your obed Ser't

RICHARD PETERS.

Colonel Wayne to Colonel Bayard.

MOUNT JOY 28th March 1778

SIR,—You are to proceed Immediately to Lancaster and call on Wm Henry Esq'r there for the Arms &cs mentioned in the two Brigade Returns.

You will also forward to Camp all such Clothing as may be provided for the Use of the Officers and Soldiers of the Penns'a Line.

I need not urge the Immediate necessity of these Articles—your Own Observations and knowledge of our Distressed Situation will be a Sufficient Inducement for you to exert every power in Dispatching this Essential duty.

You will urge the Immediate furnishing of us with two pair Linen Overalls, two Shirts, two pair Shoes—One pair *Gaiters*, one pair knee Garters, one black Stock & hair Comb for each man—Say *three Thousand men*—together with Infantry Caps and Other Clothing but the Overalls Shirts & Gaiters are the most Essential and immediately Wanted—

As soon as you can Effect this Business you will Return to Camp taking care to forward all such Recruits belonging to the Penns'a Line as may be in Lancaster first providing them with their proper Uniform Arms & Accoutrements

Interim I am Sir

Your most Ob't

Hum'l Ser't

Ant'y Wayne B. G.

N. B. Shoes we are tolerably off for—but a Store will not be amiss. If you can be furnished with Linen thread & necessarys, we will have the Overalls made up in Camp—

[Col. Stephen Bayard.]

General Wayne to President Wharton of Pennsylvania.

Mount Joy 4th May 1778

Dear Sir,—Enclosed is the Return of the 13 Regiments belonging to the State of Penns'a—you will Observe that they are very weak—the chief part of those Returned Sick at present—is for want of Clothing—being too naked to Appear on the parade— our Officers in Particular are in a most wretched Condition—I can't conceive the Reason why they are not supplied—I purchased Cloth &c at York last Jan'y Sufficient to Clothe great part of them—but have not heard what has been done with it I know it must be Distressing to your Excellency to hear so many Repetitions of our wants—but whatever pain it may give you—I hourly experience much more from the Complaints and View of Worthy fellows who are Conscious of meriting some Attention and whose wretched Condition can not be worse—they think any change must be for the better & too many have Risked Desertion—the Enclosed Order has lately put some stop to it—and had we Clothing I am Confident that we should not have any more leave us where we now have twenty.

Adieu & believe me yours Most Sincerely

ANT'Y WAYNE.

[GOV'R WHARTON.]

Colonel Bayard to General Wayne.

LANCASTER April 23d '78

DEAR GENERAL,—I wrote you a few days ago, but have not had the honor of an Answer— Mr. Mease came home yesterday, and Consented at last to let me have Linen for Twelve hundred Shirts, provided it could be made up here. Mr Howell, Major Werts and myself engaged it should and for that purpose have been in and thro' every Family in this Town in Order to get them made up, and I have the satisfaction to inform you that they are to be ready in Eight days from this— As the Expenses of staying here are great, I would gladly know whether I must remain, and bring them with me or Come Immediately to Camp. It gives me pain to relate to you the difficulty of getting Any thing from Mease. Waiting his slow Motion, dancing attendance &c are unsufferable, had I full powers it should be otherwise, but he Prides himself upon his being Confined to no particular State— The Guns and Bayonets are to be ready against the time mentioned above— I have fitted up several soldiers for Our Division— The Drummers & Fifers you have received before this time— I am heartily tired of Lancaster wou'd much rather be at Camp, a few lines from you on that head would greatly oblige

Your Most Ob't Humb Ser't

S. BAYARD.

GENERAL ANT'Y WAYNE,
   at
     Camp.

General Wayne to the Speaker of the Pennsylvania Assembly.

MOUNT JOY CAMP 13th May 1778

DEAR SIR,—I transmitted a Return of the State & Numbers of the Several Regiments in the Penn'sa Line to his Excellency the

President—in order to lay before the Honorable House at their present sessions— You will find that by Death Sickness Desertion &c &c we are much reduced—and that it will Require great exertions to Complete the Regiments to the new arrangements—altho' far short of the former Establishment—

The Recruiting business goes on very slowly owing to the enormous price given to Labourers i·e· two Dollars *per Diem* which, together with the Wages Offered by the Q M General to Waggoners & the Substitute money given to Militia (under Colour of being Servants) will in a great Degree if not totally prevent us from Completing our Corps by any means short of a *Draft*—but how this will go down with your Constituants is a Matter that may Require some serious Consideration— perhaps fixing a Certain Quota for each Battalion to furnish by a Certain day may be liable to the Least Exception— however you will be the most Competent Judges of the proper Ways & Means— I can Only say that your Consequence as a State in a great Degree Depends on your making a Respectable Appearance in the field—more Especially as the Enemy are in possession of your Capital—in which case any supineness gives ground for Censure which if I am Rightly Instructed Some States are very Liberal in bestowing—Calling us a Dead weight on their hands—with Other Language not quite so Respectful as this State at one day had a Right to Expect—and which I know she has power to Command when properly exerted.

Your Troops are Second to none in the field—They have stepped the first for Glory—for God's Sake by some means Complete your Regiments—give us Clothing and let us be Embodied together—and I pledge my life & Reputation to produce a Conviction to the World that we have a just Claim to—and will hold the first Rank in the free & Independent States of America—

I wish you to call on His Excellence President Wharton for the Return & Letter Accompanying it—that you may be the better Enabled to Estimate the Numbers & Necessaries Wanting—

Interim I am with Every Esteem

your Most Ob't

ANTH'Y WAYNE.

Recruiting Officers to General Wayne.

ALLEN TOWN, March 30th 1778

DEAR GENERAL,—Northampton County being the place appointed to Recruit in Does not turn out according to Expectation it Being so full of Tories, We have got but 15 Recruits Between us if you would be kind Enough to send an officer for these Recruits or Call us home or Give us orders to go to Some other place to Recruit in—

We were ordered to this County by the Council, Therefore we would be Glad to know how to Proceed at present and being ordered by the Council not to send Recruits to Camp without a proper Officer as they are troublesome to us here

Dear S'r We Remain your humble
Servts
WILLIAM OLDHAM Cap't
CHARLES McHENRY Cap't

Colonel Bayard to General Wayne.

LANCASTER April 11th '78

DEAR GENERAL,—your favour I received and soon after waited on the Governor & Counsil and represented the Distress'd situation of the Officers and Soldiers of the Penn'a Line. the Governor Assured me that he would Interest himself in the matter, and do all in his power to have them well Clothed, for that purpose I was desired to wait on Mr. Mcase (who was unfortunately out of Town and had been 5 days) with a message from them, but as he is not yet return'd, nothing Could be done. the Governor told me, not five minutes ago, that he was expected in every hour and as soon as he Came the Counsil would make a demand of Clothing &c which he must Comply with, or trouble wou'd ensue, that they were determined the Penn-Line should not suffer as they had done—Captain Lang will undertake to supply all the Officers this summer with under Dress (Jackets & Breeches) he having your Order for that purpose, he purchased the other day a pretty large quantity of Coarse and fine Linen, which is making up for the officers and men, but are handed Out, almost as fast as they are made to officers that pass and repass here— The Drummers and Fifers are not yet all Clothed, but most of them are, I shall send them on Monday next to Camp, sooner they could not be sent— Mr Henry will have the Guns and Bayonets and some newly Constructed Cartouch Boxes ready next week. Spontoons are about but will not be ready so soon.

The Necessary Acco't for yourself Mr. Howell unfortunately lost, he will be obliged to you for another, In the mean time he'll endeavour to procure white Cloth Trimmings &c and have them ready for you

Recruits Come in but slowly, those that do are fitted for Camp— I mean to return to Camp next week if you have no objections, bringing with me all the Clothing &c I can possibly procure—

Whose business is it to look over Captain Langs representation to the Assembly?

I am with real Esteem

your very hble serv't

S. BAYARD

General Wayne to R. Peters, Secretary of War.

MOUNT JOY 12th April 1778

MY DEAR SIR,—What are Congress doing—why is the Establishment of the Army put off to this late season?—why have not the Respective states their Quota of men in the field?—why this torpor —why this supineness?—when the season for Action has Arrived?— when the whole power of Britain is exerting itself to pour in Troops in Order to Effect a total Conquest— now is the time to strike before that force arrives— is it Possible that America means to submit—or does she expect that her *Militia* will be able to Crush the Enemy?— has the easy Conquest of *Burgoyne* lulled Congress into a state of security?— if it has, farewell to American Liberty—as Militia will never defend it— let me Assure you that the Yeomanry of the Neighbouring states in our Interest would find work Enough to keep those of a Contrary Opinion in awe— Jersey, Maryland, & Penns'a could not Effect it without Assistance from the Other states— I don't mention this from Report, but from my Own Observation—during my March through them this Winter

In Order therefore to Overawe this faction and to Crush Mr. Howe before he's Reinforced—force in twenty or thirty thousand men and leave nothing to Chance—

At present the Enemy far outnumber us—and unless speedy supplies arrive—We shall not long retain this Ground—and where we
shall make the next stand I will not undertake to say— for my own
part I have but a single Life to lose and I shall not think that worth
saving at the Expense of my Liberty or the Liberty of my Country
—I am almost out of patience with this bad World.

Adieu yours most

sincerely

ANT'Y WAYNE.

RICHARD PETERS, ESQR

at

York Town—

General Wayne to President Wharton of Pennsylvania.

MOUNT JOY 27th March 1778

DEAR SIR,—It's at last Concluded to throw the Penns'a Troops
into one Division after Reducing them to ten Regiments—which I
believe will be as many as we can fill— I have but little hopes of
being Supplied with many recruits—unless the Officers in the Back
Counties meet with more Success, than those in Phil'a and Chester—
an Officer from the Latter came in yesterday after being out five
weeks without a single Recruit— I would beg leave to Suggest the
Expediency of Employing a greater Number of Officers in that
business in Berks Lancaster, York & Cumberland Counties—as
the most likely places to meet with Success— I fear all our exertions in this way will fall far short of our wishes—and that Nothing
but a Draft will be Adequate to the business.

It's rumored that the Enemy have Evacuated Rhode Island—&
are drawing all their force to one *focus*— if this should be the
case—as we have Ground to think it is—they will be too powerful
for us in the field—unless great and Speedy Supplies are thrown in—
it therefore becomes the Interest and Duty of this State to make an
Immediate and Effectual exertion to Complete her Quota of men—
but whilst this is doing—let me Intreat you Sir Not to neglect providing the Linen Overalls and Other Clothing to enable us to take
the field with some Eclat—which will add both Spirit and health to
your Troops—for you may Rest Assured that nine out of ten of the

Deaths and Desertions in this Army are owing to Dirt and Naked-ness—

I have the happiness to Inform your Excellency that the Troops of this State Enjoy a much greater share of Health than any Other part of the Army—and I pledge my Reputation to keep them so on Con-dition that I can be provided with Linen and Other Clothing.

It's to you Sir that we look up to for these Matters—and in this case we Consider you as our Common father—

Adieu my Dear Sir and believe
me yours Most Sincerely
ANT'Y WAYNE—

[His Excellency Gov'r
Tho's Wharton.]

President Wharton to General Wayne.

In Council.

Lancaster April 2nd 1778

Sir,—I am favoured with yours of the twenty seventh of March the contents of which I communicated to Council.   They are of opinion with you that a greater number of officers should be employed on the recruiting Service and these, such as can be depended upon not only for their sobriety, but industry and expertness in that neces-sary business;—and I am fully of opinion that there should con-stantly remain in each County, officers—properly qualified to recruit, in order that the battalions should be kept complete, as well as to apprehend deserters.—

I am a good deal astonished to find that an officer could be five weeks in Chester County, and not have it in his power to recruit one man :—I doubt he has not been very attentive to that part of his duty.—The accounts that Council receives from most of the counties are upon the whole favourable ;—and I am in hopes several hundred men will in the course of a few weeks join the army, if they do not, I know of no other plan to supply our quota of troops for our common defence.—If money is an inducement for men to enlist in our regiments, this State has given generously, and the officers I think have sufficient encouragement to do their duty.—

It affords me great pleasure to hear that the troops of this State are at least as healthy, as those of any other,—and that their reputation is equal to any, is well known.—That you will continue your exertions to keep them so—I have no doubt—and it gives me no small pain to find that those brave men are not provided with such necessaries as they have a right to expect which would encourage them to persevere in doing their duty.—Council are doing all they can to provide clothing for them, but I fear their good intentions will not be crowned with the success they wish.

Mr. Howell is indefatigable in getting the clothing made up—*the want of buttons delayed them a little,* but they are now going on—

> I am Sir
> your Very humble Servant
> THO WHARTON JU'R PREST.

On Publick Service.

It is not to be wondered at that, amidst embarrassments and disappointments such as these, even the hopeful spirit of Wayne was inclined at times to give way to despair. "I hoped," he says, in a semi-official letter to his friend Mr. Peters, the Secretary of the Board of War, "to be able to clothe the division under my command, but the distresses of the other part of the troops belonging to this State were such as to beggar all description. Humanity obliged me to divide what would have in part clothed six hundred men among thirteen regiments, which was also necessary in order to prevent mutiny. . . . I am not fond of danger, but I would most cheerfully agree to enter into action once every week in place of visiting each hut of my encampment (which is my constant practice), and where objects strike my eye and ear whose wretched condition beggars all description. The whole army is sick and crawling with vermin." The only answer he can get from Mr. Peters, as late as the 15th of May, is this: "Vast quantities of clothing have been ordered, and I cannot tell why they have not been distributed."

In addition to all these troubles in supplying the physical wants of the soldiers, a new cause of embarrassment arose from the legislation of Congress in regard to the pay of the officers. He writes to his old friend and family connection Sharp Delany on the 21st of May, "The difficulty I experience in keeping good officers from resigning, and causing them to do their duty in the line, has almost determined me to give it up, and return to my Sabine fields, but I first wish" (he adds, with uncontrollable patriotic impulse) "to see the enemy sail for the West Indies! . . . We have received the vote of Congress for seven years' half pay at the termination of the war. . . . For my own part I have a competency, and neither look nor wish for any gratuity, other than liberty and honor; but the discontented say that seven years' half pay would not near make up for the depreciation of the money."

This depreciation of the money, as is well known, was a source of endless trouble with the soldiers during the war, as will more fully appear hereafter. It is very true, as has often been said, that there were some reasons outside of maladministration for the constantly recurring deficiencies in the army service at Valley Forge, especially in the matter of food-supplies. These were not in any great measure due to the disaffection of the people, as has sometimes been said, but were owing to the absolute exhaustion of the resources of the country surrounding the camp caused by the exactions of both armies. Besides, it is to be remembered that, while the territory along the coast, with the exception of New York, was open to our trade with all the world, and that this trade was largely carried on with satisfactory results during the war, notwithstanding the danger of the capture of the vessels, Philadelphia was entirely cut off from all communication with the outside world, and that land transportation upon any considerable scale did not then exist. After all, however, the grand motor in all warlike operations—real money—was not to be had, and this was the true source of the difficulty.

While the army was encamped at Valley Forge, a successful effort was made to improve its knowledge of military movements and to make its discipline more efficient. The principal agent in this most important work was the Baron von Steuben, who had formerly held high rank in the Prussian service, who had been appointed Inspector-General by Washington, and who was perfectly familiar with those details of military organization which had rendered the army of Frederick the Great the most successful of all European armies. Steuben had so great a love for the American cause that, although a general in the Prussian service, he did not hesitate to become a drill-sergeant at Valley Forge. He began with the manual of arms, instructed the soldiers, in squads at first, in tactical movements, and within a month made the officers and men familiar with army manœuvres on a larger scale. He was active, minute, and exacting in his instructions, unwearied in his efforts to teach the men the simpler elements of the drill and how to act most efficiently together, and it cannot be doubted that the ease with which the army manœuvred at Monmouth in the face of the enemy was in large measure due to his persistent instructions. He began his work on the 24th of March, and, considering all the difficulties which he overcame, not the least of which was his total ignorance of the English language, his success was wonderful. It has even been said that he taught the Americans how to use the bayonet; but any one who reads Wayne's account of the battle of Germantown will be inclined to doubt the validity of this claim.

During the winter food became scarce at Valley Forge. There was neither proper clothing for the men, nor money for the payment of their wages. The forays in the neighborhood of the city, although under the charge of Major Henry Lee, a most active and enterprising officer, did not provide sufficient food for the camp. Towards the middle of February, therefore, Wayne was sent with a considerable force to New Jersey, and the arduous duty of procuring what cattle he could find in the region between Bordentown and Salem for the use of the army, and of destroying what he could not carry off, was imposed upon him. He entered upon this work with his usual zeal and activity, and in its performance acquired from his enemies the curious *sobriquet* of "Drover Wayne." Many were the skirmishes which took place in the sands and among the pines of Jersey during the cheerless winter of 1778. Both parties found it difficult to discover the cattle they were in search of, for, although the country abounded with them, they were for the most part carefully concealed by their owners in the woods.

The following letter gives some account of his foraging in New Jersey:

General Wayne to General Washington.

HADDONFIELD 4th March 1778

SIR,—Soon after I wrote your 'Excellency from Mount Holly—I rec'd Intelligence that the Enemy had Detached themselves in small parties and were Collecting Cattle forage &c in the Vicinity of Haddonfield, Coopers, and Timber Creeks. This Intelligence Induced me (altho' my Numbers were few) to make a forced March and Endeavor to drive in or cut off some of their parties— At nine o'clock at night I arrived at one Capt. Matlacks about four Miles to the South East of this place where I was soon after joined by Gen'l Pulaski with about fifty Light Horse— Col Ellis with two Hundred & fifty Militia, being the Whole of his Command, took post at *Evesham* Meeting at the junction of the Roads leading to Egg-Harbor and Mount Holly— At Ten O'clock Genl. Pulaski attempted to surprise the Enemy's advanced post at a Mill a half a Mile Out of Haddonfield—he failed in the attempt—but Col *Stirling* who Commanded the Enemy having in the fore part of the Evening Rec'd Intelligence of our March,—and our Numbers being Exaggerated to thousands—moving in three Columns—the one to his Right an Other to his left and the third in front—the *North Briton* thought it prudent to Retreat under Cover of the Shipping, he accordingly Decamped at Eleven at night and Arrived at Cooper ferry before day—Destroying some Spirits and leaving Waggons Horses Cattle &c behind which he had stolen from the Inhabitants who have since Claimed and Rec'd their property—

The Troops being much fatigued—I could not follow before late next Morning— I advanced with Gen'l Pulaski to Reconnoitre their position—and on coming near the ferry found that they were there in full force, the Wind being too high to admit the Boats to pass—however they were too well posted to do any thing with them —being covered and flanked by their shipping— About the Middle of the Afternoon the Wind lulled when they threw over about 36 head of *poor Cattle* the whole they had been able to save from the Numbers they had Stolen.

On Observing that they were about Retreating over the River— & Gen'l Pulaski anxious to *Charge*—I ordered up Capt. Doyle with his Company consisting of Fifty men—who lay three miles in advance of the Rest, directing the Other part of the Detachment to follow as fast as possible, About the same time I Rec'd Intelligence of a fresh body of Troops having crossed from Philad'a who were Marching up Cooper's Creek and seemed pushing for our Rear— Col. Ellis being posted with his Militia on that Route I ordered him to Advance and Receive them—

About this time Capt. Doyle Arrived—near the Enemy's Covering party—whose numbers appeared to be about three times as many as ours when joined by the Horse—but as they were approachable on each flank & the Center being favourable for the Cavalry Gen'l Pulaski & Myself were determined to attack them— In Order to gain time for the main body to come up, as well as to Amuse and prevent that party of the Enemy from proceeding further up Cooper's Creek—We soon Obliged the Covering party to give way—when Mr. Stirling advanced in full force to support them—this answered my expectations and wishing to lead them from under Cover of their shipping—I Ordered the Infantry to keep up a Constant fire falling back by slow degrees until they should be joined by Col Butlers Detachment— About the same time the Hessian Grenadiers attempted to force over Cooper's bridge in face of about 100 Militia under Col Ellis—but they soon gave up that idea—finding it Impracticable.

The fire of the Enemy from their field pieces shipping and Musketry became General— however they could not be drawn out—but night coming on, and Col Butler not being able to get up until too late to see—the Enemy Effected their Retreat to Phila—before Nine at Night but not without some loss attended with Circumstances of Disgrace. Genl. Pulaski behaved with his usual bravery on the Occasion having his own with four Other Horses Wounded— The fifty Infantry being the only part that had an Opportunity of Engaging—behaved with a Degree of bravery that would have done Honor to the Oldest *Veterans*— Mr *Abercrumbie* who Commanded the Detachment that went to Salem—hearing that the Militia were Collecting in great Numbers—and that we were advancing from Mount Holly—also took the Horrors and Embarking on board His boats &c got safe to Phila—three Evenings ago leaving all his Collection of Cattle &c &c behind.—Thus ended the Jersey Expedition which has not been attended with that Advantage that those North Brittons expected of their first Arrival—

I shall begin my March for Camp tomorrow Morning it was not in my power to move until I could procure shoes for the Troops almost barefoot—

I rec'd your Excellencie's Letter of the 28th and Col Biddle's of the 25th and shall as far as is in my power Comply with the Contents—

When I have the pleasure of seeing your Excellency I shall communicate such Ideas as have occurred to me with respect to the Importance of this part of this State and the most probable mode of Covering it from the Depradations of the Enemy—who will be able to draw Great Supplies from it if left uncovered

Interim I am your Excellency's Most

Ob't & Very Hum Ser't

ANT'Y WAYNE.

[GEN'L WASHINGTON.]

One of the subjects which naturally preoccupied the mind of the commander-in-chief during the winter was the next move of the army. Many advocated an active campaign, but it seems hard for us to understand, now that we know so fully the crippled condition of the army, how such a plan could have been seriously entertained. General Reed, although opposed to such a campaign, urged the commander-in-chief, as early as December, to make a sudden move, secret as to its destination, in the hope of gaining possession of New York, then the great storehouse of those supplies of the enemy of which our army was so much in need. Although the plan was not favorably considered at the time, it was laid before a council of general officers in April, and it would appear from General Wayne's letters of the 21st of that month that he approved its general features. It was relinquished, although, besides Wayne, Generals Greene, Knox, Poor, Varnum, Muhlenberg, and Lord Stirling favored its adoption.

General Wayne to General Washington.

MOUNT JOY 21st April 1778

SIR,—I took the Liberty to suggest to your Excellency (some time since) the Idea of making an Offensive Campaign against such places as afford the Greatest prospect of Success to us & Injury to the enemy—but the Object will Depend upon your force—the first and most Desirable would be Sir Wm Howe,—the next New York—

The Question then will arise how is the Army to be Supplied and the stores secured—The Answer is—that the Magazines of Provisions & forage are to be Diffused in small Quantities through each State so as not to leave in any one place sufficient to induce the Enemy to make an expedition against us—the Military stores should be secured at Sunbury in a position Difficult of access—and Defended by a Garrison that would Oblige the Enemy to make use of a Considerable force with Artillery—and situated in the Heart of a Well Effected Country, One Hundred and Thirty Miles N. W. of Phil'a. —were they to March to such a place Phila. and New York would be left in our power—by Dividing their Army they would give us an Opening for making a Capital Stroke—On the Contrary if We still Continue on the Defensive it will be in their power to Harass us at pleasure—and lead us a March that will Debilitate and Destroy your Army more than a severe Engagement—the time and place of Action will lay with them which probably will not be the most favourable to us—

Many Reasons (in my humble opinion) both political and prudential point to the Expediency of putting the Enemy on the Defensive—their plan of Operation (perhaps) already formed in England, will by this means be Disconcerted—it will Oblige them to Evacuate New York or Phil'a, the one or the Other with its Garrison must Inevitably fall into your hands :

In either case the fruits of two hard Campaigns at the Expense of much blood and treasure, would be lost to Britain and their Glory vanished—whilst the Arms of America would become Respectable at home to both friends & Enemies and shine with Double Lustre, in the Courts of Europe—

Should you move for the North River the Militia of New York and the Eastern States will draw to your Camp—and from their being so lately flushed with Conquest they will hope to have the same good fortune— So that if Mr. Howe should attempt to succour Clinton—it will in all probability be productive of the Most Happy and Glorious Consequences—for a Conquering Army finds no Difficulties —It would be presumption in me to take up your Excellency's time on a Subject which I am Confident has not Escaped your serious thought—I shall therefore only Assure you that whatever part may be assigned to me I shall always and at all times, be ready to serve you with the best Service of your Excellency's

                    Most Ob't
                 and very
                    Humb Ser't
                       ANT'Y WAYNE.

[GEN'L WASHINGTON.]

CHAPTER IV.

EARLY in June it became apparent that the British were preparing to evacuate Philadelphia, as it was feared by them that a French fleet would soon, in pursuance of our treaty of alliance with France of February, 1778, blockade the English fleet in the Delaware. Sir Henry Clinton, the successor of Sir William Howe as commander-in-chief, arrived in Philadelphia on the 8th of June, and found preparations for the evacuation far advanced. Washington, as usual, asked the opinion of his generals as to the course to be taken. Wayne, among others, made a reply, which we annex.

General Wayne to General Washington.

MOUNT JOY 18th June 1778

SIR,—I have Maturely Considered the Matters which your Excellency was pleased to lay before the Council of General Officers last evening—and am Clearly of Opinion that any attempt on the City of Philad'a with your present force when defended by the numbers of Troops that may be brought to act against you—will be Ineligible— But it is my wish & Opinion that you cause the sick in Camp and its vicinity to be Immediately Removed further into the Country—& that the whole of the Army be put in Motion the soonest possible for some of the ferries on the Delaware above Trent Town—so as to be Ready to act as soon as the Enemy's movem't shall be ascertained— If the North River should be found to be their Object—I am for passing the Delaware Immediately,
136

Divesting the Army of every Article of Incumbrance—and then with the aid of the Jersey Militia take the first favorable Opportunity to make a Vigorous and serious attack upon the Enemy— but in Order to Complete your Victory or facilitate your Retreat (if the latter should be found necessary) I would wish that Gen'l Maxwell with his Brigade and a Body of the Militia might gain their Rear where his Action will be governed by your Motions—i.e. when the Attack is made by you—it shall be a signal for his onset which ought to be Rather a feint than Otherwise. Should your attack succeed it may be productive of the most happy Consequences—but should it prove unsuccessful the Enemy dare not nor can not pursue any great Distance, Otherwise their Baggage & provisions will be Endangered—surrounded as they will be by troops who know how to rally in case of a Misfortune and to Recoil upon their pursuers.

I am the more anxious to take this Opportunity of striking them (in case they should take this route)—as I am Confident that the minds of the Soldiers of either Army will be much Influenc'd by our Movements— On the Enemy's part it will have the Appearance of a Retreat—on ours, that of Pursuit— We may Inculcate the Idea of Besieging Clinton—he will Apprehend it—and you will more than probably effect it—

Interim I am your Excellency's &c

ANTHONY WAYNE.

It would appear from the following letter that the army was not very well prepared for the campaign upon which it was about to enter:

General Wayne to R. Peters, Secretary of War.

MOUNT JOY 13th May 1778

DEAR SIR,—Want of time—want of temper—want of Opportunity—want of everything but Inclination has prevented me from writing to you for some weeks— You will now give me leave to Congratulate you on the Establishment of the Independance of the United States of America— The Declaration of the French Embasador to the Court of Britain must Inevitably produce a War

between those powers—which never could have been better timed
—I thank my God that the Attention of Great *Britain* is likely to
be Diverted from America—Otherwise I should dread the Consequence—for altho' our Troops are daily Improving in Military Dis·
cipline by very swift Degrees—yet we are much weaker & worse
Clothed than at the Close of the last Campaign— I hoped to be able
to Clothe the Division under my Command but the Distresses of
the Other part of the troops belonging to this State were such as to
beggar all Discription— Humanity Obliged me to Divide what
would have in part Clothed six Hundred men among thirteen Regiments which also being necessary in Order to prevent mutiny and to
put a stop to that Spirit of Desertion—which has taken but too deep
a Root—and is not yet subsided—our Officers too are hourly Offering
in their Resignations—especially those who have yet *some property*
left— When or where it will end God knows—the pain I feel on the
Occasion is better felt than expressed—I am heartily tired of this
way of life—being the only General Officer belonging to the State
the whole line Apply to me on every Occasion—their real wants are
too many and too pressing to pass unheeded by—but yet I cant
Alleviate nor supply them.

I know it must be very Disagreeable to hear so many Repititions
of this Nature—but people are very apt to dwell on those subjects
that lie nearest their hearts, or that give them most Concern— I am
not fond of Danger—but I would most Cheerfully agree to enter
into Action once every week in place of Visiting each part of my
Encampment (which is my Constant practice) and where Objects
strike my eye & ear—whose wretched Condition beggars all Description—the Ball or Bayonet could only pierce the Body—but such
Objects affect the mind and give the keenest wound to every feeling
of Humanity—for God's sake give us—if you can't give us anything
else—give us linen that we may be Enabled to Rescue the poor
Worthy fellows from the Vermin which are now Devouring them
and which has Emaciated & Reduced numbers exactly to answer the
Description of Shakespears Apothecary— Some hundreds we thought
prudent to Deposit some six foot under Ground—who have Died
of a Disorder produced by a want of Clothing— The whole Army
at present are sick of the same Disorder, but the Penns'a line seem
to be the most Infected—a pointed & speedy exertion of Congress

or appointing an Other Doc'r may yet remove the Disorder—which once done I pledge my Reputation we shall remove the Enemy—for I would much Rather Risque my life Honor and the fate of America on our present force neatly and Comfortably Uniformed than on Double their number Covered with Rags & Crawling with Vermin—but I am determined not to say an Other word on the subject

I wrote a few lines to my Daughter some time since—she has not been so kind as to acknowledge it—how is the young soldier—will he be fit to take the field before the Expiration of the present War—for I think it bids fair to be a long one—if we may Draw any Conclusion from the Kings speech and the Answers of the two Houses of Parliament—who promise to Assist him with their lives and fortunes in any measure he may take to humble the pride & Chastise the perfidy of France—and to bring these States to a proper sense of their duty— *Bravo.*

Adieu and believe me yours most
Sincerely
ANT'Y WAYNE.

[RIC'D PETERS, ESQ.,
  of the Board of War.]

The following is an interesting sketch of the attempt to capture La Fayette at Barren Hill. It will be observed that it makes the singular statement that friendly Indians were employed in our army at Valley Forge.

General Wayne to Sharp Delany.

MOUNT JOY 21st May 1778

DEAR SIR,—Various are the Reports—& many are the Conjectures about the Enemy's quitting Phila—and the Quarter they are Destined for—some say New York, Others Halifax but the more prevailing Opinion is the West India Islands—for my own part (but all Accounts agree that they Intend to), I am not quite so sanguine as some Others about their Evacuating their present post without first Offering us Battle— We were so fully Confident of their being about to Embark last Monday—that a Detatchment of between 2000 and 2500 men under the Marquis De Lafayette was sent down

towards their lines to be ready to take Possession of the City as
soon as they should Quit it—but the Caitiffs made a forced March
the night before last and had thrown themselves into his Rear—and
were near on the point of surrounding him before he had any Intelligence of their Movements— However he made a happy Escape
by passing the Schuylkill at Matsons ford and possessing the Gulf
Hills— The Enemy's Advance Guards made their Appearance
on the One Side Just as the Rear of ours Arrived on the Other—
their force by every Acct. was about 7000, and they had Actually
thrown themselves in between the Marquis and our Camp—expect-
ing to fall upon him as he was attempting to gain the Bridge or
Swedes ford—but by moving lower down and Crossing at Matson's,
he avoided Inevitable Destruction— The Enemy must have made
a March of at least 20 Miles with all that Body of men totally undiscovered thro' the Inattention of the Patroles— They Returned to
Phila last evening without either Killing or taking a single man of
ours—but several Deserters and prisoners are hourly Arriving in
Camp taken by our light troops & Oneida friends the Indians (hanging on their Rear) who at the first fire Killed five of the Enemies
horse and by the War Whoop put the Remainder to flight.

I have already hinted that it's my Opinion *Mr Clinton* will offer
us battle—ie that after shipping all their Baggage stores and heavy
Artillery—they will make a forward move in force—but they will
never Attack us on this Ground—they will either Retire After a
vain parade Otherwise by taking post in our Rear near Moor Hall
Manœuvre us off this Ground—however this is but Conjecture—
they may possibly leave this State without this parade— That a
capital movement will take place in a few days I am very Confident, but time alone will Determine the Object—

We have Rec'd the Vote of Congress for 7 years half pay at the
termination of the War— I am sorry to say that it falls far short of
giving satisfaction— The Spirit of *Resignation* seems to rage rather
more than ever and is hourly taking place—for my own part I
have a Competency and neither look nor wish for any Gratuity,
other than Liberty and Honor—but the Discontented say that 7
years half pay would not near make up for the Depreciation of the
Money & the high price of every Article for this last year being on
an Average at least five to one—which would Require ten years half

pay to do even justice to them for the Deficiency of the last— How just this mode of Reasoning may be I shall not Attempt to say nor do I mean to Advocate their Cause—if they merit more I doubt not but Congress will make the proper provision—if not they will be Justifiable in adhering to what they have Done'

The Difficulty I experience in keeping good Officers from Resigning—and causing them to do their Duty in the Line has almost Determined me to give it up and Retire to my Sabine fields—but I first wish to see the Enemy sail for the West Indies—

Adieu my Dear Sir & believe
me yours most Sincerely
ANT'Y WAYNE.

[COL. DELANY.]

The British army, having evacuated Philadelphia, crossed the Delaware on the 18th of June below Gloucester, and took the route eastward across Jersey, encumbered with a baggage-train which is said to have been nearly twelve miles long. Washington crossed the same river above Trenton on the 21st, and prepared to dispute the passage of the Raritan should the enemy attempt to cross that river with his baggage-train. It was found, however, that Sir Henry Clinton kept to the southward and was moving in the direction of Sandy Hook. Washington followed on a parallel route, and on the 26th of June the armies were but a few miles from each other. On the 24th of that month a council of war had been held at Hopewell, five miles from Princeton, when certain questions as to future movements were submitted by the commander-in-chief to the general officers. The result of this council, according to Colonel Alexander Hamilton, was worthy of the "honorable society of midwives, and of no other."

Wayne and Cadwalader, and to a certain degree La Fayette and Greene, of all the generals who were consulted, advocated prompt, vigorous, and decided action. The latter, it is said, proposed an assault, but of somewhat too cautious a kind to suit the impetuous valor of Wayne. As to the rest, they were so profoundly impressed with the superiority of the English troops, due to their military skill and discipline, that they were unwilling to confront them with the ragged regiments which they commanded. The English army numbered nearly twelve thousand men, thoroughly equipped and organized, and was particularly strong in that formidable infantry which often, before and after that date, gained a world-wide renown for its skill and effectiveness in the use of the bayonet. The American army was somewhat more numerous than that of the enemy, but many of its officers, under the baleful influence of General Charles Lee, did not feel any confidence in its ability to repel the English forces in the open field. Notwithstanding, however, General Washington determined to take the advice of Wayne and reject that of the majority of the council. He probably thought that the danger resulting from the depression in the public mind which would follow from permitting a British army with a train twelve miles long to cross New Jersey unmolested should be avoided at all hazards, even that of losing a pitched battle. He determined, therefore, to attack as soon as practicable at least the rear-guard of that army by which the train was escorted. It will be observed by comparing the following letter of Wayne to the commander-in-chief with the plan adopted for fighting the

battle of Monmouth, that Wayne's suggestions were in
the main adopted:

General Wayne to the Commander-in-Chief.

HOPEWELL 24th June 1778

SIR,—The purport of the Questions Offered by your Excellency
this Morning to the Consideration of the Gen'l Officers were, first
—whether it would be prudent or Advisable to Risk a General Action
with the Enemy at Present, Considering our state, and the apparent
state of Affairs in Europe at this time— 2nd What will be the
most Eligible mode of Conduct in pursuing & Harassing the Enemy
during their March through the Jerseys—

As to the first I would not Advise Risking a Gen'l Action—unless
Circumstances should Render success Certain, or such as not to
leave you in a Worse situation, if Unfortunate, than if you had not
Attacked.

And in answer to the Other—I am with all due Deference of
Opinion that a select Corps of field & other officers—with 2500
or 3000 Effective Rank & file Commanded by a Major—and two
Brig'r Generals, or as many as may be thought Advisable, should
Immediately be Drafted, and March to gain the Rear of the left
flank of the Enemy when they should take the first favorable Oppor-
tunity of Attempting an Impression in force—at the same time
Sundry attacks ought to be made by the Militia, Maxwells Brigade,
Morgans Corps, and Jacksons and Cadwalader's troops in order to
Divert the Enemy's Attention— I would also wish the main body
of your Army to be in a position on the left of their Rear so as to
be Ready to Act effectively—but not to be Drawn into a Gen'l
Action Contrary to your Desire.

A Disposition of this or a Similar Nature would give Confidence
to your Detachments—and terror to your Enemy who dare not
pursue success,—lest they should be drawn into some Difficulty from
which it would not be easy for them to Extricate themselves, which
Consideration together with their Carriages and Baggage will Induce
them to Remain Content with the Idea of having Repulsed those
who Attacked them.

I must beg your Excellencies Indulgence for this liberty—as I could not quite meet the Other General officers in sentiment so as to sign the General Opinion with freedom.

Interim I am your Excellencies
Most Obt & very Hum'l Ser't
Ant'y Wayne.

[Gen'l Washington.]

It was necessary that Washington should act without delay, as it was feared that the baggage-train of the enemy might soon be beyond the reach of capture. So, on the 27th, notwithstanding the American army had been almost starved during the march, and was exhausted by the terrific heat of the season, La Fayette was directed to take five thousand troops, "picked and selected men," to hang on the English rear-guard, and as soon as it began to move the next morning to attack it. A considerable portion of this detachment was composed of Wayne's troops. Charles Lee, who had opposed this aggressive movement through fear of the vast superiority of the English troops, at first declined to command the detachment, but shortly afterwards, thinking better of this step, he claimed to lead it, and he was unfortunately permitted to do so. Lee's command marched about five miles in advance of the main army, his orders were to attack vigorously the rear-guard, and he was expressly told that he would be supported by the rest of the army.

Having arrived within striking distance of the rear-guard near Freehold, Wayne was directed by Lee the next morning to take with him from his division of about twelve hundred men seven hundred, to lead the advance and attack the left rear of the English. He was told by General Lee that he held the post of honor, and it soon turned out that he held at least the post of imminent danger. The enemy did not wait to be attacked, but a party of Simcoe's rangers or dragoons (American Loyalists) charged upon a portion of Colonel Richard Butler's Pennsylvania regiment of about two hundred men. They were repulsed and driven back, but could not be followed, for want of cavalry. General Wayne seems to have considered this a very brilliant piece of work. We find the following letter from him to his friend Major Henry Lee, in which he speaks with his usual pride of the gallant deeds of officers serving under him:

General Wayne to Major Henry Lee (" *Light-Horse Harry*").

CAMP NEAR WHITE PLAINS
NEW YORK 20th July 1778

DEAR MAJOR,—I wished you to have come in for a share of the Glory of the 28th Ultimo— Col Butler wanted you much— The Enemy's Horse made a Charge in force upon his Reg't Consisting of 200 men—supported by the first Regiment of Guards—he sustained the shock broke them & pursued both horse & foot the Latter having been thrown into Disorder by the former Running through them—here was a field for you to act in— Butler had no horse near to Improve the Advantage—& *Gen'l Lee*—but soft, he is now in Arrest & from present Appearances will not Continue long in the Service—a note from him to a Mr Collins printer of the Jersey paper—Savours of Insanity or flows from a *Worse Cause*— We are drawing near the Enemy's Lines—their fleet is blocked up by two French Men of War of the Line and a Number of frigates—the Cork fleet with provisions for Clintons Army is yet out—the Enemy are already on Short Allowance—come then and Assist us to Besiege them.

While Wayne's force was thus engaged with Simcoe's dragoons, the main English force from having been on

the defensive now became the assailants. At first the
force in front of Wayne was simply a covering party,
supposed by him to have consisted of about two thousand men, but it rapidly increased in numbers. Wayne
looked round for the reinforcements which had been
promised him, but was surprised to find that the rest of
Lee's command was in full retreat, leaving him to shift
for himself, and placing him in great danger of being
surrounded.   With great difficulty he made his way
through the swamp and the woods until he reached the
parsonage, just in advance of the "Tennent Church,"
and on the southern side of the road leading to Freehold, where he found all the troops which were to have
supported him falling back by General Lee's order.
There he met General Washington, amazed at the retreat of the advance corps and angry beyond restraint
with General Lee who had ordered it. The enemy,
whose whole force had by this time faced about, were in
full pursuit, and the commander-in-chief had, it is said,
but a quarter of an hour to make such a disposition of
his force as would check them. Washington's presence
and example at once stopped the retreat.   Danger
seems to have aroused all his energies.   With the true
instinct of a great general, he rallied his troops at
once, directing Wayne, who was near him, to form two
trusty regiments instantly and check the assault of the
enemy, while he would hasten to the rear and bring
forward the main portion of the army to support him.
The regiments which were called upon at this critical
moment, one of the most critical in the history of the
Revolution, to defend this most dangerous post of
honor, were those of Colonel Walter Stewart of the

Thirteenth Pennsylvania, Colonel William Irvine of
the Seventh Pennsylvania, and Colonel Thomas Craig
of the Third Pennsylvania, aided by a Maryland and
a Virginia regiment. These held the advance post
at this period of the battle, the well-known orchard of
Monmouth, until the reinforcements which made up the
second line arrived. There were hills on each side of
this orchard, which were at once occupied by these reinforcements; that on the right was held by Greene
with Knox's artillery, that on the left by Stirling. The
batteries on both these hills enfiladed the English army
on the right and the left, while the withering fire of
Wayne's command in front rendered further advance
well-nigh impossible. The British grenadiers with their
left on Freehold and the guards on their right had driven
Lee's advance to the position near the parsonage which
Wayne now occupied. Crossing a fence which lay in
their front, they advanced to the attack of Wayne's
position with dauntless courage, first on the right and
then on the left, but were repulsed in both cases with
great loss. Finally the guards, officered by the sons of
the noblest English families, who had for more than
eight months given the tone to fashionable dissipation
while Philadelphia was occupied by the British army,
and had taught their admirers there among the ladies
to look with contempt upon the brave yeomen who were
suffering the pains of nakedness and hunger at Valley
Forge, were at last to meet foemen worthy of their
steel. Their commanding officer, Colonel Monckton,
the brother of Lord Galway, was fully convinced that
the task assigned to this *corps d'élite* was one that
would test to the utmost those soldierly qualities for

which the grenadiers and guards had gained so great renown. The guards having been formed for a bayonet-charge, their colonel made them a short speech, in which he urged them, by all the motives which appeal to a soldier's pride and his *esprit de corps*, to charge home. So near were they to the American line that it is said that every word of his speech was heard there, and probably it did as much to inspire Wayne's men with courage and determination as it did those to whom it was addressed. They then rushed on with a furious charge, hoping to drive their enemies back by the bayonet. Waiting until they approached quite closely, they were met with a withering fire of musketry from Wayne's regiments, which killed not only the colonel (the speech-maker), who bravely led them on, but many of his officers. The column was driven back in the utmost confusion. How complete was this repulse is shown by the inability of the guards to rescue from Wayne's men the lifeless body of their commander, although they made the most frantic efforts to recover it. The battle raged for hours after this fruitless attempt to penetrate Wayne's column, and at last the enemy, finding that they could make no impression upon the American army, and utterly exhausted by the heat of the day, retired in confusion and with great loss.

The repulse of the bayonet-charge of the British guards and grenadiers, forming the *élite* of their infantry, and regarded by their countrymen ever since the days of Crécy and Agincourt as the most formidable warriors in the world when armed with such a weapon, by a body of American yeomen, most of whom were Pennsylvanians, under a Pennsylvanian general, men who were inferior in numbers and imperfect in discipline, who had just been rallied after an ignominious retreat, and were engaged in battle for the first time on that day, must be considered in the progress of the Revolution as a prodigious historical event. To many the orchard at Monmouth seemed a second Thermopylæ, and Wayne was spoken of as a modern Leonidas. Wayne's reputation as a military leader resting on such a basis was recognized both by the friends and by the foes of the patriot cause as one of the great forces in the Revolutionary contest. There has probably never been in our history such a spontaneous fervor in the expression of grateful hearts for any man's services, until we come to the enthusiasm with which the crushing blows dealt by Grant, Sherman, and Sheridan to the armed forces of the rebellion were welcomed. The commander-in-chief in his report to Congress speaks of his deeds in that measured phrase always characteristic of Washington. "I cannot forbear," he says, "mentioning Brigadier-General Wayne, whose good conduct and bravery, through the whole action deserves particular commendation." There was but one dissentient voice among his countrymen, and that came from his commander, General Lee, a good witness, at least, of the fearful odds against him. He says in a letter to Robert Morris, "The force opposed to the American Army was the whole flower of the British Army, Grenadiers, Light Infantry, Cavalry, & Artillery amounting in all to 7000 men. By the temerity & folly and contempt of orders of General Wain [*sic*] we found ourselves engaged in the most extensive plain in America, separated from our main body the distance of eight miles," etc.

We may be quite sure that there were few among
the patriots who were inclined to find fault with General Wayne because of his "temerity & folly" at the
battle of Monmouth. The effect on the public mind
of that battle, although the Americans could exhibit
no trophies of victory, was instantaneous, deep, and
abiding.

It cheered that portion of the people who are often
patriotic in their instincts but are apt to become timid
and desponding at the first reverses, for it helped to
convince them that thenceforth in the struggle our
armies, when properly led, could do great things against
troops hitherto supposed to be superior to them in
equipment and discipline. This hesitation in meeting
our enemies in the open field had had, as the history of
the Revolution clearly shows, up to this time, a controlling influence in the councils of war called together by
Washington. He was taught by the results of this
battle that the oftener he "acted the general," as Wayne
called it, the more likely would permanent success
follow.   Hence Wayne's example becomes a great
teaching force in our military history, for it destroyed
the charm of invincibility which in the eyes of many
always attended the British soldiery.   And it taught a
still more important lesson to all in authority, invaluable to a people in arms against oppression,—that of
self-confidence.

For our purpose it is not worth while to go into the
controversy concerning General Lee's conduct at the
battle of Monmouth. He was tried for disobedience
of orders in not attacking the enemy on the 28th of
June as he had been ordered, and for misbehavior

before the enemy in making an unnecessary retreat.
He was found guilty on both charges, and in defending himself before the court and in the newspapers of
the day he made charges against three officers, which
brought him challenges to duels from each of them:
one from the illustrious Von Steuben, to whose persistent training of the troops at Valley Forge during
the winter amidst every kind of discouragement much
of the success of Monmouth was doubtless due; one
from Colonel Laurens, an aide-de-camp of General
Washington, who sought to avenge the insulting and
outrageous abuse of which his chief had been made
the object by General Lee; and one from General
Wayne, whose action in the battle, and especially his
alleged disobedience of orders, had been very harshly
criticised by General Lee.   Only one of these proposed
duels, however, took place, that in which Colonel Laurens was the challenger, and in which Lee was slightly
wounded.   Lee's quarrel with Wayne could not be pub-
licly carried on while the latter was surrounded by
the halo of glory which encompassed him after Monmouth, and especially after Stony Point, when Lee
became the most enthusiastic admirer of his former
adversary; and as to Von Steuben, it has not been
possible to discover how his wounded honor was healed,
but there was, it is believed, no duel.

The most graphic account of the battle of Monmouth which has been printed is contained in a letter
from Wayne to his wife, and in one to his friend Mr.
Peters, Secretary of the Board of War, both of which
we give.

General Wayne to Mrs. Wayne.

SPOTTSWOOD 1st July 1778

DEAR POLLY,—On Sunday the 28th June our flying army came in view of the Enemy about Eight O'Clock in the Morning—when I was Ordered to Advance and Attack them with a few men—the Remainder of the Army under Gen'l Lee was to have supported me— We accordingly Advanced, and Received a Charge from the British horse and Infantry which we soon repulsed, however our Gen'l thought proper to retreat in place of Advancing—without our firing a single shot— The Enemy followed in force—which Rendered it very Difficult for the small force I had to gain the main body being Often hard pushed, and frequently surrounded— After falling back about a mile we met His Excellency—who was surprised at our Retreat, knowing that Officers as well as men were in high Spirits and wished for Nothing more than to be faced about and meet the British fire.— He Accordingly Ordered me to keep post where he met us with Stewarts & Livingstons Regiments and a Virginia Reg't then under my Command with two pieces of Artillery and to keep them in play until he had an opportunity of forming the Remainder of the Army and Restoring Order— We had but just taken post when the Enemy began their attack with Horse & foot & Artillery. The fire of their whole united force soon Obliged us after a Severe Conflict to give way—when a Most tremendous Cannonade Commenced on both sides, Continuing near four Hours without Ceasing— During this time every possible Exertion was made by His Excellency and the Other Generals to Spirit up the Troops and to prepare them for an Other tryal— The Enemy began to Advance again in a heavy Column against which I ordered some [torn out] Advanced with some of my Or [torn out] to meet them. The Action was Exceedingly warm and well Maintained on each Side for a Considerable time— At Length Victory Declared for us, the British Courage failed and was forced to give place to American Valour—

We Encamped on the field of Battle where we found among the Dead and Wounded a Number of the first Officers of the British Army— We have taken a Great Many Prisoners—and their men are coming in to us by Hundreds of a Day—

In this Affair we lost some brave Officers killed and Wounded with many Other Officers and men—on the part of the Enemy—the Slaughter has been great and [torn out] their Grenadiers Infantry and Guards. Their Loss is not less than twelve or fifteen Hundred men killed & Wounded

Every General & other officer (one excepted) did Every thing that could be expected on this Great Occasion, but Pennsylvania shewed the Road to Victory— Adieu my Dear Polly. Send this to my poor old Mother & tell her that I am safe & Well.

Kiss our Little People for me.

ANT'Y WAYNE.

[MRS. WAYNE.]

General Wayne to Mr. Peters, Secretary of War.

PARAMUS 12th July 1778

DEAR SIR,—We have been in a perpetual move ever since we Crossed the Delaware until yesterday—when we arrived here and shall be stationary for a few days—in Order to Recruit a little from the hard fatigue we have experienced in Marching through Deserts, burning sands &c. &c. &c.

The Enemy sore from the Action of the 28th Ultimo seem Inclined to Rest awhile. They are now in three Divisions, one on Long Island—one on Staten Island and the Other at New York—

The Victory of that day turns out to be much more Considerable than at first expected. Col Butler who remained on the Ground for two or three days after the Action says that upwards of three Hundred British had been buried by us on the field and numbers Discovered every Day in the Woods where the action commenced exclusive of those buried by the Enemy—which was not short of a Hundred—so that by the most Moderate Computation their Killed and Wounded must be full fifteen Hundred men of the flower of their army— Among them are Numbers of the Richest blood of England— Tell the Phil'a ladies that the heavenly, sweet, pretty red Coats—the accomplished Gent'n of the Guards & Grenadiers have humbled themselves on the plains of Monmouth

"The Knights of the Blended Rose" & "Burning Mount"— have Resigned their Laurels to *Rebel* officers who will lay them at the feet of those Virtuous Daughters of America who cheerfully gave up ease and Affluence in a city for Liberty and peace of mind in a Cottage¹— A Propos pray present my best wishes to all such among which Number is my Daughter.

Adieu and believe me yours

Most Sincerely,

ANT'Y WAYNE.

[NB We have not Rec'd the least Article of Clothing since you saw us at Mount Joy and are now——naked)

[RICH'D PETERS, ESQ.]

The duty of the army for nearly eighteen months after the battle of Monmouth consisted in ingloriously watching the enemy at New York lest they should sally forth and make destructive raids in Jersey or should attempt to secure possession of the Highlands of the Hudson. To retain these strongholds was of capital importance, for should the British occupy in large force the passes in the vicinity of West Point, convenient communication between the New England Colonies and those to the west of the Hudson would be cut off. The American army therefore was drawn up in the form of a segment of a circle, extending from Middlebrook, in New Jersey, to the Delaware on the south, and on the north towards Long Island Sound. For many months it performed the distasteful but necessary task of guarding this widely-extended line. Its numbers, of course, were too small to do this work effectually, and the duty was extremely harassing to the troops engaged in it. The British in New York, cooped up in their narrow quarters, also chafed at their enforced inactivity. They made occasionally destructive sorties into Jersey

¹ This is an allusion to the part taken by the British officers, while occupying Philadelphia, in the grand festival of " The Meschianza."

and Connecticut,—fruitless, it is true, as far as military results were concerned, but extremely exasperating to those who suffered from them. They also obtained possession of King's Ferry on the Hudson at the southern extremity of the Highlands, with the works erected at Stony Point on the western and at Verplanck's Point on the eastern side of the river. These places formed part of the system of fortifying the Highlands by the Americans. Hence their occupation by the enemy was regarded by Washington as a serious menace to his operations.

The first effect of the French alliance of February, 1778, was not, as many had hoped, to infuse new vigor into the prosecution of the war. It was, unfortunately, regarded on all hands as decisive of the question of independence. The treaty is spoken of in the correspondence of the time as the true Declaration of Independence, and all, friends and enemy alike, seemed to think that it would lead to a speedy settlement of the question. Within a few weeks after the hope-inspiring battle of Monmouth a large French fleet under the Comte d'Estaing, with four thousand troops on board, appeared off the coast. It was thought that the English fleet at Sandy Hook and their army at New York were at their mercy. It was soon found, however, that there was not water enough within the Hook to permit the French squadron to act with advantage. So the attempt to destroy the British fleet there was given up. It was next arranged that a combined operation of the French fleet and an army under General Sullivan should be undertaken with the hope of capturing the English garrison on Rhode Island, or at least of compelling it to evacuate that post. The attempt, as is well known, was a wretched failure. Whether the fault was due to General Sullivan, or to the French admiral, or to the storms which hindered their co-operation, the result was worse than a failure, for it bred intense jealousy and dislike between us and our French allies. The fleet with its troops sailed for Boston, and after a long delay there took part in the unsuccessful siege of Savannah. In this way were the eyes of our fathers opened to the true value of this French alliance for which they had so long prayed, and to secure which they had professed themselves ready to make such abundant sacrifices. It brought them at this time neither men nor money nor ships, but it did teach them that success was, after all, to be achieved only by their own efforts; yet the lesson was in a great measure unheeded, and our countrymen still preferred to hope great things from the alliance rather than tax themselves and put in practice the well-tried maxim that in union there is force. There seems to have been at this time in the army, in contrast with the hopeful tone which prevailed in the public, a good deal of depression from causes some of which are given in the following letter :

General Wayne to Robert Morris.

FREDERICKSBURG 5th Oct'r 1778

DEAR SIR,—Your very Polite favour of the 8th Ultimo I have just Rec'd— I wish with you that it had been in your Power to give full Satisfaction to our poor Worthy fellows in the Article of Clothing —their Distresses are great, but there is a *Distant* prospect of these Distresses being Alleviated in some Degree, though not so amply nor so soon, as the Season & their wretched Condition Require, shou'd the Enemy Operate to the Eastward as from Present Appearances they Intend it—we shall be like Mahomet and the Mountain —if the Clothing wont Come to us—we will go to the Clothing—

The Honorable mention which His Excellency was pleased to make of me on acct. of the Action of Monmouth, must be very flattering to a young soldier—Altho' I am Conscious of not having done any more than my Duty—and for which I can claim no Merit.

When Gen'l Reed was at Camp—I believe the State of Penns'a was Considered to have but two Brigades in the field— I wish to put this matter in a fair point of view— Exclusive of the two Brigades with this Army (which in health, Numbers & Discipline are second to none on the Ground) we have three Hundred Rank & file with Col'l William Butler on the Mowhawk River, five Independent Companies at West Point on Hudsons River, Upwards of three Hundred Rank & file with Col. Brodhead at Pittsburg—and Col'l Hartley's Regiment at Sunbury which was totally Raised in Penns'a and either is or ought to be Adopted by the State—so that Counting only upon two Brigades is unjust and ungenerous—as the troops I have now mentioned would if together, make a stronger Effective Brigade than any in the Service—add to this that all the troops we have in the field are Enlisted during the War, whilst the troops of almost every Other State are only Engag'd for three years or Draughted for Eight months—so that by the first of Jan'y we shall have more Continental troops in the field than any other State in the Whole Confederacy—but not so many *Gen'l Officers* having but One Brig'r General for the three Brigades—

I must acknowledge that I am much pleased to find that Gen'l Hand was absolutely appointed for N. Carol'a for was he to take a Command in the Penns'a Line we should Inevitably lose Col'l Irvine—who was a senior Col'l to Hand— Matters being thus situated is it not an Injury to Penns'a not to have the Benefit of its Proportion of Gen'l Officers which ought to be at least three Brigadiers if the number of Troops is the Criterion to Determine by and is it not a prejudice to those Officers who are Entitled to promotion to be so long neglected. If I am Rightly Instructed—there is a Resolve of Congress Reserving to prisoners their Rank and Promotion in the Line as soon as exchanged—if this is the case I doubt not but Col'l Irvine's Merit, Capacity & Conduct as an Officer & a Gent'n will Entitle him to that Rank which he would have held had he not unfortunately been made a Prisoner he was a Senior Col'l to either De Haas or Hand I have Dwelt the Longer on this Subject as I have an Intended Resignation as soon as the Campaign ends of too many of our best Officers— I am Confident that if some of the Principal Officers Lead the way that the Contagion in our Line will be very General having no Inducement to Continue in. Indeed they seem Desirous of Catching at any Pretext for Quitting a service which has or soon will Reduce them to beggary & want leaving but Rank or love of Country which will not afford them bread at an other day— for my own part I realy should have Retired to my Sabine fields before now but for fear of the ill Consequence of the Example When I once see matters in a more fixed state I may then be permitted to Retire without the Imputation of want of Patriotism or Courage—which period is most anxiously wished for by your Most Ob't & very Hum'l Ser't

ANT'Y WAYNE.

[HON'BL ROB'T MORRIS.]

While all the Colonies suffered from the illusions which reliance upon the French had fostered, and were slower during the last four years of the war in raising money or recruiting troops and providing for them than during the first three years, the burden of such a method of conducting military operations was felt with peculiar severity in Pennsylvania. Massachusetts not only had abundant harvests, but in her seaports was transacted an opulent commerce, and thus she was comparatively prosperous; Virginia at this time had on the shores of her navigable rivers large stores of tobacco, easily convertible into money when they fell into hands not hostile; but Pennsylvania was, as we have said, cut off in a great measure from commerce with the rest of the world.

In August, 1778, what remained of the three Pennsylvania brigades was formed into two, owing to the small number of recruits who were enlisted to fill the ranks of the old regiments. These brigades were composed of four regiments each. The following is a list of the field officers : *Colonels*, Chambers, W. Stewart, Thomas Craig, L. Cadwalader, Johnston, Magaw, W. Irvine, and Broadhead ; *Lieutenant-Colonels*, T. Robinson, Miller, Williams, William Butler, Frazer, Harmar, Hay, and Bayard ; *Majors*, Moore, Murray, Lennox, Church, Stuart, Talbot, Mentges, and F. Vernon.[1] The list is interesting as showing how steadily the officers of the Pennsylvania line under General Wayne held their posts. The names of nearly all those we have given are familiar for good conduct at Brandywine, at Paoli, at Germantown, and at Monmouth. So slow, however, was the progress of recruiting, that in October, 1778, the first brigade still needed eight hundred and thirteen men, and the second nine hundred and fifty, to complete their rolls.

In common with the whole army encamped at Middlebrook during the winter of 1778–79, the Pennsylvania line suffered almost beyond endurance, not only from a want of clothing and of supplies of all kinds, but also from the payment of their wages in money of merely a nominal value. Much lack of discipline grew out of "the dirt and nakedness of the soldiers," and constant discontent on the part of the officers, aggravated by disputes concerning relative rank ; in short, there was a state of suffering closely akin to that through which the army had passed the winter before at Valley Forge. Although it was hoped that the trouble would

[1] See Appendix.

be removed in a great measure by the appointment of
General Greene as quartermaster-general in place of
General Mifflin, the same complaints were made. The
true source of the embarrassment of the army service
was the want of money and of credit. There was also
a pernicious infatuation that peace could be attained
without further effort on the part of the Americans
themselves. To what indifference this blind confidence
led those at the seat of government is clearly pointed
out in the Wayne correspondence. He had sent two
of his most distinguished officers, Colonel Walter Stewart and Colonel William Irvine, while the army was in
winter quarters, to represent to the Assembly the unfortunate condition of things, hitherto without remedy,
in regard to the pay and rank of those serving in
the Pennsylvania line, and to ask for some relief from
the hardships from which the private soldier suffered.
A letter of Colonel Stewart's, like one of Washington's
written about the same time, describes the demoraliza-
tion which had seized upon men whom they met in
Philadelphia whose duty it was to find means to support the Revolutionary contest.

The picture of society in Philadelphia at that time
as drawn by General Washington is suggestive of an
anarchical condition of things. "Idleness, dissipation,
& extravagance," writes he, "seem to have laid fast
hold of the generality, and peculation, speculation, &
an insatiable thirst of riches to have gotten the better
of every other consideration, and of almost every order
of men. . . . The momentous concerns of the empire, a great & accumulating debt, ruined finances, depreciated money, & a want of credit, which is the want

of everything, are but secondary considerations, and postponed by Congress from time to time, as if their affairs wore the most promising aspect. The paper is daily sinking fifty per cent., and yet an Assembly, a concert, a dinner or a supper which costs from £200 to £300 does not only take men off from acting, but even of thinking of this business."

In a letter of Colonel Stewart to General Wayne, he says, "How much are we disappointed in respect to the representation in Congress; the pleasing ideas we had formed of it are now no more. We unfortunately find a real set of Caitiffs have supplied their places, and what still adds to my Chagrin is that I am told that Parson Duffield is to supply the place of Edward Biddle who spurned at his colleagues and refused to serve among them. Nothing but party reigns in different bodies. Every thing confirms me in the opinion that the enemy have been long enough in this country.

"Permit me to say a little of the dress, manners, & customs of the town's people. In regard to the first, great alterations have taken place since I was here. It is all gaiety, and from what I can observe, every lady and gentleman endeavors to outdo the other in splendor & show. The manners of the ladies are likewise much changed. They have really in a great measure lost that native innocence which was their former characteristic & supplied its place with what they call an Easy behavior. . . . The manner of entertaining in this place has likewise undergone a change. You cannot conceive any thing more elegant than the present taste. You will hardly dine at a table but they present you with three courses & Each of them in the most elegant manner. 'Tis really flattering to the officers of the Army, the attention paid them by the people. I have heard many of them mention it. We, I assure you, have tickets [invitations] in general for five or six days forward. God knows we deserve it. Much have we suffered while these people were enjoying all the luxury.and ease of life."

Such was Philadelphia, demoralized under the rule of Arnold, after the evacuation of the British army, and to a Congress and a State Legislature with such surroundings Wayne went in the winter of 1778–79 to plead the cause of his "naked soldiers."

Wayne determined to appeal to the State authorities until the grievances should be redressed. He writes to General Reed, President, 28th December, 1778. After complaining that his officers are suffering for want of clothing, he goes on to say,—

"You will perhaps ask why these officers did not purchase clothing for themselves. I answer for obvious reasons among others the depreciation of our money is not the least but the real cause. Congress long ago passed a resolve, recommending to the several States to furnish these officers not only with clothing, but all other necessaries, at a moderate rate and in proportion to their pay. In consequence of this Resolve, a quantity of clothing was purchased by the State of Penn'a for that purpose about this time twelve-month, and the officers were made to believe it would be sent to camp, ready made up, agreeable to the returns and measures sent for the purpose. In this they have been egregiously deceived. Not a change of uniform has come to camp and if any officer or officers have been furnished with clothing, it is not those who now are and always have been doing their duty in the field, who are not callous to their sufferings, but are conscious of meriting some attention from their State although they have not, as yet, experienced any. The officers of other States are supplied with almost every necessary suitable for a gentleman and a soldier at a moderate cost, that is at less than one sixth part of what they (the Penn'a officers) are obliged to pay for articles they can't possibly do without— This discrimination among the officers fighting in the same cause and serving in the same Army, gives a sensation much better felt than expressed.

"I know it must give you much concern to hear a repetition of these grievances, and the more so to know that they are but too just. Give me leave to assure you that whatever your feelings may be on the occasion, mine are not less, but rather heightened by a constant view of the hardships and distress which gentlemen are hourly exposed to who deserve better treatment. . . . If something effectual is not done forthwith they must be permitted to go home and leave the men unofficered. Should that unfortunately be the case I have but too much ground to believe that a very great proportion of them will never return to this army again. I have already observed that the subject must be ungrateful, but it is a duty which I owe to my country—to myself and the officers whom I have the honor to command, to represent their well grounded complaints, based upon facts which materially concern the honor of Penn'a, and the good of the service in general. I have full confidence that you, Sir, will lay the whole matter before the Legislature of the State and give it that countenance which you think it merits.

"I neither ask nor wish for any thing on my own account, and wish for nothing more than an opportunity of returning to my Sabine fields with safety to my country & honor to myself, and am determined to seize the first favorable opportunity to put that wish into execution.

"I am &c.,
"ANTH'Y WAYNE."

President Reed writes in reply on January 23, making various excuses for the non-delivery of the clothing, which amount to this: "that the State had ordered the articles to be sent, and will try to discover why none of the shirts will fit, and why the blue color

of the cloth has turned brown and white." It seems
to be a repetition of the old story of the "knavery of
contractors." He tells Wayne that such was the rapid
increase of price demanded by our traders that the
estimate of the cost of two hundred suits of clothes
for officers was found at current prices to amount to
sixteen thousand six hundred and fifty pounds.

Wayne, not yet finding redress, turns to the Continental authorities, and writes to Robert Morris and
Robert Knox about the same time, "I do solemnly
assure you that nothing but the highest sense of honor
and true patriotic zeal could have kept our officers
in a service that promises nothing but indigence and
want. Their pay is a mere *vox et praeterea nihil.* Such
as have not a little patrimony of their own (which they
are breaking in upon by very swift degrees) cannot
furnish themselves with clothing, much less with the
usual comforts of life ; so that unless something be
speedily & effectually done a very large proportion of
our best officers must inevitably leave the service.

"I have more than once expressed a wish for a favorable opportunity of quitting the army. That period is
now drawing nigh. I therefore can have no interest
in view other than wishing to see brave and worthy
officers who have shared every vicissitude of fortune
with me, and who have nobly fought and bled in every
field of action, honorably provided for, not left (when
crippled with honest wounds & grown gray in arms)
to depend upon the cold charity of men who have
grown rich under the shelter of their protecting swords."

Finding that no heed was given to his written remon-
strances, and that the officers whom he had deputed to

seek redress from the Assembly of Pennsylvania were not so successful as he had anticipated, Wayne left the army for a short time and went to Philadelphia on the same errand. The result of his appeal—and he is said to have made a pathetic speech in urging his claims— was an act passed in March, 1779, (1) extending the term allowed by Congress for half-pay during seven years to the duration of the life of the soldier, (2) fixing a reasonable price for the articles required by the soldiers, (3) providing a suitable uniform, and (4) exempting the land granted to the soldier from taxation during his life.

This was but a poor measure of justice to those who had fought with so much constancy and courage to defend their native soil from occupation by the enemy at Brandywine, at Paoli, and at Germantown, who had undergone such privations at Valley Forge and had gained fresh renown at Monmouth; but, such as it was, it was received by the soldiers with gratitude, and did much to allay the discontent which prevailed in the Pennsylvania line. This measure, it will be observed, was largely due to the personal influence of General Wayne with the Assembly. Wayne was also called upon by some of the most prominent men in the State to return and aid them in revising the constitution, as a remedy for the evils from which they suffered. The following is the letter:

General Mifflin and others to General Wayne.

November 1778

Affairs now wear a very pleasing aspect in Penn'a. A majority of the members elected to the Assembly are sincerely & warmly disposed to rescue their country from tyranny & contempt. In the

County of Chester there has been a double return of members, and a new election may perhaps be the consequence of it. Your presence in that County and in this City during this important conjuncture will be of signal service in many respects which we forbear to mention in a letter. The situation of the Army will probably admit of your absence for some time from camp. Let us therefore have the pleasure of seeing you here as soon as possible. Matters are now approaching a crisis, and in a few weeks it will be determined whether the State of Penn'a shall be happy under a good Constitution, or oppressed by one of the most detestable that was ever formed— We need say no more to induce you to be with us.

Your very humble servants,

THO'S MIFFLIN   JOHN M. POTTS
MARK BIRD   E. BIDDLE
JAMES WILSON   SAM'L POTTS

Wayne replies on the 23d expressing his sympathy with the views of these gentlemen, and adds, "The State once stood on high grounds & I have the most flattering hopes that her present leaders will place her there again where the best wishes and services of the gentlemen of the Pennsylvania line will not be wanting in helping to support her."

In the midst of the delay on the part of the Assembly in doing justice to the claims of the officers under his command for suitable clothing, Wayne was called upon to confront another source of embarrassment, which in the end well-nigh led to the disbandment of his division. This was the threatened resignation of all his field officers, who were profoundly irritated by the relative rank to which many of them had been assigned by the "new arrangement," as it was called, adopted by the State authorities in February, 1779. Before explaining the nature of this particular trouble, we must consider the position in which Wayne himself was shortly after placed by being superseded in his command of the division of the Pennsylvania line by General St. Clair.

General St. Clair was a major-general in the Continental service, and General Wayne was a brigadier only. He had succeeded Wayne in the command at Ticonderoga, and had, greatly to the surprise and disgust of Washington and the whole army, evacuated that post on the approach of Burgoyne's army without making the resistance which, as was then thought, his resources and the importance of the post demanded. He was tried by a court-martial in November, 1778, and acquitted upon charges based on these suspicions. Meantime, he seems to have convinced General Washington of his courage and capacity, and doubtless the commander-in-chief gratefully remembered St. Clair's suggestion with regard to turning the left of the British army at Trenton, which movement proved so masterly and successful a piece of strategy. He became, even while he was under arrest for his alleged misbehavior at Ticonderoga, a member of General Washington's military family, and as such (without, however, any command) he was present at Brandywine and Monmouth, but at neither battle, according to Wayne, was his conduct creditable. He had not previous to his appointment as commander of the Pennsylvania line ever led the troops of that State to victory, and he appears to have been very little known either to the officers or to the soldiers, who had been trained and made effective by Wayne for nearly three years. These soldiers were not only naturally very much attached to Wayne, but they were proud of the renown they had achieved under his command, and considered themselves as forming a special *corps d'élite* in the Revolutionary army. When, therefore, it was found by Wayne that not only did his great services at Brandywine, at Germantown, and at Monmouth avail nothing in securing military promotion, but that he was not even permitted to retain the command in which he had acquired such distinction, he prepared the following draught of a letter, which it seems was never sent, but which is valuable now as showing how deeply he felt the indignity thrust upon him.

After speaking of the ill-will borne him by St. Clair, as shown by his sneering criticism of the finding of the court-martial which acquitted him of misconduct at Paoli, Wayne goes on :

" 14 Oct 78

" I have other reasons, one of which is the conduct of that gent'n at Monmouth. An opening offered at striking the enemy to advantage. I sent for the three Penn'a Brigades to support me ; he happening to be near when my request arrived peremptorily ordered them not to advance, except three Regiments which with myself must inevitably have perished had the Enemy not been fortunately broken and routed by the unparalleled bravery of these few troops —& contrary to the most sanguine hopes of every Spectator— Although victory declared for us and the slaughter was great, yet we could not improve the advantage from the disparity of numbers —of which we were deprived either by the ignorance or the envy of this gentleman—

"Add to this, that Col. Irvine the gentleman at the head of my brigade is fully competent to the charge—and whose feelings I am determined not to hurt by depriving him of that command—

" I don't mean by this to ask for promotion. My only ambition was a Brigadier General's Command of the Penn'a line, which command I have been indulged in for two campaigns and therefore thought I had some claim to that honor in future. But to be

superseded at this late hour by a man in whose conduct and candor
I can have no confidence hurts me not a little—

"This perhaps may be a mode of reasoning that will have but
little weight. I solemnly protest that I have no such wish. I only
hoped not to be degraded, that is, reduced from the command of a
division to a brigade—and that under a man—who for reasons I
have already mentioned I can never submit to. I have therefore
determined to return to domestic life, & leave the blustering field of
Mars to the possession of gentlemen of more worth," etc.

As Wayne's passion cooled, he felt that it was his
duty, particularly at a time when all his field officers
were threatening to resign their commissions because,
as they alleged, they had been unjustly treated in the
matter of rank, to show no open sign of disaffection.
He therefore applied for leave of absence in February,
1779, and, showing a fine example of unselfish disinterestedness and patriotic devotion, asked the commander-in-chief that he might be appointed to the command of a corps of light infantry which it was proposed
to organize for special service in the spring. He
stated in his application that, although he "sincerely
esteemed" General St. Clair, he had so much tender-
ness for the feelings of the officers "that have hitherto commanded the Pennsylvania brigades that I can't
think of interfering with them on that point;" in other
words, that although for himself he was willing to become once more a brigade commander, he could not
consent that his colonels who had commanded brigades, like Irvine and Butler, should become colonels
again. General Washington granted his application at
once, and told him on the 10th of February, 1779,
"My opinion of your merit will lead me cheerfully to
comply with your request as soon as the arrangements

of the army and other circumstances permit the formation of that corps." Turning over the division to St.
Clair in February, he went to Philadelphia to work for
its interests.

But he never could forgive the injustice done his
colonels, although the wrongs to himself were forgotten.
He writes concerning it, in a letter to General Armstrong of the 25th of April, 1779, "I beg to assure you
that my only ambition was to have continued a Brigadier Commanding the Penn'a line, a command I had
long enjoyed, and in which I esteemed myself as much
honored by the confidence and affection of my officers
and soldiers as I could possibly hope from any in the
power of Congress to bestow. Whenever Congress
or his Excellency shall honor me with the charge of
troops without wounding the feelings of other officers
I shall gladly accept it, but on no other consideration."

The loyalty of Wayne to his friends was a conspicuous trait in his character, and this example of it,
insisting that Irvine's and Butler's services should be
recognized, even if it were necessary that he should
sacrifice his own position in order to accomplish the
object, is a very striking one. No wonder, when his
officers and men found that they had a man at their
head who would not hesitate to prefer their interests to
his own, that an affectionate and solid attachment grew
up between General Wayne and those under his command. No general officer was ever more warmly and
deservedly beloved by his men, or more readily obtained from them arduous and devoted service. He
was unceasing, as we have seen, in the midst of their
privations, in his efforts to promote their welfare in

camp, and in urging the State authorities to do their duty to the men enlisted in the service. While doing everything for them, he insisted that a high standard of military discipline should be kept up, so that his men might be at all times truly effective. How he succeeded, their record at Brandywine, at Germantown, at Monmouth, and at Stony Point clearly shows. Wayne was more than a popular military leader. His example, according to Colonel Frank Johnston, was a strong cohesive force in the army. "It is a matter of astonishment to me," says Colonel Johnston, "almost a miracle, that we have an Army, or the most distant vestige of an Army in being, and had it not been for the mutual and happy attachment which has uniformly existed between the officers and the men I do not hesitate to say that we should not have a single soldier in the field."

Just at this time he found it necessary to rebuke some of his younger officers for a breach of discipline, and in doing so he drew the line between what pertained to the military and what to the civil ruler in time of war. We may well weigh his views on this subject, for they trace clearly the course which a general during a civil war in his own country should follow. These letters seem to show that "Mad Anthony" was a good deal of a civilian as well as of a soldier. Nothing was further from his thoughts all through his career than the exercise of any illegal or arbitrary authority.

FREDRICKSBURG 5th Oct. 1778

GENTLEMEN,—I have caused Cap't Lieu't Henderson, Lieu't Marshall, Lieu't Ball & Ensign Smith to be put in arrest for abusing & Wounding you or some of you with their Swords.

As I am not acquainted with the Circumstances—I wish you either to Inform me by Writing or otherwise with a true Account of the Whole Affair as soon as Possible in Order that proper means may be taken to bring the Aggressors to Justice— Major Wright who Carries this will bring your Answer or Conduct you or either of you to my Quarters at the House of Mr Benjamin Haverland.

Interim I am your Most
Ob't Hum'l Ser't
Ant'y Wayne

To
Henry Birdsell
James Birdsell
&
William March

Oct'r 9th 1778

Honoured Sir,—As we were Ordered this Morning By the Court Martial to be Confined to our tents, and are Deprived of the Benefit of the Military Law, wherein we would have an Opportunity to Vindicate our Characters and Clear up that Heavy Slurr that Lies upon our Honours, By Facts which May Be Misstated to the Gen'l—

We most Humbly Request of the Gen'l to allow us the Liberty of the Camp, as it will be a Means to Prevent any sickness which May Arise to us, from Our Close and Disagreeable Confinement—

Or may it Please the Gen'l to Withdraw Our arrest and Lett us Return to Our Duty, We will Give in Security (If required) For Our Appearance when Called upon

We Are Honoured Sir
your Most Obd't Sert's
Jno Henderson Capt Lt 3. P. R't
John Marshall Lieut 3. P. R't
B. Wm Ball Lieut 3d P. R't
Peter Smith Ensign 3d P. R't

To
The Honourable
Brigad'r Gen'l Wayne—
Present—

Fredricksburg 10th Oct'r 1778

Gentlemen,—I have just seen yours of yesterday by which you Complain of being Deprived of the Benefit of Military Law.

You Certainly can't be Ignorant of the superior power of the
Civil Law over the Military—and as you have been Guilty of exer-
cising *Military Law* over the peaceable & Unarmed Inhabitants
of this State—the Governor who is the Guardian of the Civil Liberties of the People over which he presides, has Demanded you to be
Given up to the Civil power— His Excellency Gen'l Washington
has Ordered you to be Confined until he Receives Gov'r Clinton's
Directions where to send you— I am also to Inform you that however you may Conceive your Honors hurt on the Occasion—that it
has never yet been Deemed Honourable for Armed men to Assault
& Wound unarmed men in any Line Whatever—but has been particularly Reprobated in the Army.

However in a full Reliance on your Honor you may have hereby
the Liberty of the Camp till further Orders— Interim I am

Your Most Ob't Hum'l Ser't

ANT'Y WAYNE

CAPT. LIEUT. HENDERSON
LIEUTS. MARSHALL, BALL & ENSIGN SMITH

Just as Wayne had settled the question of rank in
his own case by accepting the promise of his appointment to the command of the corps "of light infantry,
which was to be raised in the spring," and, turning
over the division to General St. Clair, had retired tem-
porarily from the army, a new source of trouble, arising
from the discontent of the field officers with the relative rank assigned them by the "new arrangement"
of February, 1779, arose in the Pennsylvania line.
Owing to the diminished number of men, it became
necessary that the force should be embodied in two
brigades, and that many changes should be made in
the *personnel* of the regimental officers. For many
reasons, great objections were made to the new assign-
ment. Most of Wayne's officers had served in the
line in all the campaigns from the beginning, and they

prided themselves upon what they and their soldiers had done in these campaigns. Nothing seemed more unfair to them than that high rank should be given to men who had never, or at most for but a very short period, served in the army, the rank conferred upon them preventing the promotion of those who had borne the heat and burden of the day.

Especially was objection made to giving these coveted places to those who had been taken prisoners of war at Fort Washington in 1776 and had therefore seen no service since that date. Particularly was their anger excited by the brevet commission given by Congress to Major Macpherson, who had seen no service whatever in the American army. Macpherson, a native of Philadelphia, had been a cadet in the English service previous to the Revolution, and had reached the position of adjutant when hostilities broke out. At that time he resigned his commission, but he did not enter the American army until February, 1779, when he was made by Congress major by brevet, thus superseding all those who had faithfully done their duty as officers of the line for nearly three years. These gentlemen were so profoundly irritated by this conduct of Congress that the field officers of the different regiments unanimously agreed to resign their commissions if their grievances were not redressed by the 15th of the ensuing April. The difficulty about Macpherson's appointment was bridged over in some way at this time, but in August, 1780, the trouble was renewed, with more threats on the part of the officers of a resignation of their commissions if Macpherson were retained as major.

In this alarming condition of things, Wayne, although he had ceased to have any official connection with the Pennsylvania line, came forward, as usual, with conciliatory words and pacific measures. The occasion was one of great alarm, for the resignation of the officers meant the dissolution of the most efficient division in the army. He exerted all his influence to induce the officers to reconsider their resolution. What compromise was made cannot be clearly indicated, but the result was that through Wayne's agency these ill-treated officers retained their position in the army, ready to do in the future, as they had done in the past, loyal service to the cause the success of which they all had so much at heart.

The correspondence on this subject between Wayne and the offended officers is one of the finest illustrations to be found in his whole career of the manner in which he gained the confidence of those he commanded.

General Wayne to the Field Officers of the Pennsylvania Line.

PHILADELPHIA 14th March 1779.

GENTLEMEN,—In consequence of a Memorial of which the enclosed is a copy, a Committee [of the Assembly] was appointed with orders to call me to their assistance to form some plan for putting our officers and troops on an equal footing with those of other States—

We went a *little farther* than was expected, & presented the Hon : House with the inclosed resolves, which after some debate were carried by a great majority. Your Letter of the 7th came to hand too late, but had it been in time, it would not have been presented, as threats often irritate, & sometimes defeat the ends they are intended to obtain.—However I should have Retained it as a *Dernier résort.* The recruiting business is now before the house, who have demanded a loan of money from Congress for that purpose, & for procuring cloathing &c for the Officers who are now put on a footing equal to the British Establishment, & Superior to any others on the Continent.

You will in my name please to congratulate the Officers and Troops on the Occasion and believe me

Yours most affectionately
ANT'Y WAYNE.

THE COMMITTEE OF FIELD OFFICERS
OF THE PENNSYLVANIA LINE.

General Wayne to Colonel Harmar—Extract.

PHILADELPHIA 24th Feb'y 1779.

DEAR COLONEL,—Enclosed is the old arrangement of the Penn'a Line as made at White Plains. The Board of War have submitted a Copy of the new one to His Excellency Gen'l Washington for a *Completion* in which there are a variety of errors among Others— many Gent'n who were Capt's are now only rated as Cap't Lieut's but this being a palpable mistake you will easily have it Rectified— you will also be able to point out the Resignations—in the Respective Regiments—and supplying their place, by those next in Command.

I fear that the Major of the 11th Regiment will give some uneasiness to many worthy Captains who had Commanded him—I also feel for poor *Minzer*. However my hands are clear of every part of it as you can see by the Enclosed letter from the board of War wrote about the time I left Camp.

I wish to God that you and the Other Field Officers may be able to settle the whole with mutual satisfaction to all parties.

*   *   *   *   *   *   *   *

MILLSTONE CAMP March 8th 1779.

DEAR GENERAL,—Agreeable to your Request, I do myself the Honor of transmitting you exact Copies of the two Arrangements— The latter is likely to create great Uneasiness— General S't Clair has recommended, a Board of Field Officers to sit, & endeavor to settle it amongst ourselves— We shall have a Difficult Task of it—

The officers are greatly irritated,—yesterday they presented a letter to the Committee, signed in behalf of all the officers present, stating many well founded Grievances—desiring us to paint them in as striking Terms as possible, and to inform the House of Assembly, unless immediate Redress is granted, they would *unanimously* resign their Commissions by the 15th April—

The matter is really serious. Such a step will Dissolve the Division— We have wrote the Committee of Correspondence yesterday—informing them the *fixed Determination* of the Officers —but I suppose it will be treated as *we* have been, with Neglect and Contempt—

Should you incline to accept the Command of the Light Corps— I shall esteem it a singular Happiness to be honored with a Command under you—

I received a letter some Days since from Col Magaw on Long Island. Desires his Compliments, and believe me

Dear General

Your most obed't hble serv.

Jos. Harmar.

General Wayne.

General Wayne to President Reed.

Camp at Millstone 24th Jan'y, 1779.

Dear Sir,—I do myself the Honor of Enclosing an *Address* of the Field Officers of this Line to your Excellency, together with Copies of Resolves of Virginia & Maryland for supplying their Officers & Soldiers with Clothing and Other necessaries; also the Report of the Committee respecting the Clothing lately arrived under the Conduct of Capt. Lang with an Estimate of the Quantity of Cloth & other Materials sufficient to furnish a Suit of Clothes for each Officer.

It's with Sincere Pleasure & Esteem I join in Sentiment with the Committee in Congratulating you on your appointment to the Presidency of a State which from Internal Divisions has been Rendered feeble & will require the utmost exertions of that fortitude & abilities with which you have hitherto acted in every Vicissitude of Fortune, & from which we have the most flattering hopes of seeing Penns'a resuming that rank & Consequence which she is entitled to hold.

I am Confident that the Officers and Troops of this Line will

13

soon Experience the happy effects of having at the head of their State a Gen'l truly disposed to Redress their just Complaints, & to alleviate their distress & whom they Esteem as their Common friend & Guardian.

The Clear & Decided Opinion of the Committee of Arrangement, mentioned in your Excellency's Letter of the 14th Instant—I shall Communicate in as Delicate a manner as possible to the Gen'l who will be affected by it,—& whom I most ardently wish to Retain in the army from the *fullest Conviction* that our Line will suffer extremely by the *Change.*

It is not the *pay* or Emolument attending their Commissions that can Induce Gen'ls of Sentiment and nice feelings of Honor to Continue in this Service—the former being mere *Vox præterea nihil.*

It is the Letter & Rank alone that can Retain them—& whenever Injured in these tender points we must expect to lose Gen'ls of Spirit & Sensibility—who are the very men we want to render our arms formidable to our Enemy & Respectable to our friends.

You express a wish to know the Date of my Commission—my Colonel Com'n was dated the 3rd of Jan'y 1776 my Brig'r-Gn Feb. 1, 1777.

A. WAYNE.

On General Wayne's retirement from the command of the Pennsylvania line the following letter was addressed to him by the field officers :

Field Officers of the Line to General Wayne.

MILLSTONE CAMP March 27th 1779.

SIR,—The manner of expressing the grateful sense of a set of men conscious of their inability is harder to conclude on than is generally imagined ; especially when they know they are more indebted than the delicacy of the benefactors would choose to hear.

In this dilemma of gratitude, we are really at a loss, but fully sensible of the open goodness of your heart, are confident every reasonable allowance will be made for our want of capacity and expression.

We are (long since) acquainted with your endeavours to render the Troops of the State of Pennsylvania respectable and comfortable; and the recent proof you have given of your attachment to them, has rivetted the hearts of all ranks more firmly to you (if possible) than before.   Your manly and pathetic address to the Assembly must (*nay does*) render your name more dear to the whole line, who are confident of its effect with the House.—If there be a merit in keeping the present set of Officers in the Service, or a benefit hereafter result by it to the *State*, it is much owing to your delicate mode of proceeding on the occasion ; as they were generally determined to quit the Field :—but, as a provision is now made that will enable them to serve, we hope our friends and Country will be convinced (and see) by our future conduct, it was no licentious or parsimonious view, but real necessity and an apparent neglect, caused by the resolution.

We therefore beg leave to assure you, sir, that we have the highest opinion of your integrity and worth ; and though we have not now the honour to be commanded by you in the *Field*, we hope you will not imagine us so contracted in sentiment, as to lose any part of that sincere esteem and respect we have ever had for you as a Friend, a Brother, & Commander, and hope in a short time to see justice done to your well-known merit, and you placed in that station we are confident you can fill with honour to yourself, satisfaction to the Public, & benefit to your *Country*.

Filled with these sentiments, and conscious of your deserts, we pray you to receive, through us, the most grateful acknowledgments of your services, and the sincere thanks of the whole Line present ; with their best wishes for your health & welfare,—and in a particular manner the thanks and Friendship of, Dear General

Your most obedient &

very affectionate Humble Servants

JAMES CHAMBERS Col 10th P. Reg.

RICH'D BUTLER Col 7th P. Reg.

T. CRAIG Col. 3rd P. Reg.

JOS HARMAR Lt Com 6th P Reg.

J. MENTGES Maj. 7th P. Reg.

JNO. MURRAY Maj 2. P. Reg.

THOMAS L. BYLES Maj 3 P. Reg.

WM WILLIAMS Lt Col 3 P. Reg.

J. GRIER Maj 10th P. Reg.

No sooner was it known in the army that General
Wayne was to command the new Light Infantry Corps
than many officers, old officers of the Pennsylvania line,
as well as those of other States, expressed an ardent
desire to serve under him, and solicited him to ask
General Washington to appoint them to positions in
the new corps. Wayne, with characteristic deference
to the wishes of the commander-in-chief, writes him in
May, 1779, "I had better be absent (while the corps is
being organized) lest it should be supposed, however
erroneously, that partiality of mine for certain officers
had tended to bring them into the Corps."

The Light Infantry Corps of the Continental army,
which during its short life became so famous for its discipline, and so illustrious for its deeds of valor, notably
for its assault on Stony Point, was composed, according
to Colonel Johnston, "of one and a half battalions of
the choicest sons of Pennsylvania, taken from your own
line, and so in proportion to the other lines on this
ground [camp at Middlebrook], and, if no detachments
are made, your command is intended to number 2000
men, and is preferable to that of any in the Army."
There were two Connecticut regiments in it, under Colonels Putnam and Meigs, a Virginia regiment, under
Colonel Febiger, and the rest were Pennsylvanians,
under Colonel Richard Butler. They were formed in
two brigades, the first commanded by General Irvine,
and the second by Colonel Johnston. It was ready to
take the field towards the close of June, 1779.

So much has been said, and justly said, of the evils
in the Continental army due to sectional distrust and
jealousy among the troops, that it is only fair, in re-

counting the deeds of the men who formed this Light Infantry Corps, to recall that at least on one moment- ous occasion an appeal to their State pride proved of advantage. In his address to his men detailed for the assault on Stony Point General Wayne tells them, "The distinguished honor conferred upon every officer and soldier who has been drafted into this corps, by his Excellency General Washington, the credit of the States they respectively belong to, and their own reputations, will be such powerful motives for each man to distin- guish himself, that the General cannot have the least doubt of a glorious victory. He hereby engages to reward the first man who enters the works. . . . But should there be any soldier so lost to a feeling of honor as to attempt to retreat a single foot, or skulk in the face of danger, the officer next to him is immediately to put him to death, that he may no longer disgrace the name of a soldier, or the corps or the State to which he belongs."

Such was the martial tone with which Wayne ad- dressed his soldiers within a few days after assuming the command, and in preparation for the most hazard- ous enterprise of the war, the assault on the fortress at Stony Point.

CHAPTER V.

ON Wayne's return to the army in June, 1779, he found General Washington extremely desirous of recapturing two forts,—one at Stony Point, on the western side of the Hudson River, and the other at Verplanck's Point, opposite, on the eastern side,—which guarded the approach to King's Ferry, and which the British had forced the Americans to evacuate on the 1st of June. The forts were regarded as important, not only because they commanded King's Ferry, the only convenient line of communication between the New England and the middle Colonies, but also because, standing as they did at the southern extremity of the Highlands, they gave control, in the hands of an enemy, over West Point and its dependencies to the northward.

The strategetical value of this position, indeed, was such that it had been the objective point of Burgoyne when he strove to form a junction with the British coming from New York in 1777, and it was afterwards thought by Sir H. Clinton to be so essential to his operations in that quarter that he attempted to pur-

[1] There have been, of course, many accounts printed of the famous assault on Stony Point. That of Mr. Henry B. Dawson, written with all Wayne's papers before him, seems to me the most accurate and satisfactory, and has therefore been mainly followed in this chapter.

chase the possession of West Point by the bribery of Arnold in September, 1780.

It would appear that Washington waited impatiently for the arrival of Wayne in order to concert with him measures for regaining these posts, and, indeed, that he designed that the newly-formed Light Infantry Corps, of which he had appointed Wayne commander, should carry out his plans for this purpose.

The fort at Stony Point was built on a rocky promontory on the west side of the Hudson, about one hundred and fifty feet high. Three sides of this promontory were surrounded by water, and on the fourth a swamp or morass, which was not passable at high tide, separated it from the land. It was guarded by three redoubts, and protected by a double *abatis* of logs, which extended across the peninsula. The cannon were so arranged as to enfilade any approach to the inner works supposed to be practicable. It had a garrison of about five hundred men, under the command of Colonel Johnston, who was regarded as a highly capable officer.

The main part of Washington's army was then encamped in Smith's Clove, about ten miles back of West Point, and head-quarters were at New Windsor. It had been intended that the Light Infantry Corps, which was detailed for the purpose of assaulting the works, should consist of eight battalions of one hundred and sixty-four men each, under the command of a brigadier-general. Two only of the regiments belonging to this corps, or four battalions, were actually formed and organized on the 1st of July, when Washington issued his orders to prepare for the assault. These orders directed, in the first place, that a thorough reconnoissance of the position should be made, so that an accurate knowledge of the points to be assailed should be obtained, and especially that the manner in which these points were guarded should be carefully observed. These four battalions were supposed to form the *élite* of Washington's army, and the men composing them had been selected with great care. They were commanded respectively by Colonels Putnam and Meigs of Connecticut, Colonel Richard Butler of Pennsylvania, and Colonel Christian Febiger of Virginia.

It is curious to notice, as an instance of the maladministration of the army service, that, although the officers and men of the Light Infantry Corps were ready for any dangerous enterprise which might be undertaken, the commissariat, as so often happened at critical periods of the Revolution, was at fault, and its condition threatened the success of the movement against Stony Point. Thus, General Wayne was obliged on the 8th of July to reprimand the commissary for not providing any forage for his horses; they would, he says, "if they could speak, d—n him for starving them;" and on the next day, while he was completing the preparations for the assault, he was forced to tell the same officer, " The Light Corps under my command has been much neglected in almost every article of provision. They have had but two days' fresh provisions since they arrived here [Fort Montgomery], and not more than three days' allowance of rum in twelve days, which article I borrowed from General MacDougall, with a promise to replace it."

No privations, however, seem to have cooled the

ardor of his soldiers. His officers were all men of tried valor and enterprise, and of abundant experience in desperate undertakings. Had the army itself chosen the leaders of the expedition they would doubtless have been selected for that purpose. Richard Butler, the Pennsylvanian, as we have seen, had already shown a coolness in action in many severe engagements, especially in Morgan's Rifle Regiment, which fitted him for any emergency; Meigs and Rufus Putnam of Connecticut were well known as possessing a skill and devotion to the cause equalled only by the bravery with which they had maintained it; and Febiger, a Dane by birth, the colonel of the Virginia regiment, was recognized by all as one of the most trustworthy officers in the army. Serving under them, and sharing all the dangers of the attempt, were men whose names have become conspicuous as among the bravest in Revolutionary history. The soldiers came from widely-separated States. The men of Connecticut and Massachusetts stood shoulder to shoulder with those of Pennsylvania and Virginia, while the gallant Murfrees with his North Carolina troops was a tower of strength to both the assaulting columns.

The result of the reconnoissance made by Wayne was a decision that a storming of the defences was not likely to be successful, and that if the fort was to be taken at all it could be done only by surprise,—that is, by a sudden and overwhelming rush of the assailants, which, overcoming all obstacles, should drive the defenders from their outer works into the interior of the fort and overcome them before they had time to rally or opportunity for resistance. Such a plan, of course, increased the danger of the attempt, but if it could be carried out,—and that depended upon the firmness and fortitude of the officers and men,—success was assured. The following is the report of the careful reconnoissance of the place made by General Wayne, aided by Colonel Butler and Major Steward:

General Wayne to General Washington.

FORT MONTGOMERY 3rd July 1779
10 O'Clock A.M

DEAR GENERAL,—In Obedience to your Excellency's Orders I have Reconnoitred the Situation of the Enemy at Stoney point & the approaches to them in the best manner that Circumstances would admit & Returned late last evening to this place—

The sketch herewith transmitted (which differs but little from that made the Other day by Col'l Butler) will give you a General Idea of the Strength of their Works on the West Side which in my Opinion are formidable—(I think too much so for a *Storm*) & to attempt to Reduce it by Regular Approaches will require time as there is no ground within less distance than a half a mile but what it commands.

The works on Verplanks point are by no means so formidable as those on this side—altho' they consist of four Redoubts—Viz. the one made by us Called *La Fayette* with upraised Ditch the second situated to the N.W. on the Rising ground near the River in which is a block House—the third thrown up round a strong stone House East of Fort La Fayette & on the margin of a Rising ground Commanding the causeway from the Church—the fourth is Situate on the East Side of the Creek & march, on a high point of Rocks commanding all the Ground in its vicinity & overlooking the causeway (it has also a block House) these last three are Surrounded with *Abbatis* but not pierced nor cou'd I discover any *Embrasures* perhaps they fire in Barbet ?

I am clear that they have not more than   men on Stoney point & about   on Verplanks point in all of which I am joined in Opinion by Col. Butler & Major Steward who were with me on this duty & on whose judgment I much rely—

Upon the whole I do not think a *Storm* practicable—but perhaps a *Surprise* may be Effected—could we fall on some stratagem to draw them out— A thought has struck me that as no party of force has ever yet been down or Appeared to the Enemy—& as I have ground to believe that an Inhabitant living near Stoney point acts a double part & of course will give them every Information in his power—which goes no further than to the usual route & number of the Reconnoitring parties—they may be Induced to Attempt an Ambuscade or if they should not attempt this a few of our people appearing near may bring a party out in pursuit which may give an Opening to *enter with them.* Shou'd your Excellency Incline to Reconnoitre the works tomorrow morning or next day I will have a proper Disposition made of the Light Corps so as to Effectually cover you, or attempt the surprise in Case it meets your Approbation— The Troops at the forrest of Dane may Cooperate with us if thought necessary

Interim I am your Excellency's Most

Ob't Hum'l Ser't

Ant'y Wayne

His Excellency
Gen'l Washington.

The plan finally adopted by General Washington, after making himself a reconnoissance of the place, somewhat modified by Wayne in consequence of his greater familiarity with the ground, was the following. The commander-in-chief writes to General Wayne; July 10,—

"My ideas of the enterprise in contemplation are these :

"That it should be attempted by the Light Infantry *only*, which should march under cover of the night and with the utmost secrecy to the enemy's lines, securing every person they find to prevent discovery.

"*Between one & two hundred chosen men & officers* I conceive fully sufficient for the surprise, and apprehend that the approach should be along the water on the south side, crossing the beach and entering at the abattis.

"This party is to be preceded by a vanguard of prudent and determined men well commanded, who are to remove obstructions, secure the sentries, and drive in the guard. They are to advance (the whole of them) with fixed bayonets and muskets unloaded. The officers commanding them are to know precisely what batteries or particular parts of the line they are respectively to possess, so that confusion & the consequences of indecision may be avoided.

"These parties should be followed by the main body at a small distance for the purpose of support. . . . Other parties may advance to the works by the way of the causeway & the River on the north if practicable as well for the purpose of distracting the enemy in their defence as to cut off their retreat. . . .

"If success should attend the enterprise measures should be taken to prevent the retreat of the garrison by water, or to annoy them as much as possible should they attempt it. The guns should be immediately turned against the shipping and Verplanck's point, and covered, if possible, from the enemy's fire.

"Secrecy is so much more essential to these kind of enterprises than numbers, that I should not think it advisable to employ any other than light troops. If a surprise takes place they are fully equal to the business, if it does not numbers will avail little."

The commander-in-chief then goes on to impress upon Wayne the necessity of taking precautions to preserve secrecy, and even speaks in detail of the

hour when the attack should be made, recommending
"that the troops should move on the works at midnight rather than at the morning dawn." He concludes
by saying to General Wayne that these are, in his
opinion, the principles that should govern him in his
operations; but, after telling him that he relies absolutely on his judgment, he gives him "full liberty to
vary the plan of attack as the circumstances of the
hour may require."

This letter of instructions of General Washington has
often been printed, and it shows how he, in this as in all
his other military enterprises, pointed out with pains-
taking accuracy to his subordinates every detail of the
work to be done. It is equally remarkable as a proof
of the confidence which he reposed in Wayne when
difficult operations were to be undertaken. He dwells,
it will be observed, on the minutest particulars of the
movement, as if a careful observance of each was essential to the success of the operations in which the
Light Infantry Corps was to engage. Although, with
that modesty which was one of his strongest peculiari-
ties, he left to Wayne full liberty to modify his plans,
yet such was the accuracy with which he sketched the
work of the troops that Wayne found it unnecessary
to make any change, except, as will appear, in an unimportant detail, when it came to the actual assault.
This change, by the way, Washington calls, in his official
report, an "improvement on his own plan." The plan
adopted, then, was substantially that of the commander-
in-chief himself.

On the 14th of July Washington permitted Wayne
to make the assault on the next night should he think

the circumstances favorable. On the next day Wayne, in company with Colonels Butler and Febiger, made a last reconnoissance, when it was determined to add to the plan suggested by General Washington "a second attack," as Wayne called it, which, as he writes to the general, "is the only alteration from yours of the 10th." In the buoyancy of his spirit he concludes his last despatch to his chief in these hopeful words: "I am pleased at the prospect of the day, and have the most happy presages of the fortune of the night." He enclosed in his letter a copy of his "order of battle," as he called it, or his instructions for the assault.

The regiments must move forward in absolute silence; no one, on any pretence, to leave the ranks (to preserve secrecy), on penalty of being at once put to death by the officer in charge.[1] Arrived at the foot of the hill, Colonel Febiger was to form his regiment in a solid column of half-platoon front, Colonel Meigs to follow immediately after Febiger, and Major—afterwards General—Hull (in the absence of Colonel Putnam, on duty at Constitution Island) in the rear of Meigs. These were to form the right column of attack. The left column was formed in the same way under Colonel Richard Butler, with Major Murfrees, of North Carolina, in the rear.

Each column was to be preceded by a detachment of one hundred and fifty "picked and determined men," that on the right to be commanded by Colonel Fleury (a French officer who had done much gallant service

---

[1] This was no vain threat. While the troops were preparing for the assault, one unfortunate stepped out of the ranks to load his musket. He was at once run through by one of the officers.

during the war), that on the left by Major Jack Steward of Maryland. Each was to send forward on his march an officer and twenty men a little in advance, whose business it should be to secure the sentries and remove the *abatis* and obstructions for the column to pass through. These parties of twenty men, known in military parlance as "the forlorn hope," held the post where the danger was greatest, but where the chance of acquiring glory in case of survival was most certain. When the left column reached a certain point, Murfrees was to separate from it, and open a furious fire on the front of the works, in order to draw the attention of the enemy from the flanking columns. The right and left columns were to capture the outlying pickets, and, attacking the defenders, force their way over and around the *abatis* and enter the interior of the fort by the sallyport, driving the enemy before them.

The battalion of light horse under Major Henry Lee had been ordered to follow the expedition as a *corps de réserve*. Colonel Ball's regiment of infantry had been moved forward from Rose's farm to support the column should support become necessary, and as cover to the whole the brigade commanded by General Muhlenberg was advanced to a convenient position.

The troops marched during the evening of the 15th of July from Sandy Beach to Stony Point, a distance of nearly fourteen miles, over country roads so exceedingly bad and narrow that for a large part of the distance they were obliged to move in Indian file. They formed in half-platoons at the bottom of the hill, each column preceded by a detachment of one hundred and fifty men, and that again by the "forlorn hope," consisting of twenty men, as a vanguard. These two "forlorn hopes" were led by two young Pennsylvania lieutenants, that on the right being in charge of Lieutenant Knox of the Ninth Regiment, and that on the left in command of Lieutenant Gibbons of the Sixth; Major Jack Steward of Maryland commanded the advanced guard on the left, Colonel Fleury on the right, where Wayne in person directed the column, "spear in hand," Major Murfrees being in the centre. This was their formation close by the foot of the hill at half-past eleven o'clock, when, silent but determined and full of ardor and enterprise, they prepared to undertake the most perilous feat of the war. At that time Wayne went to a house close by. While they were preparing his supper he wrote the following characteristic letter to his dear and trusted friend Sharp Delany.[1] It is clear from its tenor that he did not expect to survive the assault, but his handwriting is as unshaken, and his faith in the cause as triumphant, as if no other sentiment than an ardent desire to do his duty to his country without regard to consequences stirred him. General Wayne's letter probably echoed the feeling of all under him.

> SPRINGSTEEL'S 11 o'clock P.M.
> 15 July 1779, near the
> hour & scene of carnage

DEAR DELANY,—This will not meet your eye until the writer is no more. The enclosed papers I commit [in their rough state] to your charge that in case any ungenerous reflections may hereafter drop from illiberal minds my friend may be enabled to defend the Charac-

---

[1] Delany was not Wayne's brother-in-law, as Mr. Dawson says. He had married the sister of Colonel Robinson, whose wife and Wayne's wife were sisters.

ter & Support the honor of the man who loved him, & who fell in the defence of his Country and of the rights of mankind.

You have often heard me default the Supineness & unworthy torpidity into which Congress were lulled and that it was my opinion that this would be a Sanguinary Campaign in which many of the choicest Spirits and much of the best blood in America would be lost owing to the parsimony and neglect of Congress.

If ever any prediction was true it is this, and if ever a great and good man was Surrounded with a choice of difficulties it is General Washington. I fear the Consequences, & See clearly that he will be impelled to make other attempts and Efforts to save his Country that his numbers will not be adequate to, and that he also may fall a Sacrifice to the folly & parsimony of our WORTHY RULERS.

I know that friendship will induce you to attend to the education of my little son & daughter. I fear that their mother will not survive this Stroke. Do go to her & tell her her Children claim her kindest offices & protection.

My best and Sincerest wishes to Mrs Delany & family and to all friends. I am called to Sup, but where to breakfast, either within the enemy's lines in triumph or in the other World! Then farewell my best and dearest friend and believe me to the last moment

Yours most Sincerely

ANTH'Y WAYNE.

At half-past eleven the word to advance was given; the right column diverged to the south for the purpose of passing the swamp and reaching the beach at the foot of the hill, and at the same time the left, under Colonel Butler, crossed the creek for the purpose of seizing the post of a picket of the enemy and assaulting the right flank of the fortification. Major Murfrees, between these two columns, advanced up the slope. The right, or column led by General Wayne in person, was obliged, in order to reach the *abatis*, to wade through water two feet deep, and this somewhat delayed the movement. Meantime, Murfrees began, as a feint, a tremendous

firing of musketry. This, of course, aroused the garrison, who in a very short time were at their stations,
striving to repel the assault with grape and musketry.
This was the crisis of danger for the assailants. The
forlorn hope of each column rushed forward to perform
the duty assigned to it, that of cutting away the *abatis*
and removing the obstructions which stood in the way
of the advance of their comrades. So fierce and terrible was the fight at this point that of the twenty men
detailed for this service on the left under Lieutenant
Gibbons seventeen were killed or wounded in the
assault.

It is significant of the kind of duty which these men
performed in this night's work that they should have
been called "the forlorn hope." Yet such was the
martial ardor which animated those who were engaged
in the expedition, and such was the ambition on the part
of the subaltern officers to reach distinction by leading the party which should force this "imminent deadly
breach," that it was necessary to select its leader by lot,
so numerous were the applicants who aspired to the
honor of the command.

The double row of *abatis* on the right seems to have
been more readily disposed of than that on the left,
where, as we have seen, resistance was overcome only
after a terrible slaughter.

The first *abatis* was turned by the column of Colonel Febiger moving along the beach under the immediate direction of General Wayne, "spear in hand."
Just as the column had climbed over this obstruction,
a musket-shot coming from a body of men on the hill
above, who were taunting the assailants and shouting

imprecations on "the rebels" as they advanced, struck
General Wayne, and inflicted a scalp-wound about
two inches long. He immediately fell, and was for a
short time dazed and stunned. Quickly recovering his
senses, however, he raised himself on one knee and
shouted, "Forward, my brave fellows, forward!" and
then, turning to his aides-de-camp, Captains Fishbourne
and Archer, he begged them to carry him to the interior
of the fort, where he wished to die should his wound
prove mortal. The men, hearing that their commander
had been mortally wounded, dashed forward, climbing
the rocks with bayonets ready to charge, and bore
down all further opposition. Colonel Fleury, who led
the right column, soon reached the flag-staff on the
bastion and hauled down the English standard. He
was the first to enter the fort, and he was quickly followed by two sergeants of the Virginia and one of the
Pennsylvania regiments, all of whom had been severely
wounded. So accurately had the movement for storming the works been timed, and so perfectly had the
plans and orders been carried out, that both columns
of assault, as well as Major Murfree's's two companies,
met almost at the same time in the interior of the fort.
They encountered, as they advanced, a persistent fire
of grape and musketry. Not a shot was fired by the
assailants (except by the men of Murfree's's companies,
whose firing was intended as a feint). All those killed
by the Americans, and they amounted to sixty-three
(the same number as had been killed by General Grey
at the so-called Paoli massacre), were despatched by
the bayonet. As soon as the attacking columns met
each other in the fort, Colonel Fleury, feeling that

resistance was at an end, shouted, in broken English, "The fort is ours!" the watchword previously agreed upon. The surrender of the fort was announced to Washington in the following note:

STONY POINT, 16 July 2 A.M.

DEAR GEN'L,—The fort & garrison with Col. Johnston are ours. Our officers & men behaved like men who are determined to be free.

Yours most sincerely,

ANTH'Y WAYNE.

GEN'L WASHINGTON.

The triumphant shout of the advancing party was taken up by the troops as they rushed on, crushing all hope of resistance on the part of the garrison. With this shout were mingled the cries of the soldiers, especially of the New York Loyalists, who a short half-hour before had defied their assailants to come on, "Mercy, dear Americans, mercy!" Although no such cry had been heeded at Paoli, Wayne made use of his returning strength to stay the arm of vengeance as soon as resistance had ceased. It is said that not a man was killed who begged for quarter. No time, of course, was lost in turning the cannon at Stony Point on Verplanck's and on the ships in the river. Two flags and two standards were captured, the latter those of the Seventeenth Regiment. The total number of prisoners taken at Stony Point was five hundred and forty-three, and the number of the English killed was sixty-three: that of their wounded is not given. The American loss was fifteen non-commissioned officers and privates killed, and eighty-three officers and privates wounded. It is worth remarking that General Wayne in his official report makes no mention of his wound.

Although the capture of the fort was a surprise to friend and enemy alike, its commander, Colonel Johnston, always insisted that he had not been taken by surprise, but that every man was at his post when the assault was made. The more glory for the assailants.

The successful attack upon Stony Point by General Wayne made a prodigious sensation throughout the country, and congratulations poured in upon him from every quarter. People seemed at a loss which most to admire, the extreme brilliancy of the courage which had led him to undertake so perilous a feat as the assault on Stony Point, the perfect coolness and self-command which he had exhibited when conducting it, the skill with which every detail, even the most minute, had been arranged, or the accuracy with which every part of his plan seemed fitted to the rest. The perfect success which had attended the whole business, the proofs which he had given of the possession of that fine temper of the true patriot, who counts as nothing personal danger if by exposing himself to it he can serve his country,—from whatever side this exploit was viewed it was regarded, amidst much that was calculated at that time to depress and discourage those who loved their country, as a unique proof that that country still possessed some men among her soldiers whose ideal was knightly valor. The immediate material gain by the possession of Stony Point was insignificant, for the post was a short time afterwards abandoned, but its moral effect in strengthening the tone of public feeling and the army was incalculable.

The congratulations partook of the character of the

men who sent them, but there was a universal chorus of joy and praise.   On the 16th of July Washington issued a general order "congratulating the army on the success of the troops under General Wayne, who last night, with the Corps of Light Infantry, surprised and took the enemy's post at Stony Point with the whole garrison."   On the 21st of July, in his despatch to Congress, the general-in-chief says, "To the encomiums he [General Wayne] has deservedly bestowed upon the officers and men under his command, it gives me pleasure to add that his own conduct through the whole of this arduous enterprise merits the warmest approbation of Congress.   He improved upon the plan recommended by me, and executed it in a manner that does signal honor to his judgment and bravery.   In a critical moment of the assault he received a flesh wound in the head with a musket ball, but continued leading on his men with unshaken firmness."

Congress immediately on receipt of the news of the capture of Stony Point adopted unanimously resolutions thanking General Wayne for his brave, prudent, and soldierly conduct, including in its thanks all Wayne's forces, specifying particularly Colonel Fleury and Major Steward, Lieutenants Gibbons and Knox, and Mr. Archer, an aide-de-camp to the general, and commending the coolness, discipline, and intrepidity exhibited by the troops on the occasion.   It was ordered that a gold medal commemorative of his gallant conduct should be presented to General Wayne, and silver medals to Colonel Fleury and Major Steward respectively, and that Messrs. Gibbons, Knox, and Archer should be appointed captains in the army by brevet.   His old

MEDAL VOTED BY CONGRESS FOR THE CAPTURE OF STONY POINT.

commander, General Schuyler, wrote to him, "It is not the least part of my satisfaction to learn that you conducted the expedition, and I most sincerely congratulate you on the increase of honor which you have acquired." General St. Clair, whose relations with Wayne were, as we have seen, somewhat strained, sent him his "cordial congratulations." "It is an event that makes a very great alteration in the situation of affairs, and must have important consequences, and more glorious from its being effected with little loss. It is, in short, the completest surprise I ever heard of." Even his old enemy Charles Lee, who had ventured, as Wayne supposed, to doubt his conduct and bravery at Monmouth, and had in consequence been challenged by Wayne to fight a duel, which was yet in suspense, spoke the genuine feeling of his heart when he wrote, "I do most sincerely declare that your action in the assault of Stony Point is not only the most brilliant, in my opinion, through the whole course of this war on either side, but that it is one of the most brilliant I am acquainted with in history,—upon my soul, the assault of Schweidnitz by Marshal Laudon I think inferior to it. I wish you, therefore, most sincerely, joy of the laurels you have so deservedly acquired, and that you may long live to wear them." To the same effect wrote Generals Greene, Gates, and La Fayette. Indeed, this is one of the few actions of *éclat* in military history concerning which popular opinion and professional opinion coincided. No adverse criticism was ever made in the army on the conduct of General Wayne in the storming of Stony Point.

The voice of his friends and of the public outside

the army was loud in praise of his gallant conduct. Dr. Rush wrote to him, "There was but one thing wanting in your late successful attack upon Stony Point to complete your happiness, and that is—the wound you received should have affected your *hearing,*—for I fear you will be stunned through those organs with your own praises." Sharp Delany, to whom the general had announced his probable death in the assault on the fort, sends him "the sincere congratulations of a friend on your safety and success. They go to you with ten-fold pleasure as I know you are determined on every opportunity to raise the reputation of your country's arms. I know you are determined to do this without any thought of self, and therefore fear much for my friend. . . . Every heart here is filled with a due sense of your bravery and the service you have done your country." The President of Pennsylvania, General Reed, wrote him a private note in which he says, "It is not the Surprise of a post or the Capture of 500 men which pleases me so much as the manner and the address with which it has been executed. You have played their own game upon them, and eclipsed the glory of the English bayonet of which we have heard so much." The Assembly of Pennsylvania, even if it had been somewhat unmindful of the wants of its own troops, claimed a share in the glory which they and their leader had achieved. It will be observed how warmly it praised their humanity.

IN GENERAL ASSEMBLY OF PENN'A.

October 10, 1779.
Resolved, That the thanks of this House be given to General Wayne and to the Officers & Soldiers of the Penn'a line for the

courage & conduct displayed by them in the attack on Stony Point, the honor they have reflected on the State to which they belong, the Clemency they showed to those in their power in a Situation, when by the laws of war, & Stimulated by resentment occasioned by the remembrance of a former Massacre, they would have been justified in putting to death every one of the garrison, will transmit their names with honor to the latest posterity & show that true bravery & humanity are inseparable.

Unanimously confirmed by the Supreme Executive Council.

Gérard, the French Minister, writes on 27th July, 1779, to Steuben, " Nothing in my opinion is more just, my dear Baron, than the eulogy you bestow upon the expedition against Stony Point. Plan, Execution, Courage, discipline, Address, energy, in short the most rare qualities were found united there, and I am convinced that the Action will much elevate the ideas of Europe about the military qualities of the Americans. I have sent an express to Baltimore to look out for a vessel which may immediately carry the news to France. As to General Wayne I believe we both entertain the same opinion of him."

General Greene writes on the same day to his wife that " Steuben thought that this gallant action would fix the character of the commanding officer in any part of the world."

The surprise of many people outside the garrison at Stony Point at its capture was almost as great as that of the garrison itself, although of a different kind. Both in and out of the army there had always been an impression produced by such men as Charles Lee and Gates that American soldiers were totally unfit to cope in the open field with an equal number of trained and disciplined English troops, and with still less hope of success when they were behind intrenchments. It will be remembered that in the previous year, just before the battle at Monmouth, fifteen general officers out of seventeen gave it as their opinion in a council of war that it would not be safe to attack the retreating British army, and that it should be permitted to escape with its long baggage-train without molestation. Neither Washington nor Wayne held this opinion, and the battle of Monmouth proved that they were right, and that the army that fought there was a totally different body from what it had been before its instruction in tactics by Von Steuben at Valley Forge. Still, there were many doubters, and probably no general officer could have been found at that time save Wayne who would have undertaken with any hope of success the perilous enterprise of capturing the enemy in his stronghold. The assault on Stony Point was an operation which every one admitted required for its successful achievement on the part of the assailants qualities of discipline and valor far greater than those needed in ordinary military operations. Wayne, however, as he was in the habit of saying, "knew his soldiers, and they knew him," and nothing which soldiers had ever achieved seemed to them too formidable for him to undertake with a good hope of success. The result was, as we have seen, the success of an enterprise more bold in its conception and more dangerous in its execution than any which had been hitherto undertaken on this continent. The history of the scaling of the Heights of Abraham by Wolfe has been consecrated in British song and story, and Wolfe has a most conspicuous shrine in the Valhalla as one of the great heroes of the English race, and yet what in point of difficulty and danger were the climbing of those heights and the subsequent capture of Quebec to a night assault on the garrison at Stony Point without the use of fire-arms, that garrison being protected by redoubts and earthworks and defending themselves by musketry and a formidable artillery?   No wonder that Washington told Wayne, when he was about to embark on this enterprise, that in such an extremity "success depended not so much upon the numbers as upon the fortitude of the men."

The great condition of success on such occasions, as we have said, is a union of discipline and valor.   Such a combination has always been the ideal of the highest military efficiency, and it has been reached in other armies by incentives to action quite different from those which controlled the soldiers of the Revolution.   We do not, of course, mean the blind obedience which is the result of a stern discipline, and which moulds men into mere machines for executing the orders of their leader, whatever those orders may be.   In modern times motives of a different kind appeal to the martial instincts of the soldier.   Take, for instance, the combat at the bridge of Lodi in 1796, as an illustration (to speak only of modern times), where the French army, under the guidance of Bonaparte, forced the passage of the bridge under a murderous fire by the Austrians, which threatened the life of every assailant, but where no one hesitated for a moment to advance.   This has always been regarded as a singularly heroic act, and much of Napoleon's early prestige was due to his having led in the assault at that time.   But it must

not be forgotten that in that day military glory was the
ambitious dream of every Frenchman. The meanest
soldier in the Army of Italy was in his own opinion
and in that of his countrymen a far more important
personage than the richest banker of Paris. He felt
and acted in the hour of supreme danger as if he carried a marshal's bâton in his knapsack. So, again,
take the siege of St. Sebastian in Spain in 1813, where
the "forlorn hope" of the British army rushed forward
to meet almost certain destruction while scaling the
walls of that fortress. When we seek the motive of
so prodigal and reckless an exposure of life, we recall
the traditions of heroic deeds illustrating the history of
certain regiments which were cherished with peculiar
pride, and which formed a powerful incentive to gallant
action in the hour of danger. We find in these motives
the source of a powerful *esprit de corps*, which has
driven English soldiers forward where the danger of
death has been greatest, but where all fear has been
overcome by a thirst for glory in the individual and by
pride in the reputation of the regiment. Motives such
as these are familiar in military history as leading to
great achievements, but none of them seem in any
degree to have actuated our Revolutionary soldiers,
although it is possible that some of the officers may
have been occasionally stimulated by a love of military
glory. Our soldiers did not form a distinct military
class, as elsewhere. There were probably few who
cared for promotion in the army, and still fewer who
were moved by what may be called professional pride.
Our soldiers did not come from that class who could
not find any other employment in life than soldiering;

on the contrary, there probably was no private man in the ranks who would not have bettered his material condition by leaving the army. They knew that there could be no permanent military establishment here as in other countries, with its aristocratic hierarchy, its social pre-eminence, and its class ascendency. As citizens they would probably have been the first to resist the creation of an army like those of other nations, for they knew, none better, that, with many noble uses, a standing army had been found elsewhere to be the greatest danger to that liberty of the citizen for which they were contending. Such an exploit as that of Wayne would have made him in England a peer with high rank and large money rewards, and have given him, in case he had fallen, a monument at St. Paul's. Here it did not even promote him to be a major-general. The truth is, the army was composed of men who were citizens before they were soldiers, whose education and habits had taught them that they were fighting not for mere military distinction and reputation, for which they cared little, but for the supremacy of law. Such men had but one motive to support them in engaging cheerfully and with determination in an enterprise so perilous as the attack on Stony Point. This great exploit is to be looked upon less as a display of the military genius of Wayne or of the intrepidity of his followers than as an example of what men who have had none of the training of European soldiers, and who are not moved by dreams of military glory, can do when called upon to face extremest danger under the promptings of sternest duty.

Many people when they speak of Stony Point remember that the attack upon it was led by a man who bore during a portion of the war the name of "Mad Anthony," and whatever was perilous about the enterprise, and about others of a similar kind in which he was engaged, they explain by supposing that their leader was a reckless madman. What has been said concerning Wayne's character and career has been said to little purpose if it does not prove that in all his military qualities he was directly the opposite to the rash, heedless, and dashing officer whom he is sometimes represented to have been. Without discussing here the question of his military genius and capacity, it may suffice to consider how it was regarded by Washington himself.

We have seen that, although he was only a brigadier-general during the war, he was always intrusted by Washington with the separate command of a division, or of large detachments, on special service of importance. He was always consulted by the general before he undertook any such movements, and although Wayne differed in opinion very often from the other generals, almost always advocating "active" measures while they did not think them prudent, Washington never lost confidence in him, but always estimated at their true value his soldierly qualities; nor was there ever an action in which he was engaged where he was blamed for any rash or imprudent movement. He was alert, active, vigilant, and these qualities sometimes enabled him to snatch victory from the jaws of defeat, when those who lacked the energy which stirred his blood faltered. When "the war-blast sounded in his ears" he was, it is true, eager and impetuous, his whole soul absorbed in the work on hand, absolutely fearless of personal risk where exposure might bring victory and success to his troops, but never foolhardy nor reckless, and sparing of the lives of his soldiers in the hour of the fiercest battle. " His impetuosity, like that of Paul of Tarsus," says Mr. Dawson, " has been mistaken for madness by some of those who witnessed its effects, but, like the madness of St. Paul, that of Mad Anthony Wayne, so called, was only the outpouring of an earnest, an honest, and a philanthropic heart."

It was also his constant care of his soldiers which won their confidence and was the cause of their strong attachment to him. It enabled him to bring the Pennsylvania line, as long as it was treated fairly and justly by the State authorities, to a condition of efficiency and discipline which made it, in his opinion, the *élite* of the army.

After all, he was not called "Mad Anthony" until 1781, and not then because he was recognized as a *beau sabreur* or a dashing dragoon. The way in which he happened to gain that *sobriquet* is a curious illustration of the manner in which certain nicknames become fastened upon illustrious personages. It seems, according to Mr. Moore, in his Life of Wayne, that one "Jemmy the Rover," as he was called, was attached to Wayne's camp in the year 1781, and with him originated the cognomen of "Mad Anthony." The real name of "Jemmy" is not given, but he was an Irishman, and regularly enlisted in the Pennsylvania line. He was subject to fits of insanity, or at least claimed to be so, but probably these were not of a very marked type, for he was employed frequently by Wayne as a spy, and he always returned from the British lines with correct and important information. At times, however, he was noisy and troublesome, and on one occasion he was ordered to the guard-house. On his way thither he suddenly halted, and asked the sergeant of the guard by whose orders he had been arrested. By those of the general, he was told. After a few hours he was released, and he then inquired whether Anthony (the name he gave General Wayne) was "mad" (meaning angry) or "in fun" when he was placed under arrest. He was told that the general was much displeased with his disorderly conduct, and that if it occurred again he would not only be confined but would receive twenty-nine lashes well laid on. "Then," exclaimed Jemmy, "Anthony is *mad!* Farewell to you; clear the coast for the Commodore, 'Mad Anthony's' friend."

General Wayne announced to the commander-in-chief the capture of Stony Point in the following despatch :

General Wayne to General Washington.

STONY POINT, 17th July 1779.

SIR,—I have now the honor of giving your Excellency a full and particular acct of the Reduction of this post by the light troop under my Command.

On the 15th Instant at 12 OClock we took up our line of March from Sandy Beach distant about 14 Miles from this place—the roads being exceeding bad & narrow & having to pass over high Mountains & thro' such deep Morasses and difficult defiles that we were Obliged the greatest part of the way to move in single files,—at 8 OClock in the evening the van arrived at a *Mr. Springsteels* within one Mile & a half of the enemy's lines & formed into columns as fast as they came up agreeable to the Order of Battle herewith transmitted (vide Order)— Col'l Febiger's & Col. Meigs's Regiments with Major Hull's detatchment formed the Right Column—Col. Butler's Regiment and Major Murfrees' two Companies the Left.

The troops remained in this position until several of the principal

Officers with myself had returned from Reconnoitring the works,—
at half after Eleven (being the hour fixed on) the whole moved forward—the van of the Right was composed of One hundred & fifty
volunteers properly Officered with fixed Bayonets and Unloaded
Muskets under the Command of Lieut. Col. Fleury preceded by
twenty picked men headed by a Vigilant Officer to remove the
Abbatis & Other Obstructions.

The Van of the Left consisted of One Hundred Volunteers also
with fixed Bayonets & Unloaded Muskets under the Conduct of
Major Steward—these were likewise preceded by twenty men under
a Brave & Determined Officer.

At 12 OClock the assault was to begin on the Right & left flanks
of the Enemy's Works & Major Murfrees to amuse them in front,—
but from the Obstructions thrown in our way & a deep Morass surrounding their whole front and overflowed by the tide rendering the
approaches more difficult than at first apprehended, it was about
twenty minutes after twelve before the assault began—previous to
which I placed myself at the Head of Febiger's Regiment or Right
Column & gave the troops the most pointed Orders not to attempt
to fire, but put their whole dependance on the Bayonet—which was
most faithfully & Literally Observed,—neither the deep Morass, the
formidable & double rows of abbatis or the high & strong works in
front & flank could damp the ardor of the troops—who in the face
of a most tremendous and Incessant fire of Musketry & from Artillery loaded with shells & Grape-shot forced their way at the point
of the Bayonet thro' every Obstacle,—both Columns meeting in the
Center of the Enemy's works nearly at the same Instant.

Too much praise cannot be given to Lieut. Colonel Fleury (who
struck the enemy's standard with his own hand) & to Major Steward
who Commanded the Advance parties, for their brave & prudent
Conduct; Colonels Butler Meigs & Febiger conducted themselves
with that coolness, bravery & perseverance that ever will ensure success. Lieut. Col. Hay was wounded in the thigh bravely fighting at
the head of his Battalion— I should take up too much of your Excellency's time was I to particularise every Individual who deserves
it for his bravery on this Occasion, however I must acknowledge myself Indebted to Major Lee for the frequent & useful Intelligence he
gave me & which Contributed much to the success of the enterprise—

& it's with the greatest pleasure I acknowledge to you that I was supported in the attack by all the Officers & soldiers to the utmost of
my wishes & Return my thanks to the Officers & Privates of Artillery
for their alertness in turning the Cannon against the enemy's works
at Verplank's point & their shiping which slipt their Cables and Immediately droped down the River.

I should be wanting in gratitude was I to omit mentioning Capt.
Fishbourn & Mr. Archer my two Aids De Camp, who on every
Occasion shewed the greatest Intrepidity & Supported me into the
works after I had received my wound in passing the last Abbatis.—

Enclosed are Returns of the killed & wounded belonging to the Light
Corps, as also that of the enemy together with the number of prisoners
taken, likewise of the Ordnance & Stores found in the Garrison.

I had forgot to Inform your Excellency that previous to the attack
I had drawn General Muhlenburg into my rear who with three
hundred men of his Brigade took post on the opposite side of the
Marsh, was to be in readiness either to support us, or to cover a Re-
treat in case of accident & have not the least doubt of his faithfully
& Effectually executing either had there been an Occasion for it.

The Humanity of our brave soldiery who scorned to take the lives
of vanquished foes calling for mercy reflects the highest Honor on them
& accounts for so few of the Enemy being killed on the occasion.

I am not fully satisfied with the manner in which I have mentioned
Lieut. Gibbons of the 6th & Lieut. Knox of the 9th Penns'a Regiment
the two gentlemen who led the advanced parties of each Column—
the first had 17 men killed & wounded out of twenty—the latter
though not quite so unfortunate in that respect was nevertheless
equally exposed—they both behaved with an Intrepidity & address
that would have been a Credit to the oldest soldier.

I have the honor to be with singular Respect,
Your Excellency's most Obt. & very
Hum'l Serv't
ANT'Y WAYNE.

HIS EXCELLENCY
GEN'L WASHINGTON.[1]

[1] The official despatches announcing the capture of Stony Point, except that of Wayne himself, and the correspondence which grew out of
the events connected with it, will be found in the Appendix, No. III.

CHAPTER VI.

IF Wayne had counted upon the Continental com-
missaries for a more regular and abundant supply of
food for the Light Infantry Corps than had been provided by the State authorities for the troops of the
Pennsylvania line, he was mistaken in his calculations.
The curse of maladministration seems to have afflicted
all those with whom General Wayne had anything to
do, whether the officials were those of the State or of
the Continent. Thus, on the 4th of October, 1779, he
thus writes to the commissary of subsistence: "The
situation of this corps requires the utmost exertion
in your department to prevent mutiny and desertion."
From the answer it seems, among other excuses, that
the teams were idle, the wagon-master being absent in
search of substitutes for those who had deserted ; and
this not in the wilderness, but in a comparatively
populous district in the State of New York.

The numbers of the corps seem to have kept up
pretty well, however, only twenty-six rank and file and
fifteen non-commissioned officers having been absent
on the 15th of October, 1779,—a fact which perhaps
may be taken to prove how much pride the soldiers
must have had in belonging to so distinguished a body,
and how admirable was their discipline. Still, in November Wayne is compelled to complain again of the
incapacity or neglect of the commissary of the Light

Corps, as it was at that time destitute of articles essential to its comfort. In the same month one hundred and twenty men of his command are reported as quite barefoot, and in the latter part of December, General Washington having directed that the Virginia line should proceed to Philadelphia, in obedience to an order of Congress, General Wayne is obliged to reply, "Colonel Febiger will march to-morrow at 8 A.M., but for want of shoes he must carry a great many of his people in wagons." No wonder that in the last order issued by General Wayne before disbanding the corps and directing them to return to the "lines" of their respective States he should speak of the accumulated distress caused by the extremity of cold, hunger, and nakedness which had rendered the troops desperate. Why it should have been determined to break up an organization so distinguished as the Light Infantry Corps, after it had rendered such gallant service, at the close of one campaign, it is difficult to understand. The action of Congress in detaching one of its most serviceable regiments (the Virginia regiment) may have rendered such a step necessary. Be that as it may, the officers of the corps parted from Wayne with sincere regret and many expressions of their good wishes. The officers of the regiment from the Virginia line, the field officers of the corps, and those commanding the artillery, as will appear from the following letters, joined in expressing their respect and affection for their commander. Wayne, as soon as arrangements for the disbandment of his troops were carried out, asked the commander-in-chief (February 4, 1780) to be employed in any capacity he might think proper.

SECOND RIVER December 9th 1779.

DEAR SIR,—The Officers of the Virginia Line, who have had the honor of being commanded by you in the Light Infantry beg leave to return you their sincere Thanks for the Repeated Marks of Esteem & Politeness you have express'd towards them.—

They entertain the highest Veneration & Respect for your Character both as a Military Officer and a Gentleman.

Under these circumstances we feel the greatest Regret especially at so short Notice to be separated from a Corps we love and a General we honour.—

Accept therefore Dear Sir these Sentiments of our Esteem, and believe us, after wishing you every future happiness, Success & prosperity to be with the most Cordial Affection and Respect

Your most obedient and Most humble servants.

At the Request and in Behalf of the V'a officers

CHRISTIAN FEBIGER Colonel.

THE HONORABLE
BRIGADIER GENERAL WAYNE.

LIGHT INFANTRY CAMP
SECOND RIVER 9th Dec 1779

DEAR SIR,—The approbation of my Conduct by a Corps so respectable as the Officers of the Virginia *Light Infantry*, must Inevitably afford the sincerest pleasure;—that attention which they are pleased to attribute to politeness, was the effect of their own *Merit*, which will always Insure the Esteem of the General who has the honor to Command them.

Permit me therefore to return my most grateful thanks to them & you for this mark of your Respect, & believe me to be with singular Esteem

Your most obt & very
Humble Servant
ANT'Y WAYNE.

COL. FEBIGER
Comm. of the Virginia Light Infantry.

LIGHT INFANTRY CAMP SECOND RIVER
Dec. 31st 1779.

SIR,—In behalf of the officers of Artillery I am to assure you that it's with the greatest reluctance they view the approaching

period of a separation from the Command of a General whose
particular attention, & politeness to them demand their most grateful
acknowledgments—

Your conduct, & acknowledged good Character as an officer &
Gentleman must ever meet with the approbation of those who have
the honour of serving under you, and altho a separation will now
take place, yet to look forward, we have a hope that at a future day,
we shall again be happy enough to meet with that General who we
are confident will lead us on to glory & crown us with honour

I am with the Gentlemen of this Corps—

Very respectfully

J. PENDLETON.

Officers of the Light Infantry Corps to General Wayne.

LIGHT INFANTRY CAMP

AT SECOND RIVER

Jan'y 1st 1780

SIR,—The close of the Campaign & the dissolution of the Corps
necessarily calls us from under your immediate Command, & in Justice to our own feelings we beg leave to tell you, that our experience
of your abilities as an Officer has justly gaind you that confidence
essentially necessary to ensure success in Military operations.   The
uniform politeness & attention you have paid to all, has endeard
you to every individual under your command ; and has in great
measure been the means of preserving a perfect unanimity & Harmony, seldom seen in a Corps formd by detachments from different
States.

Be assured, Sir, this does not proceed from the Common motives
of adulatory address, but is dictated by the warmest Sentiments of
gratitude, from a Conviction that we are eminently indebted to your
Care for the Happiness we have enjoyd thro the course of this Campaign.   We are with the Highest Respect esteem and affection

Your most obd't Hble Servts—

R. PUTNAM, Col'l L't I

Signd at the *unan-imous* request of the Officers in the Light Infantry.	RICH'D BUTLER Col'l L't I ALBERT CHAPMAN Maj'r Com'd JAS. PENDLETON Cap't Comm. of Light Artillery

LIGHT INFANTRY CAMP SECOND
RIVER 2nd Jan. 1780.

GENTLEMEN,—The pleasure I experience in your approbation of
my Conduct, gives a sensation which words can not express— the
unanimity, Mutual Confidence & friendship which (at this period
of the War) so conspicuously pervades a Corps, formed by Detachments from different States, must produce a conviction to the World,
that we are not to be Conquered, by any Idle notion of a Disunion,
—*nor forced from the field,* but by superior numbers.

The esteem & affection which you are pleased to express for me,
is truly Reciprocal & it's with sincere pleasure I acknowledge that
by your good Conduct & example this Corps has acquired the Distinction it now holds.

The Dissolution of a body of troops with which I have enjoyed so
great a share of happiness, would give me much pain, was I not
confident that those sentiments which have so firmly united the
American Light Infantry (whilst embodied) will not diminish by a
temporary separation.

Permit me therefore to wish you an easy and pleasant March, & a
joyful meeting with your friends & brother Officers in the Line of
the Army, & to assure you that I am with much Esteem

Your most Ob't
& very
Hum'l Servt.
ANT'Y WAYNE.

COLONELS PUTNAM & BUTLER
MAJOR CHAPMAN
CAPT. PENDLETON & the
other Officers of the
Light Corps.

Wayne at once returned to his home in Chester
County, but on the opening of the campaign of 1780
(on the 18th of May) Washington wrote to him, "I
shall be very happy to see you at camp again, and
hope you will, without hesitation, resume your command in the Penn'a line." Wayne rejoined the army

in a few days at Morristown, his movements being probably quickened by a letter from Colonel Johnston from
camp of the 7th of May. In this letter Johnston says,
"Shall I endeavor to paint the manifold sufferings of
the honest soldiery, the distresses of the officers, the
wounded feelings of our illustrious General, and the
complicated misfortunes attending our country in consequence of the state of our finances ?"

At this time Sir Henry Clinton had returned from
the South, and was enlisting Tory refugees with a view
of capturing the military stores deposited at Morristown.
Washington moved towards the Highlands, fearing that
the expedition might be intended to capture the strongholds there. The regular force of the British at New
York was twelve thousand men, in addition to which
they had armed about four thousand refugees. The
American army at the same time was less than three
thousand in number. The British advanced to Spring-
field, in New Jersey, which they burned, but retreated
to their post at Elizabethtown before Wayne, who had
been detached with a brigade to harass them, could
reach them.

The campaign of 1780 began under conditions even
more gloomy and discouraging than that of 1779. The
Pennsylvania troops had dwindled away in the most
extraordinary manner. By the monthly return of September, 1780, there were present in the eleven regiments of foot two thousand and five and absent two
thousand five hundred and eleven ; in other words,
more than one-half of their strength was not present
with the colors, and those who were present formed
about two-thirds of Washington's army. With this

small force he was obliged to march and countermarch between Morristown and West Point, so as to meet any assault which might be made by the British at New York on any point of this long line.

It was apparent that the difficulty with which we had to contend in achieving our independence was mainly a financial one, and that the true path out of the slough of despond into which we had been plunged was not yet discovered. One of Wayne's correspondents, writing in October, evidently thought that the crisis was at hand. He says he "met Steuben at President Reed's, and he thought that the whole army would dissolve by the first of January unless specie could be obtained." Wayne recommended the extraordinary step of suggesting to France that unless she provided specie we should be obliged to give up the contest. "Money," he says, "is now out of the question. The soldiers have not seen a single paper dollar for a long time."

General Washington writes about this time to Hon. Joseph Jones,—

"It does not require with you, I am sure, argument at this late hour to prove that there is no set of men in the United States (considered as a body) that have made the same sacrifices of their interest in the support of the common cause as the officers of the American army—that nothing but a love of their country, of honor, and a desire of seeing their labors crowned with success could possibly induce them to continue one moment in the service, that no officer can live upon his pay, that hundreds, having spent their little all in addition to their scanty public allowance, have resigned because they could no longer support themselves as officers, that numbers are, at this moment, rendered unfit for duty for want of clothing, while the rest are wasting their property and some of them verging fast to the gulph of poverty and distress.—

"TAPPAN, August 13, 1780."

The soldiers had hoped that the presence of a committee of Congress in camp would do something with that body to alleviate their sufferings, but they had been disappointed. "The army," say the committee who visited the camp at the solicitation of Washington and Wayne, "was unpaid for five months; it seldom had more than six days' provision in advance; it was for a number of days on different occasions without meat; it was destitute of forage; medical supplies were exhausted, and in short every department of the army was without money or credit, and the patience of the soldiers was on the point of being exhausted."

In the midst of all these embarrassments the sterling qualities of Wayne's character, not merely as a military leader but also as a devoted patriot, became more and more conspicuous. Surrounded by men clamorous in their complaints that the State had not done its duty towards them, and therefore ready to desert their ranks, and by officers constantly threatening to resign because they were not paid or because they were not satisfied with the rank assigned them, he was always ready to fight the enemy, if there was any prospect of inflicting injury upon them, even while he was engaged in these fruitless disputes with the State authorities and with Congress.

It was determined during the summer to capture a block-house behind Bergen Heights which had been made a place of deposit by the armed refugees of stolen horses and other property the spoils of the neighborhood. Wayne, with the First and Second Pennsylvania Brigades and four pieces of artillery, was sent to attack it.

The following account of this expedition is given in his letter to President Reed :

TOTOWAY 26th July 1780

DEAR SIR,—You have undoubtedly heard of our *tour* to Bergen— but it is a duty which I owe to you, the troops I Commanded & to myself, to make you acquainted with the Objects of that expedition —least envy, Malice, or the tongue of Slander, should attempt to misrepresent that affair— One was to take all the stock out of Bergen Neck, to prevent the Enemy from receiving constant supplies from the Inhabitants out of that Quarter—and in Case of a siege to secure to our own use those Cattle that they would Inevitably carry into New York.   Another was the destruction of a post near Bulls ferry —consisting of a Block House surrounded by a strong stockade and Abbattis Garrisoned by the Refugees & a wretched banditti of Robbers horse thieves &c—

But the Grand Object was to draw the Army which S'r Henry Clinton brought from Charlestown into an Action in ye Defiles of the Mountain in the Vicinity of Fort Lee, where we expected them to Land in order to succour the Refugee post, or to endeavour to cut off our retreat to the Liberty pole & New Bridge ; the apparent object to them was great, and the *lure* had like to take the wished effect—three thousand men Consisting of the flower of the British Army were embarked from Phillips—and stood down the river hovering off the land'g near fort Lee—where the 6th & 7th Penns'a Regiments lay concealed with directions to let them land unmolested (giving me Intelligence of the attempt) & then to meet them in the Gorge of the Defile and with the point of the Bayonet to dispute the pass at every expense of Blood, until the arrival of the first & second Penns'a Brigades when we should put them between three such fires as no human fortitude could withstand—and I may now with safety mention, that it was also designed to divert their attention from a meditated attempt upon Rhode Island, by a Combined attack by Land and Water on the French fleet & Army in that Place ; this has had the effect, by retarding them four days after they had actually embarked upwards of six thousand men for that purpose it will therefore be too late to attempt any thing at this period as the French will be prepared against it—

Inclosed is the orders of the 20th & 23d, to which & to the General's Letter to Congress I must refer you for the particulars; I always had the highest Opinion of the Troop but my most sanguine wishes—fell far short of the real fortitude & bravery, which pervades the whole, even the New Recruits—

I have it in Command from his Excellency to Inform you, that the Uniforms are all blue faced with white he therefore wishes if possible to have as much red or scarlet, sent Immediately on as will face our soldiers Coats—otherwise the officers & men will appear of different Corps—(the facings of the officers scarlet, and the soldiers white)—the other States will be in their proper uniforms it being that fixed for the Eastern States, and with a little clay may be made to appear as buff, which is the facings of New York & Jersey States so that ours will be the only officers whose uniforms will differ from their soldiers—had we the Cloth and Thread, we could in four days alter the facings for the whole line—it is the General's Intention to Clothe them all new before they meet the troops of France—Interim believe me with singular Esteem

Your most Ob't—
Humb'e Servant
ANT'Y WAYNE.

HIS EXCELLENCY
JOSEPH REED ESQ'R.

President Reed to General Wayne.

PHILAD—Aug. 4—1780

DEAR SIR,—I duly received & thank you for your favour of the 26th July inclosing your Orders on the late Excursion to Bergens— They have been spoken of here much to your Honour & with the gallant Behaviour of the Men shew that tho we did not meet with entire success we deserved it—

Neither the Object of the Expedition, nor the Conduct of it was understood fully here at first & as often happens on such Occasions were misrepresented but a few Days & better Information soon set that Matter right—if any Doubts had remained the General's Letter wiped them off tho in some Respects it tended to make the Affair of the Block House a more important Business than it really was— As to the Whispers of Envy & Malevolence & Slander, you must, my dear Sir, submit in common with your Fellow Men to a share of them, as the Tax which merit & Distinction must pay— The World would be too estimable if every Action was judged upon the Principles of Candor & its due Worth assigned it unalloyed by jealousy & Uncharitableness—

In one Respect military Merit is less subject to it than any other —as it has Witnesses & Companions & the Benefits arising to Mankind from a conspicuous Display of it are such that the World is ready to be its Friend for its own Interest. Should you be called as probably you may to any distinguished Rank of Civil Life you will find the Acts of busy wicked men more successful, & not so easily Detected or parried.—Scarce a Week elapses but some wicked Falsehood takes Wing with Respect to us, flutters about and dies— when a new one more palatable & adapted to the State of the Day arises which in its Turn gives way to a fresher. For a Time I felt myself hurt & spent Time & Labour to counteract them but I have long since learned that the best shield is Integrity & truest Remedy Patience. I am informed that there has been much Industry used this Spring & Summer in Camp on this Score & that it is very frequent at this Time— So much Pains taken to lessen me in the Opinion of Mankind while I am pursuing diligently the Interests of my Country with a single disinterested View to its success in this great Cause, fully convinces me that there are some Men who have different Intentions & who fear honest Men in publick Stations— I have at different Periods had my Passions work'd upon, my Interest assailed, splendid Prospects held forth to engage me in the Views of Party & I never experienced the full Weight of Enmity till I had fully declined every Overture of this Nature in such a Manner as left no Hope of Success—

However I trust there is Virtue & Discernment in the World sufficient to support a Man in doing his duty & that I have some Friends who will judge upon Facts not upon Suggestions especially when they come thro so corrupt a Channel.

Farmer has Directions to purchase the red Cloth for the Facings if to be had in Town & they will be forwarded as soon as possible —Lyttle has set out with a supply of stores & a good Stock of Shirts & Overalls—2000 of each which with what gets to you in other Directions will I hope prove a comfortable supply—

Adieu—my best wishes attend you & I beg you to believe me
very much

> Your sincere Friend & Obed.
> Hble Serv't
> Jos. REED—

The enemy asserted that the Americans had been repulsed from the block-house by a small garrison composed of Tory refugees only, and in some scurrilous
verses called "The Cow-Chase," which were widely
distributed, written by the unfortunate Major André a
short time before his capture and execution, the exploits
of Wayne and the other American officers are ridiculed
with a kind of pitying contempt which is very noteworthy. Wayne, whose activity as a successful forager
in New Jersey in the winter of 1778 the enemy could
never forget, and his officers, were lampooned in a way
which betokened the arrogance of the British in treating
their antagonists as men of inferior social condition.

"The Cow-Chase" closes with this significant verse,
—significant indeed, when we recall the sad fate of the
author :

> "And now I've closed my epic strain,
> I tremble as I show it,
> Lest this same warrior-drover, Wayne,
> Should ever catch the poet."

The English government thought the defence of the
block-house so noteworthy that the king sent his personal thanks to the seventy refugees who composed
that garrison. The enemy, according to Wayne, did
not discern the real object of the attack, and he explained the mystery in the letter to President Reed
which we have just given.

General Wayne during the whole summer was untiring in preparing plans for engaging the enemy to advantage. He was not disheartened by the sea of troubles which raged around him, but rather stimulated to adopt new methods of improving the military situation. On the 10th of July he proposes a scheme by which the British army at New York might be taken by surprise, and shortly afterwards he writes to President Reed one of the wisest, most temperate, and at the same time most determined letters in the whole correspondence, urging the necessity of renewed efforts on the part of Pennsylvania to carry on the conflict. It seemed as if the greater the danger the greater his resources, and that he was at his best when the fullest demand was made on his courage and energy.

General Wayne to General Washington.

CAMP AT TOTOWAY 10th July 1780.

SIR,—It was but the evening before the last that I had the honor of first seeing the General state of affairs your Excellency was pleased to lay before the Council of War on the 6th ultimo—which I have given as mature a consideration as time & Circumstances would admit of.

I find by a comparative view of our present force with that of the Enemy, after making proper allowances, for the change of affairs, by the reduction of Charlestown, & the reinforcements already arrived at New York under Sir Harry Clinton that they have a decided majority in their favor, the force of the enemy being nearly 11,000 effective rank & file regular troops, & about five thousand Militia refugees & etc etc in the whole equal to 16,000 Effectives exclusive of Marines & seamen.

The present strength of your army taking in the Garrison of West Point is not more than 7,000 rank & file being reduced (by killed & wounded, expiration of Inlistments, desertion, & other Casualties incident to all armies) at least 1000 men since your last estimate—

so that Sir Harry Clinton has at this period in New York & its vicinity a Land force more than Double your Numbers.

In this estimate I have not taken in any of the recruits or Drafts that are expected from the several States—but from the best Intelligence that I have been able to collect the number that may be expected under that description as a reinforcement to this Army, will not exceed 7,000 men.

I ground this Calculation on the following proportion viz.

New Hampshire	500
Massachusetts	2500
Rhode Island	300
Connecticut	1500
New York	600
New Jersey	600
Penns'a	600
Delaware	200

A very great part of which will be extremely raw troops, & arrive too late to afford an opportunity to reduce them to proper Discipline before they may be called to action— To counterbalance this defect—the tories refugees & Militia with the Enemy will be nearly on a footing in that respect—so that our numbers will then stand as 14,000 to 16,000 which leave a balance in their favor of 2,000 men at least.

But the assurances that his most Christian Majesty and the Court of France have given of their Generous Intention of sending a respectable Land & Naval force to act in conjunction with your Army and entirely under the Influence of American councils, opens the most flattering prospect—which by a proper exertion of the States may be productive of a Glorious Campaign.

To what point we ought to direct our Operations, will require some reflection,—there are three Capital Objects that present themselves, i. e. Canada, New York, & Charlestown.

Admit Canada to be the *first*, we are then to consider, what force will be necessary for us to furnish in addition to the French fleet & army admitting the Navy to consist of Eight sail of the Line with a few frigates, & the Land force of Seven thousand effective rank & file completely provided with all the apparatus for such an Army.—

This force is not adequate to the Reduction of Quebec and its dependencies without the addition of at least three or four thousand men from this army—& those regular standing troops—who if fortunate would also be necessary to remain in Garrison there during the Winter (which could not be expected from the drafts, their time of service terminating in January)—these troops must march by the *Cohoes* & enter Canada near the confluence of the *Sorel* with the St Lawrence— The Difficulty of transporting the Cannon provision & baggage is too Obvious to dwell much upon, for the Enemy possessing the Lake Champlain must reduce us to land carriage for the chief part of our supplies, unless the State of our Magazines will admit of sending a sufficient supply round by the French fleet—we are not to expect the Essential article of Provision in Canada,—for altho' they raise a Considerable quantity of summer wheat—there are not a sufficiency of Mills in that Country to manufacture it into flour nor have they more Cattle than what are absolutely necessary for their own consumption,—these are facts not founded upon tradition or Opinion of others—but from my own knowledge & Observation.

I beg leave also to premise, that we have little to expect from the Defection of the Canadians—those people will be very cautious how they irritate a second time the British, whilst matters remain the least doubtful—especially whilst a powerful army is in the heart of Our own Country, and the probability of the arrival of a Superior fleet from Britain to that of France in the vicinity of Quebec—during a siege that may be procrastinated longer than we expect.

The Intervention of a fleet is also a very serious matter to us— I well recollect the difficulty we experienced in effecting a retreat from that Country in 1776 when we had the full possession of the Lakes ; & have we nothing to apprehend from the exertions of Sir Harry Clinton?—will he remain an Idle spectator at the head of 16,000 men, whilst we are Operating in a distant Country?—will he not rather push his fortune against a Debilitated army, & endeavor to destroy our Magazines, & desolate the Country,—and may he not attempt this with too great a probability of Success?

I am therefore of Opinion that Canada is not the most Eligible object ;—some of these reasons, especially the last, will operate in full force against an attempt for the recovery of Charlestown, until a more favorable opening presents itself.

16

The greatest and most capital Object is New York, an Object worthy the utmost exertions of America, & which from its central position affords an Opportunity of drawing our force to a point with the greatest facility, & without those risks & Disagreeable consequences attendant upon a misfortune either in Canada or Charles Town ;—Could the eyes of this country be once opened to its true Interest—could the States be roused from the unworthy torpidity into which they have sunk—the Reduction of the Garrison of New York & its dependencies would not be attended with much difficulty—but from present appearances I fear our mode of Operation will be very circumscribed—as it will in a great degree be governed by the Numbers we have in the field.

Supposing the Drafts & Recruits to have come, & the French troops formed a junction with the other part of your Army—we may then lay our whole force at about 20,000 Rank & file—this number tho' sufficient to prevent an Incursion—will not be equal to an Investiture.   We therefore can't do with less than 12,000 good Militia in *addition*, & those engaged for a Certain term—not subject to a fluctuation which has too often,—& may again commit us at a very critical period,—and even this force will not be adequate to a Complete Investiture for unless we had two armies—each superior to the whole of our adversaries,—the Enemy by Concentering their force might find an opening to strike us in a Divided state which they dare not attempt if united.

I have not such a knowledge of the Country immediately in the Vicinity of New York as to justify me in giving a Decided Opinion as to the most proper & exact point of attack—that will require a minute & close Inspection,—but from the General knowledge I have of Staten & Long Islands—& the probable strength we may have at the Commencement of our Operations ; I don't think either very Eligible altho' they may have many real as well as apparent advantages—which the Intervention of a fleet from Europe might render very hazardous in the end.

I therefore am of Opinion (grounded upon prudential as well as Military principles) that we ought to begin our Operations against New York Island by the way of [   ] and after Establishing ourselves on that Island & securing a safe retreat in case of Accident—we may as Circumstances present effect a lodgment on Long

Island & take such position as will facilitate the reduction of the Garrison, by a combined attack from different points after securing a proper chain of communication.

I have given this Opinion on the presumption that our whole force will not exceed 30,000 or 32,000 Effectives,—should we fortunately reach as high as 40,000 I would advise two approaches to commence at the same time, i. e. by the way of [   ] & Staten Island.

I have only to add that whatever may be your decision—you may rest assured of the best services of your Excellency's

Most Ob't & Very Humb'l Serv't
ANTH'Y WAYNE.

HIS EXCELLENCY
GENERAL WASHINGTON.

General Wayne to President Reed.

CAMP AT STEENRAPIA
17 Sep 1780

SIR,—At the commencement of this campaign we had the most flattering expectations from the promised succors of his most Christian Majesty as well as from the exertions of these States, but the intervention of a superior fleet to that of our Allies in these seas, the blockade of Brest in which port the second division intended for America is shut up, and the tedious delay, and at length total prevention of operations in the West Indies, together with the recent military check we have experienced in South Carolina, and the deficiency of promised aid & supplies in the United States have materially altered the complexion of affairs.

In this situation I have been called upon to give my opinion in writing of what I think the most advisable mode of conduct or feasible point of operation— The actual arrival of Sir George Rodney with 10 sail of the line at Sandy Hook will when joined by Adm'l Arbuthnot be Equal to between 20 & 26 sail, so that the forces will be nearly on an equality. Hence we have little reason to expect any thing capital taking place—

Could any period be fixed for the arrival of the second division from Brest so as to place our allies in the sovereignty of the seas, I should not be at a loss— But as this is only problematical, or at most eventual, I must acknowledge that I see but a choice of difficulties left to determine upon, among others that of experiencing every extreme of distress at this stage of the campaign for the want of provisions is of the most alarming nature, and would of itself be sufficient to defeat the best plan in the power of a General to design.

When I look to a period fast approaching I discern the most gloomy prospect, distressing objects presenting themselves—and when I consider that the mass of the people who now compose this Army will dissolve by the first of January, except a little corps enlisted for the war, that they are badly paid and worse fed, I dread the consequence, for these melancholy facts may have a fatal influence upon their minds when opposed to a well-appointed, puissant and desolating Army— Should Sir H. Clinton profit by former error, and commence the General, and pour like a Deluge upon a naked country and once more possess your capital, I have but too much ground to dread that by an introduction of civil gov't he would find many, very many adherents and perhaps a greater number of converts than we at present suspect.

I know that you are not to learn that the fidelity of some of the Southern States is much shaken, and that the great proportion of the landed interest in your State would have little objection to submit to the former gov't and I can from my own knowledge (but not without pain) assure you that the Farmers in this State (New York) appear to wish for peace on any terms owing to the mode in which we have been necessitated to ration our troops and forage our horses, which is truly distressing to them, and affords but a very partial relief to us—yet little as it is—it has hitherto prevented the dissolution of this Army—

I know that a true picture of our situation must be very distressing to the mind and hurtful to the eye of a gentleman who from principle, as well as from his station must be deeply interested in the fate of America. Yet it is a duty which as a Citizen and as a Soldier I owe to you, to myself, & to my country to show it in its true colors, and also to assure you that I am not influenced by any apprehensions for my own liberty or Safety. I have fully & deliberately considered every possible vicissitude of fortune. I know that it is not in the power of Britain to subjugate a mind determined to be free. Whilst I am master of my own sword, I am governor of my own fate. I therefore only fear (but greatly fear) for *that* of my country, and would wish to warn her of her danger and point out the only mode that can possibly rescue her from impending ruin.

We have it yet in our power to remedy & correct former mistakes and rise superior to every difficulty and danger. This can only be done by a foreign loan, and by a completion of our regiments. The Eastern States seem fully convinced of their error, and from the best intelligence will exert every power to complete their quotas of troops for the war.

Pennsylvania in this will have greatly the advantage. The levies now in camp are enlisting upon trust. While this spirit is up, I wish we were provided with some hard cash. This is the time to take them. If we wait much longer the termination of their service will be so near, that they will begin to watch for the day when nothing will induce them to enlist. Add to this that these men are now on the spot, that there is no danger of being imposed upon by Deserters, that every man we enlist we are sure of, and that they have acquired some discipline and adroitness in exercise and manœuvring, by the close attention and indefatigable industry of our officers, while they still continue to improve with unwearied zeal.

Very Sincerely

ANT'Y WAYNE.

While beset with these anxieties and embarrassments Wayne encountered a new difficulty, or rather a revival of an old one. The year before, it will be remembered, the officers of the line had been much dissatisfied at the appointment made by Congress of Major Macpherson as a brevet major. In some way, not now easily to be explained, the difficulty was then patched up, but in August, 1780, when a new corps of light infantry was to be organized, Major Macpherson was transferred to it according to his brevet rank. This gave rise to serious trouble among the officers of the line, and they all threatened to resign their commissions if the appointment of Major Macpherson were insisted upon.

We give the correspondence on this subject between Generals Wayne and Irvine with General Washington, which is on many accounts interesting. The design of forming a new Light Infantry Corps in the summer of 1780 was abandoned, and the necessity of settling this thorny question was thus evaded.

Generals Wayne and Irvine to General Washington.

TAPPAN, 10th August 1780.

SIR,—It was not until some time after your Excellency was made acquainted with the very great dissatisfaction which the Majors of the Penns'a line experienced on the appointment of Major Macpherson to a Command in the Light Corps drawn from this state,—that we were informed of the address which they presented to you ;—the moment we discovered the effect that appointment had upon them, every means in our power was used to Conciliate matters,—& we had a flattering prospect from the nice feelings of Major Macpherson, that an opening would be made (by a voluntary resignation) for one of those Gentlemen to supply his place in the *Light Corps*— without hurting the feelings of your Excellency, or entering into an Investigation of the propriety or right of Brevets taking a permanent Command in a *full corps*—drawn from one State during a Campaign.—Upon this Ground we prevailed upon the Majors to hold their Commissions for a few days, until the Army was in a more fixed state, & to give time for cool reason to govern—hoping something might take place in the Interim that would restore harmony & Content,—but the Solemn manner in which we were called upon yesterday morning by the Colonels & Lieu't Colonels on this Occasion convinced us that the Dissolution of the Line would but too probably take place unless the *cause* could be removed—and being requested by them to make a true representation to your Excellency of their feelings & Determination,—we were Induced to wait on you at 12 O'Clock—yesterday, & to communicate *Viva Voce*—what we had in charge from them.

We have at your Excellency's request called upon those Officers to commit their Objections to writing—this they decline, saying that the Majors have already stated them in their address to you, & that they are Influenced by the same feelings and will abide the same fate as their Majors.

We shall not attempt to advocate the matter, or to give an Opinion on the usage or custom of brevet appointments—and altho' an office extremely distressing to us—yet it is a duty which we owe to your Excellency—to our Country—& to ourselves—to *declare*, that unless some happy event Immediately Intervenes—we do not believe it to be in our power to prevent the Resignation of a Corps of Officers, who have upon every Occasion produced a Conviction, that they are second to none in Esteem & attachment to your Excellency, —fidelity to the States,—or prowess in the field.

Interim we have the Honor to be with every Sentiment of respect

Your Excellency's

most Ob't & very

Humb Servt's

ANT'Y WAYNE

WM IRVINE

(Copy)
HIS EXCELLENCY
GEN'L WASHINGTON.

Generals Wayne and Irvine to General Washington.

TAPPAN 11th Aug't 1780 12 O'Clock.

SIR,—We have this moment received your Excellency's favour of this day & shall Immediately communicate it to the Field officers of the line— Could our most sanguine wishes prevail—an Immediate termination would be put to this alarming affair—

But we cannot yet flatter ourselves of any happy effects from the utmost of our exertion—which rest assured will not be wanting on this occasion

We have the honor to be with singular Esteem

Your Excellency's

Most Obed't

Humble Serv'ts

ANTHONY WAYNE.

WM IRVINE.

(A Copy)

Generals Wayne and Irvine to the Field Officers of the Pennsylvania Line.

TAPPAN 12th August 1780
6 o'Clock P.M.

GENTLEMEN,—Let us entreat you by the sacred ties of Honor, friendship, & Patriotism—well to Consider the measure recommended by us last evening—& however your feelings may be wounded—reflect that ages yet to come may owe their *happiness*, or *misery*, to the Decision of this hour.—Your own fate is so Involved with that of your Country's, that the same cause which hurts the one, will mortally wound the other.

For God's sake, be yourselves—and as a band of Brothers—rise superior to every Injury—whether real or Imaginary—at least for this Campaign, which probably will produce a Conviction to the World—that America owes her freedom to the temporary sacrifice you now make.

You will also reflect that this is a favor solicited by men who would bleed to Death, drop by drop, to defend your honor—as well as that of your very Affectionate

Hum'l Serv'ts
ANT'Y WAYNE
WM IRVINE.

N. B. at all events do not come to a final decision (should it be contrary to this requisition) before 7 o'Clock in the morning when we may have something to Offer that may meet your Approbation.

THE FIELD OFFICERS
OF THE PENNS'A LINE.

Major Macpherson to General Wayne.

12 August 1780

Major Macpherson presents his Compliments to General Wayne, & informs him, he has considered the matter he mentioned to him relative to a separate Command—and thinks it extremely improper in him to say a single word on the subject— The only reason that prevented him at once declaring himself in this manner was a wish before he determined to consider the matter maturely—tho' the same opinion struck him at the time the matter was mentioned.

With respect to the information General Wayne received from Col Stuart—Major Macpherson requests he will contradict that matter in the Division.—Colonel Stuart—as he informs Major Macpherson only said it was his opinion that if General St. Clair would request Major Macpherson to relinquish his right to the Command on the Infantry that he would do it.

The gloomy campaign of 1780 was made still gloomier at its close by the memorable treason of Arnold in September of that year. The details of this attempt (which had so well-nigh succeeded) to betray the garrison at West Point and its dependencies into the hands of the enemy are too well known to need recapitulation here. The part which was taken by General Wayne and the Pennsylvania line in defeating this treasonable scheme is not so well known, and some account of it should be given in any true story of its commander's life. His division was then stationed near Haverstraw, and in those days when there seemed a disposition to suspect the loyalty of every one, and when even Arnold could prove a traitor, it is satisfactory to find that implicit trust was placed not only in Wayne, but in the men who commanded his regiments,—Chambers, Walter Stewart, Craig, W. Butler, Harmar, R. Butler, with true and stanch General W. Irvine at their head. On their arrival at West Point, "having marched over the mountains sixteen miles in four hours without losing a man," they were placed by General Washington in charge of the post, he being well assured that they would prove its most trustworthy safeguard amidst the threatening dangers by which it was surrounded. The choice of the Pennsylvania regiments for such a duty at such a time has a significance which was very apparent at that crisis, but which has been singularly overlooked by historians.

Major-General St. Clair, in command of the Pennsylvania line, was stationed at West Point. On the 1st of October the troops under his command were the Pennsylvania division and Meigs and Livingston's Continental regiments. "Unless you think it necessary for the immediate security of the post to draw the first Penn'a (Wayne's) brigade nearer West Point," says the order of Washington, "I should wish it to remain somewhere in its present position (guarding the Defile), as it may then at the same time serve the purpose of reinforcing the main army in case of a movement against it. But on the first appearance of the enemy coming in force up the River, that Brigade should have previous orders to march to your succor." "I was ordered on here," says General Irvine, "with my Brigade (2d Penn'a) on the alarm that was occasioned by Arnold's villainous business. I made a rapid march and found the place on my arrival in a most miserable condition in every respect. About 1800 militia had been at the Post, but were chiefly detached on various pretences. Those who remained had not a single place assigned them, nor had a single order what to do. I have not heard from Head Quarters to-day, but I have reason to believe that Major André and Smith must be hung."

General Wayne to General Washington.

SMITH's WHITE HOUSE 27th Sep'r 1780
DEAR SIR,—   6 OClock A.M.

*   *   *   *   *   *   *   *

Your letter of yesterday from the Robinson house came to hand between 7 & 8 OClock in the Evening. As the troops were much fatigued for want of Sleep—no prospect of any more of the enemy up the river—& being in possession of & Commanding the pass by Storm's, &c towards West Point, with a road in our rear to file off our Artillery by Haverstraw forge under the Mountain, Gen'l Irvine & myself thought it best to remain in this position until morning— or until a move of the Enemy should take place—in the latter case to make a rapid move for West Point, sending our Artillery & baggage by the route already mentioned as soon as the latter should arrive.

I forgot to mention to your Excellency that the 1st & 2nd Brigades marched from Tappan at a moments warning leaving our tents standing, Guards & Detachments out, & pushed with rapidity to Secure this pass—where it would be in our power to dispute the Ground inch by inch—or to proceed to West Point as occasion might require, which was effected in as little time as ever so long a march was performed in.

As the wind at present is strong down the river—neither Baggage or Guard yet arrived though every moment expected—I shall take post at Williams's with the first Brigade & Artillery of the 2nd— Gen'l Irvine will move slowly to Storms & wait your further Order with regard to the Baggage Waggons horses &c

The Wind is too high for the boats to make way up the river was the baggage even arrived   The troops are at present employed in working for to day & tomorrow so that no time will be lost until I receive your further orders

I am Your Excellency's Most Ob't Hl St

ANT'Y WAYNE.

[TO GEN'L WASHINGTON.]

General Wayne to H. A. Sheel.

HAVERSTRAW NEAR STONEY POINT
2nd Oct'r 1780

DEAR SHEEL,—I am confident that the perfidy of Genl. Arnold will astonish the multitude—the high rank he bore—the *eclat* he had Obtained (whether honestly or not) Justified the world in giving it him.

But there were a few Gentlemen who at a very early period of this War became acquainted with his true Character!—when you asked my Opinion of that Officer I gave it freely—& believe you thought it rather strongly shaded—

I think I informed you that I had the most despicable Idea of him both as a Gentleman & a Soldier—& that he had produced a conviction on me in 1776—that honor & true Virtue were Strangers to his Soul, and however Contradictory it might appear—that he never possessed either fortitude or personal bravery—he was naturally a Coward, and never went in the way of Danger but when Stimulated by Liquor even to Intoxication, consequently Incapacitated from Conducting any Command committed to his charge

I shall not dwell upon his Military Character or the measures he had adopted for the Surrender of West Point—that being already fully Elucidated, but will give you a small specimen of his *peculate* talents—

What think you of his employing Sutlers to retail the publick Liquors for his private Emolument, & furnishing his Quarters with beds & other furniture by paying for them with Pork, Salt, Flour, &c drawn from the Magazines—he has not stopped here—he has descended much lower—& defrauded the old Veteran Soldiers who have bled for their Country in many a well fought field, for more than five Campaigns, among others an old Serg't of mine has felt his rapacity—by the Industry of this man's wife they had accumulated something handsome to support them in their advanced age—which coming to the knowledge of this cruel spoiler—he borrowed 4,500 Dollars from the poor Credulous Woman & left her in the Lurch.—The dirty—dirty acts which he has been capable of Committing beggar all description—and are of such a Nature as would cause the *Infernals to blush*—were they accused with the Invention, or execution of them—

The detached & Debilitated state of the Garrison of West Point—Insured success to the assailants—the Enemy were all in perfect readiness—for the Enterprize—& the discovery of the treason—only prevented—an Immediate attempt by Open force to carry those works—which *perfidy* would have effected the fall of, by a slower & less sanguine mode.—Our army was out of protecting distance—the troops in the possession of the Works a spiritless *Miserabile Vulgus* —in whose hands the fate of America seemed suspended—in this Situation His Excellency—(in Imitation of Cæsar & his tenth

Legion)—called for his *Veterans*—the Summons arrived at One OClock in the morning—& we took up our Line of March at 2— & by sun rise arrived at this place distant from our former Camp 16 miles—the whole performed in four hours in a dark night—without a single halt or a man left behind— When our approach was announced to the General he thought it fabulous—but when convinced of the reality—he received us like a God—& retiring to take a short repose—exclaimed—"All is safe, & I again am happy"— May he long—very long Continue so—

The protection of that Important place is committed to my Conduct until a proper Garrison arrives—I shall not throw myself into the Works—but will dispute the Approaches *inch* by *inch* and at the point of the bayonet, decide the fate of the day in the Gorge of the Defiles—at every expense of blood, until death or Victory cries— "*hold*"—"*hold*"— It is not in our power to Command Success— but it is in our power to produce a Conviction to the world that we deserve it—& I trust that whatever may be the Issue,—my Conduct will never require the palliation of a friend, or memory cause a blush to shade the cheek of any *tender* acquaintance. Apropo' there is one to whom you'l be so Oblig'g as to present my kindest wishes

Adieu my Dear Sir & believe me
Yours Most Sincerely
ANT'Y WAYNE.

[To HUGH SHEEL, ESQ.]

Hugh A. Sheel to General Wayne.

PHILADELPHIA Oct. 22, 1780

MY DEAR GENERAL,—Dr. Skinners sudden & unexpected departure from this gives me scarcely time to thank you for your obliging favor which was delivered to me by Mr. Litell. It made me very happy to find that our worthy and illustrious General manifested his confidence in you and the Pennsylvania Line by calling on you on so critical an occasion as the infernal treachery of Arnold produced —the extraordinary march you made invited the applause of all— but not the surprise of any who knew you—the character you gave me in confidence of Arnold several months ago, made a strong impression on my mind—it has been verified fully—his villany & machination never cou'd have been carried on, but thro' the medium of his Tory acquaintances in this place—& this points out the absolute necessity of putting an end to every kind of intercourse with disaffected & suspicious characters Female as well Male, & in the fullest manner Justifies the resolution entered into & published by you, & the other Gentlemen of the Army in this Town, last Spring— A very great number of Citizens have adopted the same measure & have associated themselves not only for that purpose, but for the removal of obnoxious characters out of the State—it is opposed by some Gentlemen here—from whom you w'd not expect opposition to so necessary a measure. We have been alarmed by an acc't of a new piece of treachery in Virginia—a Scotch gentleman, Mr David Ross of Petersburg, possessed of an immense fortune, is now in prison—for holding a correspondence with L'd Cornwallis, the Commission of Brigadier Gen'l was granted to him & found in his possession, & his dispatches with the Bearer were secured—in them were Commissions for the different Officers of a Reg't that Ross was to embody—& w'ch He transmitted to L'd Cornwallis to sign—it appears that on the arrival of a force expected from N: York—He was to arm the convention Troops— No other particulars have yet come to hand—but from the number who were commission'd it is likely that great discoveries will be made. As soon as they are made known I will transmit them to you—as I request you may any thing new that occurs in y'r part of the world.

As Dr. Skinner will give you a full detail of City news, I have but to beg you may believe me to be with sincere respect & esteem

My D'r Sir

Y'r much Obliged

& most Obed't Serv't

H. A. Sheel.[1]

Notwithstanding the devoted loyalty and high discipline which distinguished the Pennsylvania line on this

---

[1] Hugh Sheel was a native of Ireland, and a physician. He practised medicine in Philadelphia towards the end of the Revolution, and in 1780 subscribed five thousand pounds to establish the bank organized to supply the American army with money needed for supplies. He removed to Kentucky, where he was subsequently drowned in attempting to cross a river.

occasion, and which led it to undergo any privation in order to defeat the treasonable designs of Arnold, these very men were driven a few months later into open mutiny, and, desperate in their sufferings, threatened to march to Philadelphia and coerce Congress to yield to their claims and to redress their grievances. How is this strange transformation of unshaken fidelity to a mutinous spirit to be accounted for?

It is very evident that a growing feeling of discontent, which many mistook for disaffection to the cause, prevailed in the Pennsylvania line towards the close of the year 1780. This discontent arose from three causes, each of them involving an alleged violation of the contract which the State had made with the soldiers. These were, first, the non-payment of the men, or rather their payment in a nominal currency far depreciated beyond what they had agreed to receive; secondly, an insufficient supply of provisions and clothing; and, thirdly, the conviction that it was the intention of the authorities to hold all those soldiers who had enlisted for three years or the war for the latter period. The soldiers complained—and it seems to us, from all the testimony accessible, with good reason—that to keep them for an indefinite period, subject to all the privations from which they suffered, was unjust and wrongful. It may be said in palliation of their conduct in taking the redress of their grievances into their own hands, that their mutinous acts were regarded by them as protests against the violation of the contracts made on the part of the State when they entered her service. Wayne, knowing well how wide-spread was the feeling of discontent among his troops, looked forward to the first of the coming January, when the three years' enlistment of his men would expire, with ominous apprehension. "You may believe me," he writes to Colonel Johnston on the 16th of December, "that the exertions of the House [the Assembly] were never more necessary than at this crisis to adopt some effectual mode and immediate plan to alleviate the distress of the troops, and to conciliate their minds and sweeten their tempers, which are much soured by neglect and every extreme of wretchedness for want of almost every comfort and necessary of life." Again, he writes to President Reed about the same time, "Our soldiers are not devoid of reasoning faculties, nor callous to the first feelings of nature. They have now served their country for nearly five years with fidelity, poorly clothed, badly fed, and worse paid. I have not seen a paper dollar in the way of pay for more than twelve months." So Major Church writes, "As my time in the service soon expires, I am not entitled to draw rations. It is very distressing. I have not a farthing of money, nor has the regiment received any these fourteen months."

General Wayne to Colonel Johnston (at Philadelphia).

MOUNT KEMBLE 16th Dec'r 1780

My DEAR COL.,—I sincerely wish the Ides of Jany was come & past—I am not superstitious, but can't help cherishing disagreeable Ideas about that period.

I know that I have the hearts of the soldiery & that my presence is absolutely necessary in Camp

You may believe me my D'r Sir that the exertions of the House were never more necessary than at this Crisis to adopt some effectual mode & Immediate plan to Alleviate the distress of the Troops & to conciliate their minds & sweeten their tempers which are much soured by neglect & every extreme of wretchedness for want of almost every comfort & necessary of life—

Had I it in my power to assure them that as a reward for past services & their more than Roman Virtue the Hon'ble Assembly had given them a solid landed property which might at any time be turned into Specie equal or Superior to the nominal debt due them, I am confident that we should restore Content & Insure fidelity, on the Contrary we have every thing to fear from their Defection, however I am Determined to brave the storm & am

Yours most Affectionately

ANT'Y WAYNE.

COL. JOHNSTON.

This condition of the army caused the most serious apprehensions on the part of the public, and what was not done either by the Congressional or by the State authorities to afford relief was attempted by private enterprise and benevolence in Philadelphia. To relieve the wants of the soldiers the Bank of North America was established in that city, in the hope that by its means money might be raised for their pay; and the women there, headed by Mrs. Reed, the wife of the President, and Mrs. Bache, the daughter of Dr. Franklin, set to work in earnest to procure material, from which were made and sent to camp large quantities of clothing,—even more needed at that inclement season by the soldiers than their pay. But these remedies had been delayed too long or were upon too small a scale to produce an immediate impression or to prevent an explosion. Wayne endeavored by stricter restraint and discipline to bring his men completely under his control. They complained, and he replied that he would much rather be accused of severity than of a relaxation of discipline.

Between nine and ten o'clock on the evening of the 1st of January, 1781, the men of the Pennsylvania line, with few exceptions, rushed from their huts, paraded under arms without officers, supplied themselves with ammunition and provisions, seized six pieces of artillery, and took the horses from the general's stables. The following letter from General Wayne to General Washington presents a striking picture of this frightful scene :

MOUNT KEMBLE 2d Jan : 1781
Half after 4 o'clock A.M.

DEAR GENERAL,—It is with pain I now inform your Excellency of the general mutiny & defection which suddenly took place in the Penn'a line between 9 & 10 o'clock last evening— Every possible exertion was used by the officers to suppress it in its rise ; but the torrent was too potent to be stemmed. Captain Bitting has fallen a victim to his zeal and duty, Captain Tolbert & Lieutenant White are reported mortally wounded, a very considerable number of the field & other officers are much injured by strokes from muskets, bayonets & stones, nor have the rioters escaped with impunity— Many of their bodies lay under our horses' feet, and others will retain with existence the traces of our swords and espontoons. They finally moved from the ground about eleven o'clock last night, scouring the grand parade with round & grape shot from four field pieces, the troops advancing in solid column with fixed bayonets, producing a diffusive fire of musketry in front, flank & rear.

During this horrid scene a few officers with myself were carried by the tide to the forks of the road at Mount Kemble, but placing ourselves on that leading to Elizabethtown, produced a conviction in the soldiery that they could not advance on that route but over our dead bodies. They fortunately turned towards Princeton.

Colonels Butler & Stewart (to whose spirited exertions I am much indebted) will accompany me to Vealtown where the troops now are. We had our escapes last night— Should we not be equally fortunate to-day our friends will have this consolation, that we did

not commit the honor of the United States or our own on this
unfortunate occasion.

Adieu, my dear General, & believe me &c

ANTHONY WAYNE.

One of the most curious features of this remarkable
revolt was the manner in which the so-called mutineers
treated their officers. There does not seem to have
been any animosity towards them as such, and force
was employed by the mutineers only when for their
purposes it was necessary to disarm them. On Wayne's
pointing his pistols at them at the beginning of the
outbreak there were a hundred bayonets at his breast,
and those who handled them exclaimed, " We love you,
we respect you, but you are a dead man if you fire.
Do not mistake us : we are not going to the enemy ; on
the contrary, were they now to come out you would
see us fight under your orders with as much resolution
and alacrity as ever." This disposition of the soldiery
was confirmed by their permitting the general and Colonels Richard Butler and Walter Stewart to accompany
them. These officers, at apparently great personal risk,
remained with the revolters for nearly two weeks, preventing them from doing further mischief, and acting
as their mediators with the State and Congressional
authorities in an effort to bring about a settlement of
their grievances. During their march to Trenton they
kept up, according to President Reed, "an astonishing
regularity and discipline." A great alarm was, of course,
caused by the march of the revolted troops towards
Philadelphia, and Congress appointed a committee to
confer with them, who do not seem to have gone beyond Bristol. The President, with more boldness, met

them in their camp near Princeton and listened to their complaints. He was received with a military salute. "Their first demand," he says, "was that whoever was tired of the service might be discharged." This was at once refused. "Their nominal leader was," he tells us, "a very poor creature, and very fond of liquor," and he seems to think that the extravagance of his proposition is to be accounted for in that way.

After a great deal of peaceful and temperate discussion between the soldiers and President Reed and Vice-President Potter, representing the State, the following settlement was agreed upon and carried out:

1. That no soldier shall be retained beyond the period of his enlistment, and where it appears that the enlistment-paper has not been signed voluntarily the man shall be discharged.

2. In order to settle whether the man enlisted for three years or indefinitely for the war, a board shall be appointed by the government.

3. The bounty of one hundred dollars given by Congress for re-enlistment shall not be regarded as conclusive evidence that the man enlisted for the war.

4. Auditors to be appointed at once to settle the pay of the men.

5. Clothing to be issued in a few days to all the men who are to be discharged.

6. General amnesty and oblivion.

On the 29th of January Wayne writes to Washington giving an account of the final settlement of the revolt, and tells him that out of the two thousand four hundred men composing the Pennsylvania line the commissioners of Congress under the above-cited agreement had found that twelve hundred and fifty were entitled to their discharge. He says, "We shall retain more than two-thirds of the troops. The soldiers are as impatient of liberty as they were of service."

Thus terminated what seemed to the panic-stricken people of the time, and perhaps still more so to the conscience-stricken legislators in Congress and the Assembly, a most formidable and dangerous revolt. Reduced to its true proportions, it now appears simply as a lawless and irregular method of seeking a redress of grievances of an intolerable kind and of long duration, the existence of which was recognized on all hands. The people in those days felt, owing to their English traditions, a wholesome alarm at any appearance of an attempt of the military to usurp the powers of the civil authorities. Even General Washington himself was not insensible to the dangers which might result if the authority of the troops was not subordinated at all times to that of the Legislature. It is true that on the 3d of January, upon hearing of the mutiny, he wrote to Wayne, "The officers have given convincing proof that every thing possible was done by them to check the mutiny on its first appearance, and it is to be regretted that some of them have fallen sacrifices to their zeal." But on the 29th of January he writes in a different tone to the governors of the several States: "The weakness of this garrison and still more its embarrassment and distress from a want of provisions made it impossible to prosecute such measures with the Pennsylvanians as the nature of the case demanded, and while we were making arrangements as far as practicable to supply these defects an accommodation took place which will not only subvert the Penn'a line but have a very pernicious influence upon the whole army." Washington, when he first heard of the mutiny, evidently apprehending further trouble, wrote immediately to the governors of the New England States in this strain (January 5, 1781) : "The aggravated calamities and distresses that have resulted from the total want of pay for nearly twelve months, the want of clothing at a severe season, and not infrequently the want of provisions, are beyond description." So when, shortly after, a revolt of very small proportions took place in the Jersey line from the same causes, measures were taken to crush it out at once.

There were several reasons which rendered the Pennsylvania revolt in the eyes of the authorities, both military and civil, much more serious than a mere manifestation of the discontent of the soldiers. The army of Washington at that time was in a most critical condition, believed by many, including the enemy, to be at the point of dissolution, and the Pennsylvania line formed the larger portion of that army. One great fear was that the mutineers might join the British army. The English had made every preparation to receive them at Elizabethtown and Perth Amboy, five thousand troops having been detached for that purpose. Sir H. Clinton, as soon as he heard of the mutiny, despatched spies to the camp of the insurgents to induce them to join him, and offered to receive them into the English army under the most favorable conditions.[1] These proposals reached those in revolt on the 7th of January. Instead of being entertained, they were

[1] Moore, 129.

promptly rejected by the soldiers, they spurning the
idea of "becoming *Arnolds*," as they expressed it.
They placed the two bearers of these propositions in
confinement as spies, and before their submission they
were ready to hang them. They sent the overtures of
the British general to Wayne, with a solemn assurance
"that should any hostile movement be made by the
enemy the Division would immediately march under
their old Beloved Commander to meet and repel it."
Certainly such men never had any intention of desert-
ing the American cause for the purpose of joining the
British army. In the pride of their patriotism they
spurned the reward which was offered them for the
capture of the spies.

Another cause of alarm with many was the fear that
the revolters would proceed in a body to Philadelphia
and overawe Congress and the Assembly into granting
their claims. So considerable a person as General St.
Clair, who commanded the division, was disposed to
think that they should be allowed to cross the river, for
then they could not desert to the enemy ; but President
Reed and the Committee of Congress evidently thought
that in order to avoid the imminent danger of coercing
the civil authorities some binding compromise or agreement should be made with them before they came
within their reach. Much false pride was undoubtedly
sacrificed on the part of the authorities in bringing the
quarrel to an early settlement. What the soldiers
might have done had they reached Philadelphia it is in
vain to speculate, but it is very clear that the terms of
the final settlement were fair, equitable, and just.

Various theories have been put forward to explain

this revolt.   No explanation is needed beyond the intolerable condition of the men and their neglect by Congress and the State.   A curious error has been fallen into by many historians, including Mr. Bancroft, in speaking of the Pennsylvania line, that "it was composed in a large degree of new-comers from Ireland," and this has been said not only to account for the alleged lawlessness and disaffection of the men at the time of the revolt, but also (by General Harry Lee) to explain the extraordinary brilliancy of their courage on the battle-field.   These writers are evidently thinking of the characteristic qualities of the Celtic Irishman in war; but there were not, it is said on good authority, more than three hundred persons of Irish birth (Roman Catholic and Celtic) in the Pennsylvania line.   Two-thirds of the force were Scotch-Irish, a race with whose fighting qualities we are all familiar, but which are quite opposite to those that characterize the true Irish Celt.   Most of them were descendants of the Scotch-Irish emigrants of 1717–1730, and very few of them were " new-comers." [1]

[1] In regard to the statement that the Pennsylvania line was composed mainly of Irish, the following letters, one from Dr. William H. Egle, the State Librarian, the other from John Blair Linn, Esq., of Bellefonte, both of them editors of the Pennsylvania Archives, which contain the lists of the soldiers of the Revolution from this State preserved at Harrisburg, should prove satisfactorily that it was made without authority :

STATE LIBRARY OF PENNSYLVANIA.

HARRISBURG, PA., April 11, 1892.

CHARLES J. STILLÉ, LL.D.,
        Philadelphia.

MY DEAR SIR,—In reply to your inquiry of 9th April, permit me to state that Mr. Bancroft and other writers were entirely wrong in

On the whole, then, it would appear that the mutiny of the Pennsylvania line on investigation amounted to

their statement as to the nationality of the soldiers of Wayne's Division. With the exception of the Scotch-Irish, who formed about two-thirds of his force, the remainder were almost wholly of German parentage. In the French and Indian War the emigrants from the Province of Ulster were chiefly selected, while those of pure Irish descent or migration were rejected on the ground that they were Roman Catholics and that they would not be loyal to the Province when opposed by the French troops. If you so desire, when the opportune time arrives I might amplify what I have here simply alluded to. The *Irish* were not in it, although all immigrants from Ireland were thus claimed. The facts are, few *Irish* came until after the War of the Revolution. I doubt if there were 300 persons of Irish birth (Roman Catholic and Celtic) in the war from Pennsylvania.

Yours with respect,

WILLIAM H. EGLE.

BELLEFONTE, PA., April 11, 1892.

MY DEAR SIR,—Mr. Bancroft and General Henry Lee were certainly in error in stating that the Pennsylvania Line was composed for the most part of Hibernians who emigrated and enlisted in our army.

The Scotch-Irish emigration of 1717–1730 *in* its descendants furnished the bone and sinew of the Pennsylvania Line. Except in a few regiments from the neighborhood of Philadelphia there were very few. *then* recent emigrants enlisted in the Line.

Sons of German emigrants furnished quite a respectable portion of the Line, as the rolls of companies from Northampton, Bucks, Lancaster, indicate by their patronymic denomination. There were a few sons of English emigrants; but the Scotch-Irish of Philadelphia, Chester, Lancaster, Cumberland, Northumberland, Allegheny, and Westmoreland Counties composed the large majority of the Pennsylvania Line, as the names indicate, confirmed by very extensive examination of Pension applications, rolls at Harrisburg, and extensive acquaintance with families in central and western Pennsylvania, who were represented in the Pennsylvania Line.

this : It was adopted as the only method within the power of the men to compel the authorities, State and Congressional, to do them justice, or, in other words, to keep their contract with them. They asked for three things, as we have said, which having been promised them were withheld,—namely, pay, clothing, and provisions. Having enlisted for three years, they insisted that they should be discharged at the end of their term, and not be kept illegally under arms because the military authorities thought that as veterans they would prove more useful than raw recruits. The substantial justice of their claims cannot be denied, although their method of asserting them was unlawful. The authorities, therefore, in yielding did not violate the true theory of military discipline, which is based quite as much upon the justice of those who command as

They were Scotch-Irish Presbyterians : Irvines, Chambers, Butlers, Potter, Wilson, McAllister, McFarlane, Hollidays, McClellan, Grier, Buchanan, Simonton, Thompson, McClean, etc., etc., emigrants and sons of emigrants from the North of Ireland, from Antrim, Londonderry, Tyrone, Donegal, Fermanagh, and Cavan, as I have had occasion to trace them. In central and western Pennsylvania, in the frontier counties, there were a good many Scotch-Irish emigrants who came on between 1769 and 1774, who enlisted, as rolls compared with old Church records show.

There is nothing in the annals of Pennsylvania, as far as I have examined them, to sustain the assertion that Irish emigrants, as distinguished from the Scotch-Irish, formed a component portion of the Pennsylvania Line, but much to the contrary.

Respectfully
Your ob't serv't,
JOHN B. LINN.

CHARLES J. STILLÉ, LL.D.,
   Philadelphia, Pa.

upon the implicit obedience of those who are commanded.

Exactly how far the American government at that time, considering its own origin, was in a condition to exact absolute compliance with its orders when it had violated constantly the rights of the soldiers, it is not worth while to inquire. But we must remember always how completely this revolt differed in its cause and progress from ordinary military revolts. There was no disaffection to the cause for which they had for five years been fighting, there was no licentious soldiery carrying terror among the unarmed inhabitants and plundering them when free from the control of their officers, and they never asked for anything to which in the opinion of all they were not fully entitled.

It is impossible to read any faithful account of this revolt without being struck with the attachment and devotion of his soldiers to General Wayne, and the wise and judicious measures which he took to lessen the evils attendant upon it. We have seen how earnestly he pleaded with the authorities to take such measures before it broke out as would have rendered it unnecessary. When such efforts failed he was the strict disciplinarian, striving in vain to repress the mutiny with arms in his hands. When all military order and discipline had been subverted, he and his brave comrades, Richard Butler and Walter Stewart, forgetful of personal danger, remained with the men, not, certainly, with any immediate expectation of subduing the revolt, but with the hope of preventing the most dangerous consequences which were feared from it,—the desertion of the soldiers to the enemy or their coercion of Congress. When they were disposed to return to their duty upon an intimation that their reasonable claims would be granted, Wayne was the trusted mediator whose counsels brought peace and safety at this dangerous crisis. Seldom has a general with revolted troops had such a task to perform, and never was it performed more nobly and more successfully.

The following official account of the revolt of the Pennsylvania line is taken from the letters found in the collection of the Wayne MSS. :

General Wayne's Order concerning the Mutiny.

HEAD QUARTERS
MOUNT KEMBLE 2nd Jan'y, 1781

Agreeably to the proposition of a very great proportion of the Worthy Soldiery last evening Gen'l Wayne hereby desires the Non Commissioned Officers & privates to Appoint one man from each Reg't to represent their Grievances to the Gen'l who upon the Sacred Honor of a Gentleman & a *Soldier* does hereby solemnly promise to exert every power to Obtain an Immediate redress of those Grievances & he further plights that *Honor* that no man shall receive the least Injury on account of the part he may have taken upon this Occasion, & that the persons of those who may be Appointed to settle this affair, shall be held sacred & Inviolate

The General hopes soon to return to Camp with all his brother Soldiers who took a little tour last evening

ANT'Y WAYNE B.G.

General Washington to General Wayne.

HEAD QUARTERS NEW WINDSOR
3rd January 1781

MY DEAR SIR,—I this day at Noon recd. yours of the 2nd in the morning, by Major Fishbourn, who has given me a full account of the unhappy and alarming defection of the Pennsylvania line. The officers have given convincing proof that every thing possible was done by them to check the mutiny upon its first appearance, and it is to be regretted that some of them have fallen Sacrifices to their Zeal. I very much approve of the determination of yourself, Col'l Butler and Col'l Stewart to keep with the troops, if they will admit of it, as, after the first transports of passion, there may be some favorable intervals which may be improved. I do not know where this may find you, or in what Situation. I can therefore only advise what seems to me most proper at this distance and upon a consideration of all circumstances.

Opposition, as it did not succeed in the first instance cannot be effectual while the men remain together, but will keep alive resentment and will tempt them to turn about and go in a body to the enemy, who by their Emissaries will use every Argument and means in their power to persuade them that it is their only Asylum, which, if they find their passage stopped at the Delaware, and hear that the Jersey Militia are collecting in their rear, they may think but too probable. I would therefore recommend it to you to cross the Delaware with them, draw from them what they conceive to be their principal Grievances and promise to represent faithfully to Congress and to the State the Substance of them and to endeavour to obtain a redress. If they could be stopped at Bristol or Germantown the better— I look upon it, that if you can bring them to a negociation, matters may afterwards be accommodated, but that an attempt to reduce them by force will either drive them to the Enemy or dissipate them in such a manner that they will never be recovered.

Major Fishbourn informs me that General Potter and Col'l Johnston had gone forward to apprise Congress of this unhappy event, and to advise them to go out of the way to avoid the first burst of the storm. It was exceedingly proper to give Congress and the State notice of the Affair that they might be prepared, but the removal of Congress, waving the indignity, might have a very unhappy influence— The mutineers finding the Body, before whom they were determined to lay their Grievances, fled, might take a new turn, and wreak their vengeance upon the persons and properties of the Citizens, and in a town the size of Philadelphia there are numbers who would join them in such a business. I would therefore wish you, if you have time, to recall that advice and rather recommend it to them to stay and hear what propositions the Soldiers have to make.   Immediately upon the receipt of your letter I took measures to inform myself of the temper of the Troops in this quarter, and have sent into the Country for a Small Escort of Horse to come to me, and if nothing alarming appear here and I hear nothing further from you, I shall, tomorrow morning, set out toward Philadelphia by the Route of Chester, Warwick, Col Sewards, Davenports Mill Morris Town Somerset Princetown, Trenton, on which you will direct any dispatches for me.   As I shall be exceedingly anxious to hear what turn matters have taken, or in what situation they remain, you will be pleased to let me hear from you.

I am with very great Regard
Dear Sir
Your most Hble Sert.
G'e WASHINGTON—

P. S.   4 Jany 7 o'clock A.M.   Upon second thoughts I am in doubt whether I shall come down, because the mutineers must have returned to their duty or the business be in the hands of Congress before I could reach you, and because I am advised by such of the General Officers as I have seen not to leave this post in the present Situation of things—temper of the troops—and distress of the Garrison for want of Flour, Cloathing and in short everything—

BRIG. GEN. WAYNE.

Major Moore to General Wayne.

PENNYTOWN Jan'y 5, 1781

DEAR GENERAL,—On Wednesday night about eleven o'clock 80 Officers armed with Col. Craig at our head left the Hutts & proceeded to the Middlebush road when Hamilton & myself (as it was thought We could with safety pass the Troops) were detached to inform you of the approach of these Officers & the position they meant to take.   We arrived at the Borders of Prince town yesterday at 12 o'clock, were stopped by a Guard, treated with a great deal of insolence & turned back.   Col. Craig & those I first mentioned have rode round to Allentown & from there I believe will cross the river. We have arranged ourselves here in two Companies commanded by Col Harmar & wait your Orders—

The Artillery & ammunition which was left is in good order & I believe will be brought here—

Please to give my compliments to Cols Butler & Stewart. I have secured the Baggage of the former. Your Baggage to Doctor Blatchleys.

I am Sir, with confidence &
respect yours
Thos. H. Moore.

Gen'l Wayne—

3 o'clock P.M.

N.B.   I should not have been so particular but this goes by a safe hand   T. M.

General Wayne to President Reed.

Princeton 8th Jany. 1781

Dear Sir,—Being determined to bring matters to a speedy Issue at every Consequence & risk, we sent for the Serj'ts at ½ after 4 OClock this Evening & Insisted upon their marching from this place towards Trent-town in the morning, or that we would leave them to Act as they pleased, & to abide the bad Effects of their own folly. In consequence of which they had come to a Resolution of moving in the morning & bringing along the two Caitiffs [the spies], previous to the receipt of yours, by Mr. Caldwell.

I am Sir Your Most Obt.
Hum'l Ser't
Ant'y Wayne.

[To Gov'r Reed.]

General Wayne and Colonels Butler and Stewart to the Officers.

Princeton Jan'y 8th, 1781
half-past Eleven o'clock

Dear Gentlemen,—This accompanies copies of the orders, propositions, interrogations, and answers which have passed between the troops and ourselves since the unhappy night of the 1st Instant—

Yesterday President Reed, and a Committee from the Council arrived here with full powers to settle this unhappy disturbance; they were met by twelve serjeants; who Laid before them the grievances Complaind of by the troops—

Many arguments were used to Convince them of the enormous injustice which some of their demands contain, and the total impossibility of our ever receding from the just and equitable offers which we have made—

Their demand of having the 20 dollar men all discharged, seems still to remain unalterable in their minds, and you may rest assured as inadmissible in ours—

Before such a step can be taken (which will rob us of ⅔ds of the Line) a total dissolution must take place, and we must depend on Events for Collecting them together—

This morning an answer is to be received from them which will determine the line of Conduct to be in future pursued

Our attendance here, our unwearied diligence in explaining matters to the soldiery, and the Coolness of temper to which we have reduced them, will, we flatter ourselves meet the approbation of our Brother officers and fellow Citizens in General—

On hearing of your anxiety to have us with you, we determined at all events to quit this place and leave them to follow their wild & ungovernable inclinations, but this step we are prevented from taking by our Worthy Generals advice ; as well as that of Governor Reed, and the other Gentlemen

You have among the papers, proposals sent the Line by Sir H'y Clinton, the propositions as well as the Conveyers of them were both immediately handed to us. The men are prisoners, and we hope will meet the fate they deserve

It was a happy Circumstance they had us to apply to, at this alarming and important moment had we been absent, and the proposal left to work on the minds of the Soldiers—tis difficult to divine what the result might have been

An anxiety for your Situation adds much to the unhappiness and distress of our minds— We have been impatiently waiting to hear from you, but are only now and then able to have your distress pictured to us by people who have pass'd amongst you   That our anxieties, distress of mind and unhappiness of situation may soon terminate is the ardent wish of

Dear Gent.

Your aff'te friends

A. Wayne

R. Butler

W. Stewart

Colonel Hubley to General Wayne.

DEAR GENERAL,—We have just received your favor by Mr. Nesbitt— Your unwearied attention to settle the unhappy dispute, must, and is particularly acknowledged, by all who I have had any conversation with— From appearance, matters will shortly be brought to an issue—tho' not to your & our wishes, yet considering circumstances, beyond my expectations.—

I hope that every Credit will be given to you & your Colleagues, for your exertions, for my part I shall do every thing in my power to acquaint my friends & the world how much they are indebted to you.— I am with my best Comp's to Col'ls Stewart & Butler,

Your Obt hum Sert

AD'M HUBLEY JR—

N. B. From your Letters of Yesterday, I fear some erroneous representations with respect to the officers, toward you and your Colleagues, have been made to you— I hope we shall see you shortly when you will be Convinced & imbibe a very different opinion of us.

[Addressed]

BRIGADIER GEN'L WAYNE

Trenton

Proposals to the Mutineers.

His Excellency Joseph Reed Esq'r Governor & the honb'le Brigadier General Potter of the Supreme Executive Council of the State of Pennsylvania having heard the Complaints of the Soldiers, as represented by the Serjeants, inform them, that they are fully authorized to redress reasonable Grievances & they have the fullest Disposition to make them as easy & happy as possible for which end they propose—

First—That no Non-Commissioned Officer or Soldier shall be detained beyond the time for which he freely & voluntarily engaged —but where they appear to have been in any Respect compelled to enter or sign,—such Instruments to be deemed void & the Soldier discharged—

Secondly—To settle who are or are not bound to stay three persons to be appointed by the President & Council who are to examine into the Terms of Inlistment—when the original Inlistments

18

cannot be found the Soldier's oath to be admitted to prove the Time and Terms of Inlistment, & the Soldier to be discharged upon his Oath of the Condition of the Inlistment—

Thirdly—Wherever any Soldier has inlisted for three years, or during the war he is to be discharged unless he shall appear afterwards to have re-inlisted voluntarily & freely—the Gratuity of 100 Dollars given by Congress, not to be reckoned as a bounty or any men to be detained in Consequence of receiving that Gratuity— The Commissioners to be appointed by the President & Council to adjust any Difficulties which may arise on this Article also—

Fourthly—The Auditors to attend as soon as possible to settle the Depreciation with the Soldiers & give them Certificates— Their Arrearages of Pay to be made up as soon as Circumstances will admit &

Fifthly—A Pair of Shoes, Overalls & Shirt will be delivered out to each Soldier in a few days as they are already purchased & ready to be sent forward—whenever the Line shall be settled— Those who are discharged to receive the above Articles at Trenton producing the General's Discharge—

The Governor hopes that no Soldier of the Pennsylvania Line will break his bargain or go from the Contract made with the publick & they may depend upon it that the utmost Care will be taken to furnish them with every necessary fitting for a soldier— The Governor will recommend to the State to take some favorable notice of those who engaged for the War—

The Commissioners will attend at Trenton when the Clothing, & the Stores will be immediately brought & the Regiments to be settled with, in their Order— A Field Officer of each Regiment to attend during the Settlement of his Regiment: pursuant to Gen'l Waynes Order of the 2nd Instant

No Man to be brought to any Tryal or Censure for what has happened on or since New Year's Day but all Matters to be buried in Oblivion—

> Jos. REED, President
> JAS. POTTER

[GOV'R REED & GENL. POTTER's proposal to the line—1781]

The Revolters to President Reed.

His Excellency's proposals being communicated to the different Regiments at Troop beating this morning January 8th 1781—
They do voluntarily agree in Conjunction that all the Soldiers that were inlisted for the Bounty of twenty dollars ought to be discharged Immediately with as little delay as Circumstances will allow—except such Soldiers who have been since voluntarily re-inlisted, the remainder of his Excellencys & the Honble board of Committee's proposals is founded upon Honor & Justice ; but in regard to the proposals of the Honble. Board seting forth that there will be appointed three Persons to sit as a Committee to Redress our grievances it is therefore the General demand of the line, and the board of Serjants that we shall appoint as many members as of the opposite to sit as a Committee to determine justly upon our unhappy affair, as the Path we tread is Justice, & our Footsteps founded upon Honor—
Therefore we do unanimously agree that their should be something done towards a speedy Redress of our present Circumstances—
Signed
Wm. Bawser, Sec'ty—
Jan'y 8, 1781—Princetown—

[Copy of the Proposals of the Serjeants to
  the President &c Jany. 8th 1781]

President Reed to the Mutineers.

Dear Sir,—I received your Favour this Evening, & also the Proposals signed by Sergeant Bawser, which as they contain in Substance what was offered last Evening shall be granted except that appointing Persons to set with those nominated by the Honourable the Council, cannot be complied with. This implies such a Distrust of the Authority of the State which has ever been attentive to the wants of the Army that the Impropriety of it must be evident. But any Soldier will have Liberty to bring before the Commissioners any Person as his Friend to represent his Case. The Hon. the Committee of Congress have resolved that the Spies sent out should be delivered up as soon as convenient & upon that being done Congress will proclaim a general Oblivion of all Matters since the 31

December—provided the Terms offered last Evening are closed with & the Troops remain no longer in their present State. It is my clear Opinion that they should march in the morning to Trenton where the Stores are, their Cloathing expected if not by this Time arrived, by which I mean Overalls & some Blankets—
I hope they will come to a Speedy Determination & am Dear Sir
Your Obed Hble Serv't
Jos REED.

Jan. 8, 1781

[8th Jan'y 1781
from
Gov'r J. REED]

General Wayne to General Washington.

TRENTON 29th January 1781

DEAR GENERAL,—The Commissioners of Congress have gone thro' the Settlement of Inlistments of the Pennsylvania Line except a few Stragglers, and have ordered about 1250 men to be discharged out of the Aggregate of the Infantry, and 67 of the Artillery, so that we may count upon nearly 1150 remaining, including the non-commissioned officers furloughed pursuant to the Direction of the Commissioners until March & toward April, except recruiting Serg't & Music.

I shall leave this place tomorrow morning after seeing the Arms & Accoutrements forwarded to Philadelphia where I shall expect your Excellency's further Orders. General Irvine will also be anxious for your Directions, he is now there preparing for the recruiting Service.

I gave early Orders to the Regimental Quarter Masters to secure the public stores of their respective Corps, & particular Directions to Mr. Hughes the Division Quarter Master, to collect the whole and return them to Q. M. General's Store at Morris Town, except the few Arms & Accoutrements left in the Huts, which I have ordered to be sent to this place by the Return Waggons & so by Water to Philadelphia. I am happy to inform you that the loss of these essential Articles is far short of what we had reason to expect, indeed there was scarcely a man discharged or furloughed who did not produce a Receipt for the Delivery of his Arms & Accoutrements.

Inclosed are the printed Forms of Orders for Discharges—Discharges and furloughs, by which your Excellency will find that I have had my share of very Distressing Duty, attended with some disagreeable scenes at almost every Hour of Day and Night, which will also palliate for any seeming neglect in point of frequent Intelligence.

I have the Honor to be in every Vicissitude of Fortune

Your Excellency's most obed't

& affectionate hble Serv't

ANT'Y WAYNE.

☞ Inclosed is a Philad'a paper of the 24th Instant in which you'l see that *some Gentlemen* have given themselves Ample Credit for the part they have had in this unfortunate affair.

HIS EXCELLENCY

GEN'L WASHINGTON.

General Washington to General Wayne.

HEAD QUARTERS NEW WINDSOR
Feby. 2nd 1781

DEAR SIR,—In mine of the 29th of January I partly answered yours of the 21st— Yours of the 17th had been duly received, and I am since favored with that of the 29th January

I am satisfied, that every thing was done on your part to produce the least possible evil from the unfortunate disturbance in your line, and that your influence has had a great share in preventing worse extremities— I felt for your Situation— Your anxieties & fatigues of mind amidst such a scene, I can easily conceive— I thank you sincerely for your exertions—

You request to be exempted from the recruiting Service, and employed in the field—at present the last is not possible—but 'till you hear further from me, you need not occupy yourself about the first— I write to General Irvine by this opportunity

With the greatest regard

I am Dear Sir

Your most Obed't Serv't

G'E WASHINGTON

GEN. WAYNE—

General Wayne to General Washington.

PHIL'A 27th Feby 1781

DEAR GENERAL,—I was honored with your favor of the 2d Instant and experience much happiness in your Approbation of my Conduct during the unfortunate Defection of the Penns'a line.. But as I am informed that the tongue of slander (among some Individuals in the State of N. Jersey) has not been Idle on this Occasion, I hold it my duty to mention that as far as Orders & example had Influence the persons & property of the Inhabitants were protected & the strictest discipline Observed Inclosed is a Copy of one of the last Orders Issued for this purpose, which was faithfully Observed in every minutia on the part of the Officers, even at 9 OClock the night of the revolt at which hour every thing appeared favourable and all the Soldiers either in their Hutts or properly Accounted for —Indeed one of their Complaints was, that they had experienced more restraint & strict duty than usual in Winter— however I would much rather be accused of that—than a relaxation of Discipline—or inattention to the rights of the Citizen nor was any legal means left unattempted to quiet the minds of the troops which your Excely will see by the Inclosed copy of an Order of the Ultimo—

It is with pleasure I again Assure your Excellency that I am very much Indebted to all the Officers for their attention to Duty & Spirited exertions on this occasion & in particular to Col'ls Stewart & Butler who as Commanding Officers of Brigades cheerfully risqued their lives & participated in every vicissitude of fortune with me—

I now Inclose your Excellency a Copy of the General Officers answer to the Queries of the Honble. House of Assembly, & their proceedings thereon, which I hope will be productive of very salutary effects—

I have the Honor to be with
Singular Esteem
Your Excellency's
Most Obt
& very Hum'l Sert
ANTH'Y WAYNE.

[TO GEN'L WASHINGTON.]

CHAPTER VII.

THE Pennsylvania line was almost wholly dissolved by the revolt. It was a long time before the people recovered from the panic produced by it. The Board of War, indeed, was so anxious to get rid of what they considered the dangerous element in the army that they not only paid the men of the Pennsylvania line on their discharge what was due them, but issued to each soldier gratuitously a ration for every twenty miles on his way homeward. The Congressional committee, which was probably not very strict in examining the claims for discharge, set free about twelve hundred and fifty men, so that no more than eleven hundred and fifty remained in the division. General Washington complained that this commission had been imposed upon, but, upon the advice of St. Clair, the commander, the matter was hushed up. Measures were at once taken to recruit the regiments and to reorganize the division. It was decided to reduce the number of regiments to six. Of course it was necessary to retire a proportionate number of officers. Of the men who were retained many were veterans, having served continuously for five years. No greater proof could be given of the confidence they inspired, and of Wayne's high qualities as a leader, than that shown by the eagerness with which the old soldiers as well as the officers pressed forward to serve again under him. There seems to have been no effort to exclude the former mutineers from re-enlistment. Two-thirds of those whose time had expired and who had been discharged were desirous of re-entering the service under Wayne's command, and, in his language, "were as importunate for service as they had been for their discharge." The trouble was not with the service nor with the officers, but with the broken promises of the State and of Congress with regard to their pay and clothing.

On the 26th of February, 1781, Wayne was ordered to command a detachment of the Pennsylvania line which it had been determined to send as a reinforcement to General Greene, then in charge of military affairs in South Carolina. The detachment was to consist of details from each of the six regiments, in number about eight hundred, and the rendezvous and headquarters were established at York in Pennsylvania.[1] It was a long and tedious business to reorganize the men and procure the needed supplies for the expedition. In his efforts to prepare them for the campaign he was embarrassed by difficulties of the same sort that he had encountered so many times since the beginning of the war. Recruits for the expedition were scarce, the needed supplies were not forthcoming, and the worthless paper which was given him to pay his men it was soon found would purchase nothing in the way of the commonest necessaries. No allowance was made for the actual depreciation of this miscalled

[1] See Appendix, No. III.

money below its nominal value, and, as was most natural, there was much discontent on the part of the men to whom it was offered, and mutterings and threats which, according to the law-martial, came very near to mutiny. The result of this renewed attempt on the part of the State to pay its soldiers in nominal money, when it had agreed to pay them in what was real, is clearly expressed in the following letter of Wayne of May 20, 1781 :

" When I arrived at York there was scarcely a horse or a carriage fit to transport any part of our baggage or supplies. This difficulty I found means to remedy by bartering one species of public property to procure another. The troops were retarded in advancing to the general rendezvous by the unaccountable delay of the auditors who were appointed to settle and pay the proportion of the depreciation due them, which, when received, was not equal to one-seventh part of its nominal value. This was an alarming circumstance. The soldiery but too sensibly felt the imposition ; nor did the conduct or counsel of the inhabitants tend to moderate but rather to inflame their minds by refusing to part with any thing which the soldiers needed in exchange for it, saying it was not worth accepting, and that they (the soldiers) ought not to march until justice was done them. To minds already susceptible to this kind of impression and whose recent revolt was fresh in their memory little more was wanting to stimulate them to try it again. The day antecedent to that on which the march was to commence, a few leading mutineers on the right of each regiment called out to pay them in real and not ideal money : they were no longer to be trifled with. Upon this they were ordered to their tents, which being peremptorily refused, the principals were immediately either knocked down or confined by the officers, who were previously prepared for this event. A Court-martial was ordered on the spot,—the commission of the crime, trial and execution were all included in the course of a few hours in front of the line paraded under arms. The determined countenances of the officers produced a conviction to the soldiery that the sentence of the Court-martial would be carried into execution at every risk and consequence. Whether by design or accident, the particular friends and messmates of the culprits were their executioners, and while the tears rolled down their cheeks in showers, they silently and faithfully obeyed their orders without a moment's hesitation. Thus was this hideous monster crushed in its birth, however to myself and officers a most painful scene."

On the 20th of May Wayne's corps, much smaller in numbers than he had anticipated, and by no means well equipped, but according to his own account reduced to discipline and harmony by the prompt execution of two of the mutineers, marched southward from York. In consequence of the attempt of Lord Cornwallis, who had made a rapid march from South Carolina after the battle of Eutaw Springs, to form a junction with General Phillips, who commanded the British forces on the James River in Virginia, Wayne was ordered to reinforce La Fayette, who commanded in that State, before proceeding to South Carolina. Wayne joined La Fayette on the 7th of June at Fredericksburg with about eight hundred men. He formed his men into two battalions, the first commanded by Walter Stewart and the other by Richard Butler. These battalions and one from Virginia under Colonel Gaskin formed a brigade, and acted together as such under Wayne until the surrender of Yorktown. Wayne brought with him one company of artillerists, but no cannon. La Fayette's command was made up of detachments from the New England regiments and those of Jersey in Washington's army. There was also a corps of Virginia militia, varying greatly in number at different times, under La Fayette, whose effective force was, previous to the junction, not more than twelve hundred men.

Unfortunately, Wayne had been so long detained in Pennsylvania by the difficulty of obtaining supplies that before his arrival in Virginia Richmond had been burned by the predatory force under Phillips and Arnold, while the planters on the shores of the rivers emptying into the Chesapeake are said to have lost property by their depredations amounting in value to several millions of pounds. The command of the combined force of the enemy in Virginia was now held by Cornwallis, who manœuvred in such a way as to command the peninsula between the James and York Rivers. His headquarters were at Portsmouth, opposite Norfolk, which he converted into a fortified dépôt for the reception of supplies from the fleet by which, if necessary, it might be protected. The object of La Fayette and Wayne during the summer of 1781, when their army formed the only American force in Virginia, was to check the raids of the English detachments sent into the interior of the country intent on robbery and the destruction of military stores. It was also important to prevent the retreat of Cornwallis from Portsmouth into North Carolina. It was essential to the success of Washington's plan for the campaign that Cornwallis's army should be held, for the present at least, at the mouth of the Chesapeake, and until Washington with the army from the North and the French fleet should co-operate in the autumn to complete his discomfiture by blockading his army. Of course the English could not understand the significance of the movements which Washington was making so as to secure the aid of another French fleet which was expected to arrive in the Chesapeake from the West Indies. He concealed his plans under the pretext of attacking New York with the aid of the French forces under Rochambeau. By a strange infatuation, Sir Henry Clinton in New York greatly aided Washington's plan by ordering Cornwallis to establish himself at some strong point at the entrance of the Chesapeake. La Fayette and Wayne, who had been admitted to a partial knowledge of Washington's plans, were satisfied in the latter part of the summer that if they were carried out Cornwallis must surrender.

After the junction of La Fayette and Wayne, they followed the marauding army, which was then operating on the peninsula between the James and York Rivers, avoiding, of course, a general engagement, as their force was greatly inferior in numbers, and striving to find an occasion on which they could do some service by attacking the British rear-guard. This mode of campaigning involved a great deal of wearisome marching and countermarching with much distress to La Fayette's men, and inflicted, apparently, very little injury on the enemy. It certainly had the effect, however, of

confining hostile operations within a comparatively limited territory.   On the 6th of July it seemed as if the
long-hoped-for opportunity of attacking the enemy to
advantage had arrived.   Cornwallis, moving down the
James River on his way to Portsmouth, sent a portion
of his force across the river.   Intelligence was brought
to La Fayette that the English force was cut in two
by a wide river, and that consequently there was a
favorable chance of attacking its rear, which still remained on the left bank and north side of the James.
La Fayette directed Wayne to move forward at once
and attack that portion of the force which had not yet
crossed.   Upon arriving at Green Spring, near the
enemy, Wayne discovered that the intelligence that any
considerable portion of the army had passed the river
was false.   He and La Fayette, leading the advance,
in order to make a more complete reconnoissance had
crossed a swamp by a causeway with a force of about
eight hundred men before they ascertained that they
had a large portion of Cornwallis's army in their front,
and they soon found this force formed in battle array.
La Fayette at once sent back to the main American army,
a distance of five miles, for reinforcements, ordering
those left behind to join them with all speed.   " Meantime," says Wayne, " the riflemen in the advance commenced and kept up a galling fire upon the enemy,
which continued until five in the afternoon, when the
British began to move forward in columns, upon which
Major Galvan [a French officer in the Continental ser-
vice] attacked them, and after a spirited although unequal contest retired upon our left.   A detachment of
light infantry under Major Willis having arrived also

commenced a severe fire upon the enemy, but it was obliged to fall back.   The enemy observing our small force began to turn our flanks,—a manœuvre in which had they persevered they must have inevitably surrounded our advanced corps and taken position between this corps and the other portion of the army, composing the reinforcement about to join them.   At this crisis Colonel Harmar and Major Edwards with part of the 2d and 3d Penn'a regiments under Colonel Humpton, with one field piece, having joined, it was determined, among a choice of difficulties, to advance and charge the British line, although it numbered more than five times our force."   In other words, Wayne, perceiving that he was confronted by the entire force of the enemy, whose lines overlapped and endangered his flanks, decided instantly that the proper move to make was a vigorous charge.   A sudden retreat might have ended in a panic.   To await the shock of the approaching army might be ruinous.   "With the instinct of a leader and the courage of a lion," says Professor Johnston, " he determined to become the assailant,— to advance and charge."   Within seventy yards of the enemy, and for fifteen minutes, a sharp action took place.   All the horses of the American artillery were either killed or disabled.   In danger of being outflanked all the time, the Pennsylvania line was steady, and retreated through the woods and across the swamp to Green Spring, where it re-formed.

This charge at Green Spring has always been regarded as the most brilliant example of the characteristics of Wayne's military genius.   To be sent as he was with a small reconnoitring force across a swamp passable only by a narrow causeway, to find himself confronted by a force five times as large as his own, and to escape being surrounded and captured, was a feat which required absolute presence of mind on his part and the power of deciding in a critical juncture what was to be done on the instant, as well as perfect discipline in his soldiers. Wayne seems to have had that military instinct which led him to see exactly what ought to be done at the particular moment, and the courage to do it. It was a case in which what appeared to be rashness was the best—indeed, the only —course he could pursue. He had that absolute confidence in the courage of his troops which led him to undertake what seemed a very bold manœuvre, perfectly convinced that they would follow wherever he should lead. He was blamed by some military critics, but the weight of authority was entirely on his side. Washington writes to him,—

"I with the greatest pleasure received the official account of the action at Green Spring. The Marquis de La Fayette speaks in the handsomest manner of your own behavior and that of the troops in the action." General Greene, his friend and commander, says, " The Marquis gives you glory for your late conduct in the action at Jamestown, and I am sensible you merit it. It gives me great pleasure to hear of the success of my friends, but" (and he here speaks from his own experience) "be a little careful and tread softly, for, depend upon it, you have a modern Hannibal to deal with in the person of Cornwallis. Oh that I had had you with me a few days ago! your glory and the public good might have been greatly advanced." General

Wayne did not follow Greene's advice to tread "softly on the heels of Cornwallis," who was soon shut up in Yorktown, whence he "came out to vex his enemies no more." One of the most enthusiastic letters which Wayne received at this time was from Robert Morris, who paints in lively colors the effect of so gallant an action as that of Wayne in strengthening the tone of public feeling. "We have received," he says, "a full report of the action at Green Springs. It is very flattering to find our troops arrived at that degree of discipline which enables them to face with inferior numbers that proud foe who have heretofore attempted to treat our army with such contempt. It is still more agreeable to find that this handful of troops have been led to the conflict by officers revered for their public and esteemed for their private conduct through life. I do assure you, my worthy friend, that I shall think my present toils well rewarded when they enable you and your competitors for glory to enjoy the sweets while you endure the toils of a military life."

The following is the official report of the action by La Fayette to General Greene, 8th of July, 1781 :

(*From the Pennsylvania Gazette, July 25, 1781.*)

HEAD QUARTERS July 8, 1781

SIR,—I have the honour to enclose to your Excellency a copy of my letter to Maj. General Greene, containing the proceedings of the two armies since my last.

With great respect &c &c

LA FAYETTE.

HIS EXCELLENCY THE
PRESIDENT OF CONGRESS

AMBLER'S PLANTATION, OPPOSITE JAMES RIVER
July 8, 1781

SIR,—On the 4th instant the enemy evacuated Williamsburg, where some stores fell into our hands, and retired to this place, under the cannon of their shipping. The next morning we advanced to Bird's Tavern, and part of the Army took post at Norrell's Mill, about nine miles from the British Camp.

The 6th I detached an advanced corps under General Wayne, with a view of reconnoitring the enemy's situation. Their light parties being drawn in, the picquets, which lay close to their encampments, were gallantly attacked by some riflemen, whose skill was employed to great effect.

Having ascertained that Lord Cornwallis had sent off his heavy baggage under a proper escort, and posted his army in an open field, fortified by the shipping, I returned to the detachment which I found more generally engaged. A piece of cannon had been attempted by the Vanguard under Major Galvan, whose conduct deserves high applause. Upon this the whole British Army came out and advanced to this wood occupied by General Wayne. His corps chiefly composed of Pennsylvanians and some light infantry, did not exceed 800 men, with three field pieces, but notwithstanding their numbers, at sight of the British Army the troops ran to the rencontre; a short skirmish ensued with a close, warm, and well directed fire; but as the enemy's right and left of course greatly outflanked ours I sent General Wayne orders to retire half a mile to where Colonels Vose and Barber's light infantry battalions had arrived by a most rapid move, and where I directed them to form. In this position they remained till some hours in the night. The militia under General Lawson had advanced and the continentals were at Norrell's mill, when the enemy retreated during the night to James island, which they also evacuated, crossing over to the south side of the river. The ground at this place and the island was sufficiently occupied by General Muhlenburg. A number of valuable horses were left on their retreat. From every account the enemy's loss has been very great, and much pains taken to conceal it. Their light infantry, the brigade of guards, and two British regiments formed the first line; the remainder of their army the second.— The cavalry were drawn up but did not charge.

19

By the enclosed return you will see what part of General Wayne's detachment suffered most. The services rendered by the officers make me happy to think that although many were wounded we lost none. Most of the field officers had their horses killed ; the same accident to every horse of two field pieces made it impossible to move them, unless men had been sacrificed.

But it is enough for the glory of General Wayne and the officers and men he commanded, with a reconnoitring party only to have attacked the whole British Army close to their encampment, and by this severe skirmish hastened their retreat over the river.

Colonel Boyer of the riflemen is a prisoner.

I have the honour to be &c &c

LA FAYETTE.

MAJOR-GENERAL GREENE.

(*From the Pennsylvania Gazette, August 1, 1781.*)

" Extract from the Marquis La Fayette's General orders.

" AMBLER'S PLANTATION, OPPOSITE JAMES RIVER, July 8, 1781.

" The General is happy in acknowledging the spirit of the detachment commanded by General Wayne in their engagement with the total of the British Army, of which he happened to be an eye witness. He requests General Wayne, the officers and men under his command, to receive [torn] best thanks.

" The bravery and destructive fire of the riflemen engaged, rendered essential service.

" The brilliant conduct of Major Galvan and the Continental detachment under his command, entitle them to applause.

" The conduct of the Pennsylvania field and other officers are new instances of their gallantry and talents. The fire of the light infantry under Major Willis checked the enemy's progress round our right flank. The General was much pleased with the conduct of Captain Savage, of the Artillery, and it is with pleasure he also observes, that nothing but the loss of horses could have produced that of the two field pieces.—The zeal of Colonel Mercer's little corps is handsomely expressed in the number of horses he had killed."

The following letters show the care taken by General Wayne of his wounded officers :

PROVIDENCE FORGE 10th July 1781

MY DEAR FRIENDS,—Gratitude Duty & Inclination independent of those principles which ought to Inform every humane heart, leads me to use every possible exertion to render Gent'n (who have so honorably & freely bled in the defence of the Liberties of this Country) as comfortable as Circumstances will admit of, be assured that nothing but the most positive assurance of your being so would have prevented me from using every exertion to have you properly supplied & attended to

It is but this moment I was informed of the inattention which you have experienced—& have fallen upon the only means in my power to remedy it by directing the Commissioners of the County to supply you with those Comforts which wounded Officers are entitled to, & if the County will not pay it to place it to my acct.— I shall be happy to hear from you often & wish you to Command my services on every Occasion

That you may soon recover from your wounds & restored to your anxious friends is the sincere wish of your most

Obt & very
Hum Sert—
ANT'Y WAYNE.

The Wounded Officers to General Wayne.

SIR,—We have ben Hon'd with y'r kind inquire respecting Our health, and situation, generously ofering to Supply our wants, even at your own expense— Altho' our accommodations have ben but indiferent owing to the Inhospittality of the people, and a neglect in the heads of the medical department for this State—we did not think it concistent with the character of soldiers to give uneasiness to a Gentleman whos known generrosity, and Parental care, has endeared him to evry officer and Soldier under his com'd, and remov'd evry doubt of his Indefatigable assiduity to render their Situation Happy— We at present have a prospect of being Supply'd with evry thing necesary to render our Situation as comfortable as the climate will admit of.

It is the opinion of the Surgeons that a cooler Climate would be more friendly, and tend to expedite the rejoining our commands;

Strongly recommending our repairing to Penns'a until the heat of the season is over.

If such an expedient should meet with your Approbation, our reliance must be in you to enable us to proceed in character.

A light waggon for the purpose of transporting our Baggage, and orders to Draw Forage would be necessary, whether we can be supply'd with Horses, and Sadles, without y'r Friendly Aid is uncertain—

The Marquis was so good as to send one of his Aides to inquire after our wants, we informed him of our Difficulty respecting Horses &c., he said we should be supply'd, but we fear the multiplicity of buisness has prevented his recollecting the promise—

In Short, sir, our Dependance is on you, to equip us for the Tour to the North, hoping to return in a short time and prove our selves worthy the notice of that General whose Ambition is to reward the Brave.

In the mean time beg leave with evry Sentiment of Esteem, to Subscribe ourselves

Sir y'r

verry Humble Serv'ts

W. Finney

and Companions

Hanover 12th Aug't 1781

Gen Wayne

After the engagement at Green Spring Lord Cornwallis retired to Portsmouth, on the south side of the James, and began to fortify himself there. La Fayette, fearing that further raids might be made by detachments of British troops into the interior of the country for the destruction of military stores and other property, or that Cornwallis might decide to retire into North Carolina, ordered Wayne to cross the river at Westover[1] and take post at Cabin Point, on the road

[1] On his leaving Westover, then, as now, the stateliest of all the colonial houses in Virginia, Mrs. Byrd, the widow of the former

between Norfolk and Petersburg, so that any attempt to retire on the part of Cornwallis might be frustrated. But the days of Cornwallis's raids and forays in Virginia, as well as the time for his safe retreat, were at last over. He had received orders from Sir Henry Clinton, about the time that Wayne crossed at Westover, to select the most advantageous post at the mouth of the Chesapeake and fortify his position, placing himself in ready communication with the fleet, which was expected to aid him in his operations. The place which he selected, in pursuance of these orders, but contrary to his own judgment, which pointed to a retreat into North Carolina as the proper course to be taken, was, as is well known, Yorktown. The campaign in Virginia, from which the English ministry had hoped such great things, was a disastrous one, owing to the active and enterprising opposition made by La Fayette and Wayne.

All the interest in the great drama which was to terminate in the ignominious surrender of the troops they had been pursuing during the summer becomes from this time concentrated on the siege of Yorktown. Each separate part of the complicated plan which had been arranged by Washington for the destruction of Cornwallis seemed to work in wonderful harmony with the rest. All moved forward together with the certainty of an inexorable fate. On the 25th of August Washington crossed the Hudson on his march to lower Virginia, the rear of his army being reinforced by the French troops under Rochambeau lately stationed at Newport.

proprietor, wrote General Wayne a note thanking him for his great kindness and expressing her good wishes.

On the same day De Barras sailed with the French fleet from Newport for the Chesapeake, carrying with them the stores for the troops and the siege-artillery. On the 30th of August De Grasse with another French fleet coming from the West Indies, carrying three thousand troops under Saint-Simon, anchored safely in Hampton Roads before Admirals Graves and Hood, the English admirals, reached the Virginia capes. These troops were landed a few days later at Burwell's Ferry.[1] On the same day the fleet of De Barras, which had also just arrived in the Chesapeake, formed a junction with that of De Grasse, and the combined fleet (far superior in the number of ships) went to sea in search of the English squadron under Graves and Hood. The French so much damaged the English fleet off the mouth of the Chesapeake as to insure its non-intervention during the siege of Yorktown. Thus it appears that by a most remarkable coincidence—or shall we not say by a wonderful providential interposition?—all Washington's plans were successfully carried out, and the larger portion of the force which was to crush Cornwallis arrived within striking distance of Yorktown with a precision hitherto unknown in military history. During these five days while events were hastening to a crisis, La Fayette received from Washington a confidential communication telling him of the proposed combined action of his own army and its

[1] "Went down with Stewart and saw the landing of the French troops on James Island. Mortifying and surprising sight to two British flag ships that lay at this place who never heard the least whisper of this great event until the troops and vessels were among them."—*Richard Butler's Diary, September 2, 1781.*

French allies with the French fleet at the mouth of the Chesapeake. This was all that was needed to induce La Fayette to take every precaution to oppose with his own troops and those of Wayne any attempt on the part of Cornwallis to escape into North Carolina. They awaited with anxious impatience the arrival of Washington and Rochambeau.

Before the arrival of Rochambeau General Wayne wrote as follows to Robert Morris:

WILLIAMSBURG 14th Sept. 1781.

The arrival of the Count De Grasse with a large fleet of Men of War &c must have been announced in Phil'a long before this will reach you; I wish that the State of our Magazines &c had been such as to enable us to Improve the moment of his Arrival, but it was not nor is not even at this moment.

I don't know how it is, but I have not felt so sanguine on the Occasion—as the naval & land force sent us by our good & great ally would justify—probably it is Occasioned by our former disappointments when matters bore a flattering appearance.

Do you know notwithstanding all this that I have been extremely uneasy lest the Appearance of a British fleet off this Cape should Induce the Count to follow them too far & leave an Opening for the British to enter—to his exclusion. Admiral Hood with 8 (?) sail of the Line last Wednesday week made His appearance. The Count De Grasse with 22 Sail weighed anchor 14 of which Engaged Hood— the Other could not get up in time. 4 Sail of the Line were left to defend the entrance of the Cheseapeake.

The British admiral fled too soon for anything but an act of Choice—may he not wish to draw De Grasse towards New York & expose the French fleet to the Effects of the Equinoctial Storm, whilst the british lay snug in harbour— The Count D'Estaing was taken in by Lord Howe—this time three years ago—partly in the same manner—but it cannot—it must not be the case now.

Unless fortune is uncommonly unkind Lord Cornwallis & his Army must submit to the Combined force of France & America, his numbers are more than is Generally given out, we shall find them

very little short of 7000, taking in the Marines there are at least
6000 Combatants officers included exclusive of negroes—so that
During the Absence of the Count De Grasse, who has a large body
of marines on board Destined to act with us—

The french troops are the finest & best made body of men I ever
beheld—their Officers and Gen'l & I will be answerable for their
being soldiers, we have the highest Opinion of their Discipline &
can not doubt their *prowess*—(?)

[To Robt. Morris, Esqr.] [1]

On the 2d of September an unfortunate accident happened to Wayne which very nearly deprived him of
the glory of participating in the siege of Yorktown.
He had occasion one evening to visit the camp of La
Fayette, when one of the sentries mistaking him for an
enemy fired his musket and wounded the general in the
fleshy part of the leg. But no wound could check his
ardor or his enterprise on the eve of the great events
which he knew were about to transpire. He writes to
Mr. Peters on the 12th of September "that if powder
enough had been put into the cartridge, the ball which
grazed the bone would have gone through his leg."
He tells him that "this *caitiff*" (a favorite expletive
with him) "disorder is now leaving me, and I shall in a
few days take an active and interesting command in
despite of the ball, and hope to participate in the glory
attending the capture of Lord Cornwallis and his marauding army." It is interesting to notice, by the way,
the expression of the good feeling of the officers called
out by this misfortune of their general. In his private

[1] There seem to be some omissions in this rough draught of the
letter sent to Mr. Morris, but it is so characteristic that it has been
thought best to print it without any attempt to supply the omissions.

diary bold Richard Butler, who had so often been Wayne's chosen comrade in deadliest peril, writes, " The wound is mortifying to this good officer, and to the troops he commands, who love him, and wish his presence with them in the field on all occasions."

Wayne and his colonels seem to have been the first American officers to welcome the French troops under M. de Saint-Mame, brought by the fleet of the Comte de Grasse, and to aid them in selecting a suitable place for an encampment near Williamsburg. They seem to have been very soon on pleasant terms with the strangers.

On the 26th of September Washington's army, with the French auxiliaries under Rochambeau, reached Williamsburg. Washington was received with the highest honors by the newly-arrived French troops, and they and the Americans soon became very effusive in the expression of their joy that they were engaged in a common enterprise under such a general, which promised to be so successful and to produce such brilliant results. The officers of each army vied in their efforts to entertain worthily those of the other. Butler speaks in his diary of one of these entertainments, where an elegant band of music played "an introductive part" of a French opera, "signifying the happiness of the family when blessed with the presence of the father,"—a singular mixture of sentiment with warlike surroundings.[1]

[1] The opera referred to is probably the once famous opera of "Lucille," by Grétry, at that time very popular in Paris. It contained the well-known song,—

> "Où a-t-on plus de bonheur
> Qu'au sein de sa famille," etc.

There was nothing specially noteworthy in the part taken by the Pennsylvania line under Wayne at York-town. His two battalions, containing about seven hundred men, were brigaded as heretofore with Colonel Gaskin's Virginia battalion, and formed part of the division under Von Steuben. The third battalion of Pennsylvanians, under Colonel Craig, arrived too late to take part in the siege, and so did General St. Clair. The storming and capture of the two redoubts, the only operation attended with serious danger, was not assigned to the Pennsylvania line, but two of its battalions supported the attack. The truth is, the superiority of the allies in numbers, and the skill with which they made use of their siege-artillery, made the surrender of Cornwallis as certain as any event in war could be. On the 17th of October the enemy beat the *chamade* at ten o'clock. Negotiations for the surrender immediately followed, and on the 19th the garrison became prisoners of war, and Cornwallis's army was no more.[1]

The news of the capitulation was received with unbounded joy all through the country; but it seemed to be the signal, as victories in the past had been, not for renewed efforts, but for a relaxation of the vigor and energy with which the war had been prosecuted. As

[1] To show the strange course which the amenities of civilized warfare take, we insert a note of Lord Cornwallis to General Wayne declining the latter's invitation to dinner :

"Lord Cornwallis presents his compliments to General Wayne, and is sorry he cannot have the pleasure of waiting upon him to-morrow, being engaged to dine with the Count Saint Maime.

"Nov. 1st."

after Saratoga and after Monmouth, many believed that peace was not only well assured, but that it was nigh at hand ; a most fatal delusion, which added to the cost of our independence many lives and much treasure. It is worth while to reproduce here a letter from General Wayne, one from Colonel Walter Stewart, and another from his trusty chaplain, Rev. David Jones, explaining the condition of feeling in Congress and the Assembly of Pennsylvania after the surrender of Yorktown.

General Wayne to Robert Morris.

YORK, 26th Octr. 1781

The surrender of Lord Cornwallis with his Fleet & Army must have been announced in your city before this period

It is an event of the utmost consequence & if properly Improved may be productive of a Glorious & happy peace ; but if we suffer that unworthy torpor & supineness to seize us, which but too much pervaded the Councils of America after the Surrender of Gen'l Burgoyne, we may yet experience great Difficulties,—for believe me it was not to the exertions of America, that we owe the Reduction of this modern Hannibal, nor shall we always have it in our power to Command the aid of 37 sail of the Line & 8000 Auxiliary veterans— Our allies have learned, that on this Occasion, our regular troops were not more than equal to one half their Land force : and altho' our prowess was such as to establish our Character as Soldiers—our means & numbers were far inadequate to the Idea they had formed of American *resources*

Yet the Resources of this Country are great & if Councils will call them forth we may produce a Conviction to the World that we deserve to be free—for my own part, I am such an Enthusiast for Independence, that I would hesitate to enter heaven thro' the means of a secondary cause unless I had made the utmost exertions to merit it.

The Pennsylvanians with some other troops have another field of glory in view—if successful you'l soon hear from us, till when & ever believe me yours

Most Sincerely
ANT'Y WAYNE.

I dare not commit myself to paper—I wish you could take a prospective view of us for a few moments, you then would better understand me.

[To Rob't Morris, Esq.]

Colonel Stewart to General Wayne.

Philad'a Dec. 24, 1781

My Dear General,— . . . As you dreaded, our chimney corner soldiers in this place immediately on the capture of Cornwallis took up the opinion that the war was at an end. Congress were full of the idea of reduction, but this Gen'l Washington put a stop to except in the General officers. The number necessary for the army he is to mention, and Gen'l Lincoln our Secretary at War is to nominate those who remain. I have not yet heard the number mentioned, nor the mode by which Lincoln will proceed to retain them in the service. He must I think do it agreeable to their rank as he will hardly attempt to leave out Superior and keep in inferior officers. Those who retire go on half-pay for life, but I am much afraid it will be very hard to come at.

Morris has no prospect of paying the Army nor do I believe that it will be in his power for a long time— All those officers who held Brevet Commissions and were not attached to any line have their accounts settled and one fifth of their pay given them; the rest they fund with Mr. Morris at six per cent. All the French engineers who were at York in the service of America have got a step in rank. Portail is a Major-General, Gouvion a Colonel &c— Knox is trying hard for the Major General's commission, and is backed by the General. 'Tis at present doubtful, but you know our "grand body" cannot withstand regular approaches, and perseverance, both of which I am of opinion will be used in the present case. Indeed as they have broke through all rules in the present appointments, I think they ought and will attend to Knox, whose merits are Equal to any of the newly promoted.

Our Legislature have done nothing. Their whole session has been employed in the investigation of the election which I am told will prove a villainous one and will criminate in a high degree General Lacey. They have now adjourned until February and God knows what they will do on their meeting.

Philad'a is not as agreeable this winter as it has been, & I am sorry to tell you our cloth is not as much attended to as they were formerly. Be assured, the Army is the place for sociability, friendship, and happiness. You need not expect to see any recruits shortly from this State as there are no measures whatever pursuing to raise them.

Yours sincerely
WALTER STEWART.

Chaplain Jones to General Wayne.

PHILAD'A Dec 28, 1781

DEAR GENERAL,—It would take a large volume to give you a sketch of our public matters in the State of Penn'a, in short, nothing is done by our civil officers that answer any good purpose for the Army— Our taxes are insupportable, and all seems likely to be consumed in support of civil government. The old adage is true, " Out of sight out of mind." I know not when you will receive any thing, the Financier says, as I am informed. All the money lately borrowed from France will be little enough to pay the contractors for the Army— None can be spared for the pay of the Army— This should be collected by taxes, but alas! hard money is heavy, not to be drawn from the Treasury— What is lamentable is that our civil officers receive their pay, but no period is fixed to pay the Army. To-day the Assembly rise, and I believe they have done little more than quarrel about the election. I know not when it will be in my power to return, as I can get no money. Mrs. Wayne spent Wednesday evening at my house she is hearty. . . . I have no pleasure in Penn'a at present. In the Army there is some Virtue still—

DAVID JONES—

CHAPTER VIII.

On the 1st of November a detachment consisting of Colonel Butler's, Colonel Walter Stewart's, and Colonel Craig's battalions of the Pennsylvania line and Colonel Gist's Maryland battalion, was ordered to leave Williamsburg and reinforce General Greene's army in South Carolina. These troops were commanded by Wayne as brigadier- and St. Clair as major-general. On the 4th of January, 1782, this detachment joined General Greene at Round O in South Carolina. Passing by General St. Clair, Greene sent Wayne into Georgia with a very small force with general instructions to re-establish as far as might be possible the authority of the United States within that State. To understand fully Wayne's position and operations in the campaign that followed, some explanation of the condition of affairs at that time in Georgia is needed.

The people of that State were then utterly demoralized and impoverished by the partisan warfare which had been so long waged within its limits. The peculiar distress of the inhabitants was due quite as much to the bitter, malignant hatred subsisting between the Whigs and Tories of the State, with both of whom the cruel custom of putting people to death after surrender prevailed, as to the operations of the British army.

286

The population was sparse and scattered, and no set-tled law was recognized or obeyed. Taxes could not be collected, and the poverty of the State was such that the Legislature in 1782 passed a law authorizing the governor to seize upon the first ten negroes he could find, sell them, and appropriate the proceeds to the payment of his salary. Yet this was the same Legis-lature that was so penetrated with gratitude for the services of General Wayne in rescuing the State from the enemy, and in restoring peace, law, and order, that they voted thirty-nine hundred guineas for the purchase of the confiscated rice-plantation of Sir James Wright, the last royal governor of the colony, to be presented to General Wayne in the name of the people of Georgia.

Wayne began his campaign by recommending to the governor (Martin), in accordance with General Greene's instructions, that he should issue a proclamation offer-ing pardon and protection to those Tories of the State who had been aiding the British and oppressing their neighbors, on condition that they would make their sub-mission by a certain date. This proclamation, as it an-nounced the policy to be pursued towards the adherents of the royal government in the event of the success of the American arms, doubtless helped to weaken the force of the enemy in the interior. In the mean time active preparations were made by Wayne for a campaign which should subdue all active resistance.

Wayne's force in Georgia consisted of about one hundred of Moylan's dragoons, a detachment of field artillery, a body of three hundred mounted men from Sumter's brigade, under Colonel Hampton, Jackson's and McCoy's volunteers, amounting to one hundred and seventy men, and such of the militia as the governor of Georgia could induce to take the field. For the first time during the Revolutionary struggle Wayne was separated from his long-tried and well-trained comrades of the Pennsylvania line, who were retained in South Carolina by General Greene. He felt their loss sorely, as he tells the general, "Pray give me an additional number of Penn'a troops. I will be content with one battalion of Pennsylvanians. They can bring on their own field equipage without breaking in upon any part of the Army. I will candidly acknowledge that I have extraordinary confidence and attachment in the officers and men who have fought and bled with me during so many campaigns. Therefore if they can be spared you will much oblige me." With the paltry force at his disposal (raw and inexperienced troops for the most part) he was expected to subdue not only the English garrison at Savannah, composed of thirteen hundred regulars, five hundred militia, an indefinite number of refugees, and the Indians their allies, Creeks and Cherokees. Savannah, however, was the only post which was garrisoned by any considerable force of the enemy. To isolate this garrison from the rest of the State, and particularly from its Indian allies in the interior, was Wayne's first object.

He took post at Ebenezer, twenty-five miles above Savannah, on the river. He drew a line from this point to the Ogeechee, intending to cut off the garrison from its supplies as well as from aid from the hostile Indians. His force was too small effectually to guard this line, and General Clarke, the commandant at Savannah, attempted to destroy by fire all the food for man and beast to be found within the circle, and thus force Wayne to abandon his position. Wayne succeeded, however, not merely in preventing a junction between the English and the Creek Indians outside, but also in defeating each party in detail as it attacked him.

Thus, on the 19th of February, 1782, he decoyed by stratagem a large party of Indians coming from the interior within his power, and, after taking from them a considerable amount of the provisions which they were carrying to Savannah, sent them back to tell their own tribesmen that Savannah would certainly be captured by the Americans, and that the best policy for the Indians would be to remain neutral. A considerable force from the Savannah garrison came out to support the Indians; but, finding that they were too late, they retired. So, again, on the 21st of May, the garrison, under Colonel Brown, made a sortie in considerable numbers. To repel them Wayne was obliged to march at night more than four miles over a narrow causeway crossing a swamp to reach the enemy's camp. But he felt, as he characteristically says, "that the success of a night attack depends more on the prowess of the men than their numbers,"—one of his war maxims, by the way, on which he constantly acted. His vanguard charged with the utmost impetuosity the English force, and the result was the defeat and dispersion of Colonel Brown's party, consisting of a large body of cavalry and a detachment of regular infantry and of Indians.

He gives the following account of the difficulties and hardships of this short campaign:

20

"It is now upwards of five weeks since we entered this State, and during that period not an officer or soldier with me has undressed for the purpose of changing his linen; nor do the enemy lay on beds of down.

"The duty done by us in Georgia was more difficult than that imposed upon the children of Israel. They had only to make bricks without straw, but we have had provisions, forage, and almost every other apparatus of war to procure without money; boats, bridges, &c. to build without materials except those taken from the stumps, and what was more difficult than all, to make Whigs out of Tories. But this we have effected and have wrested the country out of the hands of the enemy with the exception only of the town of Savannah."

On the 24th of May some of the more violent of the Creek Indians coming from a great distance in the interior, who had not listened to the advice which he had sent them to remain neutral, made an attempt to surprise Wayne's camp at Sharon, within a short distance from the enemy's lines. These Indians were led by Guristersijo, the principal warrior of the Creeks, and attacked Wayne's camp suddenly with great fierceness on the night of the 24th. Wayne's troops recoiled for a few minutes, and lost some of their guns, but they soon rallied and advanced to the charge, supported by Colonel Posey and Major Finley, who attacked them on the right flank with such irresistible vigor that the savages were totally routed and driven into the swamp and their chief, Guristersijo, was slain. This, like the other attacks on Wayne's force, was a combined action on the part of the English and the Indians. As soon as it was daylight the British made their appearance, but they were soon driven back into the lines of Savannah by a vigorous assault. "Our trophies," says Wayne, "are an elegant standard, 107 horses with a number of packs, arms, &c. and more horses are hourly secured and brought in. Such was the determined bravery with which the Indians fought that after I had cut down one of their chiefs, with his last breath he drew his trigger and shot my noble horse dead under me."

The result of these battles decided the fate of Georgia. It is true that the British Ministry, after the vote of the House of Commons denouncing a continuance of the war, in February, 1782, regarded the question of abandoning Savannah and Charleston as one of time only, yet neither place was given up until the commanders were forced to do so by the success of the military operations of the Americans. Savannah was evacuated on the 11th of July, and Charleston in December of that year, and Wayne was at the head of the forces which took possession of both places.

The campaign of Wayne in Georgia was the only one which had been completely under his own superintendence and direction. It was regarded on all hands, at that time, not merely as most brilliant in its results, but as exhibiting generalship and military skill in a wonderful degree. He was no longer spoken of as "Mad Anthony," for his achievements made him worthy to rank as a strategist with Turenne or the Duke of Marlborough. That such a small force as his, made up for the most part of raw and inexperienced volunteers, interposed between the garrison at Savannah and

its allies the warlike Creeks and Cherokees, should so
manœuvre as to defeat each of these hostile bodies in
turn while they were attempting to support each other,
three times in three months, and compel at last the
evacuation of Savannah, the stronghold of the enemy
in Georgia, was regarded by every one as due to the
inspiration of a military genius of the very highest
order.   Nowhere was Wayne a greater hero than
among the people whom he had rescued from insupportable anarchy in so short a time.   Georgia showed
her gratitude, as we have said, by giving out of her
poverty thirty-nine hundred guineas to purchase an
estate for her deliverer.   The contrast between this
treatment and that of Pennsylvania of her illustrious
son is thus characteristically spoken of by Wayne's old
friend and comrade Richard Butler: "It gives great
satisfaction to the generous souls among your friends
here to think that the people of more Southern climes
have paid some deference to your merits, and have
demonstrated it in a more solid manner than empty
poor praise.   This is an article of no more worth here
than the Continental currency."

The British army having evacuated Savannah, Wayne
was ordered by General Greene to return with his force
to South Carolina to aid in the reduction of Charleston.
He left Georgia in August, 1782, bearing with him
kind wishes from the grateful hearts of its inhabitants,
and an expression of the great esteem in which his
military qualities and his kind and considerate treatment of the troops under his command were held by
all the officers of the auxiliary force which had served
with him.   He was also much gratified at the conclu-

sion of his labors by the receipt of a letter from General Greene in which the latter thus expresses his appreciation of the value of his services during the campaign. He had at all times the support and sympathy of his commander.

General Greene to General Wayne—Extract.

HEAD QUARTERS
ASHLEY RIVER July 14, 1782

DEAR SIR,—I am very happy to hear that the enemy have left Savannah, and congratulate you most heartily on the event. I have forwarded an account thereof to Congress and the Commander in chief expressive of your singular merit & exertions during your command and doubt not that it will merit their entire approbation as it does mine.

There was, indeed, no dissenting voice in any quarter either as to the brilliant results of the campaign or as to the skill and bravery with which it had been conducted by Wayne. He had, truth to say, just then much need of sympathy and encouragement. The war was over, and with it was gone, as he felt, all opportunity of gaining further distinction as a soldier. Almost immediately after his retirement to South Carolina he was attacked by a form of fever which has always proved dangerous to unacclimated whites on that low coast. During the three autumnal months the ranks of his little army were fearfully thinned by this plague, and he himself was so utterly prostrated by the disease that, although he recovered his health measurably, he never afterwards regained his full strength and vigor. As soon as he was able to take the field he applied for active service. In the beginning of December the light infantry of the army and the legionary corps formerly commanded by Colonel Harry Lee were added to his force by General Greene. The number of Pennsylvania troops serving in South Carolina was so reduced by disease and by casualties of all kinds that those who survived were consolidated into one battalion. All that were left were about six hundred men who had enlisted for the war, and one hundred and fifty eighteen-months men. At this time (December, 1782) Richard Butler, who was in charge of the recruiting dépôts in Pennsylvania, wrote to General Wayne that in these dépôts there were more than eighteen hundred enlisted men for the infantry, besides a considerable number of men engaged for the cavalry and the artillery. But they were not sent on, the State authorities declining to do so under the fatal delusion which had so often misled them, that their services would not be needed, and therefore that it would be useless to incur any further expense in preparing them for the field. No more men were engaged, and those who had been recruited were not paid.

During the winter General Wayne was engaged in negotiating a treaty of peace with the Creeks and Cherokee Indians at Augusta, which completed his work of the pacification of Georgia.

In October, 1783, he was appointed by Congress major-general by brevet on the recommendation of the Executive Council of Pennsylvania. It is not a little singular that a man recognized on all hands as one of the most skilful and successful officers of the army, one who had performed for several years most satisfactorily the duties of a major-general, should have gone through the war with the rank of brigadier-general only. It is due to the State authorities of Pennsylvania to say that this apparent neglect was caused by no want of effort on their part to force a recognition of his merits upon Congress. Indeed, it can hardly be said that the blame should rest on that body for not according him the rank to which his great services seemed to entitle him. The difficulty arose from the vicious system of promotion which had been adopted by Congress early in the war in order to avoid exciting jealousy on the part of the States which furnished most men for the army. The rule was that the generals should be assigned to each State in proportion to the number of men it sent into the field. Pennsylvania had two major-generals very early in the war,—Mifflin and St. Clair. It is true that her troops garrisoning Fort Pitt, Sunbury, and Fort Stanwix were in number large enough to form another brigade, as has been said, and to entitle Wayne, who was the senior brigadier, to promotion; yet Congress persistently ignored the claim of Wayne on such grounds, and at last was forced to make him a major-general by brevet, in consideration of the extraordinary value of his services.

Of this half-hearted and hesitating recognition of his services Wayne seems never to have complained. It was not his way. He and his comrades seem to have been much more affected by the unkind and ungenerous suspicions which were expressed by selfish and unscrupulous politicians concerning the motives and intentions of those who had established the Society of the Cincinnati.

Few things are more discreditable in the history of the Revolution than the aspersion of the character of those who had brought about the triumphant result, because they saw fit at the close of the war to establish a fraternal association among the survivors to aid each other in time of need, and to keep alive in their children the memory of their heroic deeds. The sorrow and indignation with which two of the most distinguished veterans of that war regarded this attempt to heap odium on them are aptly expressed in the following letters of General William Irvine and General Wayne :

General Irvine to General Wayne.

CARLISLE April 28, 1784

DEAR GENERAL,—The Society of the Cincinnati is now bandied about in this quarter, and held up as a growing evil of vast importance—in short as the fore-runner of the entire loss of liberty. For this purpose and to favor the Constitution Mr. Burk's performance is sent from Philadelphia to all true friends in the State, and propagated as a warning to rouse jealousy & enrage the populace against the members. I was informed yesterday that a scheme is on foot if the election can be carried, to disfranchise every member of the Society as a preparation ; in case they have spirit to resent—to drive every soul out of the State. How true this is I will not venture to say, but sure I am that there is base ingratitude enough interwoven in the constitution of a majority of the multitude to prompt them to greater Villainy than can well be imagined, and it is too melancholy a fact that there are not a few of their leaders of similar dispositions, and the bulk of the people have acquired the extreme liberty they now enjoy on too easy terms to feel the real use or benefit of peace, and instead of gratitude to those who have not only done the business, but are almost the only sufferers, look upon them as nuisances which must at all events be removed out of the way.

General Wayne to General Irvine.

WAYNESBOROUGH, 18 May 1784

DEAR GENERAL,—The revolution of America is an event that will fill the brightest page of history to the end of time. The conduct of her officers and soldiers will be handed down to the latest ages as a model of virtue perseverance & bravery. The smallness of their numbers, and the unparalleled hardships & excess of difficulties that they have encountered in the defense of this country from her coldest to her hottest sun, places them in a point of view hurtful to the eyes of the leaders of faction & party, who possess neither the virtue nor the fortitude to meet the enemy in the field, and seeing the involuntary deference yet paid by the bulk of the people to the gentlemen of the army,—envy, that green-eyed monster, will stimulate them to seize with avidity every opportunity (or rather pretext) to depreciate the merits of those who have filled the breach, and bled at every pore. Nor is Caitiff ingratitude the growth of any particular country or climate. The Republics of Greece & Rome furnish precedents innumerable for them to go upon, and the order of the CINCINNATI was a favorable opening for them to enter, which with the sophistical & labored performance of an angry & disappointed man has served as a baneful medicine to poison the minds of the people & prejudice them against us.

General Wayne was elected president of the Georgia State Society of the Cincinnati July 5, 1790.

In June, 1783, the soldiers of the army received six months' furlough, and in December following they were discharged, as a definitive treaty of peace had in the mean time been agreed upon. The soldiers in the Pennsylvania line received for the three months' pay due them notes of the nominal value of twenty shillings, but worth, really, but two shillings to the pound. Some recruits at the dépôt at Lancaster, indignant at their dishonest treatment, came in a body to Philadelphia as soon as they received their furlough, to demand justice, or what was equivalent to it, their just dues. So far as appears, there never was any attempt on the part of these men to overawe Congress by force. They used no threats of violence, but they insisted, as was right and natural, that the contract made with them should be observed. Some members of Congress became alarmed, frightened possibly, and that body agreed to adjourn to Princeton, alleging that their liberty was restrained by a mob in Philadelphia. Had there been any real cause of alarm, the means of quelling any disturbance were at hand. President Dickinson (the governor of the State), it is true, did not call out the militia, because it was apparent that as between Congress and the soldiers the multitude earnestly supported the rightful claims of the latter, and, besides, the people of Philadelphia had seen too much of the members of Congress during the many years it held its sessions in their city to feel any exalted respect for the dignity of that body. Had an overt act been committed by the discharged recruits (or so-called soldiers) there would have been no difficulty in checking them. It so happened that the first two companies of Wayne's veterans had just arrived from South Carolina, and were quartered in the city barracks pending their discharge. As soon as the alarm was given, these two companies fell in to a man and marched to the President's house and reported to the general in command.[1] Doubtless had their assistance been required either to protect Congress from coercion or to guard the money belonging to the government which was supposed to have been deposited in the bank, they would soon have made short work of the Lancaster recruits.

The prospect that the soldiers on their discharge would be left in a pitiable condition of want and suffer-

---

[1] Denny's Journal, p. 257.

ing excited the sympathy of all those who had profited by their labors. Wayne seems to have been impressed with the necessity of making (so far as it was in the power of the State to do so) their return to civil life easy and natural.

On the 20th of April, 1783, he writes to President Dickinson of Pennsylvania,—

"You are pleased to ask my advice on any thing respecting the troops under my command belonging to your State . . . I fondly flatter myself that the wisdom & justice of the Executive and Legislative bodies of Penn'a will remove every bar, & open wide the door of welcome and receive her returning soldiery with open arms and grateful hearts, and I cannot entertain a doubt that they on their part will cheerfully & contentedly resume the garb and the habits of the citizen."

How these hopes were fulfilled we discover when we find that the soldiers when they were disbanded were offered about one-tenth of what was due them (two shillings or two shillings and sixpence in real value for twenty that was due) in full of all demands.

CHAPTER IX.

In the month of July, 1783, General Wayne, after having seen the last of the Pennsylvania troops embarked at Charleston for Philadelphia, returned to his native State shattered and enfeebled by the fever from which he had suffered. From this cause he was unable to take part in the final ceremonies which attended General Washington's farewell to the army at New York. He was also too ill to attend the commander-in-chief as he passed through Philadelphia on his way to Mount Vernon.

In anticipation of his return, Dr. Rush wrote him in September, 1782, a most kind letter, full of generous appreciation of his services, and telling him with what honors he would be welcomed on his return to his native State by his friends.

Dr. Rush to General Wayne.

PHILAD'A 16 Sep 1782

MY DEAR SIR,—The evacuation of Savannah tho' a voluntary act of the enemy was attended with circumstances that have given you credit among your friends. Penn'a loves you. You are one of her legitimate children. Let nothing tempt you to abandon her. The strangers and the vagabonds who have destroyed her gov't can only be deposed by a union of the native and ancient citizens. There are honors in store for you here—Chester county claims you. Come, my friend, and sit down with the companions of your youth

300

under the shade of trees planted with your own hand.[1] Come and let the name of Wayne descend to posterity in your native State. If your descendants act as you have done it cannot fail of being respected while the sun shines & the rivers flow—

The exertions of the enemy for some time past have been greatly upon the ocean. This City has lost at a moderate computation £800,000 by captures since the first of January. The spirit of the ministry, it is true, is changed but the profits of the war are so immense in New York to Digby & his officers, that we can expect no mitigation of our losses at sea, until the sound of peace reaches the last British cruiser on our coast.

*   *   *   *   *   *   *   *

BENJ. RUSH.

General Wayne to Dr. Rush.

CHARLESTOWN Dec. 24 1782

DEAR SIR,—Want of health & not inclination prevented my acknowledging your obliging favor of the 16th of Sept'r. On the second of that month I was seized with a violent fever, nor have I from that period to this hour enjoyed one day's health. Frequent emetics & constant application of the Peruvian bark. I have this consolation that neither idleness nor dissipation has so injuriously affected my constitution, but that it has been broken down and nearly exhausted by encountering almost every excess of fatigue difficulty and danger in the defence of the rights & liberty of America from the frozen lakes of Canada to the burning sands of Florida.

I feel the lively force of friendship with which you so anxiously solicit my return to my native State, which I shall eventually do, not influenced by the fascinating idea of the honors you say await me (for they have lost their power to please) but from a fixed determination to revisit my Sabine field where I yet hope to pass many happy hours in domestic felicity with a few of our friends unfettered by any public employ & consequently unenvied. Until then & ever believe me with true affection & esteem,

Yours &c

ANTH'Y WAYNE.

[1] There was at this time a rumor that it was General Wayne's intention to take up his residence in Georgia.

In the Constitution of Pennsylvania adopted in 1776 there was a provision peculiar to that State, creating a body to be called the Council of Censors. It was to meet every seven years, and two censors were to be elected in each county. They had no legislative power, but their duty was to inquire whether the Constitution had since their last meeting been preserved inviolate, whether the taxes levied had been duly collected, and whether the laws of the State generally had been executed. This body had the power, in case it found that there had been any violation or neglect of the provisions of the Constitution or laws by the other branches of the government, to pass *censure* upon the offending party, and to recommend to the Assembly the repeal of all such laws as might appear to have been enacted contrary to the Constitution, and, two-thirds consenting, a revision of that instrument by a convention.

Wayne was elected a member of the Council of Censors in 1783, and consequently held that position immediately after the conclusion of the war. It will be readily understood that to perform the functions devolved upon it at such a time, which was nothing less than the substitution of legislation proper for a time of peace for that which had prevailed during the war, called for statesmanlike skill and prudence of no ordinary kind. General Wayne was evidently an active spirit in the Council of Censors while he held office. He maintained upon many questions which came before it very pronounced ideas. He was chairman of the committee appointed to ascertain how far the provisions of the Constitution had been carried out by legislation, and how far and in what way, if at all, they had been violated. The report of this committee is interesting. It treats of measures of conciliation and how far they should be adopted now that peace was restored, and recommends that a course should be taken to make the transition easy from a state of revolution to a normal condition. The committee report that many of the provisions of the Constitution had been violated by the laws passed by the Assembly during the seven preceding years, and there their action seems to have ended. The great measure recommended is a revision of the Constitution. The committee say (January, 1784), in regard to this revision of the Constitution, "It is well known how in times of danger the Constitution (of 1776) forsook us, and the will of our rulers became the only law. It is well known likewise, that a great part of the citizens of Pennsylvania from a perfect conviction that political liberty could never long exist under such a frame of government were opposed to the establishment of it, and when they did submit to it, a solemn engagement was entered into by its then friends that after seven years should be expired, and the enemy driven from our coasts, they would concur with them in making the wished for amendments. The minority in the Council is said not to represent more than one third of the inhabitants, yet the Constitution can not be amended because two thirds of the members of the Council can not be found to approve it."

General Wayne having retired from the Council of Censors was elected a member of Assembly from Chester County in the years 1784 and 1785. While there he displayed his usual activity, and lent the influence of his great name to aid the adoption of measures of justice and humanity, exhibiting the same broad and liberal spirit regarding the provisions of the revolutionary code as that by which he had distinguished himself in the Council of Censors. His great desire was to make the Revolution in its results an actual blessing, both to those who had been hostile and to those who had been neutral while the war lasted.

To accomplish this object it was necessary that the laws passed in 1777 and in 1778 disfranchising forever as *suspected* Tories and Loyalists nearly one-half of the population of the State in number, and much more than one-half if reckoned by their wealth and taxable property, should be repealed. By these acts it had been provided that no resident of the State should ever be permitted to vote for any officer of the government, or be chosen himself to any office, unless before the 1st of November, 1779, he had taken the oath—or test, as it was called—prescribed by law, by which he renounced his allegiance to the King of Great Britain, and declared his fidelity to the State of Pennsylvania. Many besides Loyalists, or adherents to the English crown, had refused or neglected to take this test. The Quakers were, of course, opposed to all political tests. Neutrals, non-resistants from a variety of causes, as well as those who from conscientious scruples were opposed to war (although after it was over most of them were well affected to the State), were included among the non-jurors, the taxation of whose property had greatly aided during the war to support the American cause. The object, of course, of this harsh legislation was to keep the control of the Revolution in the hands of its friends as long as possible. While the war lasted, such a precaution might, perhaps, be regarded as necessary; but peace once declared, such measures became, in the opinion of General Wayne, not only arbitrary but highly impolitic. At no time, it seems to me, in his whole career did Wayne's true greatness of soul and magnanimous spirit appear more conspicuously than in his unceasing efforts to rid Pennsylvania of these odious laws. No one could doubt that he had done more than any inhabitant of the State by his military services from the beginning to the end of the war in support of the cause of the Revolution. No one could doubt that that Revolution was irrevocable; hence his voice, pleading until it forced people to listen to him for a more generous treatment of those who during the war had clung to the old order and thereby had become disfranchised, became in the end most powerful in overcoming the bitter prejudices of the successful party.

As little seems to be now known of the violence of the measures of proscription adopted in Pennsylvania during the Revolution and continued in force many years after the close of the war, a slight sketch of some of the more important of them may not be out of place.

By the act of June 13, 1777, it was provided that all the male white inhabitants of the State above the age of eighteen years should, within a short time, limited by the act, take an oath of allegiance to the State, and forswear allegiance to the crown. On the 1st of October, 1778, this test was renewed and the following oath prescribed :

" I, A. B., do solemnly and sincerely declare and swear or affirm that the State of Pennsylvania is and of right ought to be a free sovereign and independent State, and I do forever renounce and refuse

21

all allegiance subjection and obedience to the King or Crown of Great Britain. And I do further swear that I never have since the Declaration of Independence, directly or indirectly, aided, assisted, abetted or in any wise countenanced the King of Great Britain, his generals, fleets or armies or their adherents in their claims upon these United States, and that I have, ever since the Declaration of the Independence thereof, demeaned myself as a faithful citizen and subject of this or some one of the United States, and that I will at all times maintain and support the freedom and sovereignty and independence thereof."

By the act of 1779 all persons who had not taken the test required by the act of 1777 were directed to take the oath of allegiance prescribed in the act of 1778 within a limited time. Those who refused or neglected to do so were rendered incapable of electing or being elected or holding any office or place within the government, serving on juries, or keeping schools, except in private houses; and after the time specified for taking such test, if they had not taken it they were forever excluded from taking the said oath or affirmation, and were deprived of the privileges of the citizens who complied with the provisions of said act.

Such were the test acts in force during the war. They and the accompanying confiscation acts were enforced with merciless severity. In March, 1784, a petition was presented to the Assembly asking that these "tests" should be abolished. It was laid upon the table, and a resolution providing that a committee should be appointed to revise the laws imposing these tests was rejected, five members only voting in its favor. In September of the same year petitions were presented stating that a large number of young men had attained the age of eighteen years since the test was established, and asking that the law might be relaxed in their favor. This was also rejected. Then, again, a proposition was made in December of that year by General Wayne and his friends in the form of the following resolution:

" WHEREAS, The Assembly is about to impose a tax for paying the interest on the State debt, and whereas it appears that a great portion of the inhabitants are disfranchised by Acts of Assembly founded on causes which no longer exist, therefore, in order to render this tax perfectly agreeable to the 8th & 17th Sections of the Constitution as well as to favor the more general circulation & credit of the paper money to be emitted,

" *Resolved*, That a Committee be appointed to bring in a Bill revising the Test Laws and admitting all persons as Citizens who have not been active or criminal in opposition to the liberties of the State."

This was also rejected. It was then proposed that all those who had not taken the oath required by the act of 1777 might enjoy the privileges of a citizen if they would now take the test required by the act of 1778. This proposition was adopted, twenty-nine yeas to twenty-two nays.

This result caused great popular excitement, the fear being that at last the claims of the non-jurors were to be recognized. On the 28th of September the Assembly was evenly divided upon a proposition to revise the Test Laws, showing how much time had done to soften the asperities of party. The Speaker voting in the affirmative, some of the members opposed to the revision, nineteen in number, arose, and left the Assembly in great confusion, without a quorum. Addresses were published by both sides, and the excitement was kept up to fever heat.

The contest was renewed in the Assembly at the next session, when General Wayne, upon a consideration of petitions from the non-jurors for the repeal of these laws, insisted upon their repeal, using the well-worn arguments in favor of his views, and especially that the necessity of continuing such laws on the statute-book was done away with by the peace, and that nearly one-half of the inhabitants of the State were deprived by them of the privileges of citizens.

These resolutions of Wayne were voted down in December, 1784, by a vote of fourteen yeas to thirty-nine nays, and the report of a committee affirming that "it would be impolitic and dangerous to admit persons who had been inimical to the sovereignty and independence of the State to have a common participation in the government so soon after the war," was adopted by a vote of forty-two to fifteen. The struggle continued with little intermission until 1789, when the contest between the non-jurors and what may be called the Revolutionary party in the State (although many of the most active Whigs had long favored the abolition of tests) reached a conclusion in March of that year. A motion was adopted at that time in the Assembly to "repeal all laws requiring any oath or affirmation of allegiance from the inhabitants of the State." Thus this strange quarrel ended. It had at least one good effect. It cured forever the people of Pennsylvania of intolerance of this kind. Wayne had fought many times in the Revolution against desperate odds with a more rapid success than in this battle against the obstinate but honest prejudices of his misguided friends and fellow-countrymen.

Wayne was a member of the Convention called in Pennsylvania in 1787 to decide upon the ratification of the Constitution of the United States. He was, as may

be supposed, one of the most active and ardent cham-
pions of its adoption, as he well may have been, for no
one had suffered more in his own person from many of
the evils which this Constitution proposed to remedy.

During these conflicts in the Assembly General
Wayne was endeavoring to cultivate to the best advantage his paternal estate in Pennsylvania and his
rice-plantation in Georgia. When he entered upon
the military service his farm and tannery in Chester
County were necessarily placed in the hands of agents,
and Wayne estimated, as we have seen, his loss from
a want of personal supervision of his estate during the
war at seven thousand pounds.

His estate in Georgia, which had been presented to
him by the State, was a rice-plantation of nearly eight
hundred and thirty acres, capable of producing large
crops if its owner could have procured a sufficient
number of laborers to cultivate it. These laborers,
according to the practice of that day in Georgia, must
have been necessarily slaves, and Wayne had not the
means needed to purchase them. He had not the
money himself, nor could he at that time secure either
in Georgia or in Philadelphia the very considerable sum
required for the purpose. Some one in Philadelphia
(probably his friend Robert Morris) suggested that he
should negotiate a loan for that purpose in Holland.
In a letter dated October 22, 1784, to Mr. Van Berkle,
the Minister Resident of Holland in this country, he
sets forth the object of the loan and the nature of the
security which he offered for its repayment. The letter
is interesting as showing the value of the estate which
had been given him by Georgia.

PHILADELPHIA 22nd Oct'r 1784

SIR,—When I had the honor of presenting the Opinion of Mess'rs Wilcocks & Lewis (two of our most eminent Counselors learned in the law) respecting the title of *Waynesborough* together with the Draught & Valuation thereof before Chief Justice McKean I informed your Excellency that I wished to give that Estate as Security for the money that might be lent upon it in *Holland* & to make remittance from time to time for the Interest &'cs in *rice* from my Plantation situate upon the river Savannah in the State of Georgia which Estate was granted and confirmed to me in fee simple by the General Assembly of that State in consideration of the Services rendered them when Commanding Officer in that Department in 1782. This Estate used to net Sr James Wright from 800 to 1000 Barrels of rice, or from between 2400 & 3000 Guineas pr Annum—it is therefore an Object of considerable consequence to me to set to work again the soonest possible, for which purpose I shall proceed for that Quarter in the course of a few weeks, in order to prepare it for a Crop in the Spring, but shall want the aid of about *Four thousand* guineas to stock it with Negroes.

I will punctually pay the Interest by annually remiting rice to Amsterdam, together with the principal in the course of two or three years if wanted.

I should have offered that Estate as Security on Mortgage in preference to *Waynesborough* but was unacquainted with the laws of Georgia as to *Aliens*. The Security by the Laws of Pennsylvania is as Valid & Certain as to a Citizen.

May I therefore take the Liberty of requesting your Excellency to do me the particular favor of writing to the Gentlemen in Amsterdam (a Copy of whose letter upon money matters you have already perused) & should I be fortunate enough to succeed in the Loan you will add to the many Obligations already conferred upon

Your Most Obt
& very Hum Ser't
ANT'Y WAYNE

HIS EXCELL'Y
P. I. VAN BERKLE
Minister of the United Netherlands
to
The United States of America—

A year later he received a letter from Mr. Morris, telling him that the prospect of negotiating a loan of four thousand guineas in Holland was not as favorable as had been anticipated, but he still thought that General Wayne might obtain the money in that country in the course of the summer. What a strange commentary all this is on the poverty of our people at that time, and of the low state of our credit abroad! Neither here nor in Europe, it seems, could four thousand guineas be borrowed on such security as Wayne had to offer, including a mortgage upon his Chester County farm.

The general was, unfortunately, too sanguine of the success of his negotiations with the Holland bankers, and, supposing the loan concluded, drew bills for the amount on his correspondents. These bills were not paid, and were returned protested. The money raised upon them in this country had been probably used for the purchase of negroes, as Wayne writes to his wife from Georgia in August, 1786, in terms which lead one to suppose that his plantation was in successful operation. It became, of course, necessary that he should pay these bills, which seem to have come into the hands of the agent of a Scotch house in Savannah, by whom immediate payment was demanded. Wayne had no money, nor could he at that time raise any, although his estate was abundantly sufficient to pay his debts. He took the only course which any honest man would have taken under the circumstances. He proposed to his creditors either that time should be given to him to meet their claims or that his Georgia plantation should be taken in satisfaction of the debt due

them.   No answer was ever vouchsafed to this proposition except a suit at law, the object of which was to
make his estate in Pennsylvania, as well as that in
Georgia, liable for the payment.   Wayne was humili-
ated and indignant beyond expression at this kind of
treatment, and stormed in his letters about the Shy-
locks who were determined to have the pound of flesh,
in a way which goes to prove, what indeed is plain from
all history, that a successful general may be, and often
is, a very bad financier.

It is not worth while to go further into the details
of the unfortunate controversy which grew out of this
generous gift of the State of Georgia.   It doubtless
did more to embitter the closing years of Wayne's life
than anything which had ever happened to him.   It
forced him to do what must have been most galling to
the pride of such a nature as his, to urge one of his
friends, a member of Congress from South Carolina, to
ask the President to appoint him to the command of
the forces which he felt quite sure must be raised to
repel the incursions of the Creek Indians.   The result
in the end was that Wayne, having paid his debt, held
his Pennsylvania estate and sacrificed that in Georgia.
Thus ended his effort to make the gift of the people of
that State produce, as it was intended it should do, an
income.   The following letter to his wife, written some
years afterwards, shows how deeply he felt the humili-
ation of being in debt.   He felt it all the more bitterly as
the debt had been incurred in order to make that gift a
real and available one.   It is strange that so much of General Wayne's sufferings, bodily and mental, should have
been due to the well-meant act of the people of Georgia.

RICHMOND, GEORGIA—
5 July 1790

I had intended writing you a long letter, but my head will not permit me, at present, to write with any degree of coherency. Persecution has almost drove me mad and brings to my recollection a few lines from " The Old Soldier,"

> " Once gay in life & free from anxious care,
> " I through the furrows drove the shining share,
> " I saw my waving fields with plenty crowned,
> " And yellow Ceres joyous smile around,
> " Till roused by freedom at my country's call
> " I left my peaceful home & *gave up all*.
> " Now, forced alas ! in distant climes to tread,
> " This crazy body longs to join the dead.
> " Ungrateful country ! when the danger's o'er,
> " Your bravest sons cold charity implore.
> " Ah ! heave for me a sympathetic sigh
> " And wipe the falling tear from sorrow's eye."

Adieu—a long adieu
Yours most affectionately
A. W.

In the midst of his financial difficulties General Wayne seems to have retained the affections of the people of Georgia. He had been obliged, owing to the necessity of his looking after his estate there, and also in Pennsylvania, to change his residence so frequently that it became somewhat difficult to determine of which of the two States he was, in his legal relations, a citizen. A large portion of the people of Georgia determined that he had all the legal requisites to serve them as a member of Congress. He was accordingly returned as having been elected on the 3d of January, 1791, a member of the House of Representatives from that State. His election was contested by his opponent,

Mr. James Jackson, and the House having taken the
testimony of many witnesses in Georgia was satisfied
that he had been unduly and illegally returned as a
member. The election seems to have been conducted
without any legal formalities, private persons having
acted as magistrates, and one of the State judges having
been convicted in Georgia of having certified as true
a false return. The whole business was so irregularly
conducted that the House of Representatives instead
of giving the seat to the contestant declared all the
election proceedings void and ordered that a new one
should take place. It was not pretended by any one
that Wayne had been in any way privy to the fraudu-
lent acts of those who acted as election officers. As he
says in a letter written shortly after the decision of the
House, "Both Federalists and Anti-Federalists pronounced in the Halls of Congress that after the fullest
investigation my character stood pure and unsullied as
a soldier's ought to be." So free was he from any
suspicion of this kind, that a few days after the question had been decided he was appointed by President
Washington general-in-chief of the army.

CHAPTER X.

IN April, 1792, General Wayne was appointed by President Washington commander-in-chief of the army of the United States. There are several circumstances connected with this appointment which are noteworthy. In the first place, it shows that the President shared the general conviction that General Wayne was not involved in the scandals which grew out of this contested election in Georgia, and that his personal character was wholly unaffected by the decision of the House of Representatives. Then, again, the position to which he was called was one which at that time required military and diplomatic skill of the highest order to fulfil the duties it imposed upon the commander. Upon his conduct, indeed, would depend, in a great measure, whether the United States should become involved in interminable war with the Indians of the Northwest, as well as with the English, whose refusal to comply with certain articles of the treaty of 1783, and notably with that which provided for the evacuation of the forts in the territory northwest of the Ohio, had led a large party in the country to clamor for war, and nearly every one to feel that hostilities were inevitable. These last campaigns of Wayne were perhaps the most arduous of any in which he was ever engaged, and certainly the importance of the interests at stake in them, which in

315

one word may be described as the peaceful and permanent occupation of our national territory between the Ohio and the Mississippi by emigrants from other sections of the country, can hardly be exaggerated.

It will be remembered that the country north and west of the Ohio having been ceded by Virginia and Connecticut to the United States, a territorial government had been organized there in 1787. Every effort had been made to induce people, and especially those who had belonged to the disbanded army of the United States, to occupy that region. The result was that a large body of emigrants from all parts of the country, as well as old soldiers and their families, soon strove to make their new homes in this region, where they were constantly exposed to the cruel incursions of the Indian savages. To such an extent did these emigrants suffer that it was calculated that between 1783 and 1790 more than fifteen hundred of them, including women and children, were slain. Of course the duty and policy of the government were plain, and that was to provide protection and safety for those whom they had invited to occupy their lands.

It is well to understand that these atrocities were not caused for the most part by any provocations on the part of the whites. The true source of the trouble among the Indians was much older and deeper than any quarrel between them and the whites occurring in the territory itself. It was nothing less than a determination on the part of the savages that the whites should never occupy the lands west of the Ohio, and that that river should form the permanent boundary between them. These Indians of the Northwest were the Shawnees and the Delawares (generally called the Miamis), who had been driven from Pennsylvania and had taken refuge in Ohio after the capture of Fort Duquesne by Bouquet in 1763. As the allies of the English during the Revolution they had proved, under a series of capable chiefs, among the most persistent and bitterest enemies of the American cause. When it was determined to subdue them by a military force, they and their numerous allies, the Wyandots, the Miamis, the Chippewas, and the Pottawatomies, were concentrated in a powerful confederacy in the northwest portion of Ohio, near the rivers Miami, the Maumee, then called Miami of the Lake, and Lake Erie. Here they had ready access to their allies, the Indians further west, to the Canadians, and to the English garrisons at Detroit and at certain smaller posts in Northern Ohio. That they were aided and encouraged by organized forces of Canadians and English not only in their forays against the settlers, but also in their hostilities against the American government, in the heart of whose lands the English had established their garrisons, no one doubted. Hence the danger that in striking the Indians we might be drawn into a war with England.

The government had undertaken several times without success to reduce these tribes to submission, first by means of treaties and afterwards by force. From the time the territory was organized until the tribes were rendered powerless by military conquest there was one stumbling-block in the way, which no effort by negotiation, and no policy of conciliation, and no successful skirmishing, could remove, and that was, as we have said, their determination that the Ohio River should form the boundary between them and the whites. Every emigrant in their view was an enemy and an invader of Indian soil, and as such might be rightfully driven off, or murdered in case of resistance. The government at last most reluctantly determined to send into the northern portion of Ohio an armed force for the protection of the settlers. In 1790 General Harmar, who had been one of the most distinguished officers in the Pennsylvania line during the Revolution, was sent by St. Clair, the governor of the Northwest Territory, with a force of fourteen hundred men to put an end, if possible, to the Indian atrocities from which the settlers were suffering. The army was a motley collection of men without training, ill armed, and totally unwilling to submit to the restraints of discipline. The men were very badly led by officers who, brave indeed, little understood how to cope successfully with the wily foe they were about to encounter. They destroyed on their march a number of Indian villages, but the savages themselves were untouched. At last they met them in force near the site of the present Fort Wayne in Indiana. Here the Indians surprised them, broke into their camp, and, after driving them from it with considerable loss, forced the army to retreat to Fort Washington (Cincinnati), disgraced in its own eyes and without inflicting upon the Indians that punishment which would henceforth keep them quiet. The result was, in fact, only to irritate to a greater degree the savages and to increase their thirst for revenge. At that time, it was said, there were only two hundred and eighty men on the lands of the Ohio Company capable of bearing arms, so that they were in no condition to defend themselves without aid. The massacres after Harmar's expedition were renewed, and the panic among the Western settlers became more alarming than ever.

To complete the work undertaken by Harmar was the reason for fitting out the expedition of St. Clair against the Northwestern Indians in 1791. His purpose originally was to establish a chain of forts from Cincinnati to the Maumee (Miami of the Lake). He had with him about two thousand three hundred regular troops, and pushed on northward, placing his forts at convenient distances. Meantime his force was much diminished by illness and desertion. On the 3d of November he reached a point in the Indian country near the junction of the St. Joseph and St. Mary, afterwards called Fort Recovery, where they were attacked in great force by the savages. The regular soldiers were for a long time steady, and met the Indians in the formation prescribed for fighting troops trained in the same military tactics as themselves. But these tactics did not answer with the Indians. Officer after officer was shot down, and to complete their discomfiture the militia, into whose camp in the rear of the regulars the Indians had penetrated, were driven into the rear of the line, a movement which was not only fatal to the success of those who were bravely holding their own against the enemy in front, but one which threw the whole army into disorder. There was no alternative left but flight, for the Indians had determined to surround the army and to destroy every man in it. They were bravely resisted for hours, but the result was in the end that more than six hundred of St. Clair's soldiers were killed or disabled. Many officers were killed, among them five of high rank. Some of these were among the most distinguished of the Pennsylvania line under Wayne's command during the Revolutionary campaigns. On that field fell General Richard Butler, one of the most brilliant and heroic officers of the army of the Revolution, the friend and comrade of Wayne, as we have seen, in many of the desperate battles of that war.

The following account of the death of General Richard Butler is given in a letter from Colonel E. G. W. Butler (his nephew) to the late General Robert Patterson, of this city :

"Having been shot through the arm & then through the body, my father [Edward Butler], then a captain in St. Clair's army, removed him [General Butler] from the field, and placed him against a tree. He then returned to the battle field and found his other brother, Major Thomas Butler, shot through both legs. He took him from the field and placed him by the side of the General. After the loss of two-thirds of our Army it gave way, and the Indians commenced a hot pursuit. Finding my father incapable of saving both his brothers, my noble uncle, the General, said : 'Edward, I am mortally wounded. Leave me to my fate and save my brother.' And so they left him alone in his glory !

"Soon after Major Gaither of his command seeing the General alone called to some men to assist in taking him from the field, when he remarked, 'No, Gaither, you will only compromise your own safety by the attempt. Take this sword & keep it for my sake, and God bless you !' "

The defeat of Harmar and St. Clair, more especially that of the latter, caused the utmost consternation and dismay throughout the country. These defeats were at once made use of by the opponents of the national administration as pretexts to accomplish party ends, and large numbers of the people were at once arrayed against the prosecution of any Indian war whatever. The cost of maintaining the army, the spectacle of its leader, St. Clair, so ill "as to be unable to stand," the utter want of discipline among the soldiery, the wretched arms with which they were supplied, and the still more wretched food which the contractor provided for them, were all spoken of as so many proofs of ignorance or gross mismanagement, and the changes were so skilfully rung on charges such as these, that an Indian war, even to maintain our unquestioned territorial rights, became the most unpopular of measures. Fortunately, there was strength enough in the administration and Congress to withstand party assaults such as these. The government determined to use an adequate force to maintain our rights and protect the settlers.

The first thing to be done was to reorganize the army and appoint Wayne to the command. By the new organization the army was to consist of one major-general, four brigadier-generals and their respective staffs, the necessary number of commissioned officers, and five thousand one hundred and twenty non-commissioned officers and privates, the whole to be denominated the *Legion of the United States.* The Legion was to be divided into four sub-legions, each to consist of the commissioned officers named and one thousand two hundred and eighty non-commissioned officers and privates. The previous army having been nearly annihilated, a new one was to be recruited. Wayne was, as we have said, appointed to the command of this force (which was not yet raised), and he was told by the Secretary of War at parting, in May, 1792, by way, it is presumed, of encour-

aging him to do his duty, "that another defeat would
be inexpressibly ruinous to the reputation of the government." The only stipulation made by Wayne on
assuming command of the expedition was that the
campaign should not begin until his Legion was filled
up and properly disciplined. General Wayne must
have been a very sanguine man if he could have looked
forward with any confidence to the success of the undertaking in which he was now embarked. We shall
see, however, from the preparations he made for the
campaign, that he trusted nothing to good fortune, and
that in all his movements against the Indians nothing
was more conspicuous by its absence than the "madness" which is popularly attributed to him.

He went to Pittsburgh in June, 1792, and there endeavored to recruit and organize his army,—his "Legion," as it was called. Many of the experienced officers
upon whose intelligent aid he had depended during the
Revolutionary War had been slain in the disastrous campaigns of Harmar and St. Clair, and others had retired
from the military service. He was forced with a most
inadequate staff so to drill and discipline his troops that
they would be able successfully to fight with the Indians.
Even among the boldest and most adventurous spirits
in the army there was neither hope of glory nor prospect of reward in an Indian war. The sad fate of St.
Clair's men, the horrible mutilations and cruelties practised by the Indians upon their prisoners, and their
savage mode of warfare generally, were not calculated
to rouse much enthusiasm among the officers. In
the private soldiers, and especially in the recruits, the
prospect of an Indian campaign excited a feeling of

horror which rendered them liable at any moment to a panic.

Desertions became so common that in a short time those who forsook their duty became almost as numerous as those who remained true to their colors. Fifty-seven recruits left a small detachment on the road from Carlisle to Pittsburgh, and such was the panicky feeling among those who remained that Wayne, in August, 1792, writes from the latter place, "Two nights since, upon a report that a large body of Indians were close in our front, I ordered the troops to form for action, and rode along the line to inspire them with confidence, and gave a charge to those in the redoubts, which I had recently thrown up in our front and right flank, to maintain their post at any expense of blood until I could gain the enemy's rear with the dragoons ; but such is the defect of the human heart, that from excess of cowardice one third of the sentries deserted from their stations so as to leave the most accessible places unguarded."

It is evident that soldiers such as these required a long training and familiarity with military discipline before they could be led against the Indians with any hope of success. Instruction in tactics and training in their military duties were persistently carried on by the commanding general and such of his officers as had any knowledge or experience. The natural result was that as the camp grew in numbers the confidence of the troops and their efficiency increased in the same proportion.

During the summer and autumn efforts were made by Wayne to ascertain whether the Indians were still disposed to be defiant. Their continued depredations on the frontier and the boastful attitude which they maintained were the answers they gave to all attempts at negotiation. It soon became clear to Wayne that the only way to secure Ohio for the settlement of white men was to march into the country occupied by the Indians and subdue them. Towards the close of the summer, therefore, he moved his camp to a position on the Ohio about twenty-seven miles below Pittsburgh, so as to be nearer the seat of hostilities. To this camp he gave the name of "Legionville." There he remained during the winter, recruiting his army, instructing it regularly in its military duties, and in the mean time (not discouraged by his hopeless efforts made hitherto) striving in vain to conciliate the Indians. During this winter the discipline of his little army was greatly improved. At the close of March he writes, "The progress that the troops have made both in manoeuvring and as marksmen astonished the savages on St. Patrick's day; and I am happy to inform you that the sons of that Saint were perfectly sober and orderly, being out of the reach of whiskey, which BANEFUL POISON is prohibited from entering this camp except as the component part of a ration, or a little for fatigue duty or on some extraordinary occasion." His force now consisted of about two thousand five hundred men, and he was inspired with high hopes of success in the event of a conflict with the red men. A characteristic act of his at this time proves his confidence and spirit. He asked the Secretary of War to send him certain flags and standards for the Legion, and on receiving them he wrote what, coming from a man of his

keen sense of military honor, had a peculiar significance:
"*They shall not be lost.*"   In May, 1793, he moved his
camp to Fort Washington, the present site of Cincinnati.   Although in the preceding January he had been
told by General Knox, the Secretary of War, "The
sentiments of the citizens of the United States are
adverse in the extreme to an Indian war," and although
a commission of men of the highest position in the
country had been named to treat with the Indians in
the hope of securing peace, still General Wayne relaxed in no way his efforts to maintain a highly disciplined and efficient army.   Most probably he felt, after
his experience with the savages, that the Indians would
yield to no terms which we could offer them.   He was
told again by the Secretary of War, "It is still more
necessary than heretofore that no offensive operations
should be undertaken against the Indians."   Still he
persevered, and it was well for the country, as will soon
appear, that he listened not to the voice of the charmer
when she promised peace.   He sent to Kentucky for
mounted volunteers to aid his own troops, who became
more disciplined and efficient every day, and calmly
awaited the result of the negotiations.

It is worth while to stop and consider for a moment
the special qualities of a military leader which he now
displayed.   His correspondence at this time was most
extensive, and on this point especially it is most instructive.   "His letters," as one of his biographers says,
"when exposed to the most critical inspection, display
extraordinary clearness of mind and felicity of expression, strength and soundness of judgment, admirable
knowledge of the duties of his profession, of human

nature, of the people of the frontiers whom he was to
defend, and of the foes whom he was commissioned to
subdue."

The negotiations with the Indians turned out, as
Wayne had expected, to be fruitless, they insisting that
the Ohio River should be the boundary. The government, forced sorely against its will to make another
effort to subdue them by force, was to the last degree timid in its measures, and it sent Wayne instructions as to his movements which clearly showed how
greatly it feared the result. General Knox writes to
Wayne in September, 1793, "Every offer has been
made to obtain peace by milder terms than the sword ;
the efforts have failed under circumstances which leave
nothing for us to expect but war. Let it therefore be
again, and for the last time, impressed deeply upon your
mind, that as little as possible is to be hazarded, that
your force is fully adequate to the object you purpose
to effect, and that a defeat at the present time, and
under the present circumstances, would be pernicious
in the highest degree to the interests of our country."

General Wayne's answer to these faint-hearted suggestions was very characteristic. As soon as he heard
of the rupture of the negotiations he made ready to
advance, and on the 5th of October he wrote the following answer to the letter of the Secretary of War from
" Hobson's Choice," his camp near Cincinnati : " I will
advance to-morrow with the force I have in order to
take up a position in front of Fort Jefferson, so as to
keep the enemy in check by exciting a jealousy and
apprehension for the safety of their women and children,
until some favorable circumstance or opportunity may

present to strike with effect. I pray you not to permit present appearances to cause too much anxiety either in the mind of the President or yourself on account of this army. Knowing the critical situation of our infant nation, and feeling for the honor and reputation of the government (which I will support with my latest breath), you may rest assured that I will not commit the Legion unnecessarily. Unless more powerfully supported than I have reason to expect, I will content myself with taking a strong position in advance of Fort Jefferson, and by exerting every power endeavor to protect the frontier and secure the posts and the army during the winter, or until I am favored with your further orders."

Such was the magnanimous spirit with which Wayne entered upon the campaign, and it is to be hoped that the expression of his confidence had an inspiring effect upon those officials who had been so utterly cast down by the defeats of Harmar and St. Clair. Wayne's acts were in strict accordance with his promises. On the 7th of October the army began its march, and on the 13th it was encamped at a place which he named, in honor of his old friend and commander, General Greene, Greeneville. This post, which was six miles in advance of Fort Jefferson and eighty miles north of Cincinnati, on a branch of the Miami, he selected for his winter quarters, and strongly fortified. There in the wilderness he passed the winter, cut off for many months from any communication with the government at Philadelphia, and, of course, without orders. He was surrounded by hostile Indians. Convoys of provisions for the camp were frequently intercepted and their escort murdered by the savages. To render his troops familiar with danger, a large detachment was sent forward to the battle-field where St. Clair was defeated in 1791, with the double purpose of performing the pious duty of interring the bones of their comrades who had perished there, and of building a fort on that site impregnable to the Indians. This fort he named Fort Recovery. The erection of this fort seemed to bring the Indians for a time to some measure of reason, and they began to hint their willingness to negotiate for peace. Wayne placed no faith in their professions, but still felt it his duty to listen to what they had to say, asking only that they should deliver to him the captives they had made, as a proof of their sincerity. This demand, which was un-answered, closed the negotiation, and nothing more was heard about proposals for peace.

Meantime the difficulties in coming to any satisfactory agreement with the Indians were increased and compli-cated by the support which they were evidently receiving in their hostile attitude from the English government. To the impressment of our seamen, and the confisca-tion of the cargoes sent by us to the French West India Islands, was added the support it gave the Indians in their depredations in Ohio. The English still main-tained strong garrisons within our territory, while the savages were openly encouraged by the authorities in Canada. Everything seemed to forebode war at no distant day, not only with the savage tribes, but with the English as well, they holding the position of openly-declared allies on the frontiers. Wayne, while he acted in his movements with extreme caution, made himself ready for any emergency which might arise. The pru-dence of the course he pursued received the unqualified approbation of his government. He was told that his taking post on the battle-field of November, 1791 (St. Clair's), and the manner in which he had treated the overtures of the hostile Indians, were "highly satisfactory and exceedingly proper."[1] The Secretary goes on in his despatch to say, "It is with great pleasure that I transmit to you the approbation of the President of your conduct generally since you have had the command, and more particularly for the judicious military formation and discipline of your troops ; the precautions you appear to have taken in your advance, in your fortified camp, and in your arrangements for a full and abundant supply of provisions on hand." This commendation is particularly valuable, as it was bestowed upon conduct directly the reverse of that pursued by his two unfortunate predecessors in similar expeditions, Harmar and St. Clair.

In order that Wayne might not hesitate in the course he should pursue in an emergency which might arise when it would be impossible to consult the government officers at Philadelphia, he was told by Secretary Knox, "If in the course of your operations against the Indian enemy it should become necessary to dislodge the party (the English garrison at the rapids of the Miami), you are hereby authorized in the name of the President of the United States to do it." Not only, therefore, was the sole conduct of the Indian war confided, with absolute powers, to the discretion of Wayne ("Mad Anthony," according to the legend), but he was given authority to take a step which must certainly have in-

[1] Moore, 186.

volved the nation in a war with Great Britain. How he used this discretionary power we shall soon see.

On the 30th of June a small body of riflemen and dragoons was attacked near Fort Recovery, and this attack was followed by a general assault upon the fort. The enemy were driven back, but renewed the assault with greater spirit, and were finally repulsed. The Indians were, no doubt, aided by the English. The Americans lost some valuable officers ; but the lesson taught the Indians by their repulse on the same spot where they had defeated St. Clair was a very important one, for they found that they had a very different man now to deal with.

A few days afterwards Wayne was joined by a considerable force of Kentucky volunteers under the command of his old friend and comrade of Monmouth, Major-General Scott. Thus reinforced, he advanced about seventy miles northward from Greeneville into the heart of the Indian country. Having disconcerted the savages by this unexpected move, he boldly confronted the English garrison established at the rapids of the Miami, and determined to meet the allies where he could strike them with one blow and thus settle the question of the supremacy of either or both of them on the frontier. He built a fort at the junction of the Le Glaize and the Miami, to which he gave a name appropriately describing his intentions and his self-confidence,—that of Fort Defiance. He then sent to the Indians a last overture for peace, and, that being spurned, prepared to fight one of the most memorable Indian battles in our history, if regard be had to the greatness of the stake which he put at issue and to the vast results which followed his success.

The following account of the signal defeat of the
Indians and their allies is given in his despatch to the
government announcing the victory:

General Wayne to the Secretary of War.

HEAD QUARTERS,
GRAND GLAIZE 28 August 1794

SIR,—It is with infinite pleasure that I now announce to you the
brilliant success of the Federal Army under my command in a general action with the combined force of the hostile Indians and a
considerable number of the volunteers & militia of Detroit (Canadians) on the 20th inst on the banks of the Miamis in the Vicinity of
the British post and garrison at the foot of the rapids.

The Army advanced from this place on the 15th inst and
arrived at Roche de-Bout on the 18th. On the 19th we were employed in making a temporary post for the reception of our stores
and baggage, and in reconnoitering the position of the enemy, who
were encamped behind a thick and bushy wood and the British fort.

At 8 o'clock on the morning of the 20th the army again advanced in columns agreeably to the standing order of march: the
legion on the right flank covered by the Miamis, one brigade of
mounted volunteers on the left under Brigadier General Todd, and
the other in the rear under Brigadier General Barber: a select battalion of Mounted Volunteers moved in front of the Legion commanded by Major Price who was directed to keep sufficiently advanced,—so as to give timely notice to form in case of action—it
being yet undetermined whether the Indians would decide for peace
or for war. After advancing about five miles Major Price's Corps
received so severe a fire from the enemy, who were secreted in the
woods and in the high grass, as to compel him to retreat.

The Legion was immediately formed in two lines principally in
a close thick wood which extended for miles on our left and for a
very considerable distance in front, the ground being covered with
old fallen timber probably occasioned by a tornado which rendered
it impracticable for cavalry to act with effect, and afforded the
enemy the most favorable covert for their savage mode of warfare.
They were formed in three lines within supporting distance of each
other and extending nearly two miles at right angles with the river.

I soon discovered from the weight of the fire and the extent of their line that the enemy were in full force in front in possession of their favorite ground, and endeavoring to turn our left flank. I therefore gave orders for the second line to advance to support the first, and directed Major General Scott to gain & turn the right flank of the savages with the whole of the Mounted Volunteers by a circuitous route. At the same time I ordered the front line to advance with trailed arms, and rouse the Indians from their coverts at the point of the bayonet and when up to deliver a close & well directed fire on their backs followed by a brisk charge so as not to give time to load again. I also ordered Captain *Miss* (*sic*) Campbell[1] who commanded the legionary cavalry, to turn the left flank of the enemy next the river, and which afforded a favorable field for that corps to act in.

All these orders were obeyed with spirit and promptitude, but such was the impetuosity of the charge by the first line of infantry that the Indians and Canadian militia and volunteers were driven from all their coverts in so short a time that although every exertion was used by the officers of the second line of the legion, and by Generals Scott, Todd, & Barber of the Mounted Volunteers to gain their proper positions yet but a part of each could get up in season to participate in the action the enemy being driven in the course of an hour more than two miles through the thick woods already mentioned by less than one half of their numbers.

From every account the enemy amounted to 2000 combatants, and the troops actually engaged against them were short of 900. This horde of savages with their allies abandoned themselves to flight, and dispersed with terror and dismay leaving our victorious army in full & quiet possession of the field of battle which terminated under the influence of the guns of the British garrison, as you will perceive by the enclosed correspondence between Major Campbell, the commandant, & myself upon the occasion.

The bravery & conduct of every officer belonging to the army from the Generals down to the Ensigns merit my highest approbation. There were however some whose rank & situation placed

---

[1] The name of this officer is written in the official muster-roll of the Legion "Robert Miss Campbell."

their conduct in a very conspicuous point of view, and which I observed with pleasure and the most lively gratitude : among whom I must beg leave to mention Brigadier Gen. Wilkinson and Col. Hamtramck, the commandants of the right & left wings of the Legion, whose brave example inspired the troops. To these I must add the names of my faithful and gallant aids-de-camp, Captains De Butts and T. Lewis, and Lieutenant Harrison, who with Adjutant General Major Mills rendered me most essential service by communicating my orders in every direction and by their conduct & bravery exciting the troops to press for victory. Lieutenant Covington upon whom the command of the cavalry devolved cut down two savages with his own hand, and Lieutenant Webb one in turning the enemy's left flank.

The wounds received by Captains Slough and Prior, and Lieutenants Campbell & Smith of the legionary infantry, by Captain Van Renselaer of the dragoons, and Captain Rawlins, Lieutenant McKenney and Ensign Duncan of the Mounted Volunteers bear honorable testimony of their bravery & conduct.

Captains H. Lewis and Brock with their companies of light infantry had to sustain an unequal fire for some time which they supported with fortitude. In fact every officer & soldier who had an opportunity to come into action displayed that true bravery which will always insure success.

And here permit me to declare that I never discovered more true spirit and anxiety for action than appeared to pervade the whole of the Mounted Volunteers, and I am well persuaded that had the enemy maintained their favorite ground for one half hour longer they would have most severely felt the prowess of that corps.

But whilst I pay this first tribute to the living I must not forget the gallant dead, among whom we have to lament the early death of those worthy & brave officers, Captain Miss Campbell of the Dragoons, and Lieutenant Towles of the light infantry of the legion who fell in the first charge.

Enclosed is a particular return of the killed and wounded. The loss of the enemy was more than double that of the Federal army. The woods were strewed for a considerable distance with the dead bodies of the Indians & their white auxiliaries, the latter armed with British muskets and bayonets.

We remained three days and nights on the banks of the Miamis in front of the field of battle during which time all the houses and corn fields were consumed & destroyed for a considerable distance both above and below Fort Miamis, as well as within pistol shot of that garrison, who were compelled to remain tacit spectators of this general devastation and conflagration ; among which were the houses stores and property of Colonel M'Kee, the British Indian Agent, and principal stimulator of the war now existing between the United States and the savages.

The Army returned to this place on the 27th by easy marches, laying waste the villages & the corn fields for about fifty miles on each side of the Miamis.   There remain yet a number of villages and a great quantity of corn to be consumed or destroyed upon Le Glaize and the Miamis above this place which will be effected in the course of a few days.   In the interim we shall improve Fort Defiance, and as soon as the escort returns with the necessary supplies from Greeneville and Fort Recovery the Army will proceed to the Miami villages in order to accomplish the object of the campaign.

It is however not improbable that the enemy may make one more desperate effort against the Army, as it is said that a reinforcement was hourly expected at Fort Miamis from Niagara as well as numer-ous tribes of Indians, living on the margin and islands of the Lakes.   This is a business rather to be wished for than dreaded, whilst the army remains in force.   Their numbers will only tend to confuse the savages, and the victory will only be more complete and decisive, and which eventually may insure a permanent & happy peace.

Under these impressions I have the honor to be &c

ANTH'Y WAYNE.

It is related of General Wayne that at the time the battle began (about ten A.M.) he was suffering to that degree from an attack of the gout that it was necessary to lift him on his horse.   His limbs were swathed in flannels, and so intolerable was his agony that it is said it forced tears from his eyes.   But by noon, in the excitement of the battle, he became wholly free from pain, and his movements were as active as those of any of his officers. The next day he seems to have recovered his strength, for, accompanied by the members of his staff, he reconnoitred the British fort very closely, a proceeding which gave great offence to the commander and led to the following correspondence:

Major Campbell to General Wayne.

MIAMI RIVER Aug 21st 1794

SIR,—An Army of the United States of America said to be under your command having taken post on the banks of the Miami for upwards of the last twenty four hours almost within reach of the guns of this fort, being a post belonging to his Majesty the King of Great Britain, occupied by his Majesty's troops, and which I have the honor to command, it becomes my duty to inform myself as speedily as possible in what light I am to view your making such near approaches to this garrison. I have no hesitation, on my part to say that I know of no war existing between Great Britain & America.

I have to honor to be &c &c

WILLIAM CAMPBELL

Major 24th Regiment commanding the Post.

General Wayne to Major Campbell.

CAMP ON THE BANKS OF THE MIAMI

Aug 21, 1794

SIR,—I have received your letter of this date, requiring from me the motives which have moved the Army under my command to the position they at present occupy far within the acknowledged jurisdiction of the United States.

Without questioning the authority or the propriety, Sir, of your interrogatory, I think I may without breach of decorum observe to you that were you entitled to an answer, the most full and satisfactory one was announced to you from the muzzles of my small arms yesterday morning in the action against the hordes of savages in the vicinity of your post which terminated gloriously to the American arms, but had it continued until the Indians *etc* were driven under the influence of the post and guns you mention they would not have much impeded the progress of the Victorious Army under my command—as no such post was established at the commencement of the present war between the Indians & the United States

I have the honor to be &c

ANTHONY WAYNE

Major General & Commander-in-Chief.

The toils and perplexities of this Indian campaign were not the only ones from which Wayne suffered in his enfeebled condition during the year 1794. The condition of affairs on the Mississippi River became in that year alarming, and had not some military measure been taken to check the excitement, a war with Spain, which then held the military posts on that river from New Madrid to New Orleans, was highly probable. Incensed by the vexatious proceedings of the Spanish authorities at these posts in interfering with what the Western people claimed was their right to the free navigation of the river, large bodies of men were enlisted in Kentucky who threatened to descend the river to the Gulf and destroy all Spanish control of it or of the country on its borders. As general-in-chief of the army, Wayne had military jurisdiction over this region, and he was obliged to send a portion of his already depleted Legion to serve as a garrison at Fort Massac, on the Ohio, with orders to arrest any armed parties descending the river and threatening hostilities with Spain. He could rely upon very little assistance or sympathy from the governor of Kentucky in the performance of this duty. He was thus placed in the painfully embarrassing position of being obliged so prudently to manage his small force that while he subdued the Indians he might not involve the country in a war with both England and Spain.

It is not easy to overrate the importance, from a national point of view, of the victory over the savages at the Falls of the Miami. It was one of the few in our history which we may call decisive. That it dissipated the cherished dream of the Indians that the Ohio River was to be the perpetual boundary between them and the whites was, perhaps, the least important of its results. In opening the magnificent national domain of the West to emigrants, secured in their life, liberty, and property by laws of their own making, it may well be regarded, when we reflect upon the history of that vast region during the last hundred years, as having given birth to a new era in the history of American civilization. The millions of freemen who now occupy the energetic and vigorous commonwealths lying between the Ohio and the Mississippi should cherish the memory of Wayne as that of the man who by his sword made it possible for white men to live in peace and security in that garden spot of the world; and the nation, proud as it ought to be of Wayne's achievements during the war of the Revolution, should never forget that it was he who by his skill and prowess changed the howling wilderness of the Northwest Territory, where the highest glory of the savage inhabitant had been the scalping of the whites, into a country where the cultivation of all the arts of peace betokens the highest civilization.

The result of the battle of the Miami was, as we have seen, the complete subjugation of the Indians of the

23

Northwest. Although their real leader, Joseph Brant, and his English allies tried to stimulate the tribesmen to tempt the fortune of war once more, they were too wise to follow such counsel. They were forced in August, 1795, to conclude a treaty with the United States at Greeneville, by which a vast tract of territory west of the Ohio and northwardly to Detroit was ceded to the national government.

The lines enclosing the Indian territory were drawn from Lake Erie along the Cuyahoga River to the Portage, thence west to the Maumee, down that river to the lake, and thence to the place of beginning. Within these lines the Indian claim to territory was acknowledged, and without them lay the lands of the whites, where for seventeen years after the conclusion of the treaty there was uninterrupted peace between the Indians and their neighbors. During this period the State of Ohio became rapidly settled by the whites, and at its close they were in no fear of the savages.

What the national government gained not only in acquisition of territory and hence in power, but in the vast sums for which their lands in this region were sold, liberated by Wayne's victory from the fear of Indian raids, it is not necessary to recount here. Wayne's victory and the treaty of Greeneville, which was its logical result, form the true "winning of the Northwest," the full story of which is that of the most marvellous achievement in American history.

Nor should we forget the influence of this battle upon our relations with England. When it took place the negotiations which ended in Jay's treaty were in progress. One point which, as we have said, was obstinately disputed between Mr. Jay and the English Ministry was the retention of the posts held by English garrisons within our territory, in violation of the treaty of 1783. When the news of this battle reached London, and it was seen that all hope of further aid from the Indians in supporting their pretensions to our territory must be given up, an agreement was soon reached, and orders for the evacuation of these posts, the chief of which were at Detroit, Oswego, and Niagara, were soon sent out.

After the conclusion of the treaty of Greeneville, in August, 1795, General Wayne, having been absent from home more than three years, spent in the most laborious and useful service, paid a short visit to Pennsylvania. His progress was a triumphal one. " Everywhere," says one of his biographers, " the people turned out *en masse* to give him welcome ; at the news of his coming all business was suspended to bestow upon him a greeting as he passed." Reaching Philadelphia, we find the following account of his reception in the newspapers of the day :

" On Saturday last (February 6th), about five o'clock in the afternoon, arrived in this city, after an absence of more than three years on an expedition against the Western Indians (in which he proved so happily successful), Major-General Wayne. Four miles from the city he was met by three troops of Philadelphia Light Horse, and escorted by them to town. On his crossing the Schuylkill a salute of fifteen cannon was fired from Center Square by a party of artillery. He was ushered into the City by the ringing of bells and other demonstrations of joy, and thousands of citizens crowded to see and welcome the return of their brave general, whom they attended to the City Tavern, where he alighted. In the evening a display of fireworks was exhibited."

The President of the United States (General Washington) in a message to Congress referred in fitting terms to the achievements of General Wayne and to the vast consequences likely to follow from his victory. An attempt was made in the House of Representatives to recognize the wise counsels and the intrepid bravery of the man to whom the success of the campaign was chiefly due. Here party malignity interposed with its venomous spirit, and the House, with singular inconsistency, while refusing to give to the leader his due meed of praise, adopted the following resolution : " *Resolved unanimously*, That the thanks of this House be given to the brave officers and soldiers of the Legion under the orders of General Wayne for their prudence, fortitude, and bravery."

Had these short-sighted politicians been endowed with a gift of prophecy which would have enabled them to look forward for fifty years into the future of their country, they would doubtless have owned to their own confusion that even such triumphal honors as were awarded to Roman conquerors would have been a fitting tribute to Wayne. Pompey the Great when he presented to the Senate and people of Rome the submission of Syria, Phœnicia, and Palestine as the trophies of his conquering army, and the illustrious Cæsar when he forced Egypt, Africa, and Gaul to bow to the supremacy of the Roman authority, by the voice of public gratitude were made masters of the Republic. What is due to the memory of the man whose prudence and valor gave to the American people the peaceful possession of the magnificent domain of the West?

Wayne was permitted on his return home to enjoy but a short holiday. During the winter of 1796 the opposition to the enforcement of Jay's treaty had become so violent that it seemed at one time probable that the House would not make the appropriations necessary to carry the provisions of the treaty into effect after its ratification by the Senate. The alternative, of course, was war with Great Britain, and war was clamored for by vast numbers of people, who could not speak of the capture of our vessels and the loss of our commerce, still kept up by the English cruisers, except in terms of violent indignation. If the treaty negotiated by Mr. Jay had not been carried out, then, in addition to other evils, the English posts on our northern frontier would have been retained in the hands of our enemies, and they, held as a vantage-ground within our territory and supported by the alliance of the Indians, would have practically abrogated the treaty of Greeneville and opened anew the country west of the Ohio to all the horrors from which that agreement had delivered it. Hence it may be understood with what anxiety the administration of Washington regarded the opposition and delay of the House in making appropriations to carry Mr. Jay's treaty into effect, and how momentous was the destiny which hung upon their decision. On the 30th of April the memorable debate on this bill was concluded, and principally through the influence of Fisher Ames the House decided, by a vote of fifty-one to forty-eight, to make appropriations to carry the treaty into effect.

This measure happily closed another most critical juncture in the history of the West. When the news of its adoption reached that region, the arrangements which had been begun during the winter for an alliance between the English garrisons and the Indians for

a new campaign in the Northwest Territory suddenly
ceased, and the government received the welcome
news that the officers in command of those garrisons
had at length received orders to surrender them to the
Americans in pursuance of the terms of the treaty.

In order that there might be no delay or interruption
in the proceedings connected with the delivery of these
posts, it was necessary that some one should be appointed as the agent of the government who was not
only perfectly familiar with its policy, but who also, from
his position and character and general acquaintance
with the parties to the controversy, could be trusted to
carry out that policy. General Wayne was the man
appointed by the government to conduct what it was
supposed might prove a very difficult and delicate negotiation. His qualifications may be summed up in a
very few words : " He knew the English on the border
and their allies the Indians, and they knew him. His
appointment was a notice to those who had opposed
the treaty that there would be no trifling nor delay
while the business was in his hands."

The treaty stipulated that the English should surrender into our hands the posts at Niagara, Oswego, the
Miami, and Detroit. At the beginning of June Wayne
was ordered to visit these posts and take possession of
them in behalf of the United States. His commission
invested him with the powers of a civil commissioner as
well as with those of a military commander. He executed his task with wonderful tact and discretion. He
was received by the English officers commanding the
garrisons not only with official courtesy but in a kind
and friendly spirit which indicated their readiness to

close the dispute. He visited the different forts in succession, and in no case was any obstacle interposed to carrying out the formalities of the transfer to the American government. He reached Detroit in September, where he found many Indians, his former foes, by whom he was welcomed with many noisy demonstrations of admiration, for with all their defects the Indians never fail to recognize the truly brave man, even if he is, as he was in this case, their conqueror. He remained at this post for more than two months, his evident sincerity and kindly disposition being a powerful means of influence in cementing a lasting friendship between the Indians and their former enemies.

On the 17th of November he sailed from Detroit for Presqu'isle, the site of the present city of Erie, which was the last post he was ordered to visit. Within a day's sail of that place he was suddenly seized with an attack of gout, and he reached Erie in a dying condition. He was removed to the quarters of the commander of the post or block-house at that place, Captain Russell Bissell, where he seemed for a time to recover his strength. Neither the kindness of the family of Captain Bissell, however, nor the skill and attention of the surgeon of the post, Dr. George Balfour, could relieve him. The disease reached his stomach and gave the general intolerable agony for several weeks, all efforts to revive him or to mitigate his sufferings proving vain. At last, on the 15th of December, he breathed his last in the arms of Dr. Balfour. He was buried, according to his wish, at the foot of the flag-staff on a high hill called "Garrison Hill," north of the present Soldiers' Home. The fort or block-house was destroyed by fire about thirty years ago, the parade-ground graded off, and every trace of the hero's grave was lost. Previous to this, however, his son, Colonel Isaac Wayne, in 1809, caused his remains to be removed and reinterred in the family burial-ground attached to St. David's Church at Radnor. The very impressive ceremonies which took place on this occasion are fully described by Mr. Lewis in the Supplementary chapter of this book. In 1876 the empty grave was discovered at Erie, and in 1879 the Legislature of this State appropriated one thousand dollars, which was afterwards supplemented by an additional appropriation of five hundred dollars, for the erection of a suitable monument at Erie. With rare good taste the committee charged with the duty adopted as a monument a model of the old block-house in which he died, which is thus described :

"A new stone was placed over the grave, and over it was built as a monument to 'Mad Anthony's' memory an exact copy of the old block-house which Wayne himself had first built in 1791. The present one is made of squared oak logs well notched together at the corners. The first story is sixteen feet square and ten feet high, with a door on one side. The upper is octagonal in shape, and made to project several feet over the lower, thus making it difficult of access except through the interior of the lower room. A flight of winding steps permits of ascent to the upper octagonal room from the ground-floor of the block-house. The roof is also octagonal, and finished to a centre pole, which forms the flag-staff. The upper story is the height of a man at the sides, and increases with the rise of the roof to the centre."—*The American Architect and Building News*, vol. xxi. p. 159.

The following is the inscription on the monument erected by the Society of the Cincinnati in St. David's Cemetery :

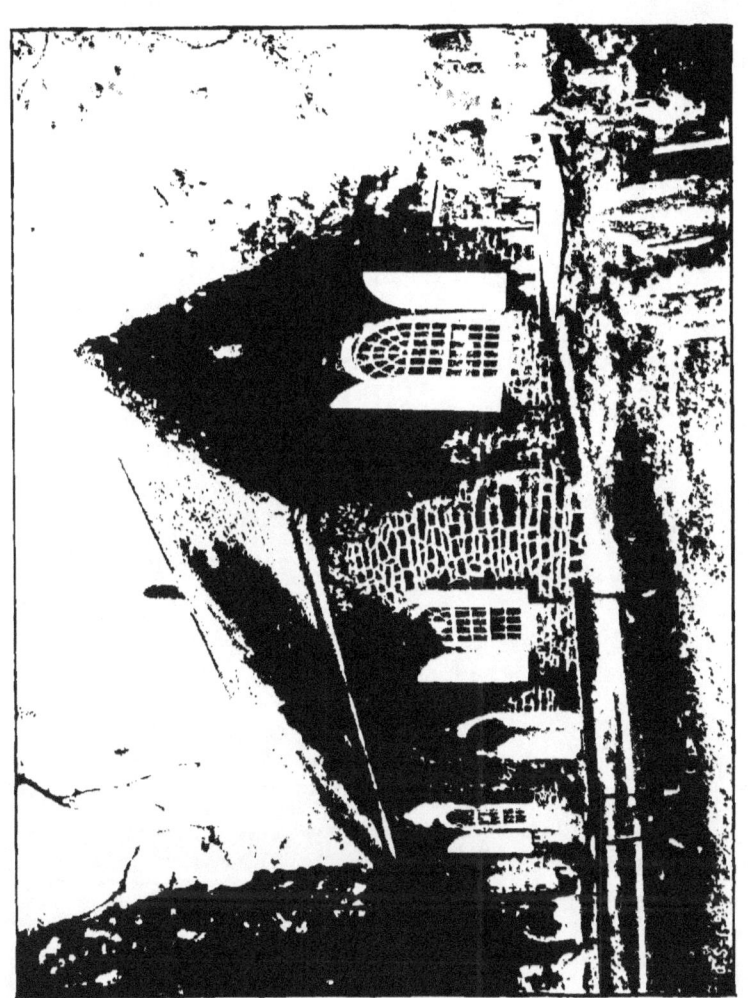

ST. DAVID'S CHURCH, RADNOR.

[*North front.*]
MAJOR GENERAL
ANTHONY WAYNE
was born at Waynesborough
In Chester County
State of Pennsylvania
A.D. 1745.
After a life of Honor & Usefulness
He died in December 1796,
At a military post
On the shores of Lake Erie
Commander-in-chief of the Army of
The United States.
His military achievements
Are consecrated
In the history of his country
And in
The hearts of his countrymen.
His Remains
Are here Deposited.

[*South front.*]
In honor of the distinguished
Military Services of
MAJOR-GENERAL ANTHONY WAYNE
And as an affectionate tribute
of respect to his Memory
This Stone was erected by his Companions
In Arms,
The Pennsylvania State Society of
The Cincinnati,
July 4th A.D. 1809,
Thirty fourth anniversary of
The Independence of the United States,
An event which constitutes the most
Appropriate Eulogium
of an American Soldier and
Patriot.

Thus died in the full maturity of his powers, and with undiminished capacity for further usefulness, ANTHONY WAYNE, true type and exemplar of that lofty virtue, of that unfailing constancy, of that perfect disinterestedness of purpose, and of that knightly valor with which we love to invest the memory of our Revolutionary heroes. His whole active life was given ungrudgingly to the service of his country. From the snowy battle-fields of Canada to the burning sands of Florida, there is no region which is not full of his labors in his country's cause. Amidst all the trials and sufferings and dangers of the Revolution he never faltered. He began his work when the Colonies were feebly struggling against ministerial oppression, and he did not finish it until, twenty years later, he had laid the solid foundations of an empire. As he lay a-dying, and looked back over his chequered career, full of difficulties and dangers through which he had been safely led until that hour, he may well have thought, as he knew his work was done, that the history of his country must ever be resplendent with the glory of his achievements, and that the hour of his death was the hour of his complete and assured triumph.

When one reads the story of this hero's life as told in his correspondence, and reflects how little has been done since his death to requite his services or to honor his memory, one is tempted to ask himself, What would have been his fame and reward had he done for our enemies what he did for us? A contrast with the fate of Wolfe, the greatest soldier ever sent by England to America, and the captor of Quebec, naturally occurs to us. Wolfe's name is consecrated in English song and story. Had he lived, doubtless a peerage and large money rewards would have been bestowed upon him ; and since his death a most conspicuous position in the Valhalla dedicated to the heroes of the English race has been occupied by him. One act of heroism made his name famous for all time ; and yet Wayne's exploits, each inspired by the same dauntless valor, seem almost forgotten by his countrymen. Wolfe, it is said, gave Canada to England; but Wayne gave the whole territory between the Ohio and the Mississippi, comprising four States, to that peaceful immigration which has made that region the home of a noble civilization.

But it is more grateful to consider the points of resemblance between these two heroes than to contrast the manner in which their fame has been preserved by their countrymen. They were both misunderstood in their lifetime save by their own soldiers. Wayne, like Sherman, was called "mad," and Pitt hoped that God would forgive him for confiding the interests of England on this continent to so reckless a dare-devil as Wolfe. What is there romantic or daring about the exploit of climbing the Heights of Abraham, and the subsequent capture of Quebec, which is not paralleled by the midnight assault of Stony Point and the capture of that stronghold? If Wolfe could exclaim, when told that the French were fleeing, "I die happy!" what must we think of Wayne, who, finding himself, as he supposed, mortally wounded at Stony Point, begged his aide-de-camp to carry him into the interior of the fort, that he might die there? Even in the tender emotions of these two heroic hearts there is a wonderful likeness. Wolfe, as he was descending the St. Lawrence in his boat, repeated a portion of the famous Elegy of Gray, and said to his companions that he would rather be the author of that poem than gain all the glory the capture of Quebec would give him. Wayne's letter, written but a half-hour before the assault on Stony Point, with the evident expectation that he would not survive it, while it is full of tender care for his wife and children, is also full of pathetic solicitude for the fame and success of his great chief, Washington.

There is no adequate reward which a country can bestow for the great deeds of such men. None know better than they that "the paths of glory lead but to the grave." But let us not forget that in all great soldiers the incentive to great deeds is the hope that their names and their memory shall not be forgotten by their countrymen.

SUPPLEMENTARY CHAPTER.

[The following chapter was prepared by the late Hon. Joseph J. Lewis, of West Chester, as the concluding one of a memoir of General Wayne which he proposed to write, but which, unfortunately, he was unable to finish.]

IF General Wayne had lived eighteen days longer he would have completed his fifty-second year. He died in the meridian of his life and in the full maturity of his powers. Although he had been accustomed to share with his men the hardships and privations of a soldier's life, his general health had been uniformly good, except a protracted spell of malarial fever contracted in the swamps of Georgia and occasional attacks of gout. The first of these attacks he experienced during the war in that State. Before he was forty years old his constitutional tendency to the gout, which had been hereditary in one branch of his family, became manifest. Having with several of his officers dined with a planter during his campaign in Georgia, the party returning to head-quarters late in the evening were mistaken for Indians and were fired upon by some of his men. A musket-ball struck him on the shoulder and caused a slight wound and the loss of a few ounces of blood. This was immediately followed by an attack of gout in the great toe of one of his feet. The disease, having thus effected a lodgement in his system, advanced in repeated visitations from the extremities towards the vitals, and at length, having

349

reached the stomach, put an end to his life. His remains in the first instance were interred at Erie. In 1809 the Pennsylvania Society of the Cincinnati determined to erect a monument to his memory in the cemetery of the church of St. David's, in Radnor, Delaware County. In consequence of this resolution, Colonel Isaac Wayne, the general's son, visited Erie in June of that year and caused his father's remains to be exhumed, and they were removed to Waynesborough.

The 4th of July was appointed for the reinterment of the remains at St. David's. The funeral was attended by an immense concourse of people from Chester and the adjoining counties, and by the Philadelphia City Troop under the command of the mayor, Robert Wharton. The procession was more than a mile in length. An old soldier, Samuel Smiley, who had served in the Pennsylvania line during the war of the Revolution, refusing every means of conveyance offered him, walked the whole distance from Waynesborough to St. David's in front of the hearse. He took this way to show the affection with which he cherished the memory of his beloved commander. The Rev. David Jones delivered the funeral oration. He had been a guest at the general's table before the war of the Revolution. He had been his chaplain; he had been with him in camp, in council, and on battle-field; and no one had a better opportunity of forming a proper estimate of his character as a man and as an officer ; and he was enabled to furnish graphic illustrations of his theme from his own observation. This he did with excellent effect. A high platform was erected close by the open grave to serve as a stand for the speaker, and from this Mr.

Jones addressed the multitude. Thirty-three years before he had preached within the church building, appeal-
ing to the young men of the period to take up arms in
defence of their liberties, and now at the age of seventy-
three he came to speak of the merits and services of
the hero who may have led some of those same men
to victory. The speaker was himself of heroic mould,
and his statements of what had passed beneath his eye
had the value of history. The curiosity to hear "the
old man eloquent" was universal, and the interest was
intense. The people in a compact mass crowded around
the stand, and many even climbed the surrounding
trees and sat among the branches, the better to catch
the words of the speaker. He spoke particularly of
the night of the battle of Paoli, where he had himself
narrowly escaped death, and corrected by his own rec-
ollections of the events some erroneous rumors then
current. No report of the address, we believe, is now
extant, except in some unimportant particulars. The
day was extremely hot, but the heat was not permitted
to interfere with the proper celebration of the obsequies.
It was without doubt the intention of the Pennsylvania
Society of the Cincinnati to dedicate the proposed
monument on the day of the reinterment of the general's remains. The date upon the structure, July 4,
1809, indicates this. Its actual erection did not occur
till the 5th of June, 1811, at which time the members
of the Society attended in a body, accompanied by the
Philadelphia and Montgomery volunteer cavalry, and
there was again on the ground a very large number of
citizens.

The estate which General Wayne derived from his

father, according to the standard by which fortunes were measured in the ante-Revolutionary times in Chester County, raised him above those who occupied the middle station of life, and if he had devoted his attention to its improvement he might with little effort have become wealthy. But his thoughts took a direction which gave other objects a preference to pecuniary gain. During the latter part of the year 1774 and the whole of the year 1775 his time was much occupied by duties of an official or semi-official character. This was especially the case while he was acting as a member of the Committee of Safety. After he entered the army he could for a number of years give but little attention to his private affairs. The conveyance from his father in 1774 of the Waynesborough estate made him at the same time the proprietor of an extensive tannery, which had produced for a number of years considerable profit. He knew nothing of the business of a tanner, and was obliged to trust the management of it to other hands. His agent, a Mr. Shannon, was believed to be capable and trustworthy. Yet under his agency General Wayne ascertained, at the termination of the war of the Revolution, that he had sustained a loss of not less than seven thousand pounds (£7000). When Wayne in 1777 was appointed brigadier-general, he considered that a due regard to his official position required him to maintain a table to which he could invite his brother officers and such members of the government as might occasionally visit the army. He accordingly acted upon the idea. The expense was considerable, and it has been stated that it sometimes exceeded his pay, received as it was in depreciated

Continental currency. The excess was necessarily drawn from his private income. The cost he thus encountered, however, had no effect upon the liberality with which he dispensed his hospitality. His most important pecuniary loss occurred in consequence of an attempt to improve the lands which had been granted to him by the State of Georgia in consideration of his military services. As large sums of money could not be obtained on loan at that time in this country, he made arrangements with an agent of certain bankers in Holland to borrow one hundred thousand florins, and gave as security a mortgage on his Chester County property, dated January 9, 1785. He drew bills for that amount on the bankers, which were discounted, and he received the proceeds. The bills, owing to the bad faith of those with whom he dealt, came back protested. This subjected him to great annoyance and embarrassment. He succeeded, however, in overcoming his difficulties, and on the 7th day of August, 1787, satisfaction was entered on this mortgage. His improvement project, on which he had spent considerable sums, was, however, abandoned, and the lands were ultimately disposed of for less than the money he had laid out upon them. The Will of General Wayne was executed at his head-quarters on the Miami July 14, 1794, when he was in daily expectation of a battle with the Indians. It shows on its face the real estate of which he was the owner at the date of the Will, and we believe also at the time of his death. He acquired by purchase a valuable tract which lay adjoining Waynesborough on the east, and this tract has since been considered as a part of the Waynesborough farm, and

24

passed with it to the present possessor. Of the other pieces of property mentioned in the Will, the house on Second Street, in Philadelphia, of which he appears to have owned a moiety, was the most valuable. The lands in Nova Scotia, and the several donation tracts granted in consideration of his military services, had more prospective than present value, and constituted no considerable addition to his fortune. The truth seems to be that although General Wayne exhibited his usual energy in whatever effort was necessary to relieve himself from the pressure of any existing need, he felt no such interest in the acquisition of property as was required to sustain any prolonged struggle in that direction. His mind was too much occupied with public affairs during the twenty-two years he survived his father to admit of much attention to his private fortune.

He devised to his son Isaac (as stated in his Will) the Waynesborough estate, then increased to five hundred acres, a building-lot in Harrisburg, Pennsylvania, fifteen hundred acres of land granted to the testator by Congress for his military services, and a large tract of rice-land in Georgia. He devised to his son Isaac and his daughter Margaretta (Mrs. Atlee) his large landed estate in Nova Scotia; to his daughter Margaretta a house and lot on Second Street between Market and Walnut in Philadelphia, Isaac to release to her his interest therein, a tract of fifteen hundred acres in the western part of Pennsylvania, a donation by the State in consideration of his military services ; and he made his son and daughter residuary devisees and legatees. This Will was admitted to probate on the 15th of February, 1797, by the register of the city and county of Philadelphia, and letters testamentary were issued to Isaac Wayne. The other two executors, Sharp Delany and William Lewis, Esq., an eminent lawyer of the Pennsylvania bar, appear to have declined the trust.

Some years after the general's death, Colonel Isaac Wayne, as executor of his father's Will, received a letter from the Treasury Department at Washington, containing a statement of an account against the estate of General Wayne, and claiming the payment of a balance of some five thousand dollars to the United States government. Colonel Wayne, knowing his father's habits, was satisfied that he at the time of his death owed nothing to the government, and proceeded to examine his private papers. In them he found evidence of payments made by the general for the use of the government to an amount considerably exceeding the balance claimed in the Treasury statement transmitted to the executor. With his vouchers in hand, he drew up an account and repaired to Washington with a view of obtaining a settlement. The delays usual in such cases on the part of the accounting officers of the government were interposed. At length, wearied with waiting on the slow circumlocutory processes of the department, he petitioned Congress, setting out his claim, and an act was passed January 21, 1811, by virtue of which, on the 21st of February of the same year, the sum due to the general's estate, five thousand eight hundred and seventy dollars and eighty-four cents ($5870.84), was paid.

Although General Wayne's achievements belong to the history of the country, with which every well-informed

citizen ought to be familiar, his character, in one respect
at least, seems to be strangely misunderstood. It is supposed by many, perhaps by a majority of readers, that
he was a sort of military madcap, a modern knight-
errant, by whom considerations of prudence and expediency were disregarded, whose romantic and chiv-
alrous courage sought display in rash and perilous
adventure, and whose claim to distinction rested solely
on his personal prowess and contemptuous disregard
of danger. The *sobriquet* of "Mad Anthony" has been
thought to have been justly applied to him as indicating
the recklessness with which he rushed to an encounter.
One writer of no inconsiderable celebrity speaks of him
as a "constitutional fighter, always ready for a fray,"
without an intimation that he had other qualities which
fitted him for command. Mr. Irving, in his "Life of
Washington," who rarely mentions the name of Wayne
without coupling with it the odious appellation of "Mad
Anthony," remarks, "That brave commander had conducted the war with a judgment and prudence little
compatible with the hare-brained appellation he had
acquired by his *rash* exploits during the Revolution;"
thus giving us to understand, without a semblance of
authority for the imputation, that his rashness was
habitual and his prudence exceptional. When authors
of eminence write thus loosely and inconsiderately upon
a subject with which they may be reasonably believed
to have some acquaintance, it is not surprising that
readers should be misled. It is true that General
Wayne was distinguished for his bravery,—he was,
indeed, the "bravest of the brave;" his valor shone
conspicuously in every battle in which he was engaged;

yet he was none the less a skilful general of singular discretion and sobriety of judgment.

He possessed that rare faculty which the French call the *coup d'œil*, which consists in detecting, by a glance at the battle-field, the purpose of an enemy, or any fault in his arrangements of which advantage may be taken ; and he also instantly, as if by intuition, decided how to frustrate the enemy's purpose. Thus, at Green Springs, having been ordered with a detachment of seven hundred men to pursue the rear-guard of the enemy, he found himself on emerging from a wood within musket-shot of the whole force under Cornwallis drawn up in battle array. The design was to attack the American army, which was following in a loose and fragmentary way, before it should be concentrated, and to cut it up in detail. Wayne instantly comprehended the purpose of Cornwallis and the whole peril of the situation. He therefore ordered a charge to be sounded, and rushed upon the British line, which he broke and threw into confusion. He then retreated in good order and in such manner as seemed to invite pursuit. The British general was utterly disconcerted, and, fearing that Wayne's movement was a stratagem to draw him into an engagement with the whole American army or to lead him into an ambuscade, he hesitated to move till the opportunity to profit by his advantage was past. By this bold stroke the object of Wayne was gained, and the American army was saved from disaster, if not from destruction. The amazing audacity of the charge contributed largely to the successful result. It was inconceivable to Cornwallis why so small a body should attack ten times its number, unless in pursuance of some device by which he should be drawn into a hidden danger. The hesitation on his part was, therefore, natural and reasonable, and was just what Wayne anticipated.

During his campaign in Georgia, when marching to meet the enemy, he unexpectedly met a large body of British and Indians, superior to his own, on a narrow causeway over a swamp. Both parties were taken by surprise. Wayne, perceiving that the enemy were hesitating and apparently uncertain how to meet the emergency, gave them not a moment for deliberation, but charged at the head of his column, and, where almost any other commander would have deemed himself fortunate to escape defeat, gained a complete victory. Other instances occurred in the experience of the general in which the service profited by his exercise of this faculty, and established his claim to the credit of superior generalship. In the opinion of closet-critics, who know nothing of war but what they read of it in books, such exploits may be considered rash, and they may be subject to the same imputation from duller minds, who regard all enterprise as savoring of temerity. Yet it is by such strokes as these that genius is distinguished from mediocrity,—the chief who is fit to command from one whose only duty it ought to be to obey. The two instances in which the daring of Wayne approached most nearly to the verge of unwarrantable temerity were his assault on Stony Point and his attack upon Cornwallis at Green Springs. Yet the first was originally suggested by Washington, who outlined the plan ; and the second was applauded by both Washington and Greene. In the one, every step, from the capture of

the sentinels to the surrender of the fort, was carefully
studied, and every probable contingency provided for,
and nothing was left to be overcome by force that could
be surmounted by strategy. In the other, the apparent
rashness was merely a phase of consummate prudence,
in which the risk of a bold advance was less than that
of a retreat.

If the exploits of Wayne were rash, as Irving sug-
gests, it is strange that Washington, who was a close
observer and an excellent judge of character, failed to
discover it during the whole of the seven years that he
served under him. Upon no other officer of his rank
did the commander-in-chief devolve duties of equal
gravity, and in no instance did he find cause to complain that his orders had not been faithfully and intelli-
gently executed. Before Wayne had been a year in
active service he was directed by Washington to lead
the advance in an expected collision with Howe in New
Jersey. At Brandywine he was stationed at the ford
to oppose Knyphausen, supported by the brigade of
Grey, while Washington went himself with the bulk of
his army to meet Cornwallis on Birmingham Heights,
thus committing to the young brigadier the maintenance
of a position of the highest importance. At Germantown Wayne led the attack, and needed only the proper
support, which the ill-advised delay at Chew's house
prevented, to convert the half-won battle into a complete and overwhelming victory. At Monmouth he
was again at the head of the attacking column, and
was so efficient in staying the British advance, after
Lee had treacherously ordered a retreat, and in turning the tide of battle in favor of the Americans, as to

obtain special commendation for gallantry and good
conduct in Washington's letter to Congress, while the
name of no other officer is particularly mentioned.
Washington's project for the assault on Stony Point
was communicated to no other officer than Wayne,
and he alone was consulted about that most daring
and dangerous enterprise.[1]

When Arnold's treason had struck the army and the
country with consternation, it was to Wayne that the
commander-in-chief committed the defence of Stony
Point, the most important fortified post on the Hudson,
thus affording the highest proof of his confidence.
When Georgia was overrun by a large British force
aided by several tribes of hostile Indians, to Wayne
was assigned the duty of driving out the invaders, and
for that purpose he was intrusted with an independent
command. After the American army had suffered two
disastrous defeats west of the Ohio and had become
thoroughly demoralized, to Wayne was committed the
duty of restoring its discipline and its confidence in

[1] Mr. Irving, in a foot-note on page 503, vol. iii. of his "Life of
Washington," says, "It is a popular tradition that when Washington
proposed to Wayne the storming of Stony Point the reply was, 'I'll
storm hell, if *you* will only plan it,' " and Mr. Lossing, in his "Field-
Book of the Revolution," repeats the story. We doubt, nevertheless, its authenticity. The same thing substantially has been told of
others than Washington and Wayne, and we may well believe that
it was told of Wayne merely from its supposed fitness to his character.
It is probable that we should never have heard the story in connection with his name if he had not been called "Mad Anthony," as
he never was chargeable with the rashness imputed to him, and
especially as he was not asked by Washington to storm Stony Point,
but merely to consider the practicability of that enterprise.

itself and of protecting a long line of settlements along the Ohio. Either Washington was mistaken in the character of Wayne and committed to a *rash*, "harebrained" officer duties requiring the utmost prudence and discretion as well as military skill, or Mr. Irving's estimate of Wayne is absurd and preposterous. When such alternatives are presented, it is not difficult to decide which is the more conformable to truth.

If Mr. Irving had made the proper inquiries before he ventured a stab at the military reputation of Wayne, he would have found that the general was as cautious in laying his plans as he was courageous in carrying them into execution; that, as a rule, in every enterprise in which he acted on his own judgment he was justified by success; that when intrusted with independent command his vigilance was never relaxed and his forecast provided for every emergency, and every step by which he advanced was calculated with mathematical precision. There was, indeed, nothing in his conduct in any instance that justified the imputation of rashness, much less was it warranted as a general characteristic.

An anecdote is told of Wayne that gives some support to the proposition that "fighting was constitutional with him." It is said that when summoned to councils of war he usually attended carrying with him a book,— "Tom Jones" or some other interesting novel,—which he would read, sitting apart in a corner of the room, while the anxious company were discussing the measures proper to be pursued. When they had severally given their opinion, the commander-in-chief would inquire of Wayne, "Well, general, what do you propose to do?" "Fight, sir," is said to have been the invariable answer. It is possible that this anecdote may have a basis of truth so far as relates to a single occasion when the circumstances were peculiar. Wayne knew that, as a rule, councils of war never fight. He was also aware that ordinarily their decision was a foregone conclusion, and that the commander-in-chief, after listening with attention to the reasons which his subordinates had to present, would be guided by the dictates of his own judgment, even if a majority of the council should entertain opinions different from his, and Wayne may have thought it unnecessary to do more than signify his dissent from the opinions of his brother officers. We know that Washington did give battle repeatedly against the advice of his council, and that Wayne agreed with him in the expediency of doing so ; that Washington called a council of war to decide whether he should attack Sir Henry Clinton on his route from Philadelphia to New York in the summer of 1778, and that the council, true to the traditional proclivities of such bodies, decided in the negative,—Wayne and Cadwalader being the only brigadiers that favored the attack out of seventeen who sat in council. Whether Wayne indicated his opinion by the monosyllable "fight" we are not told, nor does it seem probable that such was the case, as the question was one of great importance, and he was deeply interested in the decision, which he foresaw might be attended by momentous consequences. The attack was ordered, and if he had commanded the attacking corps instead of Lee the great probability is that the triumph at Yorktown would have been anticipated at Monmouth, and the independence of the Colonies would have been secured without aid from France. In one case only, so far as we know, did Washington and Wayne differ as to the eligibility of striking the enemy, and that was when it was proposed to storm the British fortifications north of Philadelphia. Wayne and Stirling favored the measure, the rest of the council opposed it, and Washington after much hesitation agreed with the majority. Wayne certainly did not give his voice for fighting at all hazards. When first consulted by Washington about assaulting Stony Point, he considered the fortifications too strong to take in that way, and it was not until after careful observation and reflection that he changed his opinion. While it is conceded that there may be some truth in the story of Wayne's behavior in councils of war, so far as regards some particular instance where the circumstances were peculiar, it is much to be doubted whether the whole story is not a fabrication. It is so suitable to the character of a military madcap that it invites the suspicion of its having been fabricated to suit the absurd *sobriquet* that has been applied to him. Wayne was not a man to treat his brother officers, assembled in council to deliberate on a grave subject, with disrespect, much less was he disposed to behave to his commander-in-chief, whom he revered, in the offensive manner described. Wayne was at heart a gentleman and accustomed to genteel associations. He was the intimate friend of Dr. Benjamin Rush, John Dickinson, Benjamin Franklin, and Robert Morris, and we are not very ready to believe that he had the manners of a boor.

The epithet "Mad" in connection with the Christian name of the general is said to have originated with a silly camp-follower, who, by reason of his oddities of speech and demeanor, was the butt of the soldiers and somewhat of a privileged person in camp. For some misbehavior he was put under arrest by order of the general. After his release, being rallied on the subject, he averred that he had been arrested not because he had done anything to deserve it, but because Anthony was mad. " He was a 'mad Anthony,' and that was all there was of it." The word "mad," in old English, is a synonyme with "angry," and was doubtless so used here. · This, in substance, the fellow repeated whenever the matter was mentioned, and thus the term " Mad Anthony," dropped casually from the lips of a simpleton, obtained some sort of circulation, and became used in a jocular way among the rank and file of Wayne's command, but never in a sense intending disparagement or disrespect. Wayne was too much admired and beloved by his men to be the proper subject in their eyes of an injurious misnomer, and they would have resented any indignity cast upon his character.[1]

As far as the appellation of " Mad Anthony" was used in the army, no reference whatever to him as a com-

[1] An enemy of Wayne, some years after his death, standing by his grave, placed his foot upon it, and addressed some visitors to the spot, saying, " Here lies the body of a scoundrel." One of the visitors, afterwards a man prominent in politics in his State, who had served in the Pennsylvania line during the war of the Revolution, instantly, by a blow of his clinched fist, felled the speaker to the ground. This rude demonstration by the assailant of his respect for the memory of his old commander is not to be justified even by his great provocation, and yet it may be said with some confidence that almost any other survivor of the gallant band whom Wayne had led in battle would have acted in the same way.

mander was intended or understood. It was deemed to have a meaning in no wise derogatory to him personally, but rather as a compliment—rugged and coarse, indeed, but still a compliment—to those qualities which the common soldier most highly appreciates and most truly admires. None of his contemporaries of the Revolutionary era ever charged him with rashness in his exploits or enterprises. The charge originates with writers of books and of magazine articles of a subsequent period, whose opinions on military matters must be taken with many grains of allowance. On such a subject, however, the judgment of Washington may be properly considered as decisive ; and as he, with full knowledge of all that he did and of all that he advised to be done, found nothing in his conduct to disapprove, but much to commend, we may safely conclude that the offensive epithet "mad" had no just application to his character, and that it may be properly relegated to the use of that class to which the camp-followers of armies belong. It has no rightful place in history, for it represents an idea which is false.

The love of glory was Wayne's master-passion. This supplied incentives to action to which his high-wrought patriotism gave additional stimulus. He was jealous of his honor, and he preserved it as bright and pure as the empyrean, and whatever faults he had were not those of an ignoble nature. His spoken word was as binding upon him as his written bond. His popularity with the people, which was due mainly to his valor, was enlivened by other qualities which are usually found associated in characters of heroic type. He was generous, frank, confiding, warm-hearted, and impulsive. His temper was quick, but his anger passed away with the first flash; and though hasty to take offence, he was placable, and his forgiveness was hearty and thorough.   Direct and straightforward in his methods, he despised the meanness of intrigue and the machinations of secret cabals. He preferred to fail in his purposes rather than to accomplish them by sinister means.   He was habitually outspoken, and was strong and decided in the utterance of his opinions.   He was apt to indulge in his criticisms of the conduct of public men with more freedom than discretion.   His judgment was nice, accurate, and discriminating, and he was not easily deceived in his estimate of those who came within the sphere of his observation.   His unfavorable estimate of some of his contemporaries while they were in the flush of an undeserved popularity has been fully ratified by time. Among those whom he denounced early in the war as utterly untrustworthy and corrupt was Benedict Arnold, whose treason, though a surprise to many, appeared to Wayne but the natural and logical termination of a base and profligate career.   He long regarded Charles Lee also with distrust, although many believed him ill used and his treachery remained for many years unknown and even unsuspected.   Of the fidelity of another general officer to the cause of American liberty he openly expressed his doubt, and if that doubt has not been confirmed, the grounds of it have not been removed. He had many friends in the army of the highest rank and of the most solid reputation, who were warmly attached to him.   Among these were Schuyler, Greene, Lafayette, Stirling, Sullivan, and Knox.   If he did not refrain from censure, neither did he withhold his praise, and where it was well deserved he was liberal and even lavish of it. Of envy and jealousy he was absolutely free, though frequently the object of both by reason of the conspicuous part he bore in the operations of the army and of the confidence reposed in him by the commander-in-chief. His perceptions were quick, and his mind readily took hold of the prominent points of his subject, and when the exigency demanded a prompt decision he decided without hesitation and allowed no doubt to embarrass or delay his action. His self-possession was perfect, and in every extremity of danger it was fully maintained, and the severer the pressure upon him the more complete appeared to be his command of his intellectual resources. He had great self-reliance, and to his resolution once taken he adhered with immovable firmness and tenacity. The idea that the freedom with which he exposed himself to the bullets of the enemy was due to his insensibility to danger is a mistaken one. He went into battle fully prepared for whatever might befall him. In two instances, at least, when about to engage in extraordinary hazards, he made his Will and wrote farewell letters to his family, to be forwarded in case of his fall. At other times he reminded his children of the perils which beset him, and of the probability that by the fortune of war they might at any moment be deprived of his paternal care. Considerations of this kind, however, had no effect upon his conduct. When once engaged with the enemy his whole soul was absorbed in the effort to obtain success.

It has been said of him that he was imperious, and, with his temperament, habituated to command and accustomed to rely wholly on himself, it would be surprising if it were not so. He had a strong will, which, within the sphere of his authority, governed with absolute sway, bending men and circumstances to his purpose. He was egotistic and somewhat sensitive, and felt more keenly than a wise man should have done any calumnious statement affecting his conduct or character. He was not destitute of vanity, and he was too susceptible to flattery. He estimated highly the value of discipline, and was not merciful to those who voluntarily violated its rules. He was well assured that no such soldiers as those who constituted the Pennsylvania line could be made without severe preparatory training, and that such training was one of the necessary means for securing efficiency. His severity in this respect was not in his apprehension a subject of choice, but of duty. He certainly owed to it much of his success. His restless activity and unremitting vigilance in the supervision of every department of the service kept his subordinates constantly on the alert. In his last campaign as well as in his first, his keen observant eye was always open to detect whatever was amiss. During the winter of 1793–94 he slept on the ground and endured the rigors of an Ohio winter with no other accommodations than those of a common soldier, and he rose at four o'clock in the morning to visit the outposts and to see that every sentinel was awake and in his proper place. War with him was serious work, and not a holiday recreation, and his primary concern was that the interests of the country should not suffer in his hands. No thirst for revenge could stifle in his bosom the instincts of humanity. Although at Stony Point the cry of "No quarter to the rebels!" raised by Grey's ruffians at

Paoli, was still ringing in his ears, and the horrors there enacted were still rankling in his bosom, he would suffer no stain of cruelty to rest on the American arms, and no blow was struck after resistance ceased. In dealing with the Indians on the Miami, while he carried the sword in one hand he held out the olive-branch in the other, and when he had made himself sure of victory he declined to attack till every offer of peace was rejected. When compelled at length to strike, the blow was delivered with such effect that it was unnecessary to repeat it. By his vigor he won the respect of the savage tribes, and by his fairness and magnanimity their confidence. In the conduct of this war his instructions left him a wide discretion, which if rashly or injudiciously exercised might have involved the country in a war with England. But his every step was marked with the tact and prudence becoming a statesman, and in no act of omission or commission did he fail to realize the just expectation of the country. In fact, in whatever relation he stood to the public service during the whole period of his connection with it, whether as chief or subordinate, he was distinguished above his peers, and in whatever conflict he was engaged he won deserved applause. We do not propose to compare him with Washington. They were different in many points of their respective characters, and in some there were strong contrasts between them. Both were gifts to the nation from that beneficent Power which, from feeble beginnings, led this nation by the hand gradually up to its present pitch of greatness. Though not equally eminent, each was peculiarly fitted for the part he was appointed to act in the drama of the

25

American Revolution, and we may as soon expect to see another Wayne as another Washington.

Isaac Wayne, the only son of the general, was born in East-town, Chester County, in 1768, and died at Waynesborough, the old family seat, on the 25th of October, 1852, at the venerable age of eighty-four. He was educated at Dickinson College, Pennsylvania, and after graduating at that institution he studied law under William Lewis, Esq., in Philadelphia. He was admitted to the Philadelphia bar in the fall of 1794, and to the Chester County bar August 21, 1795, and immediately entered upon the practice of his profession, in which he continued for eighteen months. At the end of that period, at the request of his father, he went to reside at the paternal mansion, in order to attend to the management of the Waynesborough estate, which, owing to the long absence of his father in the public service, needed better care than that which was bestowed by his tenants. On the 25th of August, 1802, he married Elizabeth Smith, a young lady of excellent family and of good estate. Five children were the issue of this marriage. Isaac Wayne was a man of very respectable talents. In politics he was a decided Federalist and exceedingly popular with his party. In 1800 and 1801 he was elected a member of the Assembly. In 1806 he was elected a member of the

State Senate, and in 1810 he was re-elected, but served only one year of his term. In 1814 he was nominated by the Federal party as candidate for the office of governor of Pennsylvania, and also as a candidate for Congress for the district composed of the counties of Chester and Montgomery. Although he ran far ahead of his ticket, the Democratic majorities in the State and the Congressional district were too large to be overcome. In 1822 he was again nominated for Congress as one of the representatives of Chester, Lancaster, and Delaware Counties, with James Buchanan and Samuel Edwards as colleagues, and was elected. He declined a re-election in 1824, and did not again enter political life.

Prior to the war of 1812 he raised a regiment of cavalry, of which he was elected colonel, and, when that war broke out, he offered his services and those of his regiment to the government. He was ordered to Marcus Hook, and spent the summer of 1814 in Camp Dupont at that place when an attack on Philadelphia was expected. He had much of the martial spirit of his family and many of the traits of character which distinguished his father, but he lacked the opportunity to acquire reputation as a soldier. After the death of his children his affections reverted to his father, whose memory he cherished with a devotion amounting almost to idolatry. In 1829 and 1830 he published in "The Casket" a short memoir of the general, in which he studiously presented the most important of the documents relating to his military career. At that time he destroyed a large number of letters relating to his private and family affairs. This he did, as he declared,

in obedience to the injunction of his father, although
they contained matters of much interest. Before he
complied with his father's directions he placed the
papers in the hands of the Hon. Charles Miner, his
successor in Congress and proprietor of the *Village
Record* at West Chester, with the request that he would
write the last chapter of the memoir. While the papers
were in Mr. Miner's hands, the writer of this paragraph,
who was the legal adviser of Colonel Wayne, was permitted to examine the papers, and availed himself of
the opportunity of doing so, and afterwards suggested
to Colonel Wayne that he might reasonably exercise
his discretion as to the letters he would destroy, as
among them there were those which the public would
be glad to see, and which reflected credit upon his
father's character. To this suggestion he replied that
the request of his father he considered it his duty to
obey, and that duty he would perform to the letter.

   Mr. Miner prepared the final chapter with much
care and pains and delivered it to Colonel Wayne. It
gave an accurate and singularly graphic account of
General Wayne's financial difficulties owing to his
efforts to improve his Georgia estate, and set forth in
a striking light his energetic and honorable character,
and the masterly manner in which he had managed to
fulfil his engagements and to preserve his credit at a
time when the industries of the country were in a depressed condition and money difficult to be procured.
Colonel Wayne gave the MS. a careful perusal, and
justly regarded it as an admirable conclusion to the
memoir. But he could not endure the thought that
his father's pecuniary troubles, though surmounted by

praiseworthy efforts, should be exposed to the world. He therefore burned what Mr. Miner had written, and finished the memoir in his own way.

General Wayne had one daughter, Margaretta, who married William R. Atlee, a lawyer of reputation. Mrs. Atlee had one child, a daughter, Mary. She married Issachar Evans. She left one child, William Evans, to whom Colonel Wayne devised all his real estate and a considerable part of his personal property. William Evans having become the owner of the Waynesborough estate (under the will of his uncle, Colonel Isaac Wayne), upon application to the proper court obtained a decree by which the name of Evans was exchanged for that of Wayne, he being the only lineal descendant of the general in the third generation.

APPENDICES.

APPENDIX I.

GENERAL WAYNE'S DIVISION ORDERS, 20TH DECEMBER, 1777.

The following promotions of Field Officers in the Penns'a Line has taken place Viz

George Nagle Col'l of the 10th Reg't.
Henry Bicker Col'l of the 2nd Reg't.
Ric'd Butler Col. of the 9th Reg't.
Thomas Craig Col. of the 3rd Reg't.
Matthew Smith Lieut. Col. of the 9th Reg't.
Henry Miller Lieut. Col. of the 2nd Reg't.
Josiah Harmar Lieut. Col. of the 6th.
Thomas Robinson Lieut. Col. of the 1st.
Rudolph Bruner Lieut. Col. of the 3rd.
Stephen Bayard Lieut. Col. of the 8th.
Caleb North Lieut. Col. of the 11th.
Francis Nichol Major of the 9th Reg't.
Thos. Church Major of the 4th Reg't.
John Hulings Major of the 3rd Reg't.
James Moore Major of the 1st.
Frederick Vernon Major of the 8th.
James Taylor Major of the 5th.
Jeremiah Tolbert Major of the 6th &
Michael Ryan Major of the 10th Reg't.

The Justice done to the merits of these Officers has Open'd the way for the promotion of the Subaltern Officers in the Respective Regiments whose bravery and good Conduct equally Entitle them to it—the pleasure and satisfaction the Gen'l experiences on this Occasion he can much better feel than express—it must Afford the greatest Satisfaction to a grateful mind to see a Corps of Officers

375

Honorably provided for—who has more than shared the Danger and Difficulties of this hard campaign

The General's State of Health as well as Other Considerations Require a little Respite—he hopes soon to be able to Rejoin the Army—in the Interim every exertion of his shall be used to provide not only Comfortable Clothing—but the Neatest Uniform for his Worthy fellow Soldiers whose bravery and Conduct have made them formidable to their foes—and endeared them to their Country and their General—whose greatest Ambition is to deserve their Esteem and Confidence and to share every vicisitude of fortune with them

Genl. Wayne most earnestly wishes the Officers in General to exert every power in Covering themselves and men in Speediest and most Comfortable manner possible & to pay every Attention to the Discipline Health and Cleanliness of the Soldiers—

Col. Broadhead will take the Command of the Division until the Genl— Returns—

APPENDIX II.

ARRANGEMENT OF THE PENNSYLVANIA LINE (WAYNE'S DI-VISION, EIGHT REGIMENTS), AS MADE AT WHITE PLAINS IN 1778.

First Regiment.

Dates of Commission.

James Chambers, Colonel........................28th Sept'r 1776.
Thomas Robinson, Lt. Colonel ....7th June   1777.
James Moore—Major........................ .....20th Sept'r "
Captains—1. James Parr...........................9th March 1776.
        2. James Hamilton ....10th "   "
        3. Samuel Craig.......................1st October "
        4. Michael Simpson...................1st Dec'r   "
        5. James Wilson.......................16th Jan'y 1777.
        6. William Wilson.....................2nd March "
Capt. Lieutenant—Thomas Buchannan (Rank
        as Capt)...........................1st Oct.   1777.
Lieutenants—1. John Dougherty................ "   1776.
        2. David Zeigler...................16th Jan'y 1777.
        3. Abraham Skinner...............13th May   "
        4. Benjamin Lyon...................6th July   "

First Regiment—Continued.

Dates of Commission.

5. John McClellan................11th Sept'r 1777.
6. Aaron Norcross.................14th "   "
7. Thomas Boyd....................14th Jan'y 1778.
8. John Hughes....................20th March "

Ensigns— 1. James McFarland (ranks as
              Lieut)......................13th May 1777.

All these 2. William McDowell (ranks as
rank   Lieut)......................6th July . "
as 2nd   3. Edward Crawford (ranks as
Lieut'ns   Lieut)......................11th Sept'r "
from the   4. David Hammond (ranks as
13th P. R.   Lieut)......................14th   "   "
           5. Andrew Johnston Q M. (ranks
              as Lieut).....................24th March 1778.
           6. Joseph Collin..................18th April 1777.
           7. Samuel Beard..................2nd June 1778.
           8. Benjamin Chambers...........   "   "
           9.

Second Regiment.

Dates of Commission.

Walter Stewart, Colonel.....................17th June 1777.
Henry Miller, Lieut. Colonel...................1st March   "
John Murray, Major..............................5th Feb'y   "
Captains—1. John Marshall....................13th June 1776.
           2. George Tudor....................13th July   "
Date   3. Jacob Ashmead..................6th Sept'r   "
not   4. John Bankson..................25th   "   "
settled 5. John Patterson..................1st Jan'y 1777.
           6. Samuel Tolbert....................
Capt. Lieutenant—Peter Gosner (Ranks as
   Capt).................................   "   1778.
Lieutenants—1. John Cobea..................   "   1777.
           2. John Irvine......................   "   "
           3. John Stoy......................   "   "
           4. Jacob Snider..................18th April   "
           5. Henry Piercy..................12th March "
           6. James Morris Jones...........   "   "

Second Regiment—Continued.

Dates of Commission.

Lieutenants—7. William Moore.................18th April 1777.

8. James Whitehead..............2nd June 1778.

Ensigns—   1. Philip Waggoner.............12th March 1777.

2. John Gugg—from 13th Regt.10th April "

All here   3. James Brickham...............   "   "

rank as   4. Thomas Norton Q'r M'r...24th April "

2nd   5. John Striker..................1st October "

Lieutenant   6. Henry Purcell..................4th   "   "

7. John Park.....................1st Aug   "

8. Patrick Fullerton.............13th April "

9. Jacob De Hart.................2nd June 1778.

Surgeon—Benjamin Parry

Mate—Robert Harris

Third Regiment.

Dates of Commission.

Thomas Craig, Colonel ....1st August 1777.

William Williams, Lt. Col......................5th June   "

David Lenox—Major.........................8th   "   "

Captains—1. Thomas Lloyd Moore.............21st May 1776.

2. James Chrystie ....9th Aug.   "

3. Thomas Butler ....4th Oct.   "

4. John Reily.......................20th May 1777.

5. Isaac Budd Dunn ....1st June   "

6. William Craig.....................4th July   "

Capt. Lieutenant—John Henderson ....1st October 1776.

Lieutenants—1. James Black....................3d   "   "

2. George McCullouch ....4th   "   "

3. James Armstrong...............4th   "   "

4. John Marshall..................10th Jan'y 1777.

5. Daniel St. Clair..............1st April   "

6. Robert King....................20th May   "

7. John Boyd......................   "   "

8. Persival Butler..................1st Sept.   "

Ensigns—   1. Blackall William Ball.......17th October 1776.

These rank   2. Andrew Engle...............11th Jan'y 1777.

as 2nd Lieuts 3. John Armstrong.............11th Sept.   "

Third Regiment—Continued.

Dates of Commission.

4. John Wigdon, P. M ....2nd June 1778.
5. Peter Smith...........................   "   "
6. Richard Fullerton...................   "   "
7. Thomas Hulings....................   "   "
8.
9.

Surgeon—James Tate

Fourth Regiment.

Dates of Commission.

Captains—1. Evan Edwards.....................23rd March 1776.
   2. Edward Scull.......................3rd Jan'y 1777.
   3. William Gray ....   "   "
   4. Benjamin Fishbourne.............   "   "
   5. John McGowen.....................   "   "
   6. Benjamin Bird......................   "   "
Capt. Lieutenant—William Henderson.........   "   "
Lieutenants—1. John Dover.....................   "   "
   2. David Brown.....................   "   "
   3. William Sprout ....   "   "
   4. Edward F. Randolph ....   "   "
   5. Thomas Campbell..............   "   "
   6. George Blewer.................   "   "
   7. Arcurius Beatty....... ....2nd June 1778.
   8. Peter Summers—Q M.........   "   "
Ensigns (from Col. Shea's)—1. Jacob Weaver
   (ranks as 2nd Lt.)................16th Nov. 1776.
   2. George Boss, Adj't.................2d June 1778.
   3. Gilders Bevans......................   "   "
   4.
   5.
   6.
   7.
   8.
   9.

Matthew Potar to be an Ensign from............2d June.

Fifth Regiment.

Dates of Commission.

Francis Johnston, Colonel.........................27th Sept'r 1776.

Persifor Frazer, Lt. Colonel.......................1st October   "

Christopher Stuart, Major........................28th Feb'y 1777.

Captains—1. Benjamin Bartholomew...........2nd October 1776.

        2. John Christie........................23rd October "

        3. Samuel Smith ....1st March 1777.

        4. William Oldham................ ..24th March "

        5. Isaac Seely...........................20th Sep'r "

        6. Thomas Bond ....23rd "   "

Capt. Lieutenant—Michael Ryan (Capt'ns

        rank).......................23rd Jan'y 1778.

Lieutenants—1. Job Vernon.......................1st Jan'y 1777.

        2. John Bartley ....   "   "

        3. Levi Griffith......................   "   "

        4. Alexander Martin..............   "   "

        5. John Harper......................   "   "

        6. George North...................   "   "

        7. James Forbes...................   "   "

        8. James McCullouch. ....   "   "

Ensigns—
Rank as
2nd Lieut.
{ 1. Andrew Lytle.................30th Dec'r 1776.

    2. David Marshall.................   "   "

    3.   Bickham ....2nd June 1778.

    4. Henry Hankly.................   "   "

    5.

    6.

    7.

    8.

    9.

Surgeon—   Davidson.

Sixth Regiment.

Dates of Commission.

Robert Magaw, Colonel............................3rd Jan'y 1776.

Josiah Harmar, Lt. Colonel....................... 6th June 1777.

Jeremiah Talbot, Major.............................25th Sept. "

Sixth Regiment—Continued.

Dates of Commission.

Captains—1. John Nice.............................13th June 1776.
   2. John Doyle ....16th July "
   3. Walter Finney.......................August   "
   4. Jacob Humphries ....15th Feb'y 1777.
   5. Jacob Bower .... "   "   "
   6. Robert Wilkin......................28th "   "
Capt. Lieutenant—Thomas Bull (Capt'n Rank)1st Aug't "
Lieutenants—1. William McHalton ....17th Octob'r 1776.
   2. Richard Collier.................16th Feb. 1777.
   3. Isaac Vanhorn...................17th Feb'y "
   4. James Gibbon ....18th Feb'y "
   5. James Glentworth ....17th June "
   6. Benjamin Lodge ....11th October 1777.
   7. Garret Stediford ....12th Oct'r 1777.
   8. Stewart Herbert.............. 9th Jan'y 1778.
Ensigns—1. Thomas Doyle (2d Lt. Rank)...1st Jan'y 1777.
   2. Farquhar McPherson (")...15th Feb. "
   3. Philip Gibbons   (")...17th Oct'r "
   4. Edward Speer   (")...7th Feb. 1778.
   5. John Mackland....................20th Aug. 1777.
   6. Charles Macknel ....23rd Oct'r "
   7. Thomas Dungan...................2nd June 1778.
   8. James Allen........................ "   "   "
   9.
Surgeon—John McDowell.

Seventh Regiment.

Dates of Commission.

William Irvine, Colonel...........................9th Jan'y 1776.
Samuel Hay, Lt. Colonel........................2nd Feb'y 1778.
Francis Mentges, Major...........................3rd October 1776.
Captains—1. William Alexander...............1st June "
   2. William Bratton...................12th Jan'y 1777.
   3. John Alexander...................20th March "
   4. Alexander Parker .... "   "   "
   5. Samuel Montgomery.............. "   "   "
   6. Andrew Irvine.....................25th Sept'r "

Seventh Regiment—Continued.

Dates of Commission.

Capt. Lieutenant—William Miller (Capt'n
Rank)......................2nd Feb'y 1778.

Lieutenants—1. William Lusk..................20th March 1777.

    2. Samuel Kennedy.............. " " "

    3. John Bush..................... " " "

    4. Samuel Bryson................. " " "

From 13th

    Reg.—5. James McMichael ....20th June 1777.

    6. Thomas McCoy.................13th Aug. "

    7. Robert McPherson.............1st Sep'r "

    8. Alexander Russel...............25th Sep'r "

Ensigns— 1. Joseph Torrence..................20th Jan'y "

    2. John Blair........................ " " "

All these 3. James Williamson..............19th March "

Rank 4. Robert Peble.....................24th April "

with 2nd 5. James Milligan...................1st Sep'r "

Lieuts. 6. John McCullum.................25th Sep'r "

    7. John Hughes—Q M .... " " "

    8. Thomas Alexander—B Q M...2nd June 1778.

    9.

Surgeon—John Ross.

Mate—   Berry.

Eighth Regiment.

Dates of Commission.

Daniel Broadhead, Colonel......................29th Sep'r 1776.

Stephen Bayard, Lt. Colonel....................23rd Sep'r 1777.

Frederick Vernon, Major........................7th June "

Captains (from 11th)—1. Samuel Dawson......16th July 1776.

    2.   Van Swearingen.9th Aug't "

    3. John Finley.......... " " "

from 13th Reg't—4. John Clark...........10th April 1777.

    "   5. James F. Moore ..... " " "

    "   6. James Carnagan..... " " "

Capt. Lieutenant—Samuel Brady................17th July 1776.

Lieutenants—1. Basil Prather....................9th Aug't "

    2. John Harding..................

    3. Gabriel Patterson..............

Eighth Regiment—Continued.

from 11th

Dates of Commission.

Reg't.—4. John Stotesbury.................9th April   1777.
from 13th.—5. Joseph Brown Lee.............10th April   "
from 2d. —6. William Honyman...............15th Jan'y   "
    "   —7. Benjamin Boyer.................12th March   "
from 11th —8. Nathanael Martin..............30th October   "
Ensigns—1. William Amberson (rank 2d Lt.)..9th Aug't   "
       2.   Graham   ("   ).. "   "   "
       3. John Crawford, Adj't.............2nd June 1778.
       4.   Reed, late Paymaster......... "   "   "
       5.
       6.
       7.
       8.
       9.

Surgeon—Abel Morgan.

APPENDIX III.

ARRANGEMENT OF THE PENNSYLVANIA LINE (SIX REGI-
MENTS), JANUARY 17, 1781.

First Regiment.

Commissioned.

Colonel Daniel Brodhead..........................Sep'r 29, 1776.
L't Colonel Thomas Robinson...................June 7, 1777.
Major James Moore ....Sep'r 20,   "

Captains.

1. John Davis (of the 9th)......................Novem'r 15, 1776.
2. John Clark (of the 8th)......................February 28, 1777.
3. William Wilson...............................March 2,   "
4. Jacob Stake (of the 10th) ....Novem'r 12,   "
5. David Zügler.................................Decem'r 8, 1778.
6. John Steel (of the 10th) ....March 23, 1779.
7. Ebenezer Carson (of the 10th).............April 1,   "
8. John McClellan..............................October 1,   "
9. Edward Burke (of the 11th)................October 2, 1780.

First Regiment—Continued.

Subalterns.

Commissioned.

1. Lieutenants William Feltman (of the 10th)Novem'r 2, 1777.
2. James McFarland..............March 21, 1778.
3. William McDowell..............March 22, "
4. Edward Crawford..............March 23, "
5. Joseph Banks (of the 10th) ..June 2, "
6. David Hammond...............Decem'r 8, "
7. Andrew Johnston..............May 12, 1779.
8. Joseph Collier ....May 17, "
9. Francis White (of the 10th)..August 2, "
10. Robert Martin .... April 1, 1780.
11. Michael Everly.................July, "
12. James Camble...................July 18, "
13. Ensign Robert Nesbitt (of the 10th)......Sep'r 15, "
14. Brooks (of the 10th)..........
Surgeon John Rogers ....Commiss'd.
Surgeon's Mate John Rague (of the 10th).....August 19, 1778.

Second Regiment.

Colonel Walter Stewart...........................June 17, 1777.
Lt. Colonel Caleb North (of the 9th)..........October 23, "
Major James Hamilton...........................December 10, 1778.

Captains.

1. Joseph McClelland (of the 9th)..............July 15, 1776.
2. John Bankson....................................Septem'r 25, "
3. Samuel Tolbert...................................October 2, "
4. John Patterson...................................January 1, 1777.
5. John Pearson (of the 9th)....................September 7, "
6. Joseph Finley (of the 8th)...................October 20, "
7. Andrew Walker (of the 11th) ....January 23, 1778.
8. William Lusk (of the 7th)....................May 12, 1779.
9. Samuel Kennedy (of the 7th)...............April 17, 1780.

Subalterns.

1. Lieutenants Henry Piercy ....March 12, 1777.
2. James Whitehead.............. " " "
3. James Morris Jones.............. " " "

Second Regiment.—Continued.

Commissioned.

4.	William Moore	April 10, 1777.
5.	Enoch Reeves (of the 10th)	March 1, 1778.
6.	John Striker	May 1, 1779.
7.	Henry D. Pursell	Sept. 3, "
8.	Ensign William Munen	May 19, "
9.	John B. Tilden	May 28, "
10.	Anlavin D. Marcellan	Sept. 21, "
11.	George Le Roy	" "
12.	Lts John Ward (8th)	April 2, "
13.	John Holtsberry (8th)	

Surgeon.

Benjamin Perry ....July 10, 1777.

Surgeon's Mate.

Robert Harris ....August 1, "

Third Regiment.

Colonel Thomas Craig ....August 1, 1777.
Lt. Colonel Josiah Harmar....................June 6, "
Major William Alexander......................April 17, 1780.

Captains.

1. James Christie ....August 9, 1776.
2. Isaac B. Dunn ....October 4, "
3. Lawrence Keene (of the 11th) ....January 13, 1777.
4. George M. Cully..............................October 20, "
5. Abraham G. Claypoole (of the 11th).......June 10, 1778.
6. William Sproat (of the 4th) ....
7. John Henderson ....May 12, 1779.
8. John Marshall ....August 13, "
9. Samuel Bradey (of the 8th)..................August 2, "

Subalterns.

1. Lieutenants Daniel St. Clair ....April 1, 1777.
2. Percival Butler....................Septem'r 1, "
3. Blackall W'm Ball ....Septem'r 11, 1778.
4. Andrew Engle...................December 20, "

26

Third Regiment.—Continued.

Commissioned.

5. Lieutenants James Pettigrew (of the 11th) April 13, 1779.
6. John Armstrong ....May 12, "
7. Richard Fullerton.............. " " "
8. John Wigton.....................August 13, "
9. Peter Smith..................... " " "
10. Jacob Whitzel (of the 11th)..March 11, 1780.
11. Robert Alison (of the 11th)..March 16, "
12. Francis Thornberry (of the 11th)...........May 25, "
13. Samuel Read (of the 11th) ...October 2, "
14. Ensign Peter Cunningham ....July 1, 1779.

Surgeon.

Alexander Stewart ....October 10, 1779.

Surgeon's Mate.

Robert Wharry ....June 20, 1778.

Fourth Regiment.

Lt. Colonel William Butler.......................January 22, 1779.
Major Frederick Vernon (8th)..................June 7, 1777.
Major Evan Edwards (11th)......................December 16, 1778.

Captains.

1. Benjamin Fishbourne ....January 3, 1777.
2. John Alexander (7th)...........................March 20, "
3. Alexander Parker (7th)........................ " "
4. Samuel Montgomery (7th)..................... " "
5. Andrew Irvine (7th)........................... " "
6. James Carnahan (8th)..........................April 18, "
7. Henry Becker...................................May 15, 1778.
8. William Henderson.............................May 16, "
9. Thomas Campbell..............................January 1, 1781.

Subalterns.

1. Lieutenants Samuel Bryson (7th)............March 20, 1777.
2. James McMichael (7th).........June 20, "
3. Garret Stediford....................October 12, "

Fourth Regiment.—Continued.

Commissioned.

4.	George Blewer..................May 16, 1778.	
5.	Arcurius Beaty.................June 2,	"
6.	Peter Summers................. "	"
7.	George Boss....................June 4,	"
8.	Robert Peebles (7th)..........April 15, 1779.	
9.	James Milligan (7th).........April 16,	"
10.	John McCullam (7th)......... "	"
11.	John Hughes (7th) ....April 25,	"
12.	Wilder Bevans ....May 11,	"
13.	John Pratt.....................	
14.	Henry Henley..................	
15. Ensign	Andrew Henderson..................July 4, 1779.	
16.	John Rose (7th).....................	
17.	James Gamble (7th)................	
18.	Ebenezer Denny (7th)..............	

Surgeon William Magaw.........................June 15, 1775.
Surgeon's Mate John Wilkin.....................

Fifth Regiment.

Colonel Richard Butler (9th).....................June 7, 1777.
Lt. Colonel Francis Mentges.....................October 9, 1778.
Major Thomas H. Moore (9th)...................May 12, 1779.

Captains.

1. Thomas B. Bowen (9th)......................September 2, 1776.
2. Benjamin Bartholomew.......................October 2, "
3. John Christie....................................October 23, "
4. Samuel Smith..................................March 1, 1777.
5. Isaac Seely....................................Sept'r 20, "
6. Thomas Boude..................................Sept'r 23, "
7. John Finley (8th) ....October 22, "
8. Job Vernon......................................June 13, 1779.
9. William Vanleer (9th)..........................October 10, "

Subalterns.

1. Lieutenants Levi Griffith......................January 1, 1777.
2. John Harper...................... " "
3. George North.................... " "

Fifth Regiment.—Continued.

Commissioned.

4. Lieutenants James McCullough ....January 1, 1777.
5.   Andrew Lytle....................January 20, "
6.   John McKinney (9th).........March 18, 1778.
7.   David Marshall...................Novem'r 5, "
8.   Ephraim Douglass (9th) ......January 20, 1779.
9.   Edward Butler (9th)............January 28, "
10.   John Bispham....................February 1, "
11.   Abner M. Dunn (9th).........May 31, "
12.   Benjamin Marshall..............June 13, "
13.   Llewellyn Davis (9th) ....August 10, "
14.   Nathaniel Smith (9th).........
15.   David McKnight (9th)........
16. Ensign James Gilchrist.......................July 1, "
17.   Joseph Irwin (9th) ....July 20, 1780.
18.   Joseph Reed (9th)................... " "

Surgeon.

James Davidson.......................................April 5, 1777.

Surgeon's Mate.

Richard Alison ....March 16, 1778.

Sixth Regiment.

Colonel Richard Humpton (10th)...............October 1st, 1776.
Lt. Colonel Stephen Bayard (8th)..............Sept'r 23, 1777.
Major James Greer (10th)........................October 23, "

Captains.

1. John Doyle...July 16, 1776.
2. Walter Finney.....................................August 10, "
3. Robert Wilkin.....................................October 10, "
4. George Bush (11th)............................January 13, 1777.
5. Jacob Humphrey.................................February 15, "
6. Jacob Bower....................................... " "
7. John Crawford (8th)............................August 10, 1779.
8. Robert Patton (10th) ....March 1, 1780.
9. Jeremiah Jackson (11th).......................March 16, "

Sixth Regiment.—Continued.
Subalterns.

Commissioned.

1. Lieutenants Edward Hovenden..............February 15, 1777.
2.   James Gibbon (Brevet Capt.).   "   "
3.   James Glentworth......... ......   "   "
4.   Benjamin Lodge.................October 11,   "
5.   Stewart Herbert.................January 9, 1778.
6.   John McMahon (11th).........June 1,   "
7.   James F. McPherson...........January 15, 1779.
8.   Samuel Morrison (11th).......February 13, "
9.   Thomas Doyle..................March 15,   "
10.   John Markham ....July 1,   "
11.   William Huston (11th)........Feb'y 24, 1780.
12. Second Lt. Edward Spear.....................Feb'y 7, 1778.
13. Ensign Thomas Dungan......................June 2,   "
14.   Sanky Dixon...........................Aug't 25, 1779.
15.   John Humphrey.....................   "   "
16.   John Vankoort (10th)..............Sept'r 15, 1780.

Surgeon.
John McDowell ....February 5, 1778.

Surgeon's Mate.
Ezekiel Downey ....Sept. 11, 1780.

APPENDIX IV.

MUSTER ROLL OF THE OFFICERS IN THE LEGION OF THE UNITED STATES, 1793.

Commissioned.

Anthony Wayne...Major General.
James Wilkinson....................................Brigadier General.
Thomas Posey.....................................   "   "
Michael Rudolph.................................Adjutant & Inspector.
James O'Hara ....Quarter Master.
John Belli...Deputy Quarter Master.
Caleb Swan..Paymaster.
Richard Allison....................................Surgeon.
John Hunt...Chaplain.

Cavalry.

Commissioned.

Michael Rudolph..............Major...............5th March 1792.
Henry ....Captain............. " " resign'd.
William Winston .... " ....8th May.
Robert Miss Campbell........ " ....7th October.
William Aylet Lee............ " ....25th "
Tarleton Fleming.............Lieutenant.........8th May.
Solomon Van Rensalaer...... " ....18th September.
James Taylor................... " ....7th October.
Leonard Covington .... " ....25th "
John Webb ....Cornet.............8th May.
George H. Dunn......... ..... " ....18th September.
Abraham Jones................. " ....7th October.
Dan'l Torrey................... " ....25th "

Artillery.

Henry Burbeck. ....Major ....4th November 1791.
Mahlon Ford..................Captain............4th March "
John Pierce..................... " ....15th October "
Moses Porter.................... " ....4th November "
Daniel McLane................ " .... " "
Abimael Youngs Nicoll......Lieutenant.........4th March "
George Ingersoll.............. " .... " "
Staats Morris................... " ....26th July "
George Dembar .... " ....5th March 1792.
Piercy Pope..................... " .... " "
Joseph Elliot................... " .... " "
Ebenezer Massey.............. " .... " "
Peter L. Van Alen............. " ....6th September 1792.

First Sub Legion.

John F. Hamtramck......... Lieut. Col. Com-
              mand't ....18th Feb. 1793.
Thomas Doyle..................Major...............28th Sept'r 1792.
Thomas Hughes............... " ....27th Nov'r "

First Sub Legion—Continued.

	Rank in the Legion.	Commissioned.
John Pratt.........................Captain....	3	......4 March 1791.
William Hersey................. "	 4	......4 June "
William Peters .... "	 5	......4 November "
Jacob Kingsbery............... "	 8	......28 December "
Thomas Martin................ "	 9	......5th March 1792.
Thomas Pasteur .... "	...10	...... " "
Cornelius R. Swan............ "	...11	......23d April "
John Jeffers..................... "	...12	......15th May "
Abner Prior.. .... "	...13	......2 June "
Asa Hartshorne................ "	...15	......1 September "
Jacob Melcher................ "	...16	......28th September "

. . . Vacancy to be filled by Ensign Morgan if acquited.

James Clay.....................	1 Lieutenant	.....28th December 1791.
Daniel Britt.....................	2 "	.....29th "
Hamilton Armstrong	3 "	....10 January 1792.
Bartholomew Shomberg......	5 "	.....5 March.
Bernard Gaines................	4 "	..... "
John Wade	6 "	..... "
Ross Bird.......................	7 "	.....23 April 1792.
Hastings Marks	8 "	.....15th May "
William H. Harrison..........	9 "	.....2 June "
Robert Hunter................10	"	.... 1 Sept "
Lewis Bond.....................11	"	.....28 Sept'r "
John Whistler..................12	"	.....27 Nov'r "
John Morgan...................Ensign		..............May 1790.
Daniel Bissell 3	"	............5 March 1792.
John Michael 5	"	.... " "
Jacob Krumer.................2	"	.... " "
Henry Montford..............1	"	.... " "
Charles Hyde.................4	"	.... " "

Second Sub Legion.

David Strong..................Lieut Col. Command't	..........19th February 1793.
Thomas Hunt.................Major................18th Feb'y	"

Second Sub Legion—Continued.

Commissioned.

John Mills......................Major...............19th Feb'y 1793.
John H. Buell.................. " ....20th " "
Rich'd Brooke Roberts......Captain *promoted.*4 March 1791.
Thomas H. Cushing.......... " " " "

Rank in
the Legion.

Joseph Shaylor................. " No. 1...... " "
Jonathan Haskell.............. " 2...... " "
Bezaleel Howe.................. " ......4 November.
Daniel Bradley................. " ...... "
Cornelius Lyman .... " 14......30th July 1792.
Richard Trucombe Howe... " ✕ ....27th Nov. " dec'd.
Richard H. Greaton.......... " ....18th Feb'y 1793.
Russell Bissell.................. " ....19th " "
Joseph Dickinson.............. " ....20th " "
Edward Miller.................. " ....21st " "
John Tillinghast..............Lieut'nt *promoted* 4 Nov'r 1791.
Daniel Tilton jun.............. " No. 1... " "
Samuel Andrews.............. " promoted " "
John Bird....................... " " " "
Micah McDonough............ " No. 2...5th March 1792.
Edward Turner................ " 3...13th July "
Theodore Sedgwick........... " 4...30th " "
John Sullivan.................. " 5...27th November "
Andrew Marschalk........... " 6...18th Feb'y 1793.
William Marts.................. " 7...19th " "
John Lowry... .... " 8...20th " "
Andrew McCleery............. " 9...21st " "
Samuel Drake..................Ensign 11...5 March 1792.
✕ Felix Long.................. " ... " "
Peter Shoemaker.............. " 12... " "
Isaac Younghusband.......... " 10... " "

Third Sub Legion.

. . . .Lieut. Col. Command't ....
Henry Gaither ....Major..............5 March 1792.

Third Sub Legion—Continued.

Commissioned.

George M. Bedinger..........Major...............3 March 1792 resig'd.
Jonathan Cass................. " ....21st Feb'y 1793.
Isaac Guion.....................Captain............5 March 1792.
Zebulon Pike.................... " .... " "
Richard Sparks................ " .... " "
Uriah Springer................. " .... " "
Nicholas Hannah.............. " .... " "
John Heth....................... " .... " "
Joseph Kerr..................... " .... " "
William Faulkner............. " .... " "
Thomas Lewis.................. " .... " "
William Lewis.................. " .... " "
Howell Lewis.................. " .... " "
John Cummins................. " ....30th June.
John Reed.....................Lieutenant........5 March 1792.
William McRea............... " .... " "
Robert Craig................... " .... " "
Nathaniel Huston............ " .... " "
John Boyer .... " .... " "
Samuel Vance.................. " .... " "
William Smith................. " .... " "
Samuel Finley................. " .... " "
William Richard.............. " .... " "
Aaron Gregg................... " ....30th June "
John Pothimers............... " ....25th Sept. "
John Steele .... " ....21st Feb'y 1793.
Reason Beall..................Ensign.............5 March 1792.
Peter Marks..................... " .... " "
Samuel Davidson............. " .... " "
Charles Wright................ " .... " "
Nanning I Nischer............ " .... " "
David Hall ✕.................. " .... " "
Archibald Gray............... " .... " "
Houtman Lightner........... " .... " "
Andrew Shanklan............ " .... " "

Fourth Sub Legion.

Commissioned.

John Clark......................Lieut Col. Com-
mand't..........21 February 1793.
Thomas Butler.................Major..............5 March 1792.
William McMahan............ " .... " "
* Ballard Smith............... " ....2nd June "
   * To be filled by Captain Ballard Smith who was suspended for six
months by the sentence of a General Court Martial.
Edward Butler.................Captain ....5 March 1792.
Henry Carbery X.............. " .... " "
William Buchanan X......... " .... " " resigned.
Jacob Slough................... " .... " "
Joseph Brock.................... " .... " "
William Eaton.................. " .... " "
John Crawford................. " .... " "
John Cooke..................... " .... " "
William Preston............... " .... " "
Alexander Gibson............. " .... " "
Benjamin Price................. " ....9 June "
Henry De Butts............... " ....28 Decem "
Robert Thompson............Lieutenant.........5 March "
Henry B. Towles.............. " .... " "
Maxwell Bines... .... " .... " "
Daniel T Jenifer............... " .... " "
James Glen..................... " .... " "
William Clarke................. " .... " "
James Underhill............... " .... " "
William Stedman.............. " .... " " resigned.
Benjamin Lockwood.......... " .... " "
Benjamin Strother............. " .... " "
William Dwen.................. " ....9 June "
Peter Grayson.................. " ....28 Decem "
Robert Purdy.................Ensign ....5 March "
Hugh Brady...................... " .... " "
William Pitt Gassaway....... " .... " " deceased.
Campbell Smith .... " .... " "
Robert Lee...... .... " .... " "

Fourth Sub Legion—Continued.

Commissioned.

Stephen Trigge ....Ensign..............5 March 1792.
Patrick Sharkey ✕............ " .... " " resigned.
Jonathan Taylor............... " .... " "

Surgeons.

John Elliot.
John Scott.
John F. Carmichael.
Nathan Hayward.

Surgeon's Mates.

Elijah Tisdale.	James L. Clayton.
Charles Brown.	Thomas Farley.
Joseph Philips.	Joseph Strong.
William McCrosky.	Joseph Andrews.
Frederick Dalcho.	John C. Wallace.
William A. McCrea.	John Hammill.
Thomas Hutchins.	Charles Watrous.
John Sillman.	Samuel Boyd.
George Balfour.	Elihu Lyman.

Provisional Ensigns to be called into service at the Discretion of the President of the United States.

Levi Hause.	Richard Butler present.
John Lamson.	William Davidson.
Nathan Woodward.	Ferdinand Leigh Claiborne.
Aaron Catlin.	Charles Turner.
Francis Johnston *present.*	Charles Harrison.
Garret Voorhis.	George Lee Davidson.
John Wallington.	Howell Cobb.
George Baynton.	Edmund Taylor present.
Jesse Lukens.	John Bradshaw.
Charles Lewis present.	Elijah Strong present.
Levi McLane "	John Brick "

APPENDIX V.

FORT MONTGOMERY 5 July 1779

To COL'L RICHARD BUTLER.

SIR,—You will proceed with your detachment as near the enemy this evening as you think proper; your own judgement will best govern you in what mode, or manner to reconnoitre their situation, so as to remain undiscovered— You will fix on the most proper ground for the troops to take post who are destined for the charge, as also the point from which the feint is to be made. Could you take a prisoner, or any person well acquainted with the Sally port, or ports, & the Saliant angles of the works it may have a happy effect— I shall expect to hear from you at Storms; should you make any important discovery, you will communicate it the soonest possible— I wish you every happiness, & am Sincerely yours

Signed by order for Gen'l Wayne   J. ARCHER.

General Wayne to General Washington.

FORT MONTGOMERY 10th July 1779

DEAR SIR,—Your Excellency must have Observed how wretchedly your Officers were armed—many of them without any—of Consequence should they ever come to a charge, in place of producing an example of Fortitude to their men, they must Inevitably be the first to give way—an example much easier adopted by the Human mind than the former—especially by the private Soldier who can't conceive his Honor or duty Concerned further than his Officers & will be governed by his example as well in a *Retrograde Manœuvre* as in a pursuit—

I have no reason to doubt the bravery of any Officer belonging to the Corps—& will be answerable for their Conduct in every Vicissitude of fortune let them but be properly Armed—which I believe is in our power to—to effect as a considerable Number of Espontoons were sent forward to Camp before I left Phila. which must have Arrived— Will your Excellency be so obliging as to Order about fifty of the neatest & best to this place with all possible dispatch—

I mean to *practice with them* in the Course of two or three days, of which you shall hear further, I shall also expect your Excellency's Advice and Instructions on the Occasion which shall be faithfully executed—

Adieu & believe me yours most
Sincerely
Ant'y Wayne—

General Washington to General Wayne.

New Windsor 10th July 1779

D'r Sir,—Immediately upon receipt of your letter of this date I ordered the Q. M. Gen'l to furnish the Espontoons you wrote for, and presume you will get them in a day or two. My ideas of the enterprise in contemplation are these— That it should be attempted by the light Infantry only, which should march under cover of night and with the utmost secrecy to the enemy's lines, securing every person they find to prevent discovery.—Between one and two hundred chosen men and officers I conceive fully sufficient for the surprise, and apprehend the approach should be along the water on the South Side crossing the Beach & entering the abbatis.—

This party is to be preceded by a van-guard of prudent and determined men, well commanded who are to remove obstructions— secure the sentries & drive in the guard— They are to advance (the whole of them) with fixed Bayonets and muskets unloaded.— The officers commanding them are to know precisely what batteries or particular parts of the line they are respectively to possess, that confusion and the consequences of indecision may be avoided.—

These parties should be followed by the main body at a small distance for the purpose of support and making good the advantages which may be gained—or to bring them off in case of repulse & disappointment—other parties may advance to the works (but not so as to be discovered till the conflict is begun) by the way of the causeway & River on the north if practicable, as well for the purpose of distracting the enemy in their defence as to cut off their retreat. —These parties may be small unless the access and approaches should be very easy and safe.—

The three approaches here mentioned should be well reconnoitred before hand & by persons of observation.

Single men in the night will be more likely to ascertain facts than the best glasses in the day.

A white feather or cockade or some other visible badge of distinction for the night should be worn by our troops, and a watch-word agreed on to distinguish friends from foes.—If success should attend the enterprise, measures should be instantly taken to prevent if practicable the retreat of the garrison by water or to annoy them as much as possible if they attempt it—and the guns should be immediately turned against the shipping & Verplanks point and covered if possible from the enemy's fire—

Secrecy is so much more essential to these kind of enterprises than numbers, that I should not think it advisable to employ any other than the light troops— If a surprise takes place they are fully competent to the business—if it does not numbers will avail little—

As it is in the power of a single deserter to betray the design—defeat the project—& involve the party in difficulties & danger, too much caution cannot be used to conceal the intended enterprise to the latest hour from all but the principal officers of your Corps and from the men till the moment of execution— Knowledge of your intention, ten minutes previously obtained, blasts all your hopes; for which reason a small detachment composed of men whose fidelity you can rely on under the care of a judicious officer should guard every avenue through the marsh to the enemy's works by which our deserters or their spies can pass, and prevent all intercourse.—

The usual time for exploits of this kind is a little before day for which reason a vigilant officer is then more on the watch, I therefore recommend a midnight hour—

I had in view to attempt Verplanks point at the same instant that your operations should commence at Stoney Point, but the uncertainty of co operating, in point of time and the hazard thereby run of defeating the attempt on Stoney point, which is infinitely most important—the other being dependent—has induced me to suspend that operation.

These are my general ideas of the plan for a surprise, but you are at liberty to depart from them in every instance where you think they may be improved or changed for the better—a dark night and even a rainy one if you can find the way will contribute to your success— The officers in these night marches should be extremely attentive to keep their men together as well for the purpose of guarding against desertion to the enemy as to prevent skulking.

As it is a part of the plan, if the surprise should succeed to make use of the enemy's cannon against their shipping & their post on the other side, it will be well to have a small detachment of artillery with you to serve them— I have sent an order to the Park for this purpose and to cover the design have ordered down a couple of light field pieces—when you march you can leave the pieces behind—

So soon as you have fixed your plan and the time of execution I shall be obliged to you to give me notice. I shall immediately order you a reinforcement of light infantry—& more Espontoons— I am with great regard

D'r Sir

Y'r most obe't servant

G'o WASHINGTON.

BRIG'R GEN'L WAYNE—

General Wayne to General Washington.

FORT MONTGOMERY 15th July 1779.

11 OClock A.M.

DEAR GENERAL,—On the 11th Colo's BUTLER & FEBIGER and myself Reconnoitred the Enemies works at Stony point in the most Satisfactory manner possible—and are decidedly of Opinion that two real attacks and one feint ought to be made agreeable to the Enclosed plan & Disposition which I now do myself the Honor to transmit—by the Unanimous Voice of the field Officers present as well as your Excellencies permission I have ventured to add the Second Attack which is the Only alteration from yours of the tenth— I perfectly agree with your Excellency that an Enterprize of this Nature don't so much depend upon Numbers as on Secrecy & prowess—yet the Mass of our Soldiery will derive Confidence from the Reputation of Numbers—from this Conviction I have taken the Liberty to Order Colo' BALL's Regiment Stationed at Rose's *farm* to follow in my rear & shall give out that the Whole Virginia Line are to Support us—it can have no bad Effect—but it may have a very happy one.

I have taken every possible precaution to secure the passes Leading to Stoney point—for which purpose I have detached three small parties of picked men under prudent & Vigilant Officers with direction to Approach near the Revene little before night so as to Reconnoitre & fix on the proper places to plant their Sentries as soon as it's dark also to secure Certain persons to serve as Guides

I shall meet Majr LEE at CLEMENT's or between that & STORM's.

I am pleased at the prospect of the day & have the most happy presages of the fortune of the night

adieu my Dear General

& believe me with every

Sentiment of Esteem

Your Most Ob't & Affectionat

Hum'l Servt.

ANT'Y WAYNE.

General Washington to General Wayne.

HEAD QUARTERS NEW

WINDSOR July 14th

1779

DEAR SIR,—I have reflected on the advantages and disadvantages of delaying the proposed attempt, and I do not know but the latter preponderate. You will therefore carry it into execution tomorrow night as you desire, unless some new motive or better information should induce you to think it best to defer it. You are at liberty to choose between the different plans on which we have conversed. But as it is important to have every information we can procure, if you could manage in the mean time to see Major LEE, it might be useful. He has been so long near the spot and has taken so much pains to inform himself critically concerning the post, that I imagine he may be able to make you acquainted with some further details. Your interview must be managed with caution or it may possibly raise suspicion—

I am D'r Sir

Your most Obed't Serv't

G'o WASHINGTON

BRIGADIER GENERAL WAYNE.

Order of Battle, July 15, 1779.

The troops will march at   OClock and move by the Right making a short halt at the Creek or run next on this side Clement's —every Officer & non Commissioned Officer will remain with & be answerable for every man in their platoons, no Soldier to be permitted to quit his ranks on any pretext whatever until a general Halt is made & then to be attended by one of the Officers of the platoon. When the Head of the Troops arrive in the rear of the Hill Col Febiger will form his Regiment into a solid Column of a half Platoon in front as fast as they come up—Col'l Meigs will form next in Febigers rear & Major Hull in the rear of Meigs which will form the right Column

Col'l Butler will form a Column on the left of Febiger—& Major Murfree in his rear

every Officer and Soldier is then to fix a Piece of White paper in the most Conspicuous part of his Hat or Cap as an Insignia to be distinguished from the Enemy—

At the Word March Col'l Fleury will take charge of One Hundred & fifty determined & picked men properly Officered with their arms unloaded & placing their whole dependance on the Bayn't, who will move about twenty paces in front of the Right Column, by the Route 1 & enter the sally port—he is to detach an Officer & twenty men a little in front whose business will be to secure the Sentries & Remove the Abbatis & Obstruction for the Column to pass through the Column will follow close in the Rear with shoulder'd muskets Led by Col'l Febiger & Gen'l Wayne in person— When the Works are forced—& *not before* the Victorious troops as they enter will give the Watch Word " The fort is ours" with Repeated and loud voice & drive the Enemy from their Works and Guns which will favor the pass of the Whole Troops—\ Should the Enemy Refuse to Surrender—or attempt to make their Escape by Water or Otherwise, effectual means must be used to Effect the former & to prevent the Latter.

Col'l Butler will move by the Route 2, preceded by One Hundred men with fixed Bayonets properly Officered & unloaded—at the Distance of about 20 yards in front of the Column which will follow under Col'l Butler with shouldered muskets and Enter the Sally port " C" or " D." These Hundred will also detach a proper Officer &

27

twenty men a little in front to Remove the Obstructions : as soon as they gain the Works they are also to give & Continue the Watch Word—which will prevent Confusion and mistake

Major Murfree will follow Col'l Butler to the first figure 3 when he will divide a little to the Right & left & wait the Attack on the Right—which will be his signal to begin & keep up a perpetual and Galling fire & endeavor to enter between & possess the works a. a.

if any Soldier presumes to take his musket from his shoulder or attempt to fire or begin the battle until ordered by his proper Officer he shall be Instantly put to death by the Officer next him, for the Misconduct of one man is not to put the whole Troops in danger or disorder—& be suffered to pass with life :—after the troops begin to advance to the works the strictest silence must be Observed and the closest attention paid to the Commands of the Officers—

The General has the fullest Confidence in the bravery & fortitude of the Corps that he has the happiness to Command—the distinguished Honor confered on every Officer & soldier who has been drafted into this corps by His Excellency Gen'l Washington—the Credit of the States they Respectively belong to, & their own Reputation will be such powerful motives for each man to distinguish himself that the General can not have the least doubt of a Glorious Victory—& he hereby most Solemnly Engages to Reward the first man who enters the works with five Hundred Dollars & Immediate Promotion ; to the second 400 to the third 300 to the fourth 200 & to the fifth 100 Dollars and will Represent the Conduct of every Officer & Soldier who distinguishes himself on this Occasion, in the most favorable point of View to His Excellency whose Greatest pleasure is in Rewarding merit—

But shou'd there be any Soldier so lost to every feeling of Honor, as to attempt to Retreat one single foot or skulk in the face of danger, the Officer next to him is Immediately to put him to death—that he may no longer disgrace the name of a Soldier, or the Corps or State he belongs to—

As General Wayne is determined to share the danger of the night —so he wishes to participate of the Glory of the day in common with his fellow Soldiers—

Colonel Fleury to General Wayne.

"EXTRACT OF BRIGADE LIGHT INFANTRY ORDERS.
"15 JULY, 1779.

"The general Solemnly engages to Reward the 1st man who enters the work, with *five* hundred Dollars, and immediate promotion. to the Second 400D; to the third 300D; to the 4th 200D; to the 5th 100D; & will Represent the Conduct of every officer, and Soldier, who Distinguishes himself on this occasion, in the most favourable point of view, to his excellency who allwais Receives the greatest pleasure in Rewarding merit."

The following is an extract from Col. Fleury's report:

"It is unanimously acknowledged that the 1st man on the Rampart has been

    1st.......Lt. Colo. FLEURY.
    2D   Lt.......... KNOX........pensylvania Line.
    3........Serj......... BAKER.......virginia.........4 wounds.
    4........Serjeant... SPENCER.....virginia.........2 wounds.
    5........Serjeant... DONLOP......pensylvania....2 wounds.

"DR. GENERAL.

"I beg—the money to which I am entitled to be Delivered to my men 2d. Lt. KNOX begs the same.

"for my promotion, If I am obliged afterwards to Leave my command in the L. infantery I Decline it. but I would be very glad to Receive from his excellency, or from Congres some public mark of their satisfaction. My military fortune at home Depends on it."

Wayne's Supplementary Report to the President of Congress.

[From *The Pennsylvania Packet, or The General Advertiser* (Dunlap's), Philadelphia, Thursday, August 26, 1779.]

WEST-POINT, August 10, 1779.

SIR,—Your very polite favor of the 17th ult. with the extract of an act of Congress, I have just now received. The honorable manner in which that respectable Body have been pleased to express their approbation of my conduct in the enterprize on Stony-Point, must be very flattering to a young soldier; but whilst I experience every sensation arising from a consciousness of having used my best endeavours to carry the orders of my General into execution, I feel much hurt that I did not in my letter to him of the 17th of July, mention (among other brave and worthy officers) the names of Lieut. Col. SHERMAN, Majors HULL, MURPHY and POSEY, whose good conduct and intrepidity justly entitled them to that attention.

Permit me, therefore, thro' your Excellency, to do them that justice now which the state of my wound diverted me from in the first instance: And whilst I pay this tribute to real merit, I must not omit Major NOIRMONT DE LANEUVILLE, a French gentleman, who (in the character of a volunteer) stept amongst the first for *glory.*

I will only beg to add, that every officer and soldier, belonging to the light corps, discovered a zeal and intrepidity that *did* and ever will secure success.

I am,

With every sentiment of esteem,

Your Excellency's most obedient humble servant

ANT'Y WAYNE.

HIS EXCELLENCY JOHN JAY, ESQ;
    President of Congress.

Published by Order of Congress,

CHARLES THOMSON, Secretary.

Washington's Official Report to Congress.

[From *The New Jersey Gazette*, vol. ii. No. 84, Trenton, Wednesday, August 4, 1779.]

HEAD-QUARTERS, NEW WINDSOR, July 21 1779

SIR,—On the 16th instant I had the honour to inform Congress of a successful attack upon the enemy's post at Stony-Point, on the preceding night, by Brigadier-General WAYNE, and the corps of light infantry under his command. The ulterior operations in which we have been engaged, have hitherto put it out of my power to transmit the particulars of this interesting event. They will now be found in the inclosed report, which I have received from General WAYNE. To the encomiums he has deservedly bestowed on the officers and men under his command, it gives me pleasure to add, that his own conduct throughout the whole of this arduous enterprize, merits the warmest approbation of Congress. He improved upon the plan recommended by me, and executed it in a manner that does signal honour to his judgment and to his bravery. In a critical moment of the assault, he received a flesh wound in the head with a musket ball, but continued leading on his men with unshaken firmness.

I now beg leave, for the private satisfaction of Congress, to explain the motives which induced me to direct the attempt.—

It has been the unanimous sentiment to evacuate the captured post at Stony-Point, remove the cannon and stores, and destroy the works, which was accomplished on the night of the 18th, one piece of heavy cannon only excepted. For want of proper tackling within reach to transport the cannon by land, we were obliged to send them to the fort by water. The movements of the enemy's vessels created some uneasiness on their account, and induced me to keep one of the pieces for their protection, which finally could not be brought off, without risking more for its preservation than it was worth. We also lost a galley which was ordered down to cover the boats. She got under way, on her return the afternoon of the 18th. The enemy began a severe and continued cannonade upon her, from which having received some injury, which disabled her from proceeding, she was run ashore. Not being able to get her afloat till late in the flood tide, and one or two of the enemy's vessels under favour of the night, having passed above her, she was set on fire and blown up.

It is probable Congress will be pleased to bestow some marks of consideration upon those officers who distinguished themselves upon this occasion. Every officer and man of the corps deserves great credit, but there were particular ones whose situation placed them foremost in danger, and made their conduct most conspicuous. Lieut. Colonel FLEURY and Major STEWARD commanded the two attacks. Lieutenants GIBBONS and KNOX commanded the advance parties or *forlorn hopes*, and all acquitted themselves as well as it was possible. These officers have a claim to be more particularly noticed.

Mr. Archer, who will have the honour of delivering these despatches, is a volunteer Aid to General WAYNE, and a gentleman of merit. His zeal, activity, and spirit, are conspicuous upon every occasion.

> I have the honour to be,
> With the greatest respect and esteem,
> Your Excellency's Most obedient
> humble servant
> G. WASHINGTON.

I forgot to mention, that two flags and two standards were taken, the former belonging to the garrison, and the latter to the 17th regt. These shall be sent to Congress by the first convenient opportunity.

General Wayne to President Reed.

NEW WINDSOR 26th July 1779

DEAR SIR,—Your very polite favor of the 20th I had the pleasure of Rec'g last evening—and am much honored by the manner in which you are pleased to express your approbation of the Enterprize against Stoney Point—the particulars of which you undoubtedly have seen before this time

I think it my duty to Inform your Excellency of the good Conduct of the two young Gent'n who led the Van of each column & who are Entitled to some marks of Distinction for an Intrepidity & Address that would have done honor to the oldest Soldiers Mr. Gibbons of the 6th & Mr. Knox of the 9th Penns'a Regiments

I have not put pen to paper on the Occasion except to His Excellency Gen'l Washington— Indeed my head has been too much disordered to attempt it— You will therefore have the goodness to excuse a *seeming* neglect & do me justice by attributing it to the cause I have mentioned which will also apologize for the shortness of this

> My best wishes to Mrs Reed & believe me
> with every Sentiment of Esteem
> Your Excellencies most Ob't
> & very Hum Serv't
> ANT'Y WAYNE.

HIS EXCELLENCY
GOV'R REED.

Colonel Meigs to General Wayne.

[From the original manuscript.]

LIGHT INFANTRY CAMP, 22d Aug. 1779.

SIR,—I think it my duty to inform your honor, that the account contain'd in your honors letter to his Excellency of the Reduction of Stony Point, is exceptionable to many Officers in the Brigade— It is thought that as the Acco't now Stands, the Public must be induced to believe, that L't Col'o FLEURY, Major STEWART, Lieu'ts GIBBONS & KNOX, forced their way into the Works, which made the advancing of the Columns comparatively easy— While the fact is that the volunteers of the Right Column did not Suffer more in proportion than the Columns in General—the Gentlemen don't object to the encomiums given in your honors letter of any one of the Officers there mention'd, who upon ev'ry principle ought to be distinguishingly noticed But think that there is the appearance of partiallity, in not mentioning any wounded Officer except L't Colonel HAY, whose wounds are equally honorable & no more so than the Others—the Officer who voluntarily took charge of the Pettiaugre on board of which were a considerable part of the Stores, & under a Severe cannonade rowed her off, it is thought deserves some notice I would not think that your honor would deliberately shew a partiallity to any particular Corps or State. On the Contrary I am convinced that you are actuated by Sentiments as great as the magnitude of the cause in which we are mutually combin'd.

The multiplicity of matters which crowded upon your honor at the time you wrote his Excellency, exclusive of the attention necessary to your own wound, made it impossible for you to take up ev'ry circumstance of the attack— I beg leave to submit it to your honor Whether the names of the other wounded Officers; & two or three others who enter'd the Fort nearly at the same instant with Col'o FLEURY; ought not to be mention'd in a subjoin'd account. I know they claim it as due to them Since others are mention'd— Our feelings in these matters are exquisite, & are absolutely necessary to us as Soldiers— The honorable mention made of my name with the other Colonels is to the utmost of my wishes— As Major HULL Commanded a Reg't in the Attack, I could have wish'd that his name had been mentioned with the Colonels— A Sincere wish

that the most cordial harmony may ever Subsist thro : the States &
Army—and more particularly in the Light Corps at this time, has
induced me to write—

I have the honor to be

with great esteem & respect

your honors Obed't Serv't

R. I. MEIGS, Colonel

Lieutenant-Colonel Sherman to General Wayne.

[From the original manuscript.]

LIGHT INFANTRY CAMP 22d Aug. 1779

SIR,—Can it be supposed that the officers of the New England
line are totally void of sentiment, that those fine and delicate feelings which ever distinguish the generous and manly soul are incapable of making any impression on them. Honor and glory are,
together with a desire of rendering our country great, happy, and
respectable the grand incentives to our continuing in the army.
And what can be more agreeable to the man of feeling, or what can
be a greater inducement to urge him on to the performance of
actions great and hazardous, as well as glorious, but the happiness
of his country, a desire of the grateful applause of his fellow citizens, and of transmitting his name in an amiable point of view to
the world. These are the united motives that have inspired you to
tread the scenes of carnage ; for no one will believe the welfare of
your country separate from every other consideration, was the only
incentive. The glory you have acquired by the last daring and well
conducted enterprise, has gained you a name which will be coeval
with the annals of american history; which, perhaps, time herself
will be unable to efface. Similar motives you must think warm our
bosoms, and stimulate us to similar actions.

When first appointed to the Light Infantry was happy to hear the
command was given to you. Your brave and spirited behaviour in
the action of Monmouth endeared you to your brethren in the field,
and merited the highest applause ; but /your letter to gen'l WASH-
INGTON on the reduction of Stony Point, in the minds of many
judicious persons, has in some measure tarnished the lustre of your
character, and rendered your command less agreeable./ However,

we wish to believe it was owing to the variety of business that demanded your attention at that time, rather than any other cause—that your only view was to give an impartial history, to state facts as they really were, without any design of partiality—

I wish not to depreciate the merit of any officer, neither would I presume to do it, as it is descriptive of a base degenerate mind; but I wish, if any discrimination was necessary to be made, that every officer might be noticed according to his merit in the action, and if any were deficient in duty, they may be particularly pointed out.—

There appears in the account you have given evident marks of a State partiality; all distinctions of which kind I detest, and ardently wish they may be for ever banished from the mind of every friend to his country; they have a tendency to lay a foundation for future broils: for when once a man is sensibly injured, if he is possessed of the least feeling he doth not soon forget it. Why cannot we consider ourselves as one and walk hand in hand like brethren? Are we not embarked in the same cause, and does not our independance rest on our united efforts? But rather than be injured, rather than be trampled upon and considered as insignificant beings in the scale —*my blood boils at the thought. Nature recoils, and points out a mode, the only one of redress*—

I am not anxious to have my name transmitted to publick view, neither do I think any thing can be said of me more than barely attending to duty— I am not writing for myself, but I feel for those officers under my command as well as others who merit as much as those most distinguished by you.

Duty, separate from the ties of friendship is sufficient, to induce me to acquaint you with the sentiments and uneasiness of many officers under your command, which, perhaps, is more extensive, than you may imagine. It is still in your power to place things in their proper channel, to gain our affection, and confidence, and then, when called into the field, inspired by your example, animated with a desire of crowning you with fresh laurels, every thing will conspire to induce us to play the man.

However conspicuous you may appear in the eyes of the world, you cannot imagin your reputation is so firmly established as never to be sullied, and that the affections and confidence of your officers is unworthy your consideration. You have not arrived beyond the regions of censure, and our feelings as well as interest require that there should be a more full and impartial representation of facts than you have made.—The integrity of my intentions I hope, will apologize for my troubling you on this subject.

I have the honor to be,

with the greatest respect,

your most Obed't Serv't

ISAAC SHERMAN

L't Col

GEN'L WAYNE

General Wayne's Reply to Colonel Meigs.

FORT MONTGOMERY 23rd Aug't 1779

SIR,—I was presented with yours of yesterday on my way to Head Quarters—& as I sincerely believe your Inducement for writing that Letter proceeded from the motive you mention—I shall therefore answer it with that Candor, which I hope will always govern my Actions whilst honored with the Command I now hold

If I know my own heart,—I am as clear of Local prejudices as any Gentleman on this ground—perhaps *full* as much so, as those who *effect* to suspect me of it,—& who *feel* themselves so much hurt at my Letter of *the 17th Ultimo* to His Excellency Gen'l WASHINGTON on the Reduction of Stoney Point.

I have re-examined that letter with Attention, & am well convinced that it contains a true & *Impartial* relation of facts, *too well known* to admit of a Contradiction,—& that the mention made of such *Officers only*, whose particular Commands, Situation or Circumstances, rendered it Necessary, is warranted by example, & founded upon just & Military principles—

Let us suppose for a moment, that I was to name every Officer who *had*—or in Similar Circumstances would have equally distinguished himself on that Occation,—I am confident that I shou'd have to recapitulate the names of every Officer in the Corps, otherwise not have done justice to their merit,—& perhaps it would not have rested here, but must have gone down to every Non commissioned Officer & private,—the Absurdity is too Obvious to admit of a serious comment,—no but says *Suspicion*—" you ought to have placed Other " Officers at the head of the *Volunteers*, and not have given one

"Command to Lieu't Colo' FLEURY—who was *a frenchman*, & not "belonging to any *particular State*,—and the other to Major STEW-"ARD—a *Marylander*, & the *forlorn hope* to Messrs GIBBONS & "KNOX who were Pennsylvanians"

In answer to which I need only observe—(& it will strike every Military Gentleman—) that the two former were the only Field Officers in the Corps except Colonels BUTLER, & FEBEGER, Lieut Col'o HAY and Major POSEY (who had other Commands Assigned them) that had a Competant, if any knowledge of the Situation of the Enemies works, or Approaches to them,—and which they had for many days previous to the Storm, made it their particular business to Obtain,—I therefore say, that upon every Principle, Military, as well as Prudencial, they ought to have been placed at the Head of the Columns, and on this Ground I trust I shall stand justified to my General, & in the eye of the World for my Conduct.

But why GIBBONS & KNOX,—why are two Officers belonging to "the State of *Penn'a* to be honored with the *forlorn hopes*, & so "particularly mentioned *to* in your *Letter* of *the* 17th *July*"

As to the first, I am Informed they Obtained it by lot,—for my own part I did not even know, that they were among the Volunteers until they had taken post in their Respective Commands.

The following extract of a Letter from His Excellency, added to their own good Conduct, will best answer the latter.

/ In yours of the 16th "you do not mention *the names* of the two "Officers who led the Advanced parties to the two Columns,—you "will be pleased to do it with all the Circumstances of Conduct, & "loss which they Sustained"

So that after I had despatched my first Letter to His Excellency, I again wrote it over & Inserted the very particulars which seem to give so much uneasiness—and shou'd Certainly have done the same had they been Officers belonging to *any Other State*, than that of Penns'a

but why was not the Gentlemen mentioned who Voluntarially took charge of the Boats with the Ordnance & Stores on the Evacuation Of Stoney Point,—for the very reasons already assigned, and because every Officer & Soldier are Generally, & honorably mentioned, in that very exceptional Letter to His Excellency, & because it is actually dated two days previous to the Circumstance you allude to

"But why was not Major *Hull* & some Other field Officers taken "notice of—they were not many, & surely might have been men-"tioned"—true, & I was not a little hurt on account of the Omission,—but the politeness of Congress put it in my Power to do that justice to their Merit, which they certainly deserved—& which you'l find in the Enclosed copy of a Letter to His Excellency JOHN JAY Esq'r—& which I flatter myself was Published by Order of Congress previous to the date of your's

I must therefore Request you to place this matter in its proper point of View—not only to the Officers of your Regiment—but to Others who may have read my Letters & Returns with a Prejudiced, or Inattentive eye,—and assure them that I wish for nothing more than an Opportunity of Producing a Conviction to the World that I detest *Local Prejudices*, as much as I pity the man who would unjustly suspect me of them—and that I hope the day is not far distant when an Other Brilliant Action or Actions may put it in my Power—to do justice to their Merit and to recapitulate their good Conduct on a former Occation i.e. when I can do it in a Military way

Interim I am Your most Ob't
& very Hum'l Ser't
ANT'Y WAYNE.

☞ I have rec'd a letter dated yesterday from Lieu't Col'o SHERMAN, of a very extraordinary Nature,—which at a Proper Season will require a very *Serious* & particular explanation,—for altho' I don't wish to Incur any Gentlemans displeasure, yet, *I put up with no man's Insults*

A. WAYNE

COL'O MEIGS

Colonel Sherman to General Wayne.

LIGHT INFANTRY CAMP 24th Aug. 1779

SIR,—I find in the Postscript of your letter to Col. Meigs, you think mine of the 22d instant to be of an extraordinary nature ; and which will require a serious and particular explanation ; that you wish not to incur the displeasure of any gentleman, and that you mean not to receive an insult from any man.

These are sentiments which ought to inspire the mind of every man of honor, and are entirely correspondent with my own feelings.

An explanation of my letter, I wish and am ready to give when required.

To insult you, I declare upon my honor, never was my intention ; my view was to acquaint you there was an uneasiness among the officers of your command, and the cause.—They imagined themselves sensibly injured, and wished you to be acquainted with it.—I therefore wrote you on the subject, with an expectation that matters would be adjusted to our mutual satisfaction. I am sensible that I expressed myself with a good deal of warmth, arising from my feelings at that time—While on the one hand, I considered we had attended to duty, and merited at least your notice ; so on the other, I thought we were viewed of no consequence in the Scale of Beings—the thought awoke all my sensations—it would have animated a dead man—So far from thinking to make use of compulsive measures to gain redress that I can assure you ; it never entered my mind.

I am, with the greatest Esteem

Your Obed Ser't

ISAAC SHERMAN.

GEN'L WAYNE.

Major Hull to General Wayne.

LIGHT INFANTRY CAMP 25th Aug't 1779

SIR,—When I first saw your Honours Letters to his Excellency giving an Account of the Expedition against Stoney Point, no Arguments that I could use with myself could convince me, that a Degree of Injustice was not done me—Lest I should judge wrong in the Matter, I consulted some of my Judicious Friends on the Subject, and found their Sentiments coincided with mine—desirous that no Broils should be created in the Corps on my Account, I pointed out to his Excellency with as much Modesty as my Situation would admit, the Grounds of my Uneasiness, and only requested Permission to retire to my Reg't   In Consequence of this Request, his Excellency was pleased to send me a Note, desiring my Company at his Quarters for the Purpose of giving me a Satisfactory Explanation of the Subject of my Letter—I was happy to find the Explanation satisfactory, and have been made doubly happy since in seeing your Letter of the 10th inst (to the Presid't of Congress) wherein ample Justice is done me, and the Cause of the first Omission clearly pointed out—I am only unhappy that I imputed the Neglect to the wrong Cause, and am now firmly persuaded that you was actuated by no other Principles, than equal and impartial Justice to your Corps —I shall now Sir, consider myself happy to remain in your Corps, and shall make it my Study to cherish & cultivate Harmony & Union with my Brother Officers—I have the Honor to be with perfect Esteem your most Obed't Serv't

W'M HULL

[Addressed, "GEN'L WAYNE Present."]

General Wayne's Reply to Major Hull.

LIGHT INFANTRY CAMP Aug't 1779

DEAR SIR,—The Candid manner in which you have in yours of this date deliver'd your Sentiments, gives a Sensation which I can much better feel than express—my highest Ambition is to Merit the Esteem & Confidence of every Officer of the Light Corps—

Conscious of the Rectitude of my Heart I feel doubly happy in your Approbation of my Conduct—& I have the most happy presages, that by Mutual Confidence and a Strict & due Observance of Orders & Discipline this Corps will produce a Conviction to the world that the sons of America deserve to be free

I am with true Regard yours
Most Sincerely
ANT'Y WAYNE

General Wayne's Reply to Major Posey.

[From the original draught in General Wayne's autograph.]

FORT MONTGOMERY 28th August 1779

SIR,—Your very *Laconic* note of the 12th Instant enclosing a Copy of a long letter to His Excellency Gen'l WASHINGTON—I purposely delayed Answering until you had an Opportunity of being convinced that I had made use of the first Opening of doing justice to your merit.

You'l now permit me to make some Observations on your Letter to his Excellency of the 10th Instant, you say—"it is perfectly well "known to General WAYNE that I led the Battalion which Com-

"posed the front of the Right Column, where he himself marched "until we came to the beach—when Gen'l WAYNE *left the Head* "*of the Column* After which *I had the sole Guidance & Direction* "*of it*"

Surely Sir you had forgot that the brave & Intrepid Lieut Col'o FLEURY was Immediately in front of you who had some claim to the *Guidance of it*, & that if Gen'l WAYNE *had left the Column Intirely*, yet a MEIGS, a FEBIGER, a SHERMAN, & a HULL (were present) and each of them Senior Officers to you) would have claimed the *Direction of it*

But I am Certain they have too much *Modesty* to assume it—as it's too well known that I myself continued to *direct it* even after I had Rec'd my wound—& that at the point of my Spear—I at least help'd to *direct* the greater part of the Column over the Abbatis and into the Works, & to take measures to Secure them & the Prisoners after (which perhaps may not be so well known to you Sir as to Other Gentlemen)

You ask a number of Queries of Gen'l WAYNE all tending to prove that you did *at least* your duty,—Gen'l WAYNE answers you, that you did,—& that he highly approved of your Conduct appears in his letter of the 17th Ultimo Viz

"I should take up too much of your Excellency's time was I to "particularise every Individual who deserves it for their bravery "on this Occasion"—(& again)—"Its with the greatest pleasure "I acknowledge to your Excellency that I was supported in the "Attacks by all the Officers & Soldiers to the utmost of my wishes"

but not content with this, as soon as Congress put it in my power, I did that further Justice to your Merit which I thought you Entitled to—as you'l see by the enclosed Copy of a Letter to JOHN JAY Esq on the Occation.

I now request you to read my Letter to His Excellency Gen'l WASHINGTON & the Returns of the killed & wounded with an Attentive & unprejudiced eye, together with the Copy of a letter herewith transmitted— Re examine yours of the 10th to His Excellency Gen'l WASHINGTON—& then consult your own feelings,— perhaps on cool reflection you may find that there are some expressions made use of tending to hold up an Idea of *want of Prowess in me*—which was Supplied *by you*

Was that really your Intention, and you still Continue in the same Opinion—I know that you will have Candor enough to acknowledge it,—(not to me as your Superior Officer) but to me as a Private Gentleman very tenacious of my *Honor*,—which honor is now plighted to *meet you* on that ground only.

But should you have no Intention to cast a Shade on my Military Character (as a Gentleman of those nice feelings which I believe you to possess)—I now call on you to place that matter in a proper point of View

Interim I am with due Esteem
Your most Hum'l Ser't
ANT'Y WAYNE

MAJOR POSEY

APPENDIX VI.

Description of the Medals voted by Congress for the Capture of Stony Point.

The following descriptions are from Dr. MEASE'S *Description of some Medals*, etc., in the *Collections of the Massachusetts Historical Society*, Third Series, vol. iv. pp. 301–303.

GENERAL WAYNE'S. "*Device.* An Indian Queen crowned; a quiver on her back, and wearing a short apron of feathers; a mantle hangs from her waist behind: the upper end of the mantle appears as if passed through the girdle of her apron, and hangs gracefully by her left side. She is presenting, with her right hand, a wreath to General Wayne, who receives it gracefully. In her left hand, the Queen is holding up a crown towards the General. On her left, and at her feet, an alligator is stretched out. She stands on a bow; a shield, with the American stripes, rests against her left knee.

"*Legend.* ANTONIO WAYNE, DUCI EXERCITUS COMITIA AMERICANA.

"*Reverse.—Device.* A fort with two turrets, on the top of a hill; the British flag flying: troops in single or Indian file, advancing in the front and rear up the hill: numbers lying at the bottom. Troops advancing in front, at a distance, on the edge of the river: another party to the right of the fort. A piece of artillery posted on the plain, so as to bear upon the fort: ammunition on the ground: six vessels in the river.

" *Legend.* STONY POINT EXPUGNATUM.

" *Exergue.* XV JUL. MDCCLXXIX."

It is said of this medal, in another place in the same volume (p. 302), that it " is superbly executed, and most tastefully designed. The description is taken from the original in the possession of General Wayne's son. It weighs 63 dwt. 18 grains."

LIEUTENANT-COLONEL FLEURY'S. " *Device.* A soldier helmetted and standing against the ruins of a fort: his right hand extended, holding a sword upright: the staff of a stand of colours reversed in his left: the colours under his feet: his right knee drawn up, as if in the act of stamping on them.

" *Legend.* VIRTUTIS ET AUDACIÆ MONUM. ET PRÆMIUM D. DE FLEURY EQUITI GALLO PRIMO SUPER MUROS RESP. AMERIC. D. D.

" *Reverse.* Two water batteries, three guns each: one battery firing at a vessel: a fort on a hill: flag firing: river in front: six vessels before the fort.

" *Legend.* AGGERES PALUDES HOSTES VICTI.

" *Exergue.* STONY PT. EXPUGN. XV. JUL. MDCCLXXIX."

The following, from *The Pennsylvania Packet and General Advertiser*, No. 1650, Philadelphia, Thursday, January 22, 1784, contains a narrative of the presentation of this medal:

" Paris, *Oct.* 17. Dr. Franklin has lately delivered to the sieur DE FLEURY, major of the regiment of the Saintonge and lieutenant-colonel in the service of the United States of America, a medal which has been decreed for him by Congress, after taking of Stoney Point. That fort which was defended by 30 pieces of cannon and 600 picked men, was carried in the night of the 15th July, 1779, by a detachment of 1100 men under the command of gen. WAYNE. The sieur DE FLEURY who commanded the van guard, leaped first into the intrenchments, and struck down with his own hand the English flag."

MAJOR STEWARD'S. " *Device.* America personified in an Indian queen, is presenting a palm branch to Captain Steward: a quiver

28

hangs at her back: her bow and an alligator are at her feet: with her left hand she supports a shield inscribed with the American stripes, and resting on the ground.

"*Legend.* JOANNI STEWART COHORTIS PREFECTO COMITIA AMERICANA.

"*Reverse.* A fortress on an eminence: in the foreground, an officer cheering his men, who are following him over *abatis* with charged bayonets, in pursuit of a flying enemy: troops in Indian files ascending the hill to the storm, front and rear: troops advancing from the shore: ships in sight.

"*Exergue.* STONEY POINT OPPUGNATUM, XV JUL. MDCC-LXXIX."

LETTERS FROM GENERAL WAYNE.

INDEX.

423

THE END.

www.ingramcontent.com/pod-product-compliance
Lightning Source LLC
Chambersburg PA
CBHW022021110726
47901CB00006B/1610